Only Gossip Prospers

A Novel

of Louisa May Alcott in New York

D1496224

Only Gossip Prospers

A Novel

of Louisa May Alcott in New York

Lorraine Tosiello

PINK UMBRELLA BOOKS

pink umbrella
books

Published by Pink Umbrella Books (www.pinkumbrellapublishing.com)

Lorraine Tosiello-Author

Only Gossip Prospers/Lorraine Tosiello

Louisa May Alcott visits New York in the winter of 1875 and encounters a host of historical and fictional characters whose lives become intertwined.

ISBN: 978-1-949598-11-7
Library of Congress Control Number: 2019950793
Edited by Merry Gordon and Marnae Kelley
Cover design by Adrienne Quintana
Photo by Gautam Krishnan on Unsplash
The figure of the woman on the cover is a detail from a photograph by Robert Bracklow, *Fifth Avenue at 42 Street, 1888,* used with permission from the Department of Image Collections, National Gallery of Art Library, Washington, DC.

To

Jane, who told me I should do it,

and

Louisa, who showed me how.

Illustrations

Contents

Chapter 1

A Winter Escape

"It wouldn't be Saturday without the hordes." Louisa snapped the parlor curtains closed and turned to her sisters. "Girls, I'm itching to be off somewhere this winter. Someplace where I can disappear into the crowd and doff my mask as the staid and famous Miss Alcott."

"How nice it would be to be off by myself for an adventure just once, without the boys tugging at my apron strings," sighed Anna, looking down at her widening middle. Louisa considered her sister's matronly spread, wondering where the years had flown since they planned their castles in the air.

"It would have to be somewhere that keeps little girls and their mothers out of the hotel lobby, or I shall continue to be inundated with autograph seekers and swooners and generally cracked young ladies waving their dog-eared books in my face," said Louisa.

"You'd have to go to Timbuktu to escape recognition, I fear— though I've lately heard your smart little books are being translated into Songhay, so you ought to go soon," quipped May, tossing her curls.

"You should take some time for yourself, dear. You have been working altogether too hard, and I know how the New England winters affect your moods and your joints," said a bonneted being sitting quietly in the corner. Marmee put aside her book and spread her arms wide, seeming ready to draw all three of her grown daughters onto her lap should they need inspiration, comfort or instruction.

Louisa looked lovingly at the women in her life. "My word, you three are becoming more like the March family than your very own selves!" Perhaps they were cozier due to the warmth of the new furnace and thick rugs she had been able to purchase using the profits from her popular children's novel, but otherwise not much had changed about the stout-hearted and determined Alcott women. They still came together in the quiet evening to peg away at their household tasks, to crack jokes about their Concord neighbors, and most of all, to speak words of encouragement to each other.

"Oh, yes, Anna glows with tranquillity and acceptance of her dismal lot as a doting mother and housewife," May joked.

"And May is ever the perfect snow goddess," Anna joined in.

If I had to describe them each with one word, Louisa thought, *Anna would be 'contentment,' May, 'grace,' and dear Marmee, 'wisdom,' of course. And what of me? What word best describes me?* Lou knew that some thought her opinionated and blunt, others considered her jovial and honest, and far too many fanatics hoped that she was the impersonation of Jo March herself.

Her sisters often remarked on how her tomboyish, scattered look had matured into a composure close to elegance. She was glad there was no mirror in their little parlor, as she never was satisfied with her angular looks. She and May had inherited their gangly height from their father. Still, her forty years rested well on her. She was tall and straight, almost imposing, and her mass of thick, dark hair gave her even more stature. Her sarcastic steel gray eyes were softened by a youthful twinkle. But what words could she use to describe herself, as if she were a character in a book? *Energetic, determined, creative, ambitious, responsible*—each word was part of her, but missed the true mark. She tapped her foot, fidgeting as she thought of the best words and threading errant tendrils of hair behind her ear. *Restless*—

that's what I am. Restless to do more, to see more, to achieve more.

Louisa surveyed her little universe—the alcoves filled with books, the scattered water colors on hearth and wall, Beth's lonely melodeon in the corner—and ached as much for things as they had been as she did for a complete change. The enduring home her father had forged from a ramshackle building and two farm sheds now both embraced and stifled her. Louisa loved her family to distraction, but the burdens of the homestead exhausted her. Try as she might to ennoble the art, Louisa could not justify the hours she spent with broom in hand, or rolling pin, or most of all, the entire day spent at the washtub. She tried to reconcile her responsibility to family with her responsibility to an ever-percolating mind. During each spring and summer she ran Orchard House, providing in every way for her parents' needs, always disgruntled at the time away from her craft and livelihood. As soon as May stepped in to take up the load, Louisa would race off to a Boston garret or hotel or flat and work furiously at her writing for as long as she could hold out. But Louisa liked her new idea of spending the winter in a different location altogether, one which might energize her flagging spirits and add grist to her story mill.

"I sometimes feel that I cannot make one honest acquaintance since I have become all the rage," said Louisa, gesturing to the closed curtains. "I need to go somewhere where I can hide my identity and approach people without fanfare. Where shall it be, ladies? Where would you think your shabby Lou can get both stimulation and anonymity? I will be off to the Women's Congress in Syracuse in a few weeks and shall make my getaway from there."

"You could easily reach Cleveland by boat from that town and meet Father on his way back from the West," ventured Anna.

"If you're going by ship, then why not go to Havana?" suggested May, again with a smirk. "You could put a red rose in your hair, disguise your face with a lace mantilla and succumb to the sensuous life you described in your short stories."

11

"My sailing days are over," lamented Louisa. "We all rejoiced when I survived gales and seasickness and the smallpox on board that last ocean voyage, and I swore never to try it again. What do you think, Marmee?" Louisa still turned to the good counsel of her mother, who was closer to her than anyone else in the world.

"Go to New York, dear," Abigail offered.

New York—how perfect! New York would be seething with new ideas and unusual people. There, she could completely melt into the mass of humanity, revel in the creative life and accumulate experiences to turn into new stories. The pleasure of invisibility would be part of the allure. She need not be hampered by the self-consciousness that always stymied her in Boston, where she was lauded for her fame but denied the respect of the literary giants. In New York, she needn't worry about the intricacies of European social maneuvering, which always left the Alcott women just barely adhering to decorum. It didn't put her off at all that the city had at its core the adulation of wealth and power, either. She could hold her head as high as anyone when it came to making money. Despite her success, or because of it, she could scoff at the pretentiousness of high society. She was ready to pit her independence and savvy against the New York grain. In New York, she could be every bit as adventurous as she chose.

Louisa shook her head in the direction of her mother and smiled slowly. New York! She had sent Jo March there to learn to be herself apart from her family, to write unfettered by chores and even to find her heart's true love. Why had she denied herself the same?

"I smell the wood burning in her noggin,'" May said. "It's a wonder her brains aren't singed."

"I think she's wild about the idea and doesn't want us to know," Anna added.

Marmee went on to press her point. "I have read that they have outstanding health establishments, baths and saunas where you will get the care you need to be restored at the same time that you enjoy the society and the bustle. Mrs. Botta still keeps her salon and I will write her to look out for you."

Louisa smiled at her sisters over her mother's head. Though they were mature women, Marmee always looked to protect and shield them within the web of family social connections. Marmee knew that Louisa would find a network of energetic and conscientious women in New York.

Though Lou felt a rush of enthusiasm about New York, even hope, she reined herself in. She had long ago learned to hide her own emotions, especially the most turbulent ones, so that by now she was an expert at turning notable or sentimental moments into playful ones for her family.

"Marmee's sending me off to her gaggle of friends again, as if I would be a lowly worm without their welcome," Louisa spoke as she rolled her eyes. Louisa never deliberated long. If it felt right and she had the means, she would act abruptly and be off within the week. The clock on the mantel barely ticked a beat as her family turned to her for the verdict.

"Well?" asked May.

"New York! Just the place! I shall eat oysters, drink champagne, and go to the theater every night!" Louisa thundered.

"Will you really stroll past the mansions on Fifth Avenue?" said Anna.

"And see the pictures in the new museum?" said May.

"And tour the slums at Five Points and write a story about it just to rile the upper crust!" finished Louisa, for as much as she tried to enjoy luxury she would always be the most comfortable when she was helping others.

"And come back with a street urchin to raise, no doubt, to comfort you in your old age," May added archly.

Louisa was almost immune by now to May's comments. As sociable and charming as May could be, she still managed to blurt out remarks that could sting, usually when she was feeling sorry for herself. May would likely be thinking that it should be her luck to go to the city where the Art Students League had just formed and was accepting women into their program. Instead, Lou would go to New York, and the daily grind would fall to May.

"I know you will be a dear and handle all the home drudgery while I am away," Louisa said, turning to May. "I love you for being my right hand. And you will deserve a trip of your own when I return."

May brightened immediately. "I shall go back to Europe, then! There is so much changing about Continental art and I have been stagnating here in Concord."

Louisa quickly calculated in her head the expenses related to her own sojourn and May's extended trip. She hid her chagrin. Naturally, May thought three months in New York should be paid back with a year or more in Europe. "I'll have to come back and work like a steam engine on the sequel that Tommy Niles expects about Rose and her boy cousins," said Louisa, remembering her editor's persistence. "But it's worth it! I must try my hand in the great and bustling city of New York."

"You can't go to New York with the tatters you've got for a wardrobe," said May.

"I'm not like you, who always knows how to add a ruffle or feather to a tired outfit and appear the image of refinement and elegance," lamented Lou, shaking her head at the memories of the hand-me-downs the girls had endured.

"We all learned the art of sprucing up throwaways," May said. "We shall have to sew like the dickens to get you outfitted as befits your great literary personage."

Louisa no longer had the need to remake her clothing from the cast-off finery of her wealthy cousins but she still loved the challenge of taking an old gown and restoring it to something brand new—something her own, and only barely recognizable. She rummaged in her storage, pulling out an outdated crinoline and last year's walking

14

suit. She hauled them down to the table in the study where May and Anna sat with their piecework baskets. Grabbing the crinoline, May draped it across Louisa's waist, drawing in the front panel tightly. "See, this slim silhouette is all the fashion now, and look at the fabric left to spare for flounces in the back," she muttered through pins in her mouth.

"Perhaps it is too youthful," Louisa protested.

"Never admit your age." May shook her head, still a girlish coquette in spite of her years.

Anna was already at work on the walking dress, separating the bodice and the skirt. "I would like to see that bodice changed to a long sacque,' said Louisa.

"It would make you look even taller and could be used with different skirts," said Anna. Louisa saw the admiring look that Anna cast her way. "Your taste always did run to the refined, Louisa."

"In New York I will allow myself a lifelong desired luxury: a full silk gown from one of the great establishments on Broadway."

While the women ripped and stitched together, Louisa was transported back to one of the most serene memories of her girlhood, the sweet circle of mother and sisters sewing together, each head bent on one hem of a single sheet, singing softly or blithely transposing their geography lesson onto the four corners of the sheet in front of them and listening with glowing eyes as Louisa entertained them with a story. It was the hushed evening time before bed, filled still with industry, never marred by intrusion from the male world. That world sat only a room way in her father's study, discussing the noble thoughts of the times—but perhaps not producing anything so necessary or comforting or definite as a sturdy, well-hemmed bed sheet.

Amid the bustle of packing, a letter arrived filled with dubious advice for her trip. Louisa's father had spent months in New York two decades before and wanted to direct her to his old haunts. With only a touch of irritation, Louisa read his advice in a missive filled with eloquent reminisces. She was aware that any practical guidance he could give her would be obsolete.

Bronson's letter rambled and took an otherworldly flight. "Ah, too bad, too bad the lusty Walt is no longer in New York. He would have welcomed you in Brooklyn," he wrote. "And the venerable Mr. Greeley, the editor of the nation's mind, no longer uses his pen to right our society's wrongs." With Walt Whitman gone from Brooklyn and Horace Greeley now dead, with its power brokers, transportation magnates and imposing architecture, the New York of 1875 would baffle Bronson. She wondered what effect it would have on her.

Marmee had only practical and encouraging suggestions. She entered the kitchen where May and Louisa were soaking currants, the first step in May's recipe for currant wine. "Look, dear, here is an advertisement for just the kind of establishment I was hoping you would find," she said, waving a newspaper. "It's not unlike the water therapy resort where I worked one year."

"*Dr. Eli Peck Miller's Turkish Baths combines all the advantages of a good hotel and home with those of a first-class health institution*," Louisa read aloud, flourishing the journal and upsetting a bowl of raisins.

"Really, my only requirements are to have the chance to roam, the peace to write, and the good health to do both," said Louisa as she absentmindedly massaged her thigh. Just bending to scoop up the raisins gave her a shooting pain down her right leg. In New York, she hoped for a spell of good health and the water cure could only help. "I don't know if the good doctor will allow me a diet of oysters and champagne, but I will give his program a try!" she exclaimed.

A letter of inquiry was sent and her room was engaged for the social season.

May chattered as they rearranged her trunk, adding warm stockings and a fur muff. Louisa shuffled her books and considered whether she should bring Goethe or try to purchase the volumes the family did not own while she was in New York.

16

"Goodness, Louisa," May said, lifting out a ragged brown parcel. "Are you really going to carry this silly good luck charm with you to New York?"

Louisa colored and snatched the package from May's hands. "Humor me. I have had it with me ever since my first trip to Europe, and with it I have survived many a scrape. It brings me good luck."

"You really are a romantic, you know, carrying that old hat about."

"It's just a reminder of a happy time in my life," said Louisa, placing the tattered bundle gently back in the trunk.

"Well, you should sweep those tired memories out of your brain and collect some new ones. I think you just might adore New York," May said, folding a woolen shawl. "It has all your favorite charms: poverty, greed, child labor, horrid prison conditions. By now, I think it is more Londonier than your beloved London."

"*Londonier* isn't a word, dear. But if it means that special combination of grit and wealth, bustle and crime, ambition and avarice … all those things I treasure so much, then yes, it is Londony." Louisa struck a dignified pose and proclaimed in her favorite stage voice, "I shall be happy to reveal the plight of the underpaid seamstresses, the women subjugated to tyrannical marriages, the children working in sweatshops." She paced the room like a grandstand. Finally, with a theatrical bow, she concluded. "All this I will do through the gentle messages in one of my 'simple stories.'"

"Sometimes I think you are more subversive than our Mr. Thoreau was," May laughed, shaking her head at her rebellious sister. "Whether New York welcomes you, swallows you, or remains completely indifferent doesn't concern you, I see. You will be the one observing and recording, writing of its wonders or exposing its injustices."

"You know the Alcotts are destined to fight inequity and unfairness," Louisa declared. "I remain bewildered as to why the role of the 'Children's Friend' has been cast upon me. But since I'm playing that part, I will play it dramatically."

17

She was ready to dip her toe into the roiling whirlpool of New York City. Louisa was not one to make waves, but she was not at all averse to starting a ripple.

"Slow down, Louisa. This is a sojourn, not a crusade." May shook her head at her excitable sister. "Remember to get some rest and by all means, drink some champagne!"

Chapter 2

The New York Central

Louisa stared out of the window as her train lurched toward New York City. She left Syracuse behind with relief. The Women's Congress there had been both stimulating and nerve-racking. On the one hand, she was at her best with the beloved group of activists who made up the American Women's Suffrage Association. She was humbled to know that her presence at the conference had given special significance to the proceedings, that her letters of support and her commitment to the cause made an impact. That was the positive aspect of her fame. Still, she rejected as ridiculous all the attention she attracted due to her celebrity. She had been besieged by girls and their mothers, kissed and accosted and entreated for autographs. Being the center of attention was exactly what Louisa was hoping to avoid for the second part of her trip, the upcoming months in the New York sprawl.

She had hastily boarded the train at the Syracuse depot, barely evading the throngs of young ladies who had also ascended, chattering about the ideas and energy they had inhaled at the conference. Louisa settled into a corner, collapsing her long legs and lanky arms and adjusting her broad-brimmed hat and veil to shadow her face. She scrutinized the occupants of the car. Two middle-aged men, their newspapers shielding their sidelong glances, ogled a trio of fresh-faced young women in hats that brimmed with carnations and lace. The girls had left the conference with enough fire to color their cheeks and warm their dreams, rendering them completely oblivious to the attentions cast their way. A mother quieted her children, who clamored for her to read aloud to them. "Children, we cannot disturb the others on the train. You will have to read silently," she shushed them.

"But we've only got one *St. Nicholas*," blubbered the youngest boy. "And the last chapter of Miss Alcott's bully story is in this one." Louisa slunk further into her chair, grabbing a newspaper that lay about. Using the two gawking gentlemen as her guides, she opened it wide.

She scanned the news, looking for coverage of the women's meeting. Police raids, political news and stock market reports took precedence, and the never-ending Beecher-Tilton scandal was being revived again. It sold so many papers that the press seemed unable to let it rest. *Ah, here's our meeting's coverage, page seven, bottom right, sandwiched between the horse racing bets and an article about a suicide attempt by an unrequited lover. How chipper that the ladies should be recognized so,* she thought, finally ferreting out the headline: *Women's Congress---Officers for 1876---An Immense Audience.* Still, she appreciated her anonymous people watching, and kept her gazette in place. *No wonder the old fellows assume this posture immediately on the train. They might be eavesdropping or sleeping, and it is all the same to us.*

The train trundled through woodlands and rolling mountain scenery, bright with the magnificence of a New York autumn. Utica, Schenectady, Troy—with each town, more ladies descended. Across from Louisa, a matron and her two adult daughters stirred restlessly. "We had a glorious few days," one young woman brooded as she watched another small town fly past the window. "Only a few more stops left."

The second sister nodded. "We best rouse ourselves," she said, fumbling in her bag and drawing out her knitting. Louisa knew, for she understood how it was with the lives of women everywhere, that they had carved out a few days away from domestic responsibilities. But now the women turned industriously to their piecework or darning, picking up where they left off before their galvanizing trip. Watching them, Louisa imagined an endless skein of wool, unbroken, fashioned into shawls and jumpers and stockings, enveloping with its warmth and comfort while entangling the hands of the faithful darners. The women's fingers moved, wrists flapping, the rhythmic clack of the train echoing the gentle click of the needles. Women's work never would stop and never did get noticed.

At Albany, all the passengers and baggage had to be ferried by boat across the Hudson River to board the line that would continue to New York. In East Albany, Louisa sat in the depot commissary sipping tea and chewing a bland boiled beef dinner. Her bones and stomach were both starting to ache, and she still had to suffer an overnight passage to New York. She scanned the other faces and noted that some of the women from the conference remained among the passengers. She could not let her guard down yet. It wasn't easy to eat with her veil in place and she soon gave up the effort with relief at not having to stomach the unpalatable food.

The bell rang to board. Louisa collected her belongings and strolled to the locomotive, settling at a window seat. A wave of activity on the platform caught her attention—a passenger needing assistance to board, no doubt. Porters loaded a cumbersome wheeled chair into the baggage car. A valet entered the car and looked about for suitable seating for his party. Two porters followed, supporting a thin young man. They nearly carried the man between them and his face contorted in pain. Once settled, the valet covered the invalid's frail legs with a shawl, adjusted some pillows at his neck, and offered him a cup of tea from a thermos. The young man declined with a shake of his head and shifted slightly to look at the receding train station.

"This will be a most unpleasant evening," the man said.

21

"But we hope the effort will be worth it, Mr. Hahn," the valet responded.

While the pair were fashionably dressed, the young man exuded neither airs nor haughtiness and the valet showed only genuine concern. They spoke together pleasantly, with the cordiality of trusted friends rather than the constraints of master and servant.

The young man appeared near thirty years old, with dark, wavy hair and a gaunt face. He seemed deep in contemplation as he looked at the bright autumn foliage, squinting at times, then closing his eyes contentedly for a moment. Soon, his face creased with pain. He sat almost motionless, his face sullen, lips taut. When the train lurched or swerved he grimaced and once or twice let out a groan.

"Can I get you some quinine, sir?" the valet offered. The young man smiled at his assistant kindly, but waved away the suggestion. His hands were gnarled and misshapen. Louisa took note of the angry red joints and the wildly curving fingers, so distorted that they resembled swan's necks. He suffered from an advanced case of rheumatoid arthritis.

After the third groan, Louisa was in action. She never travelled without a well-stocked medicine bag. "Excuse me," she ventured, approaching the pair and addressing the ailing man. "I could not help but see your discomfort. I think I might be of assistance."

There was an awkward pause. The young man looked quickly at his valet and then away from Louisa. The valet stood, as if to protect him from view. Louisa felt she had blundered badly.

"Is my condition so very apparent … and appalling?" the man said gruffly, still turned away from her.

"I beg your pardon," she said meekly. "It's just that I have done some nursing in my time and I never travel without a little pharmacy for my own ailments." Perhaps her intrusion would be interpreted as strange, even insistent, but Louisa persisted nonetheless. "I'll just leave you some arnica—it's a salve that can help the pain and inflammation," she said hurriedly, poking about in the well-worn valise.

"Use it if you like. It's tip top for my own twinges and soreness ...."

Louisa looked up, raising the apothecary jar in her hand. The two men shared a smile, then looked at her with amusement and interest. "How fortunate, sir, that this kind lady has a suggestion for your comfort," the valet said, with a more sincere tone in his voice than Louisa expected. The young man looked weary but his manner turned more gracious. His cautious eyes met Louisa's, half bemused and half exasperated. He nodded and waved his hand for Louisa to proceed. Soon she was instructing the valet on the amount to use on the hands, wrists, elbows and knees.

Not long after, the frown relaxed on the young man's face. He turned to Louisa with a brightened mood and stretched out his inflamed, misshapen claw. She took it as gently as she could.

"Thank you so much for your kindness, ma'am. You can grasp my hand a bit tighter now, because the salve has lessened my pain for the moment," the young man said. "I am Augustine Hahn. This is my assistant, Robert Cooper. You are a veritable sorceress with your concoction. You have placed a spell on me, if only a temporary one, for I am at peace."

Louisa saw that their conversation had attracted the attention of two women whom she had been avoiding since they clamored aboard at Syracuse. She thought they might have been reporters from a women's gazette. She stood awkwardly, holding Mr. Hahn's hand, knowing that she should introduce herself.

His eyes looked at her questioningly.

"I am Charlotte May," Louisa announced, flustered at her inability to concoct a better subterfuge. She had just spent the week in Syracuse with a cousin by that name and it came to her immediately. She had a warm relationship with Lottie May and Louisa knew she would feel comfortable in her new role.

"Miss May, we are heading to New York to attempt a hydrotherapy cure for Mr. Hahn's benefit. And your treatment has started his cure already," said Robert.

In the morning, the three acquaintances met in the dining car shortly before the arrival in New York. Judging from his fatigued expression, Louisa was certain that Augustine had not slept at all in the Pullman car overnight. He seemed to be counting every milepost, and gratefully recognized the final approach to the city.

"We are in the Bronx already," Augustine noticed. "Take a look at the last bit of picturesque landscape before we enter the tunnel." Louisa admired a charming vista of wooden colonial structures surrounded by gentle rolling lawns. A rustic mill at the waterside was roiled by the churning motion of a small but turbulent sluice of water. "The Dutch named this creek 'Spuyten Duyvil' because it has such a treacherous current," Augustine said. "It separates the upper tail of Manhattan from the countrified district of the Bronx."

"I am fortunate to have such a knowledgeable guide," said Louisa.

"I have dreamed about this trip to New York since I was a schoolboy," Augustine replied. "I just never imagined I would arrive in such poor condition."

Louisa thought of her own joint aches. *Marmee always said that if you look about, you will find someone in more need than yourself.*

Suddenly, the train plunged into darkness. A few moments later, a streak of light illuminated a dusty, broad avenue, wooden shacks and a few granite buildings before another plunge into darkness. "This is the new Fourth Avenue tunnel," Augustine said. "Before this, the train lines coming into the depot had literally cut the city in two, dividing east from west along Fourth Avenue. People couldn't cross the tracks safely. Now the train lines are buried under the street level, and above, the promenade of Park Avenue was added." Augustine's energy and interest seemed to be surging more and more as they approached the city. "Watch this now! Right here, the engine

24

disconnects ... and glides off to the track on the right ... and we roll slowly on to Grand Central Station, with no noise or smoke to disturb the platforms."

"I am glad you seem to feel better today," Louisa said, "even before you start the water therapy."

"Bah—it's my mother, and a newfound brother, who hope for some kind of cure. I am not coming to New York for that! I am here to immerse myself in the art world and to work on something new, perhaps my masterpiece." Augustine fumbled at the front of his coat, but the fingers could not work the buttons and he turned sheepishly to Robert for help.

How pathetic. Louisa was touched by the tableau of the master and devoted valet. *He is an artist and cannot even manage his coat buttons.*

Augustine's enthusiasm was undeterred, even once he was deposited in his wheeled chair in the grand terminal. "Look, Miss May, at this magnificent room: all iron and glass, not one pillar in sight. There's not a room in the country that is larger. At night, it's all illuminated by gas lamps—it glows like a beacon. I might be able to do something on canvas that shows the glistening light, don't you think, Robert?"

"People would like to see that, Mr. Hahn. This place is almost as popular as the Capitol Building in Washington," he replied.

"Forget the Capitol. New York aims at nothing less than being the Capital of the World."

Louisa's interests lay neither in architecture nor politics. The mass of humanity—their struggles, their delights and their foibles—always captivated her. She followed the back of the wheelchair toward the hansom stand, clutching her shawl strap and stumbling a bit to keep up with the pace. The number of people herding about her was breathtaking, reminding her of the urban crush she had experienced before at Paddington Station in London.

"Excuse me, ma'am."

"Pardon ... sorry." She was already being jostled by commuters hurrying for departing trains.

"I expect my half-brother will be able to find me, as I am a bit of a spectacle in this condition," Augustine grumbled. "He is to meet us here. I hate to be a bother to someone I hardly know, even if he is a relation. Growing up, I longed to know him, but now I feel I will be nothing but a burden."

"Brothers of any kind should be the closest relations in the world," Louisa said. "Unless, of course, you consider sisters."

"A gentle sister might be better suited to my needs right now." Augustine shifted uncomfortably in his chair.

"Can I help you get a cab to your destination, Miss May?" asked Robert, heading off to acquire a carriage.

"No, thank you, I need to stretch my legs and get a glimpse of the city," answered Louisa. Actually, she pined to witness the poignant meeting of the two long-lost brothers, but having learned that Augustine was sensitive to observation, she determined not to be meddlesome and turned to bid her fellow traveller goodbye. But her escape was too late, for a stocky, energetic man burst out of the crowd and encircled Augustine in a genial embrace. While the two brothers made their somewhat awkward introductions, the mystery of their estrangement was starting to make sense. The older brother, with his gray flecked beard and handsomely creased face, seemed some fifteen years older than Augustine. He spoke in a thick German accent.

"Excuse me if I fly off—you gentlemen have much to talk over." Louisa tried to make her exit.

"Miss May, I cannot thank you enough for the comfort you gave me last night. This is my brother, Herr Josef Hahn. I have known him a full moment longer than you have," Augustine said.

Herr Hahn turned to Louisa. "Ah, so you be a goot Engel watching over my brother. I vould like very much to be of assistance to you during your stay. You vill find us at the Dr. Eli Peck Miller Hygienic Institute. Eet is on Twenty-Sixth Street."

Well, this cannot possibly get more inopportune. Louisa had just been introduced under a false name and now the brothers were staying at her hotel. She blushed and stammered again, caught in her lie. Augustine scrutinized her with those same questioning eyes he had when she had falsely introduced herself the night before. It certainly would not do for her to introduce herself as Louisa May Alcott in the middle of Grand Central Station. She imagined the crowd which was milling about them, pausing and pushing in her direction.

"How extraordinary! I am staying at the very same facility," Louisa heard her own voice maundering. Why could she not recover from her falsehood with a quip or a laugh like other women, the way May might do? How like herself to complicate her introductions at the hotel, to bumble with her new relationships!

"Glorious!" Augustine gushed. "I feel better already knowing that you will be there."

And with a beguiling wink, the middle-aged Herr Hahn twirled the young Mr. Hahn about in the wheelchair, heading toward the hansom stand where Robert beckoned.

Figure 1. **Grand Central Depot**

Chapter 3

Streets of New York

Louisa watched the backs of the mismatched American and German brothers become engulfed by the crowd in Grand Central Station.

"Where are the Red Caps to be found?" A young mother with a carriage, a toddler and an impossible amount of luggage begged assistance. Louisa noticed that young boys seemed to be loitering about the place. Some were bootblacks hawking their trade, but others seemed not quite as industrious. She noted a coy young pickpocket eyeing her purse all too intently. She pulled the drawstrings taut and looped them over her belt to secure the pouch to her waist. She stared the surprised boy down and he sidled away, looking a bit cowed by her unspoken but not unkind reprimand. She quickly engaged a porter and sent her trunk and baggage ahead to the hotel.

Exiting the depot on to Forty-Second Street, she looked up at the imposing structure. Made of brick with marble and granite trim and sporting three towers topped by mansard roofs and three gleaming clocks, Grand Central Station impressed her as some imaginary vision of a French Empire style that could only be built in New York. She turned her face toward the whole pulsing city to the south and saw the new mall of walkways and gardens that made up Park Avenue. Smiling to herself, she ventured to cross the street, but had not the slightest idea how it would be managed, given the carriages, street cars, stages and omnibuses all in confusion in the streets around the depot.

"Need help, ma'am?" This query came from a rosy-faced young lad, neatly but simply dressed, clutching his newsboy's pouch across his chest. His shoes were worn and the cap covering his very short, red hair was decidedly too big. "No offense, ma'am, it's just that you look new here."

Louisa's kind eyes showed that she was *not* offended. In fact, nothing pleased her more than to be starting her adventure conversing with a gallant lad of the streets. "If you can give me some pointers about how to cross the street, I would be ever so grateful, young man," she laughed.

The boy raised his eyebrows and looked a bit peeved. "Golly, you talk funny," he blurted. Louisa smiled. Her Boston accent had startled him. She knew, too, that her appearance could be rather forbidding due to her gangly height, so she was satisfied when he added, "But you look rather merry and I bet you're a good egg even with that queer speech. It's easier if you cross near the policeman, and"—here he glanced at her polished boots—"I can find you a crossing sweeper, too."

A tangle of horse carts, delivery wagons and barouches filled the intersection. Horses reared and drivers backed up or stopped to unload passengers. The mess in the muddy street was horrific. Louisa hitched up her skirts and followed the wiry boy between the carriages as he jostled and elbowed his way, keeping close to the limber back of a girl who swept a path across the street before him. She practiced her skill with no shame for the benefit of the awkward but grateful parade that followed her. Louisa's heart went out to the two enterprising youths who managed to make themselves useful and asked only for their due in return. She fingered her purse for a few coins, turning first to the girl, who seemed impossibly young and vulnerable. The child grasped her coins, dropped a half curtsy, and was off in the other direction, forging another path for other customers in an instant.

"I've got a lot more pointers than just how to hop 'cross the street," the boy said, brushing away her attempt to tip him. "I can show you the lay of the land."

"I trust you already, my lad, and am ready to follow your lead," Louisa said, and he scampered ahead of her, heading west on Forty-Second Street.

Now that she was safely distanced from the din of the station, Louisa was able to look about her. Across Forty-Second Street, in the direction that the newsboy pointed, she saw a gigantic Egyptian tomb looming two boulevards away on Fifth Avenue.

"My goodness, son," said Louisa, "from French Empire to Thebes on one boulevard! It's so very odd. I will take your advice and head in that direction. Let's see if we can saunter where the blue bloods live." Ivy enveloped the thick granite walls of the Egyptian structure, and high above her, Louisa saw small groups of visitors gathered on the promenade that circled the rim of the massive monument. A plaque on the corner of Forty-Second Street explained this was the terminus of the famed Croton water system.

"They say we have the freshest city water in the world," the newsboy boasted. "It comes from thirty-two miles away. This pool holds fifteen days of water for us to use."

"What the desert of Egypt has to do with water I certainly cannot understand, but this is the most magnificent mass of building I have seen in a long time," Louisa acknowledged.

The jaunty newsboy paced at her side, offering tips. "You can't get lost—everything here is a grid. Each block is exactly the same length and twenty blocks makes one mile. The long avenues run in a north-south direction. Fifth Avenue runs straight down the center of the island, and everything is marked either east or west from there. Everything's straight 'cept Broadway, which runs kinda slanting through it all. Every time Broadway crosses an avenue, there's a triangle and we have a square or plaza there."

As the pair wandered south along Fifth Avenue, Louisa approved of the sedate and gracious homes. The Bottas, the family friends Marmee had mentioned, lived nearby in this refined neighborhood. All the affluence and gentility of the city were on display in the brownstone-clad buildings with high stoops, large windows and impressive entablatures. Elegant women strolled with their children and the clip-clop of private carriages on cobblestone made a pleasant sound, unlike the din of the station she had left earlier. Men in somber broadcloth frock coats brightened by vibrant neckties accompanied women in fine silks. Nursemaids in starched aprons minded perfectly attired, mannered children. The promenade reminded her more of Europe than Boston in the noticeable way that the pedestrians displayed their finery.

Several blocks south, the elegant houses gave way to fanciful recreations of European power. The serenity of the Federal style was replaced by small imitations of Italianate palazzos, medieval fortresses and French chateaux. Louisa had seen the originals of these faux castles, and sensed the strained attempt at a new aristocracy. Her father, a homespun architect, revered the integrity of a building in its environment, keeping their home in character with the surrounding land as a reflection of the place. The dull brown of their homestead was selected expressly because it blended with the Concord elements. Here, standing out seemed to be the main ambition.

An elegant woman walking a poodle passed by with an air of aloofness. *House of Worth*, Louisa guessed, looking at her dress. Louisa didn't care much for keeping up with those wildly expensive fashions.

She chuckled a bit to herself, thinking of the little French bonnet she had packed at the last moment. It wouldn't do at all on this modern street. Louisa's secret treasure was a purchase made during a glorious spree on the very first day she had ever spent in Paris. It was a delight selected by her dear boy, Ladislas, who had insisted that she should own the charming article. The imitation chateaux and the counterfeit French femme must have set her daydreaming.

Louisa and her newsboy had reached the intersection of Fifth Avenue and Thirty-Fourth Street. "We got the Vanderbilts on one corner and the Astors on the other here," said her informative guide. On opposite corners, as if challenging each other's superiority, the two wealthy families vied over the opulence of their mansions. Enormous red brick buildings swarmed with architraves, cornices and columns made of Nova Scotia freestone.

"I think I must be trapped in some insane person's idea of luxury," Louisa said. "What a bunch of poppycock this is!"

"They say they've got ballrooms, pich'ure galleries, even their own theaters inside," the newsboy marveled.

"And what is that gleaming white marble palace?"

"Why it's the most expensive home in the whole wide world!" said the boy. "It belongs to Mr. Stewart. He's the richest man in the city and he comes from Ireland." Louisa understood the source of the boy's pride, taking in his red mop and freckles.

"He owns the biggest store in town, doesn't he? A merchant prince," she replied.

The building glittered and dazzled in the afternoon sunglow. It soared four stories high, clad in white marble as pure and soft as the Carrara Louisa had seen in Italy. The building was ringed about with a stone balustrade, and a watchman paced a slow, deliberate walk from end to end. Double rosewood doors made up the front entrance, surrounded by twin sets of Corinthian columns. Suddenly, the doors opened, and an entourage of elegant women descended the front steps. The foyer blazed with gas torches and a globed chandelier. The boy's eyes grew wide and his face blanched. Louisa stared at the marble columns, mirrors and coffered ceilings. The boy stared at the nude nymph statues.

"Come here." Louisa drew him to the right side of the door. "Look at that statue and tell me what you think." She pointed to a regal woman, fully clothed, wearing a crown.

"She's a queen, I reckon," said the lad. "But she's got chains binding her."

"It's a depiction of Zenobia, the Syrian queen who was captured by the Romans. Do you see how nobel she is, not allowing her captors to defeat her? The artist is a woman." She could thank May for her instructions about the art to see in New York. "I believe she is trying to say that women are still shackled today," Louisa told the incredulous boy.

"Take a look at them gals," the newsboy said, jerking his thumb to the departing socialites. "They ain't sufferin'."

"I like to say that women have been called queens for a long time, but the kingdom given them isn't worth ruling," said Louisa. "You have no idea how much being male improves your chances in life, son."

The boy eyed her doubtfully. "Well, I'm about to improve my chances by my own self. It's time for me to get my afternoon papers." He looked at the back of the watchman, who was pacing his beat away from them. With a quick move, the wiry boy jumped to the top of the balustrade and was suddenly airborne toward the closest gleaming column, grasping it with two hands and swinging about it one time. He leapt back to the street and raced off before the watchman could even respond. From the far corner, the guard raised his fist and the boy scuttled off, giving him a mocking wave.

With his dramatic exit, Louisa realized she had missed an opportunity to compensate the boy for his services. She didn't even know his name. He was certainly an extraordinary character. She continued down Fifth Avenue but the affluence and ostentation oppressed her. At sedate Madison Square, she turned off the avenue to Broadway.

Broadway, the most crowded, bustling, fashionable artery in the city, filled with characters. Peddlers with carts or brimming baskets extolled their wares. A messenger in a drab green jacket with brass buttons held his bag protectively. It could be contracts he was scuttling to a railway magnate, stacks of gold for the Treasury or just a dozen pastries for the boys in the mail room. The serious man with a top hat and mustache could be a music impresario or a renowned financier. A dapper fellow on the corner, eyes shielded and cigarette dangling, impressed Louisa as either an insolent idler or a sharp-eyed detective. She must have stared at him for a moment too long and he winked in her direction. *That's impudent!* she thought and then realized that she had encountered a character who could comfortably enliven one of her "potboiler" stories.

She looked about to see if she should be easy walking in this neighborhood unaccompanied. She was immediately encouraged to see that young ladies were making a mark of their own in the energy of New York. Groups of school girls chattered, young shop girls hastened to work, and housewives, their baskets filled with produce, strode from vendor to vendor. The mood was cheery, exuberant, almost impetuous.

Louisa was aware of her footsteps keeping cadence with the pace of the throng. In Concord, she had never felt alone. Even when she strode through the town early in the morning on one of her jaunts, she knew that the townspeople were watching her every move. Already she felt liberation here as she merged with the populace—together, yet completely solitary. One might do anything here, she thought, and do it in complete anonymity.

The shop windows enticed with live displays of their wares. Louisa smiled at her own reflection in a toy store window as she watched tiny steamships wound with springs ply across the waters of a miniature lake. In another, a Shaker woman demonstrated a mechanical clothes washer. Marmee had always been wary of the burden of work placed on the Shaker women at their utopian village. How clever of them to take women's most onerous chore and motorize the hard work! Behind another plate glass window, two store clerks worked side by side. One man wrote in elegant script on parchment. Dipping his pen and blotting frequently, he made slow progress. His counterpart demonstrated a piano-like machine. He pecked and pounded deliberately, revealing printed letters onto paper and far outstripping his partner's output. Louisa had heard of these curious ways of producing type in the office or home. She could not imagine being able to complete her stories without a pen in her hand. She liked the feeling of her thoughts flowing directly through her fingers into the pen, resulting in an ink trail that, though slightly messy and always rushed, revealed her thoughts.

She entered Union Square and stopped to admire the grand equestrian statue of George Washington. The huge bronze was not unlike the statue of Marcus Aurelius that she had seen in Rome, traditional in every way. The horse strode resolutely while the leader was steadfast, gazing forward with hand upraised. Louisa felt sorry for General Washington's horse, though. *If the President dismounted right now, I think he would stand taller than that overworked beast*, she thought. She never could admire static works of art, no matter how much May had tried to instruct her.

The park's foliage was at the peak of its many-colored autumn show. Leaves of gold and orange still clung to the trees, blocking out the sounds of the chiming clock towers, the piercing whistles of the policemen, the rumble and rattle of the passing vehicles. Half sequestered from the city hum, she felt a calming breeze—a warm, hazy wind, the kind of summer current that returned in autumn to bring the New York residents one last frolic before the calamitous winter. They called it an Indian summer and knew when it was over the wretched, icy weather would begin.

The aromas from a cluster of street stands on Fourteenth Street reminded her that she had not eaten since breakfast. The voices of the women as they bartered and haggled rang with the Irish brogue. Some had delightful candies and sugar plums, others had russet and yellow apples piled into pyramids, some had plump molasses cakes. She selected a fine red apple from one stand and coffee and hot cakes at another.

The mild weather, the simple meal, the excitement of a new adventure—all combined to give her a feeling of complete contentment. Despite the coffee, Louisa was fatigued. Ever since her typhoid pneumonia during the war, she had to push her body to match the energy of her spirits and the activity of her mind. Perhaps the bath treatments that she would begin would restore some of her vigor.

Red and yellow omnibuses pulled by gigantic horses ran on double rails up and down the center of Broadway. Louisa clamored aboard for her return trip uptown to her lodgings. It seemed that all the mass of humanity that thronged on the streets had followed her into the cars. Although the carriage was furnished in high style with upholstered chairs and brocade curtains, all intentions of comfort were abandoned by the crush of bodies lurching with the tramp of the horses. Clustered at the trolley stops, groups of newsboys shouted and thrust their wares through the windows. As no one could have raised a hand to accept a newspaper, this seemed to be an ineffective method of business.

Not knowing what to do with her lanky limbs and oversized personage, Louisa stared straight out the window. Suddenly, a red-haired gamin dangled dangerously from the roof of the bus, thereby outwitting his competition and having exclusive rights to sales between stops.

"Evening edition, miss?" He thrust his paper just under Louisa's nose.

Recognizing the same lad who had been her guide earlier in the day, she smiled. "Are you here to save me again by getting me out of this infernal situation and back to the street safely?"

"What's ya stop, lady?" the conductor barked, overhearing her and apparently offended by her discomfort in his vehicle.

"Twenty-Sixth Street."

"Just here, then. Come on, folks, let the lady out."

Louisa descended the steps of the bus while the lad up top tumbled down to her side.

"Need an escort, ma'am? I can deliver you safely to your rooms."

The boy was as energetic and enterprising at the end of the day as he had been earlier. Louisa appreciated his industry.

"Lead on, brave pathfinder. I will follow." This little walk allowed Louisa to get a better look at her protector. By his demeanor and ability, she took him to be near his eleventh year. His confidence and authority were belied by his slight frame and light step. "I could use a guide for some of my outings in the city and I see that you are the very man I need. Would you please come in the morning to deliver my paper, and we can discuss terms of your employment as my escort?"

"That's awful nice of you, ma'am, and you could not find a better man for the job!" The young face beamed with pride at his new assignment.

The congestion of Broadway intensified in this part of town. Skittish horses stopped suddenly, then backed up, kicked and bit. A horse in front of a tavern had stalled and the horses behind were restless. There were enough horses in the street to start a stampede. Louisa crossed to the quieter side of the street, keeping the boy in tow and hugging close to the buildings. Just as the pair turned into Twenty-Sixth Street, a loud thud and a wail pierced the air. The crowd surged forward in rabid interest. Crumpled beneath a rearing horse lay the writhing body of a messenger boy. He grasped his crooked leg and bawled loudly, in fright and pain combined. Louisa intuitively drew her startled little guide to her, covering his head with her shawl. A huge police man in blue, who seemed to have jurisdiction on Broadway, waded into the crowd.

"Make way, make way, get along, nothing to see here," he barked to the crowd. By mere physical force he was able to subdue the horse, lift the boy, disperse the crowd and send a relay to the precinct.

Louisa felt the newsboy tremble in her arms, and then with an abrupt movement he freed himself from her grasp, crammed his hat down and grumbled, "Schucks, ma'am, it ain't like this don't happen every day. He'll be a'right. That ain't the way a man screams when he's real hurt." Louisa wondered how he knew that so confidently. "Besides, every precinct has a direct telegraph wire to the hospital. That big cop, he's a member of the Broadway squad. They all need to be over six feet tall. He's already sent the alarm."

"He's got such authority and expertise I half expected that he would set that bone right here in the street," Louisa said as the policeman set about clearing the road for the expected ambulance.

"This chap is lucky. The closest hospital is Bellevue and they have seven ambulances. They tear through the streets, the horses all white—wish I could stay to see that!" He had recovered himself. Louisa thought, with the snarl of carriages and wagons, that it would be some time before an ambulance could navigate anywhere near them, and she convinced the newsboy to carry on to her door.

The Miller Hygienic Hotel had a double wide facade: one side for the hotel entrance and one for the Turkish Baths. The boy gave a low whistle. "What kind of place *is* this?" he wondered aloud, cocking his head.

"Never mind that for now. It's not as exotic as it sounds. If you haven't got rheumatism, this isn't of any interest to you." Louisa laughed at his confusion. "Stop daydreaming, lad! I need to make sure you are capable of coming to me tomorrow in the late morning." This time she was able to slip the deserved coins into the boy's hand. "I will pay you in advance for my papers for this week," Louisa said.

He grasped the quarter joyfully, tipped his cap, and leapt down the steps in one bound. As he scampered away, she realized that she did not know his name. "What do they call you?" she shouted after him.

She was just able to hear his muffled response as he tore down the street: "Casey. Casey McDermott."

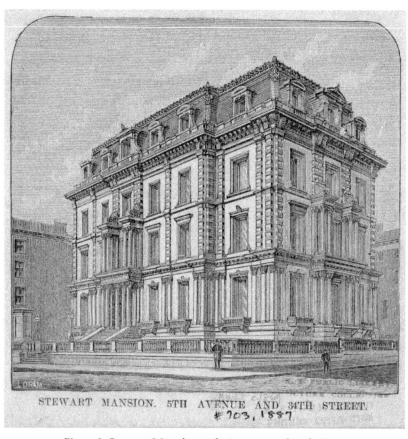

STEWART MANSION. 5TH AVENUE AND 34TH STREET.

Figure 2. Stewart Mansion, 5th Avenue and 34th Street

Chapter 4

Dr. Eli Peck Miller's Hotel

Forty-One West Twenty-Sixth Street was on a quiet block between Broadway and Sixth Avenue. Louisa had chosen Dr. Miller's Bath Hotel for its proximity to all the rail lines and shopping as much as for its claims for hygienic cures. She hoped that the clientele would be more sedate than those at the usual hotels filled with tourists and socialites—perhaps her fellow lodgers would be more intent on their cures than on uncovering secrets. Louisa detested gossips and nosy people, but knew the intrusions of life at a boarding hotel. She wanted to protect her privacy absolutely even while she thrived on observing others, guessing at their affairs and imagining their inner thoughts. It fueled the vivid portraits and honest relationships in her work. As Louisa climbed the high stoop to the hotel entrance, she wondered about the characters she would be able to spin from the community inside.

She was delighted to find her first character just behind the entry-way. The door girl was a dainty young Negress, thin and spry, barely out of childhood but with the grace of a woman. She wore a crisp white cap and an apron which did not obscure the coarse brown linen dress beneath. The girl welcomed Louisa to the warmth of the hallway and, taking her shawl and bonnet with a shy, sidelong look in Louisa's direction, nodded toward the adjoining office. "Who shall I say has arrived?" she asked.

"You can call me Miss May, and what is your name, dear?"

"I am Rebecca Grant," she said. "But here, I am just Rebecca."

"I shall call you Miss Grant, for you are a young lady."

"Oh, no, miss, that wouldn't do. It might make Mrs. Miller ornery."

With that recommendation about her hostess, Louisa stifled a grin as she turned to the hotel reception office. "Then no need to introduce me to your matron. I will handle it myself." She waved to Rebecca. She didn't know where to begin with an explanation about how two of the hotel guests thought she was someone she wasn't. Or that she really wanted to be someone else completely for her sojourn. She might as well just continue with her little charade for a few days to see how much peace and solitude she could get. She didn't have the strength or interest to work at fulfilling anyone's image of the famous Miss Alcott while she attended to her own health and relaxation here.

Mrs. Miller rose from a desk that was organized precisely with folders and ledgers, lists of menu items, hotel receipts and small devices that represented models of the hydrotherapy equipment. She wore an anticipant, fixed smile as she greeted Louisa with reserve. "Welcome, Miss Alcott. We are humbled by your attendance at our facility." For years, people had been as obsequious toward her as Mrs. Miller was right now. Louisa knew this smile of slight hesitation, of idolization, of expectation—expectations she felt she might never measure up to.

"No, it is I who should be humbled by your work with the ailing," Louisa began decorously, then hastened to add, "but while I am here, I would very much like to be considered just a needy client. Perhaps I could be introduced as Miss Charlotte May, just to keep the patrons and the staff more relaxed around me."

Mrs. Miller blinked and cleared her throat. A slight look of panic flashed across her eyes. "That is hardly necessary, Miss Alcott. I would not allow your rest to be interrupted regardless of your celebrity," she said icily. Perhaps Louisa's hostess had been looking forward to advertising 'the great authoress' residing at her hotel. For all she knew, she was already on the next broadsheet.

"Nevertheless, for the comfort of others, you must agree that we do not want autograph seekers clamoring at the door. I am trying to escape that part of my life just now. I certainly won't be able to recuperate if people expect me to regale them with stories," Louisa replied firmly. *No expectations, no demands, no adulation, no whispers.*

"As you wish." Mrs. Miller paused a moment, composed her face and bustled efficiently back behind her desk, drawing out a pamphlet. "Miss Alcott—er, Miss May—as you know, our goals are to treat and cure the chronically ill without the use of medicines, or 'poisons,' as we in the hygienic culture call them," she said, "while furnishing you with a pleasant, genial atmosphere for your daily relaxation. I hope you will appreciate our healthful meals, quiet rest times and attention to your needs."

"My needs will be very few. Just the quiet you mention to work, and some vigorous treatments to get my old bones in tip-top shape." Mrs. Miller looked a little deflated by her candor and joviality. Whatever image Mrs. Miller had of Louisa May Alcott, she was dispelling it grandly.

"Very well, yes, then. We have the Turkish Baths, electric baths, vapor baths. Also the Swedish Movement Cure, machine vibrations, lifting cure, water cure and magnetism." Louisa had an urge to make a joke about electricity and water, but opted instead to meekly choose a system of treatment that would leave her afternoons free for writing and exploring and her evenings open for theater, dinner, soirées and lectures.

Louisa was not completely sure that she could accept all of hydrotherapy's amazing cure claims. Baths, especially sulfur springs, had been used for millennia in Europe. There, the chemical compositions of the waters were considered the essential elements in the cure, which could be applied as baths but also ingested or inhaled.

Mrs. Miller pointed out the latest thoughts about hydrotherapy in modern institutions. "Our theory of relief is based on temperature shifts, sweating to release toxins and rubbing to induce circulatory changes," she explained.

"If only I can find relief from my chronic insomnia and get some rest, I will pronounce your treatments a success," Louisa said.

"Please let me show you to your rooms. You have an hour to freshen up before supper. I will send Lizzie to help you with your things. As your trunk arrived earlier, she has been able to unpack and iron as necessary." They stepped out into the hallway that lead to the upstairs quarters. Augustine's wheelchair sat waiting at the bottom of the stairs. Mrs. Miller showed the way up the curved stairway and down a silent, carpeted corridor to Louisa's chambers.

The rooms were compact but delightful, providing all that Louisa would need. There was a tiny sitting room papered in green and white stripes, a small green and yellow sofa and matching tasseled draperies. Louisa was charmed to see a petite spinet in the corner, giving her the immediate feeling of home and grounding her back to both fond and poignant memories of the family. This anteroom was followed by a pale yellow bedroom with a writing desk near the window, where Lizzie had already placed her paper and pens.

"Your girl has done everything to make me comfortable. I don't need any other help tonight. Really, I don't need anyone to lay out my clothes or help with the lacings, as there are none," blurted Louisa. Mrs. Miller looked deflated, and with a shrug and a wan smile, retreated to her office.

An hour later, Louisa descended to the dining room. Potted ferns, an overhead fan and calm, neutral colors made the room serene. Two tables were set for nearly two dozen guests, some of whom were chatting familiarly while others, new to the proceedings, looked about themselves expectantly.

Mrs. Miller breezed in on the arm of her distinguished husband. Louisa appraised and approved of the understated beauty of her gown. Shawl collar, ruffled skirt, modest train—all were of pale pink silk. She wore neither lace nor tassels nor beading; just some quiet ruching along the skirt adorned her dress. Mrs. Miller's elegance was relaxed and casual, putting her guests at ease while announcing her as a woman of some social standing. Her transformation from the efficient matron of a health establishment to a fashionable mistress of the house was impressive.

Mrs Miller nudged her husband. "Miss May, this is my husband, Dr. Eli Miller."

"Ah, Miss May, welcome. It seems that you need some rest and nutrition. We hope to relieve your ills and restore your energy." Dr. Miller's gaze seemed intent on diagnosing her instead of meeting her. Did she really look that scrawny and ill? Perhaps she was beginning to resemble the image that the public now had of Miss Alcott: middle-aged, sedate, restrained. She did better meeting the other guests. As "Miss May," the introductions went along capitally. She could be as relaxed, boisterous and anonymous as she desired.

The Hahns entered the hall. After a quick review of the seating arrangements, Robert pivoted the wheelchair to a table with a small coterie of young men whom Mrs. Miller admitted for their desire for healthful meals and proximity to their businesses alone. Robert remained at the table with Augustine and Herr Hahn settled into a seat at the end of the second table, where he greeted the diners with familiarity.

Louisa sat next to a sweet-faced young girl. Herr Hahn beamed at her from the far end of the table. He chatted comfortably with those about him. His ruddy face easily broke into a smile after one of his own quips, and he stared down the length of the table through his monocle to judge the effect on his audience. His hair stood askew, his tie was akimbo, and his lively demeanor belied any lapse of health. He appeared to be a hale and sturdy middle-aged specimen, ready to imbibe his dinner with gusto and animate the meal with interesting banter.

"Herr Hahn is a fixture at the hotel," said Dr. Miller. "I wish my treatments could be considered the genesis of his vitality."

Louisa immediately decided that if he had any diagnosis at all it would be, perhaps, malingering. "Share the secret of your good health, sir," Louisa called to Herr Hahn. "I am eager to follow a program that might give me as much energy as you."

"Goot habits, pleasure in mein vork, and so many blessings that are not of mein own making," Herr Hahn answered warmly, but looked about him at the less fortunate guests. All along the table, Louisa saw signs of weariness and indisposition. At one end, an elderly man with a tremor leaned on his thin, pallid grandson, the one no fitter than the other. At the other end sat a timid old woman who stared stone-faced and uncomprehending as her assistant tried to interest her in the food before her. Mrs. Miller introduced these new guests as Marchesa Contini and her ward, Marienne Ayers. The marchesa wore a black ensemble that would have been fashionable three decades before and her young ward was so demure and simply dressed that she nearly disappeared into the drab draperies behind her.

An energetic and beautiful girl of about twelve chatted with her companion. "Perhaps just some cool milk and a bit of toast tonight, and then I shall feast on berries to my heart's content." The young lady exuded a grace and presence rarely found in one so young. A white-faced woman with downcast eyes sat silently nearby. She might be a widow or spinster or wife awaiting the return of her husband from an overseas business expedition. She was introduced only as Mrs. Cutney. And finally, a mother with her two sons, their throats and chests wrapped as after an asthma therapy, rounded out the group. *Well,* thought Louisa, *jolly fun this is!*

Herr Hahn gestured to the healthy fare before them. "Miss May, behold the meager meal we haf got. Cakes and toast and fruit and nuts. You vill not see any meat in this house, except perhaps mine own self. I am the rooster in this coop."

46

"You have no complaint from me, Herr Rooster. I was raised to abstain from meat." That had all changed when Louisa travelled to Europe, where she tried everything from frogs' legs to tripe and washed it all down with white Montefiascone wine. There were nights when the meals ended with a coffee and cigarettes, too. How far had she gone from those carefree days? She felt as impassioned and adventurous as ever, though the public had assigned her the role of a staid spinster who entertained children with cozy bedtime stories.

Louisa spoke aloud to the table. "I am rejecting vegetarianism in general now, just as I find it might be necessary to reject the use of alcohol. At the Women's Congress, which I just attended, some of the clearest speeches were about the connection between alcoholism, debauchery and the subjugation of women." She looked down the table to see the reactions of her fellow guests. Herr Hahn peered through his monocle. Marienne Ayers lifted her young face toward Louisa as if to ask for more guidance. The lovely Mrs. Cutney started, raised her eyebrows, and then stared almost crestfallen at the tablecloth.

"It seems that the vomen's movement vould haf to move ahead together vith the legal questions of alcohol," Herr Hahn spoke. Louisa nodded in his direction. Marienne leaned toward the speakers, her eyes alert and hopeful. Louisa read the interest in her face and knew she would have to address this in one of her novels soon. The story percolating in her head about Rose Campbell and her cousins would be the right spot. Charlie was enough of a dandy to fall under the influence of alcohol. The question would be whether Rose could rescue him from his demons and save herself in the struggle.

"Why are you rejecting vegetarianism?" Dr. Miller asked.

"I suppose I sometimes have a hankering for frogs' legs," Louisa quipped. The children gagged and screwed up their faces, and the adults laughed. In truth, this talk brought back reminders of the darkest hours in her family's story, recollections which Louisa could not utter aloud. Her father's adherence to his own strict vegetarian principles nearly killed his family when they tried to eke out an existence at the communal farm at Fruitlands. For most of that year, the family existed on flour, squash and apples, with only water to drink. *To this day*, Louisa thought to herself, shivering, *I think back on those poor children as if I was not one of them, it seems so remote and sad.* Since then, Louisa could not tolerate seeing a hungry child.

She turned to the young girl who sat with so much composure and confidence at her side. The girl's dark eyes wore a placid expression. "Do you enjoy this simple fare day after day?" Louisa asked her.

"Oh, I appreciate simple things. It's so refreshing after all I have been through in a day!" the girl said.

Louisa smiled at her theatrical response. "And how *have* you survived your trying day?"

"Such a long rehearsal it was! We rehearse for months, and sometimes the play will only perform for a week or two, depending on how the people like it."

"Oh, Miss Helene, your public always adores you," said her female companion.

"My name is Helene, but on the stage I am called Bijou Heron," the girl said by way of introduction.

Louisa knew the name and both the fame and tragedy attached to it. "My dear, I saw your beautiful mother, Matilda, play Camille many years ago in Boston. She gave a most arresting performance."

"Mother can not perform any longer," the girl sighed. "She is too weak, but always instructs me in the best methods and elocution. She took me on the stage when I was a youngster, hand in hand, playing her child."

Louisa and Anna had dreamed of becoming actresses when they were young, but neither had the heart for the hard life or the pitfalls that can befall a single woman in the profession. But this child was as serene and elegant as royalty. Matilda had introduced her daughter in a production of *Medea*, as one of the sons doomed to matricide. Louisa looked at the girl with sympathy. It was such a dark start to her career and a dismal end to her mother's.

"Well, when I was a child, I was romping around in the family barn, the instigator of all my family's productions. I kept performing regularly in the community players in … town." Louisa stopped. Perhaps she had said too much. She would have to be careful not to mention Concord. "I was always assigned the comical parts."

"That shows that you understood the playwright's motives," interjected Dr. Miller. "I suspect you are a keen observer, Miss May."

"Before the war, my rendition of 'Mrs. Jarley's Waxworks' was popular enough to raise a bit of aid for the war effort. I even wrote some dreadful plays of my own back then." Louisa reddened. It was hard to speak naturally of herself when she was supposed to be Lottie May. *Surprising what a poor actress I am right now.* She had underestimated the pitfalls of her little bluff.

Luckily, a gale of guffaws from the table of young men attracted the attention of the room. Augustine was enjoying the camaraderie. Louisa followed Herr Hahn's concerned eyes and saw that Augustine kept his hands in his lap. *He's not able to eat the soup,* Louisa observed. Robert stayed nearby but Augustine gave no sign of accepting his help in public.

Turning back to Helene, she went on. "I love the theater," said Louisa, wishing to encourage and compliment the girl. "It's one of the main reasons I came to New York."

"I would like it ever so much if you would come to a performance," replied the young actress. "I always stay at the Miller Hotel when I am performing nearby, as it is so calming and restful and I enjoy having my 'neighbors' come to the theater to see me." Helene smiled at the asthmatic boys, the trembling elders, the weary caretakers and the jocular young men, and all smiled and nodded back at her, the little Bijou of the theater—except for the solitary, pale woman who sat as if disconsolate, almost in a trance. Mrs. Cutney slipped easily into a light slumber and then with a jerk aroused herself. She turned her teary eyes toward Louisa. Something about this woman's demeanor deeply troubled Louisa. She nodded meekly and assuringly in Louisa's direction and resumed a sort of slow, careful attention to her meal. Dr. Miller seemed unconcerned. As the meal concluded, the woman's head rose. She yawned deeply, smiled a sad smile, and followed the others to the parlor.

Louisa's day had been exhausting, starting with the overnight train ride from Syracuse, her long walk in the city and the confusion and excitement of her new surroundings. She excused herself from the party and headed to her rooms.

The city sounds lessened only a little from the midday ruckus. Voices rose up from the street—parties returning from the theater or gaming houses, discussing their evening. A fire engine wailed in the distance. Two cats quarreled in the alley and a tin can clattered as it overturned in their struggle. Softly, gradually, the city calmed, until the only sounds were the firm footfalls and low whistle of the policeman on his beat and the occasional clip-clopping of a horse and carriage. Louisa always slept well in a city.

Louisa took a candle and headed to the water closet. Standing at the top of the stairs she was arrested by two visions, the first as angelic as the next was ghastly. Sitting on the middle landing, Helene and Rebecca, the door girl, huddled together. Rebecca recited her lessons and the little actress encouraged the performance with attention and gentle corrections. Past the candle glow surrounding their heads as they bent together in concentration, the front door opened stealthily. A figure shrouded in a black hooded cloak entered. Louisa stood, frozen by the terrifying image.

Just as she was about to raise the alarm, an upraised white arm fastened the latch. The apparition dropped the hood, revealing the ashen face of the mysterious Mrs. Cutney.

The girls continued their lessons undisturbed and Louisa realized that their clandestine study sessions were as regular as Agnes Cutney's nighttime wanderings. The woman raised watery eyes to Louisa's, then dropped her lids and turned her back while she attended to her cloak.

Chapter 5

The Bath Cure

The next morning, Louisa descended the same staircase where she had seen her two mysterious nighttime visions and entered a quiet breakfast room. There were signs of some hastily taken meals, but no other guests appeared while Louisa munched her toast and jam. Lizzie clattered away in the kitchen and popped her head into the room to check on Louisa's needs.

"Have I slept terribly late to have missed all the others?" Louisa asked.

"Oh, the young gentlemen prefer to take their breakfast out on their way to business and the children are off at school. Herr Hahn takes his treatments early, so it's quiet here most mornings," Lizzie replied.

There was no sign of disturbance on her face, so Louisa persisted in satisfying her worries about the night before. "Does Rebecca go to school?"

"Oh, yes, miss." Lizzie nearly beamed. "She's a regular scholar. We're all right proud of her, and do all we can to encourage her. She works here evenings after school and you will always find a book in her pocket or somewhere handy."

"And Mrs. Cutney, does she not come to breakfast?"

"No, ma'am, she's not one to be seen before the noon bell

strikes."

"She does look as if she needs some rest, the poor thing," Louisa offered. If Lizzie had any inkling of the nighttime habits of Mrs. Cutney, she made no indication. The only response was a quick clearing of the table and a shake of the tabletop doilies.

Thinking that she had hinted too much, Louisa hastened to cover her inquiry by adding, "And Herr Hahn, he doesn't appear to miss many meals."

"Aye, that man, he has four eggs before the bell is rung for breakfast, and follows it with bread smeared with butter and cheese. Some days he wheedles me into making his German pancakes with sausage. The missus mustn't know about the meat at breakfast, you know. It goes against the nutrition rules. But what can you do with a man that ravenous?"

There are wurst ways to start the day, Louisa punned to herself.

Just a moment later, Mrs. Miller appeared and with the hint of a scowl announced, "There's a small streetboy here asking to speak to you. Shall I send him away?"

"By no means. He is my guide and escort and I value him dearly," was Louisa's mischievous response. *I do think I will be able to irritate this woman every day by just being myself.* She smiled.

Louisa had never had a doubt that she would see this upright lad again, though others would have called the prior evening's payment before services a folly. "Good morning, Casey. Before we come to our agreement, I must know if your parents approve of your employment with me."

"I have no parents to look after me, miss. I'm on my own and doin' fine. I live at the Newsboys' Lodging." Louisa's affection for the boy only increased with this new information since boys of all kinds, but especially orphan boys, held a special place in her tender heart. She looked at this ruddy waif and thought of Anna's sons, who had lost their father at a young age, and then the young orphan sculptor, Frank Elwell, whom she mentored and supported through

52

his art studies. Louisa was resigned to the fact that a bit of her earnings, attention and energies went to the needs of orphan boys. She couldn't help herself, really. Ever since she had created the utterly beguiling orphan boy Theodore Laurence, she remained devoted to the species.

"And why are you not in school right now?"

"I do my classes in the evening, miss. The Lodging sees to that so we boys are able to make our living when the news breaks."

"It sounds like a fine place for boys. I would like to visit there with you one day," said Louisa. "But first, I need to satisfy my curiosity about that magnificent boulevard, Broadway. I was there for some time yesterday but did not learn half of what I want to know about it. Would you walk with me as far south as we can go?" Louisa asked.

"It goes clear to the end of the island, miss, right to the spot where the river enters the ocean."

"I would follow you to the edge of the ocean, though it be my nemesis. Come, my Hermes, let's go where we may. Perhaps we will get as far as Park Row and you will show me where your great newspaper originates, or maybe we shall reach the sea!"

Casey stared at her, partly fascinated and partly befuddled. She could tell that he didn't understand half of what she was saying but enjoyed the conversation twice as much because of that. "I will see you tomorrow afternoon, then," he offered eagerly. As Casey left with his usual bound down the stoop, Mrs. Miller watched him from her office with a sour twist on her lips.

Herr Hahn and Robert assisted Augustine down the staircase, carefully keeping one to each side, and placed him in the wheelchair. "I am off to my first water treatment, Miss May. Let's hope it helps as much as your gentle salve," Augustine said.

"It was such a trifle, and my pleasure to offer. Please don't mention it again," Louisa replied. The elder brother stood behind the wheelchair protectively, but relief settled upon his face when he

53

heard her humble tone. "Indeed, you have a way of doing good so urgently that it seemed an impertinence not to accept your offer." Augustine's smile was warm and a bit impish. He had a knack of cutting straight to the truth.

"I am sorry if I was too brusque. It's just my way—when I see suffering I dive in and flail away and mostly make things worse," Louisa confessed.

"No, you were perfect, just what I need. You see my affliction but you also see me—not like most others, who either try to ignore my infirmity or seek to make me an invalid before my time."

"I have had some experience with prolonged illness and can tolerate it better than most," Louisa confided. Beth's lingering illness had taught her that infirmity did not change a person's worth and sometimes it might even strengthen the soul of both patient and nurse.

"Ach, you are a gentle nurse and a vomen's rights believer. A most modern voman." Herr Hahn smiled at her, as he pushed the wheelchair toward the baths. She wasn't sure if he was mocking or complimenting her.

Louisa herself was more anxious about her first water treatment that morning than she admitted. Before beginning her program, she was slated for a consultation with Dr. Miller. His office was on the lower floor and Louisa found it just past the gymnasium. Through the gym door, which was slightly ajar, she glimpsed a number of wooden contraptions and exercise cycles. The equipment looked like something from an Inquisitor's den and Louisa doubted she would find a cure there. She was relieved to see that Dr. Miller's office was not equipped with a rack or manacles, but still she looked at him skeptically. He had long, pale hands, perfectly manicured, and small spectacles that he put on and off but never seemed to peer through. His limber frame looked as if it had rarely done any strenuous labor.

"Tell me your symptoms," he said, pen hovering over her medical record.

"After I contracted typhoid more than ten years ago, I began to have bouts of aches and swelling of the joints, a throbbing head, sore throat, and most of all, intractable pain." Louisa had told this tale to so many doctors that she almost always used the same words. "The infuriating part is that the disease runs in spurts. I might have several weeks of calm, and then be nearly homebound for stretches of time. At the worst, I cannot walk, sit or be at peace in any way. One English doctor thought I had mercury poisoning from the calomel treatments I took for the typhoid. Another doctor said I had familial inflammation, since there are eye and joint and ear conditions in my family. But I am never completely sick nor completely well. Our family friend, Mr. Emerson, used to call it 'lukesick.'"

"Ah, rheumatism, cephalgia, pharyngeal inflammation, neuralgia." The doctor ticked off her conditions, unimpressed that Emerson had labeled them otherwise. "What makes it worse?"

"Well, usually an episode might be started off by overwork or cold weather or stress," Louisa offered.

"And what makes it better?" The doctor gave a long look, actually through his glasses this time.

"Getting some rest, being by myself … and laudanum, when I couldn't stand it any longer." Dr. Miller wrote furiously, his head down. Louisa braced herself for his professional condemnation. She knew well enough that any medicinals were frowned upon by the hydrotherapists. She stopped using laudanum years ago, after having a deuce of a time trying to get off of it. The memories of the griping abdominal pain, palpitations and sweats were impossible to forget. The doctor raised his pen and shook his head. "Please, have no worry about my use of 'poisons' any longer," she added. "That cure was worse than the disease."

Louisa grasped the little paper on which Dr. Miller had scribbled instructions to the therapists. She had a strong desire and just a little faith that the hygienic cure would help, or at the least, be harmless. The Turkish bath used heat, steam and cold plunges to affect the temperature changes so necessary for improvement. They claimed results in any of a number of chronic diseases: gout, rheumatism, diabetes, hysteria, "female weaknesses," epilepsy and hypochondria, according to the pamphlet Mrs. Miller had given her yesterday.

Louisa presented herself to the bath attendant in the building adjoining the hotel. The young woman escorted her down a flight of stairs to a comfortable room filled with easy chairs and lined all around with little curtained changing rooms. An assistant gave Louisa her bath garment and demonstrated how to tie it effectively, not unlike a Roman toga. In keeping with the Roman theme, she learned that the cool room they were in was called the Frigidarium. Thinking of herself as a Roman senator helped Louisa overcome her shyness and discomfort at the odd surroundings. As much as she wanted to embrace the new therapies, her practical mind remained skeptical. But she liked the costume, and hoped that her acting experience would at least help her to hide her uncertainty.

The attendant signaled for her to move on to the Tepidarium, a warm room lit by soft light filtering through stained glass windows. *From a Roman bath to a gothic cathedral,* Louisa thought. *If that blasted Egyptian motif appears in the next room, I will know I am in New York.* Here, the woman wrapped a warm, wet towel on Louisa's forehead and placed her feet in hot water. In a short time, Louisa began to perspire. This was the sign that she was ready to move to the sauna. After a few moments lying on a couch she broke out into a disturbing perspiration. The humidity smothered her. Just when the heat became unbearable, the attendant reappeared to soap her body and cool her down with a shower. In Mrs. Miller's pamphlet it had been billed as "the perspiration that does not exhaust," followed by the "rubbing that electrifies" and "the cleansing bath more refreshing than a summer shower on withered plants." One more brisk rubbing, this time with alcohol, and the procedure commenced in reverse: back to the Tepidarium, then the Frigidarium, where Louisa reposed, wrapped in a warm, dry woolen blanket and covered over in three more. There, she reclined at peace, undisturbed, left alone for as long as she needed to feel the effects of the treatment.

Louisa lay in the dim room, sinking into the soft blanket and the even more relaxing couch. She wanted desperately to achieve some benefit from the therapy and she knew that she would have to quiet her mind as much as refresh her body. Even while she was lying comfortably in silence, her mind raced through plans for her stay and the stories she would need to write to pay for these luxuries. She took a deep breath to calm herself. She stared into the dark and tried to breathe rhythmically and mindfully. She had read the Bhaga-vad-Gita in her classics stage and had heard of those who repeated a mantra until their minds were empty and thus achieved oneness with the universe.

Filled with nervous energy, Louisa kept assessing if she was re-laxed. She tormented herself over whether she had achieved the right mental state. Her inability to give her mind over and relinquish complete intellectual control interrupted her peace. *Let's hope these wraps and vapors at least relieve my aching muscles.*

Instead, she concentrated on concocting a reverie of scenarios for her next novel about Rose and her seven boy cousins. As boys were always her special delight, she intended to reveal them in all their varied characters: the dutiful son, the dandy, the scholar, the athlete, the precious youngest rascal. Their names and attributes swirled in her head. "Archie, Charlie, Mac, Steve, Will, Geordie, Ja-mie," she sang softly to herself. "Archie, Charlie, Mac, Steve, Will, Geordie, Jamie, Archie, Charlie, Mac, Steve, Will, Geordie, Jamie," she repeated until she achieved a delightfully cozy state.

"Angelina! Renata! Mama! Angelina! Renata! Mama!" Louisa awoke in a sweat to a shrieking voice repeating the series of names. But this was no rhythmic mantra—this was a terrifying voice of des-perate agony.

The door to the Frigidarium opened and the attendant spoke to her in apologetic tones. "Pay no mind, miss, it's one of our older patients having a fit."

Pay no mind indeed! Louisa understood the mad sounds of delirium and every bit of her nursing skills were at the ready to help. "Please take me to her," she told the attendant. "I think I can be of some assistance."

"Really, miss, it's a sorry case. You best not get involved."

"Sorry cases are my greatest specialty," Louisa shot back as she plunged into a thick robe and followed the young lady in the direction of the shrieks.

In the adjoining treatment room, she found the tiny source of the big scream. Marchesa Contini, the frail matron Louisa had seen at dinner the evening before, writhed against the bondage of the cool, damp treatment sheets. The attendants tried to cajole her while her sweetly ineffective young ward wiped her contorted face with a camphored cloth and whispered words of comfort.

"Angelina! Renata! Mama! Angelina! Renata! Mama!" the elderly woman cried.

She was calling for her mother, and who were the other names that poured off her tongue hysterically? Nodding to the ward to keep up with her gentle ministrations, Louisa asked, "Angelina and Renata are her sisters?"

"Were," was the solemn answer.

Louisa bent down to the shivering, tearful face and murmured, "Mother is just near, dear, waiting for you after your bath."

"I am so cold and wretched. I need to sit by the fire with Mama," the old woman replied timidly.

"Ladies, you have succeeded in terrifying this dear old head. She has no idea what your purpose is," Louisa whispered to the attendants. Turning back to the quaking woman, she said, "Let's get you out of these wet things and warm you up and then you will feel just as cozy as ever you did with Mama and Angelina and Renata at home."

The distant eyes swung slowly to look into Louisa's and found only calm compassion there. The fragile mind sought a memory and, finding it in the sincere smile and warm touch of Louisa's hug, she responded innocently, "Yes, we always sit together near the hearth after our baths, don't we? And Renata always gets the place closest to the warmth, because she's the baby, you know."

"Oh, I know all about baby sisters," Louisa laughed. "They get the best of everything but they are worth it, every bit!"

Docile now, the sweet, demented woman was led away to be pampered and repaired and Louisa turned to her frightened young companion, who sat down disconsolate in a nearby chair. "You have a big job for someone so young. But your care was a sweet relief to your lady."

"Oh, thank you, miss! Marchesa Contini is all I have in this world and there is nothing I would not do to help her," Marienne said.

So alone in the world, thought Louisa. *What a sad situation for this young girl!* "I am having my tea served in the library this evening. Will you join me for a nice chat?"

"Oh, miss, that would be so very kind of you! I will come if the marchesa is calm and asleep by then!"

LORD & TAYLOR'S STORE—Broadway and 20th Street.

Figure 3. **Lord & Taylor's Store - Broadway and 20th Street**

Chapter 6

Marchesa Contini

Marienne tapped on the library door and slipped inside. "The marchesa is asleep," she said quietly. Louisa was impressed again by her winsome vulnerability. She was pale and lithe, with brown curls framing her face. The brown eyes met Louisa's with a cautious hope and modest dignity that Louisa found touching.

"How do you like your tea, dear? I will draw it for you," offered Louisa, smiling and gesturing for Marienne to have a seat on the yellow divan. "And then you will tell me all about your aunt and yourself. How is it that your aunt has such an exotic name?"

"Oh, Aunt Carlotta's life is as romantic as a novel," said the young girl, sitting on the edge of the couch. "Where should I start? She was born in Genoa but her father was an American seaman. He married an Italian woman and they had three children. He wasn't often at home with them, but a good provider who always returned to his family when he was in port."

"So that left months for Carlotta, Angelina, Renata and Mama to sit by the hearth together," Louisa said, nodding.

"Carlotta was the oldest daughter and a renowned beauty known for her intelligence and seriousness," Marienne said, munching on a tea cake.

"Then you have inherited your great-aunt's family traits, Marienne."

The girl blushed and shook her head. "No, Aunt Carlotta was truly exceptional. The nuns at the convent school noted that she had a special talent for poetry. She wrote beautiful verses in Italian. She did it all her life."

Louisa roused. "Your aunt is a writer?"

"She was something of a prodigy, it seemed. First the nuns, then the clergy, then the local nobility started to notice. It became a special entertainment to have her at their banquets where she would recite poems she had written especially for the occasion."

Louisa listened to the young lady's words and, from the details, spun a touching tale in her own mind, not unlike one of her own early romance stories, a tale of lovers in Italy.

She is not cowed by the lush garments or the shining embroidery. She is the mistress of her craft and her words are golden. The murmurs of the room lessen, the clink of the forks on the silver chargers stop and the room listens to Carlotta recite.

Marienne's words completed the tale. "That's when her husband fell in love with her. The son of the marchese. He was more dazzled by the poetry than any wealth an arranged marriage would offer," Marienne said. "Of course, once she was married, Carlotta was happy with her new life, her husband and her sudden prosperity. She was ready to extol her bliss in poetry. She wrote and wrote, but her husband stopped the public readings."

"She was not the first woman to have her talents diminished by her husband," Louisa said. "That must have been hard for her, especially after she grew up in a home of women." *Not unlike my own,* Louisa thought. "Hadn't she learned that a woman must speak and act in the world for herself?"

"Well," Marienne went on, gazing at Louisa with the same dazzled look she had when hearing the dinner conversation about the Women's Conference, "Aunt Carlotta had more to worry about than her poetry. One year after their wedding, Federico Contini was taken with a sudden fever. As he lay dying he asked Carlotta to promise never to perform her poetry publically again."

"She kept that promise? How could she deny her work?" Louisa demanded.

"She took this vow so firmly that though she continued to write, she never read her poems in public again. She rejected offers to have them published, too."

"That must have been like being wrenched from her firstborn," Louisa said hotly.

Marienne looked at Louisa quizzically. Louisa swallowed hard and bit her lip to keep herself from interjecting again. "As I said, Carlotta had more to bear than losing her poetry," Marienne continued a bit haughtily. "Not long after, her mother and sister Angelina died in an epidemic of petechial fever. Carlotta was twenty years old and a widow of small means, but Renata, my grandmother, was only a young girl."

"Her husband, her mother, her sister, all at once," Louisa said softly.

"Their father, with his itinerant life, and overcome with loss and grief as he was, couldn't provide a home for them. He decided the two sisters must set out for the country of his parents."

"Here? In New York?" Louisa asked.

"They intended to go to their grandparents but the old people had never forgiven their son for deserting them. I heard so many times the story of how they were turned away. 'We have no son,' the grandmother said. Even worse were the words of her husband: 'We have no need of foreign vagabonds making demands on us.'"

"And they never returned to their homeland?" Louisa asked.

"Their letters to their father were never answered," Marienne said. "Maybe he died, maybe he wanted to forget," she mumbled, then shrugged. "My grandmama and aunt were able to maintain a genteel kind of existence. Nonna Renata offered Italian lessons and worked embroidery, which was her special skill, and Zia Carlotta had her small inheritance. They got by. Carlotta became a bit of a curiosity in the small circle of Italians here, once the story of her secret poetry became known."

"It sounds like your aunt had not only a tender heart, but much bravery and resilience," Louisa said.

"The two sisters were everything in each other's world, and when Renata married, she and her husband stayed within the warm embrace of Carlotta's home. She needed all that bravery you speak of, for the family remained together only a few years. Two years after my mother was born, Nonna Renata and my grandpa died of cholera," Marienne continued haltingly. "Now you know why I cherish Aunt Carlotta."

"She nurtured your grandmother and your mother and now you are doing the same for her, dear," Louisa said, knowing that as the marchesa's ward, this girl had a sad story of loss all her own. "How did you come to be your aunt's caretaker?"

"My parents both died," Marienne said bluntly. Louisa winced. Perhaps she was prying too much. But the girl looked up and began her story. "I was born in Brooklyn. My father was a schoolmaster and my mother, Elizabeth, was his partner in every way, at home and at school. Our home was filled with warmth and love, and my parents bound together by interest and devotion."

The girl had a luxurious way of using words. Louisa smiled.

"Father was a scholar who taught his students to know about the modern world and to examine the thoughts and lessons of the past."

"How like my own father," Louisa said, interested to hear how that legacy had stamped itself on this dutiful daughter.

"My mother admired his knowledge and his goodness and did all she could to make his school room bright and welcoming." Marienne recounted sweet memories of the three of them walking to school in the early morning light. "There was a dutch door, I remember, for I was just able to peer over the lower half."

"Not more than five years old, then," Louisa concluded.

Marienne's face grew wistful as she continued. "Papa would let me ring the bell to gather the students to school. I would see them streaming from down the hill after I rang the summons."

"And did you spend your day at school with your father?" Louisa asked. "My sister and I did the same when we were small."

"Yes, I would sit quietly in the corner, marking my paper with letters. I learned to read from the routine of listening while the students read aloud the passages written on the chalkboard. To this day I love reading and composition."

"Books and literature, the best friends a woman can have!" Louisa added.

"I wish my story ended like a fairytale, but it doesn't. All our bliss was shattered when the war came. My father ... he enlisted ...."

"I imagine your father was too avid a supporter of the North to avoid it, even though it meant leaving his family behind," Louisa ventured. Louisa pictured the train pulling away, the recruits hanging out the windows, waving bravely, the mother and daughter trotting alongside the train until it picked up steam and sped away. She remembered how many letters she had written from the war front for her wounded boys. She imagined that Marienne and her mother had anxiously awaited and then savored their letters, until the final letter, which wrung so many tears and left a little girl without hope of ever seeing her father again.

Louisa did not need to reopen the deep wound. Seeing Marienne's sad expression, she took the girl's hand, gently saying, "I know. I know—go on, dear."

"After my father's death, my mother was shattered. She was an orphan, nearly alone in the world. Just trying to support our small family of two was a struggle. When Mother's parents died, her mother's sister, Aunt Carlotta, raised her. It was only natural that she would return to her care," the girl continued. "Mother lived only two years longer than Papa."

"Such a weight and sadness," Louisa said.

"She could neither eat nor sleep, and though she tried to be lively for me, I believe I reminded her too much of Father. One night she took a sleeping draught and never awoke." The girl said this in a soft voice and held Louisa's hand even more tightly.

Whether she intended to end her life or if it was a tragic mistake matters little, Louisa thought, *for each option is pathetic.*

"Aunt Carlotta has become all in all to me since then," said Marienne, her eyelashes damp. "She raised me as her own. Though she was already on in years, she was the light of my life and the protectoress I needed."

Three generations of loss and tragedy. But always, for each loss, it was Carlotta who offered protection and love. "So Carlotta became the mother, father and provider for your grandmother, then your mother and now yourself."

Marienne's eyes grew moist. "I have brought her here in the hope that the treatments will stimulate her mind. She is so confused now that she trembles nearly all the time, and sometimes mistakes me for her mother."

There was little comfort that Louisa could render, but the girl seemed more at peace having told her story. "You have done a good thing to bring your aunt here for medical attention. But don't forget that you need to keep yourself vigorous, or you will be no help to her."

"It helps when I write. It clears my mind," the girl said, brightening.

"I often keep a journal to examine my own moods and successes," Louisa said.

"I write more seriously than mere journaling," the girl said with that slightly chiding way she had. "I think seriously about a profession in writing. If that comes to be, it will be because of my parents' and my aunt's examples." Marienne added, "I have some manuscripts that I have never shown anyone, but I keep working at them over and over to become the best writer I can."

Louisa gulped and nodded. How could she remain Lottie May to this girl who was revealing her family story and her own fervid dreams?

"Let me help you with some small tasks. I want you to take a good, bracing walk every morning and I have a jolly lad who will do that with you right after breakfast. Then, you must let me be the one to stay with your great-aunt for an hour every day so that you can write as you would like. I know how important it is to get the steam out of your kettle, to stop it from banging your brains around. I have written a bit in my time, too."

"Oh, Miss May, it seems a long time since I have had a friend to assist me." The girl's simple gratitude and look of relief nettled Louisa's conscience. As Miss May, she had listened to the girl's most intimate story as an imposter.

"Marienne, can I trust you with a secret?"

The girl looked tentative, almost alarmed. "Yes, miss," she said timidly.

Louisa would have liked Marienne to swear to secrecy in a more fervent manner. But it was her guiding principle that women should assist each other. She was determined to mentor the young writer. She and Marienne could forge a sisterhood of mutual respect.

Louisa plunged on. "Marienne, I haven't revealed my true identity to the others here at the hotel."

Marienne's eyes grew sharp.

"Don't look so alarmed. I won't be asking you to harbor a criminal," Louisa laughed. "But I do need you to keep my secret for a while. It's just that ... I am Louisa May Alcott. I am glad you are a writer, for I like to help women help themselves. I suspect we will be great friends."

Marienne's startled look turned to one of joy. She grasped Louisa's hand again. "I had no idea! Oh, Miss Alcott, I am so ashamed of ever telling you I am a writer. Not a writer like you! My goodness, never such a grand writer as you!"

"No gushing—that's my first rule," Louisa cautioned the girl. "Gushing is exactly what I was hoping to avoid by being Miss May."

The girl looked at her quizzically. "Is that the *only* reason you told the others a lie?"

Louisa blushed at the incriminating way the girl continued to stare at her. "Not a lie, dear." Louisa was unnerved by her charge. Lousia cleared her throat. "Just a little story. It's a silly story. I will tell you someday … or better yet, I will write about it. I just haven't figured out all the turns in the plot just yet."

Louisa rose and walked Marienne to the door.

Chapter 7

Broadway

The next morning, Marienne came home breathless from her walk, her cheeks glowing, her nose red. She and Casey had raced back from Fifth Avenue and the burst of activity gave her a bright look that Louisa had not seen before. The two came tumbling through the doorway, occasioning a start, a long stare and another shake of the head from Mrs. Miller.

Day one of our exercise program is a success. Louisa smiled to herself as she rose from the breakfast table. She wondered if Mrs. Miller thought she was corrupting the respectability of the marchesa's gentle ward.

It was a quiet Saturday morning and the hotel residents dawdled over their morning meal, planning the day's excursions or reading the morning papers. Several diners held their papers wide, the headlines blaring the adultery accusations against the grand preacher Henry Ward Beecher again. One of his parishioners, the newspaperman Theodore Tilton, had publicly accused the preacher of seducing his wife. This most intimate of family matters had been adjudicated publicly, culminating in a trial where the husband equated his wife to a piece of property which had been devalued. This trial ended with no verdict, the jury neither able to condemn nor exonerate the minister. Still the story smoldered, and there was talk of retrying the case.

"It's that woman, Mrs. Woodhull, who's instigating all this turmoil," one guest announced over her paper. "She is a chameleon: part financial advisor, part newspaper editor and part free love advocate."

Louisa turned from the conversation. She shook her head and sighed at the conduct of everyone involved in the incident as well as those who repeated the sordid details. That the two powerful men had each tried to bring the other down was clear. That Mrs. Woodhull, an ardent suffragist and an editor and lecturer, had sought to advance her own interests was also clear. And Mrs. Tilton, her only intent was to hide her shame.

The woman continued. "A vixen, that's what Victoria Woodhull is. Her objective was to expose the hypocrisy of the men."

"But it is Mrs. Tilton's reputation which has suffered," Louisa interjected.

"Yes, it's that busybody, with her 'belief in justice' who brought the whole business to light," the woman continued, undeterred.

"And every other woman and man who reads and reports the details keeps it in the spotlight," snorted Dr. Miller, glaring over his glasses at the tittering women. Louisa was glad that the doctor discouraged gossip. These women were drawing conclusions based on salacious reports and their own prejudices. That the burden of guilt had fallen only to the women in the situation irritated but did not surprise Louisa.

Herr Hahn diverted the children's attention from the conversation of their elders. Casey lingered at the threshold of the dining hall, watching as Helene and Marienne and the asthmatic fellows circled in a raucous ring around Herr Hahn. He held a peeled hard boiled egg above his head in one hand and an empty milk bottle in the other. "Who thinks I can fit thees very fine egg through the very leettle neck of thees bottle?" Herr Hahn challenged the youngsters.

"No! Impossible!" they shouted.

He nodded to Casey to draw nearer. "And vat is your answer, young man?"

Casey sized up the bottle and egg and the sly grin on Herr Hahn's face. "Without breaking it? I think you've got something up yer sleeve," was the artful response.

"Ah, ve have a man who doubts mein honesty." Herr Hahn winked at Casey and proceeded to remove his jacket, roll up his shirt sleeves above his biceps, and spread his fingers wide in an exaggerated display of openness.

"Stand back and I vill reveal mein secret."

Herr Hahn ripped a portion of the back page from his newspaper, put a match to it, dropped it into the glass bottle and placed the egg firmly in its neck. The egg began to vibrate, then wobble. It plunked down into the bottle in one sudden rush.

"How'd that happen?"

"Is it magic?" the children cried.

Rebecca silently observed the spectacle from near the sideboard she was helping to clear. "The heat must have warmed the air inside the bottle and as the air rushed out, the egg was pushed into the vacuum."

"I'd say it's a waste of a good egg," said Casey, eyeing the remnants of the breakfast table. Rebecca noticed his hungry look and slipped a muffin into his pocket.

Louisa surveyed the happy faces, none happier than Herr Hahn himself. He was an awkward caricature of her beloved Professor Bhaer—or maybe just a real man, with real kinks and quirks.

"You have a flair toward the theatrical, Herr Hahn," Louisa said as they walked together to the front hallway.

"The children, they need to be children for a vhile yet, no?" he answered. "I missed the entire boyhood of mein own brother."

Louisa looked at him with interest. "Your separation must have been a worry to you," she suggested.

"My father remarried a young American vhen I was almost a

71

man. He died right after the second son was born. Augustine's mother brought her boy home to her family in Albany. I never saw him after that. But vhen I came to New York and heard of his illness, I knew I must bring him here."

"So you have confidence in the bath cure?" Louisa asked.

"Do not ask a German about the power of the bath cure." Herr Hahn smiled. "Eet is a piece of our life. Eet may not cure but it alvays refreshes." He picked up a stack of envelopes which lay on the front hall table, collecting a considerable number addressed to him. He broke the seal on a large envelope and stood, reading and shaking his head.

Casey dawdled about the front door. Louisa plopped down on an elaborately carved mahogany bench and drew up her skirts to remove her slippers. "Casey McDermott, you are all mine now," she said as she pulled on her walking boots and covered them over with her manly gaiters. "Young man, you look as scandalized as if I were entering the ballot box. Why should men have all the advantages of tramping, carefree and unaccosted by the dust and mud they stir up? Someday, I'll have the ballot, but for now, I have my gaiters."

Louisa looked at her masculine audience. Casey seemed impressed. Herr Hahn looked up from his letters and parcels and glanced quickly at the gaiters and then directly into Louisa's eyes with no sign of disapproval. She saw a glimmer of a smile, then he regained his composure quickly.

"Casey, you are about to show me the New Yorker's New York—if you are not too embarrassed to be seen with me, that is." In fact, the newsboy looked eager to see what adventures a day with this strange New Englander would bring. He already had his hand on the doorknob.

At the top of the stoop, they looked right and left along West Twenty-Sixth Street. To the east was Broadway and Fifth Avenue, the offices of the famed John Jacob Astor, and the sedate Madison Square Park which Louisa had traversed on her first day in the city. To the west, past a few doctors' and dentists' offices, was Sixth Avenue, becoming known as "The Ladies' Mile" for its stretch of fine department stores. Louisa turned west. From here she could crisscross between Broadway and Sixth Avenue and not miss an important purveyor of women's clothing.

A strong rainfall the night before had washed the pavement clean but filled the gutters with mud. "Step lively, Miss May. The street-cleaning brigade has not reached uptown yet," Casey warned, as Louisa sidestepped to avoid the mud seeping toward the intersections. Despite the muck in the corridors, Louisa was determined to keep her head up to catch every impression of New York. The clopping of the iron hooves on cobblestone, the crashing sounds of the omnibus, the high whistle of the newsboys surrounded Louisa. Countering this were the quiet almost whispering calls of a colporteur, who offered his pamphlets from a billboard type apparatus that unfolded across his chest, and the eerie coos of the pigeons ensconced in the eaves of the storefronts.

Between Sixth Avenue and Broadway from her doorstep to Tenth Street, the city was one huge caravansary for a stretch over a mile. Signboards hung from each storefront and flagstaffs rose from nearly every building. There were bookstores, tea purveyors and hat stores in the ground floors of elegant hotels. Department stores with six stories above ground and two below towered over them. At Twentieth Street was a grand building with an angled corner tower and a huge mansard pavilion on the roof. The lacy columns and arched windows proclaimed that this building was proudly constructed of iron. No sign was needed to know that it was Lord and Taylor, acclaimed for its show windows filled with the most magnificent display of fine goods and the latest styles.

"Jewels, silks, hosiery, gloves … this store is my dream, Casey," Louisa announced, stopping to peer into the windows piled with silver services, laces and hats. She read the poster board at the entrance of the store: "*Our silk department contains all the celebrated makes of the* best *Lyons manufacturers. We offer 250 pieces in plain colored silks. We are offering taffetas, cashmere and plain Gros Grains in seal brown, myrtle green, navy blue, Corbean prune, Fumce de Londres, tea rose, eglantine, gris perle and all fashionable shades for street, dinner and evening wear.*" Louisa had used some of these very colors and fabrics to magnificently clothe the "blood and thunder" heroines of her early stories. The listing went on: "*Elegant Lyons Brocades in pink, sky, pearl, ecru, cream and white.*"

"Casey, here's two cents for a baked potato. Rest a moment and refresh yourself. I need to order something in this store." Louisa could not keep out of sight from the literary and artistic friends who awaited her in the city, and they expected her to appear as a wealthy authoress. *The time has come … my treasured silk awaits.* A uniformed boy swung open the plate glass door to the emporium.

"Can I direct you, madam?" a suave manager asked.

"Silks," Louisa whispered breathlessly, "for an evening dress."

The gentleman made a slight bow and directed her to the second floor, toward the rear of the store where an efficient salesman took over while she selected her fabric. Louisa caressed the orchid, prune and tea rose fabrics, but knew that for her purposes only a staid and traditional black silk would do. The red velvets, phosphorescent greens and magenta lace would have to be relegated to the fantasy creations in which she clothed her *femmes fatales.*

Next, an accomplished matron seamstress took her measurements and helped her select the style. The dressmaker stood by demurely while Louisa fumbled with the gaiters, only raising her eyebrows a touch as she draped the lush fabric for Louisa to appraise in the mirror. Louisa chose an elegant gown from the store pattern book. It had a row of tiny buttons down the front of the bodice, a band of ruffles on either side of the buttons, a wide skirt with ruching in the front, two layers of ruffles on the bottom and a small bustle. An adaptable train could swing over her arms, like a shawl. A detachable lace collar and cuffs would be used for more formal affairs. To soften the look, she ordered a large, contrasting bow.

The entire ensemble required an underskirt, an overskirt, a blouse, a bodice and vest, plus the sashes, neckpieces and cuffs which would make the same dress wearable over and over. Louisa approved of the efficient operation. By choosing from the Lord and Taylor catalogue, she would have the dress made to order at a savings. *It's alright to spend a bit on myself.* After all the years of success, she still had to convince herself that money was available for finery.

Louisa stopped and considered her purchases, then turned to the seamstress. "My sisters deserve to share in some of this luxury and sophistication," she said. *Anna used to call me "Shakespeare" when I wrote those silly plays at home*, Louisa thought, *and May thought my romances quite as good as those by Hawthorne.* But none of them had envisioned that Louisa's years of hard work and sacrifice would one day propel her into the finest shop in New York City, buying yardage for her humble sisters.

"Tell me about them, miss, and I will help you select a fabric for each," the kind woman offered.

"Well, one is very pretty and feminine but she spends most days at home with her children. She's a widow and doesn't go out much," said Louisa. The woman pointed to a silvery gray sateen fabric, practical but attractive, for Anna.

"My other sister is all artistry and whimsy," said Louisa. "She works hard but knows how to enjoy herself, too." The seamstress selected some Byzantine blue voile, fanciful and filled with illusion, for May.

"Is there another sister?" the woman asked, seeing Louisa still musing. It wasn't that she was considering the memory of Beth, who had never seemed to want more than a gray cloak to clasp tightly while going about her errands. She thought instead of her generous cousin, Louisa Willis, who had taken her under her wing in Boston, the first winter that Lou set out from home. Cousin Louisa had surveyed her hand-me-downs and thoughtfully given her a scarlet crepe shawl to wear to the theater, and more prudently, a soft, warm Talma cape to replace her shredded, old-fashioned one. The irregular shape and full folds were just as dramatic as Louisa cared to be. That it was worn by both men and women made it especially delightful and appealing to her. *How I wish I could repay my dear cousin's generosity. A claret silk would have been grand for her,* Louisa thought, caressing the fabric. But the gentle friend had died, even before Louisa had achieved any of her success.

She closed her eyes and thought, *Cousin Lou, I'm on Fifth Avenue buying silks.*

The shop girl shifted a few bolts of fabric, awaiting an answer. Louisa shook her head and grasped the questioning woman's hand. "No. Nothing more," she said.

She found Casey outside enjoying the antics of an organ grinder with his monkey. The squealing cadence of the barrel organ and the droll capers of the monkey made a clamorous scene. Despite the jocularity, the tenderness between the organ grinder and his pet was affecting and Casey watched their little pantomime with a sad smile. Surrounding the organ grinder was a crowd of destitute little vagabonds—bootblacks, thieves, street musicians. The little musicians seemed the most vulnerable, listless and slow. Two grimy lads roamed about singing plaintive songs, one strumming an untuned guitar, the other plucking a pitchy harp. Each child was ragged and hungry, but singing, nevertheless, for their lives depended on it. Louisa felt there were thousands of these lost children in the city. They were more abused than this little well fed monkey.

Looking to her own self-sufficient boy, Louisa noticed for the first time that his shoe soles flapped wildly as he walked before her, worn and almost detached from their seams. At Nineteenth Street, she saw a sign on the far avenue: Cantrell's Shoes.

"Casey, we need to look at that shop."

'Ironclads' strong, serviceable shoes for boys and youth. 'Waukinphast' English shoes and all kinds of overshoe for men and women, the sign read.

"I don't think you'll find what you need to match yer new gown,"

76

drawled Casey.

"No, but we'll find what *you* need to continue to be my guide. Come in, Casey, let's see your size."

"Oh, no, ma'am, the Lodging gives us our new stockings at Christmas, and I'll soon have enough saved to have these ugly old boats repaired."

"Since I will be responsible for the thinning of those socks and the scuffing of the 'old boats,' I must be responsible for their replacement. Come, my man, it's only a business deal."

Figure 4. **Printing House Square.**

Chapter 8

Printing House Square

Louisa never felt better than when she was giving, and giving to a child raised her to the pinnacle of bliss. She was certain that she felt even happier than her grateful little guide. Casey carried his old stockings and shoes carefully wrapped in newspaper, determined to repair them and use them in rainy weather, as he stepped lively down Broadway in his new shoes.

At Fourteenth Street the odd pair admired the treasures of art and jewelry in Tiffany's windows. This area was the piano sector of the city, both a sales and manufacturing center, and they peered into windows filled with grand pianos and small organs, upright and console keyboards. The prices seemed aimed at the pockets of any middle-class family, reflecting the passion for parlor music at the heart of every home. They passed Brentano's, the grandest bookshop in the country. Louisa noted the address in order to return to peruse at her leisure. She would send her father some hidden treasures from the bookstore.

As they passed Fourteenth Street, the streets downtown were cleaner, but more crowded, with workmen and businessmen all treading with a buoyant confidence in their own industry. Soon after, the sidewalks became monopolized by elegant ladies, animated and gay. The exquisite costumes, both on the shoppers and in the store windows, delighted Louisa. One window featured a ball gown, white satin with point lace in a perfusion of flounces, which looped up at the sides with bands of pinks, roses and forget-me-nots. Louisa noticed that almost every shopper wore a bouquet in her bosom made possible by a literal legion of sidewalk peddlers, all young girls, hawking small floral clusters and adding to the sweet scene of femininity.

One approached Louisa, offering a basket overflowing with pinks and baby's breath and heliotrope. A bouquet of fragrant mignonette was just the thing to brighten Louisa's walking outfit. As she stopped to fasten it to her lapel, the crowd parted and streamed about her.

"My word, Casey, where is this herd heading?"

"That's Mr. Stewart's, over near the church. It's the biggest and best in the city, ma'am."

Louisa looked one block down Broadway and saw a spire and behind it, a massive building. She followed Casey and stopped in front of Grace Church. Even in this city of churches, it was particularly beautiful. Its airy spire and Gothic Revival architecture reminded Louisa of the watercolor of Westminster Abbey that May had painted on her last trip abroad. The quiet garden, rectory and fountain called to her just as the green and peaceful landscape of England had charmed her on her own first trip to England. The patch of countryside, however, had now fallen into the shadow of the looming six-story palace of commerce across the street, A. T. Stewart's. This ironclad mammoth was festooned with arcades, columns, glass windows and a center rotunda which soared from the ground floor to the roof. It was owned by the exuberant man who had built the marbled mansion on Fifth Avenue where Casey had spun and launched himself so acrobatically on their first walk.

The pair entered with the intention of gawking at the huge atrium and the elevators. Casey's eyes scanned the one hundred counters of merchandise, and up the atrium to the colonnaded galleries that thronged with shoppers. From men's furs and ice skates to kitchen chairs and books, the store reflected the excesses of its eccentric owner.

The boy poured over a display of embroidered handkerchiefs. His face had a faraway look. "I'm sorry I am dragging you through these ladieswear departments," Louisa said.

Casey blushed and pulled his eyes away from the lace-trimmed linen squares. "I'll be looking at the baseball bats," he said, shuffling off.

"I can't very well live in one silk gown for the entire season," Louisa deliberated aloud, as a tidy cash boy smiled and nodded. "A cashmere walking suit would be necessary, I think." She chose a deep gray suit of two pieces, the bodice with puffed sleeves and the skirt with a slim silhouette, and two blouses, one cream and one a dark blue with a white lace collar.

Louisa left excitedly with Casey in tow, satisfied and not a little abashed. "My goodness, what temptation there is on this street! I have been enticed by fashion. Of course, there is a real charm about fine clothes. Let's hope I can be as grand as befits these extravagant items," she reasoned to her little guide, assuaging her conscience more than convincing him. More astonishing to her than the fact that the finery had gone so quickly to her head was that she had parted with hundreds of dollars so willingly. How many short stories would she have to churn out to keep pace with the bills she was accumulating on this trip?

One block away on Eleventh and Broadway was the stunning McCreery's Dry Goods Store, made of cast iron from prefabricated columns and arches. A billboard announced the sale of opera wear and leopard and tiger skin wraps. The massive buildings of cast iron that lined Broadway for the next ten blocks to south of Houston Street reached to ten floors high.

Casey took Louisa's hand as they entered the Haughwout Emporium on Broom Street. The façade of the building was modeled after an Italian renaissance library. "I remember this place," he said softly, looking around as if in paradise. "My father used to like to take us here, after work, to ride the first elevators in the city. Mama and Papa would put on their best clothing—otherwise the clerk would not let us in. They got wise to the rabble that only came in to take a ride."

"We can ride it again, if you would like," Louisa offered. But Casey looked sad and shook his head, turning away from the elevator line.

Louisa diverted his attention. She wanted to set foot in the store, not particularly to see its selection of cut glass, crystal, porcelain and chandeliers, nor the famous elevator. She had developed a kind of reverence for this establishment before ever seeing it. "President and Mrs. Lincoln ordered table settings for the White House from here, Casey. Maybe the clerk can show us the sample display. Look, here it is on the front wall!" They surveyed the white china, bordered in solferino purple, with a central image of an American eagle bearing a banner with the motto *E Pluribus Unum*. Louisa would never stop honoring the man who had kept the country as one through the most vicious division it could ever face.

After passing the gamut of stores on Broadway, they continued past the theaters, insurance companies, banks and hotels that lined the chasm down to Wall Street. White marble, brown stone, gray iron and red brick all aligned in a single file down the broad street, which now offered an unobstructed view to the Bowling Green.

"Casey, you've been a most patient companion," Louisa noted. "It is time for some dinner." At the corner of Worth Street, Casey perked up and pointed in the direction of the popular restaurant, Henry Henne's. Louisa would have found the establishment without her little guide, for the smells of hearty cooking engulfed the whole intersection, along with the jumble and clank of the boisterous sounds of a popular eatery. Louisa was happy to have her escort since the entire dining room was filled with businessmen, street boys and strident workers. Casey slid into the green leather booth and looked hungrily at the plates of beef and gravy that the waiters ferried to the noisy tables.

"What do you say to a plate of roast beef with potatoes and onions, Casey?" The boy looked at her with the most grateful smile, as if he hoped this day would never end. As he plied into the steaming plate and Louisa enjoyed an oyster stew, a snicker and sarcastic voice interrupted their comfort.

"I knew that mamma's boy had a sugarpot somewhere," said a sassy hobbadehoy to his gang of street boys. "No wonder you're the sweetest smelling newsboy in the Lodge."

Louisa wanted to charge over to the big-mouthed ragamuffin and lash into him for his smirking. She was the only woman in the restaurant. She stayed seated. Staying still was as hard for Louisa as holding her tongue. Casey shifted in his seat.

"Do those boys taunt you every day, Casey?" asked Louisa.

"No, ma'am, they're bad apples. They never would follow the rules and got locked out so many times from the Lodge that they are not welcome there anymore. They're just jealous of what anyone who follows the rules has got. That noisy one, he's been picked up more'n once by the police for burglary."

"And he's hardly past thirteen, it seems," mused Louisa, thinking again about the easy access to so many temptations in a city like this. Liquor, cheap entertainment, gambling—all were in reach of these vagrant children.

She looked at Casey, his slender neck beneath the slouching cap, his voice that had not yet achieved any semblance of masculinity, his sparkling innocence and spirit despite the urgency of his want. She thought of how cruel boys could be. She shuddered to think how Casey may have been abused at the hands of these ne'er-do-wells. She tried to smile at him. "You'll tell me if they bother you again, won't you?" she asked. He offered no confidences, nor any inkling about what kept him optimistic, or what dread he hid inside.

The manager moved the rowdy group along and Casey's shoulders relaxed. Louisa noticed that he had neatly devoured all his food.

"How about some baked beans to fill you out while I finish my stew?" said Louisa. "And then some pie and coffee!"

Casey walked a little slower as they continued south after dinner. They headed downtown with the tapering brown spire of Trinity Church as their guide, but stopped at City Hall Park, just across from Park Row and the massive clock tower of the Tribune building.

"Your City Hall is built to rival the capitals of Europe," Louisa told Casey. It faced a delightful park with a massive fountain, the strength and clamor of which Louisa had never encountered in any European piazza.

"It shoots a full fifty feet into the air," said Casey. The fountain water tumbled, spurted and finally exploded furiously into high arches. The sparkling arc bathed the park in a mantle of rainbows. Casey stretched his hands to the spray and wiped his sweaty face. The pair had attained the southern limit of their stroll for the day. On the eastern side of the park was their destination, the center of the newspaper and publishing world, Park Row.

"You're in the right business for this town, Casey," Louisa said. "It seems that after commerce, printing and publishing is New York's leading industry. The editors here are among the most respected men in the city." Louisa agreed with their grasp of the modern condition, which included a real cosmopolitanism, a hope for the future and a commitment to growth and change. Indeed, their breadth of outlook, their inclusion of diverse opinions, and their ultimate point of view spoke for the American situation. "New Yorkers are not naming public squares after famous forefathers such as Jefferson or Franklin, like the rest of the nation," Louisa observed, "but after the titans of publishing—Greeley Square and Herald Square."

"I never heard of anyone having four fathers and don't know how you would tie tans, Miss May," Casey said, trying to follow her oration.

"Never mind my silly talk, Casey. I see you are in your element now," Louisa said. "*The Herald, The Times, The Sun, The World, The*

Tribune and *The Evening Post* are all right here in those magnificent buildings across the street."

"We call it Printing House Square," replied the newsboy. "It could not be closer to City Hall and it's a short run from here to the courts, the police headquarters and the stock exchange. Look about—everyone here has something to do with the press."

Having crossed Broadway, Louisa saw the stressed and urgent faces of the telegraph boys, proofreaders, advertising men and reporters who traversed the busy plaza. The throb of the crowd was matched by a literal droning sound from the pavement. "There's two huge engines in a basement a street over," shouted Casey, straining to be heard. "They run the belts and shafting that power one hundred and twenty-five printing presses." The square actually hummed with the industry of printing. "The Newsboys' Lodging used to be on the sixth floor of the Sun building--that one on the corner with the big flag. They only had room for fifty lads back then. We live in a better place than that, all the floors for us, across town on Duane Street. You've got to come, Miss May."

The boy emitted pure exhilaration in this atmosphere. For the first time, Louisa thought of him as a link to the world of the daily newspapers. Casey had access every day to the breaking news. He might idle about the square in off hours. What if an astute reporter had already recognized her and asked him for a story? He knew how many outfits she had purchased and what she had for lunch. And that she wore gaiters. It would come out that she was in town under an assumed name. The tabloids could spread some jolly gossip.

The afternoon sun was sinking and barely filtered any warmth through the low clouds. The buildings threw long shadows across the square and the wind swirled dry leaves between the caverns in whirling gusts. The newsboys waiting for the late edition congregated on the square. They could feel the heat of the press rooms actually penetrating the flagstone pavement. Some boys curled up there together for warmth and rest.

"I can grab the evening edition here sooner than through the distributor uptown," Casey said. "I'll get a jump on my pals if I start my afternoon sales now."

He was guileless, honest, straightforward. How suspicious and sinister she had become to think that he would sell her story for profit. She hastened to compliment him. "You're an industrious lad, my boy. I wouldn't be surprised if some day you are working as a reporter behind one of those glass panes." Casey's eyes first misted and then beamed, as if the thought of such success was a castle so high in the air that he had never thought to even dream of it. "Get to work. I'll be fine getting home on my own," said Louisa.

"Take the cars right here on Broadway," Casey advised. "Don't wander north from here anywhere but on Broadway. You will be directly at the Five Points if you wander away, and I will be darned peeved if you get into any trouble, Miss Louisa."

"Don't swear, Casey. I intend to see Five Points sometime, but perhaps going alone in the late afternoon is not a wise plan."

As she watched Casey's small frame disappear into the crowd, Louisa sat down on a bench, exhausted and aching. It had been a grueling day—not only because she and Casey had walked almost three miles, but because her head whirled with so many worries. Thoughts of her sisters and cousin, her finances and immoderate purchases, her concern about the destitute children and now her recurring unease about being identified all rattled her brain.

It wouldn't do to sit in Printing House Square for long. Someone would spot her and start a fuss. She knew many editors in the buildings that surrounded her, or at least corresponded with them. They regularly sent her checks for the stories printed in their family and children's gazettes. When she was first starting out, she had been encouraged by the editors and publishers who printed her short stories in newspapers and popular magazines. They cheered her and kept her working and hoping and striving. She was grateful.

The crowd bustled as a curious entourage crossed the far end of the square. At the center of the maelstrom stood a debonaire man with a beautiful woman on his arm. He seemed to be barking orders and suggestions to the men around him. Some peeled off on errands and others jotted notes as he spoke. From his bowler hat to his buttoned boots, the man exuded charisma. He sported a broad plaid jacket, two fobbed watches and an unkempt beard. There was a swirl of energy, of imperative motion about him.

The woman on his arm was not young. She was glamorous, but seemed made of steel. She had a presence that declared she belonged in the turmoil; in fact, that she thrived on it. At times, the man turned to ask her a question, then nodded at her reply and barked it to the lackey nearby.

They approached closer to the bench where Louisa sat. "Mr. Leslie!" someone called out to him.

Louisa drew in her breath and turned her head sharply away from the scene. Frank Leslie! And then the woman at his side must be Miriam Squire Leslie, his wife. They were among the most notorious newspaper people in the land, not only for their often tawdry reports but for the scandalous way they conducted their lives. They had openly lived together along with her first husband and co-editor for ten years. The gossip was that Mrs. Squire herself had finally set up her first husband in a scandal with prostitutes and then had it reported in Leslie's paper. She divorced him for the escapade, committed him to a madhouse and went on to marry Frank Leslie.

Louisa groaned at her bad luck at encountering the pair. In her early years, the editor who gave her the most recognition and incentive was Frank Leslie. He had sponsored a contest which she won, over a hundred other submissions. Her prize was one hundred dollars and the appearance of "Pauline's Passion and Punishment" in *Frank Leslie's Illustrated Newspaper*, a revolution in publishing with a circulation of half a million readers. For years after that, Leslie was one of her greatest supporters, printing dozens of her short stories in his various publications. His new wife had worked as an editor on his ladies' magazine and five or six years ago had regularly published Louisa's romances peppered with spunky or vengeful heroines.

Louisa admired how this newspaper mogul brought vivid stories and startling illustrations within reach of every home. He ran the first likeness of Lincoln in his paper before the election, making his face as reassuring and familiar as Washington's. He had every intention of swaying public opinion. Most of what Leslie reported became a phenomenon.

Frank Leslie was just as flamboyant and titillating as his publications, frequently involved in the city's gossip. Two years before he had been indicted for obscenity. He published a rag called *The Day's Doings*, which concentrated on romantic liaisons, wayward women, and any other tantalizing bit of scandal he could dredge up. But it was the suggestive and lascivious personal advertisements in the back pages that got him in trouble. Louisa had seen the columns of print devoted to treatments for venereal disease, lewd books, marriage manuals with illustrations. Leslie had beaten obscenity charges over those advertisements and seemed to have come out of the scuffle with no repercussions on his own notoriety. But his wild assertions and virulent prose could damn another's reputation.

The group approached. She did not have time to rise and leave without crossing their path. Leslie knew of her unmitigated success and the part he played in it. She looked down and away. She hoped he knew why she couldn't greet him. It wasn't just his wife, or his obscenity rap, it was Louisa's own secret, too.

Those stories—all of her "blood and thunder stories," including the first prize winner—had been written either anonymously or under a pseudonym. Writing for Leslie's tabloids and other newspapers, Louisa had delved into a world of intrigue peopled with passionate, sometimes outrageous, characters. Stories of mesmerism, cross-dressing, experimentation with hashish and purloined wills were scattered about in periodicals and journals—her first work, but not linked to her now. No one had yet publicly made any connection. So far, Mr. Leslie and his colleagues were keeping their part of the bargain by not revealing her exuberant creations.

Though most of the brash and confident heroines she had created in those stories were among her favorite characters, Louisa could no longer claim them. Now, she was known as the revered author of the young ladies' favorite novel. Her upright young characters never cavorted in Frank Leslie's world.

The vortex approached, and the great man pulled up suddenly. He consulted one of his watches. While he made a show of checking the time, Louisa saw his eyes dart to the right and take a long look in her direction. Then he snapped his watch closed and hurried on.

Louisa was sure the shrewd newspaperman had seen her. She pulled her shawl more closely around her as the evening shadows deepened. Frank Leslie was not a man with whom Louisa May Alcott, the "Children's Friend," could afford to associate. She had worked too hard for her impeccable name. She had recently written to an old friend, "One's best defense is one's life and character." And indeed, Frank Leslie was a *character*. What he would do with the information that she was in town concerned her.

Later, as Louisa jolted northward on the Broadway line streetcar, she gazed east across Worth Street toward the notorious intersection of Five Points. Casey had warned her against its squalor, but Louisa's life had often skirted and many times reported the types of experiences found in the wretched hovels, the beer cellars and opium lairs that stretched east of Broadway. One world existed in the glistening light and industry of Broadway and another in the shadows of poverty, down the crooked narrow lanes of the most destitute neighborhood in the city. Fifth Avenue and Printing House Square were as far away from this habitat as different cities. Here, the Bowery Boys and the Dead Rabbits squared off against one another. Louisa knew that a woman alone, even a respectable man, might not pass there safely.

A trickle of pedestrians trod deliberately from the intersection, some appearing inebriated, others only trying their best to evacuate the place before nightfall. A cavalcade of tattered boys raced off, scattering in all directions as a policeman came after them, blowing his whistle in vain. A figure descended from a shabby tenement, looked furtively left and right and assuming an attitude of dignity, slipped away gracefully.

Louisa blinked at the black hooded cloak and swallowed hard, for she knew that cloak and those pale, white arms.

Chapter 9

Treatments

Late one afternoon, Louisa returned from another walking tour and, bidding Casey good evening, she entered the warm and bright hallway. Rebecca scrambled to the door, thrusting the book she was reading into her apron pocket. This industrious youngster was never idle. The thin, muscular girl had a strength and power in her limbs that reflected her mettle.

"The afternoon sun is so low here and these November evenings fall so swiftly, I am always surprised," said Louisa as she shed her cape and bonnet, turning to hang them herself on the stand behind the door. "What are you reading today, Miss Grant?"

"*Oliver Twist*, miss." Rebecca dropped a half curtsy in reply to the respect Louisa had given her.

"I should give myself the treat of reading that again on the next rainy day." Louisa had been fascinated with Dickens's novels when she was young. "I know that the poor, abused little boys in London don't seem very different from the pathetic gangs of pickpockets I saw at the Five Points here," she chattered to the girl. Suddenly, Rebecca looked past Louisa and sprang up behind her to reach for a black cloak. A distracted Mrs. Cutney hurried to the door, taking her wrap. Her face looked startled and apprehensive at Louisa's comments, and Louisa had the distinct thought that the mysterious woman might be returning to the Five Points.

"My good lady, I can certainly call my little escort back immediately to assist you in your outing so late in the day," offered Louisa. Except on a lively stretch of Fifth Avenue, a woman out alone after dark in New York was suspected of the saddest occupation to which a woman might descend.

A brief look of annoyance passed over the pale face before her, the blue eyes intense, but the woman recovered herself. "Thank you for your concern, but I am really without need of an escort." She smiled through watery eyes as she stepped out into the dusk. Louisa resolved to speak with this aching soul at the next possible private moment. She chose to think the best of her erratic behavior. Perhaps she could help her with the missions she needed to accomplish so urgently at strange hours.

Every afternoon punctually at three, Mrs. Cutney attended her hydrotherapy session and then exercised at gymnastics for an hour. She seldom asked for assistance from the staff and encouraged no intimacies with the other guests. She remained impassive at the dinner table, polite but aloof, revealing no clues to her nocturnal outings. Most evenings, she could be found quietly reading or knitting. She never joined the conversations or games of whist which took place in the hotel drawing room.

Louisa engaged a gymnastics session to coincide with Agnes Cutney's usual time at exercise. She was determined to hear the cryptic woman's story. Louisa approached the room warily, unsettled by the metallic clanking sounds that came from within. She loved to exercise out of doors. Running, skating and hiking had always been her joys. But sweating against a load of weights had never stimulated her energy or her moods.

The atmosphere was close and humid. Mrs. Cutney stood, her back to Louisa. She was strapped to a machine with a number of steel balls on a corset-like apparatus that hugged her back. The attendant began to crank a wheel, moving the balls up and down Mrs.

Cutney's spine. Mrs. Cutney's face was reflected in the mirror at the end of the room. Her eyes were closed as if in resignation, but her face winced with each revolution of the wheel.

"I hope my presence won't bother you," Louisa said as she was led to a contraption with a bench surrounded by a scaffold. Handles hung from wire cords that were connected to weights. Louisa sat on the bench and pulled one handle down, while her other arm was pulled up by the synchronous action. She took it that she would be sweating and aching today.

"No bother at all Miss May," said Mrs. Cutney. "I have reached the part in my routine where my assistant does all the work. I merely must submit."

"It seems that you have a lot to endure," Louisa said. "And you do it so quietly." She pulled with the opposite arm. Her assistant added a weight.

"I suppose my reserve around the others has been misinterpreted as aloofness," Mrs. Cutney said.

"Oh, not at all. I can see you suffer every day," Louisa replied. "Everyone can see that." Another weight was added.

"I wonder what else everyone can see," the woman said a bit sharply.

Louisa paused. Mrs. Cutney offered no explanation.

Louisa was directed to straddle the bench. Here, she had stirrups to push in order to lift the weights. Sweat, breathlessness—a new pain shot down to her left great toe. This was getting intolerable. "This is the first time I have been strapped to the rack and I think it may be my last." Louisa exhaled. "I have never been the same since I had typhoid." Louisa nodded at Mrs. Cutney, ready to hear her story. "I guess we are all a bit broken."

"Actually, I've been blessed with a lot of improvement here. I came to the facility crippled, unable to walk, my back fractured," Mrs. Cutney said as she was released from her torture. She lingered a bit near Louisa's exercise bench. "I was thrown from a carriage. My husband was killed."

"I'm sorry," Louisa said. *Pain, debility and grief, so much to bear.* "Your recovery has been a remarkable one, then, given the severity of your injury and the sadness you abide."

"Thank you. I try very hard, but I am not the woman I was. Perhaps it is too soon after my loss to find any peace, or perhaps it is too late." Fatigue clouded Mrs. Cutney's face. She tottered a bit and appeared to swoon. An attendant ran to her side.

"You are not well, Mrs. Cutney," said Louisa, unable to disengage herself from the apparatus.

"No need for concern. I have some comfort at times," replied Mrs. Cutney. She sweated and trembled softly. "I have merely done too much today and will cancel my session tomorrow," she said to the attendant as she was assisted from the gymnasium.

Louisa had the same mind to cancel her further sessions, having gotten no closer to information about Mrs. Cutney's errant wanderings. Besides, her days were too full already. Treatments, outings, lectures, dinners and theater consumed her time. She tried to balance the entertainment with work. She already had obligations for stories she owed to *The Youth's Companion.* She was crafting some of her impressions of the characters around her for use in those tales. Her extravagant clothing purchases served her well when she attended Mrs. Botta's soirée for literary and artistic types. Once she was introduced there, one invitation led to another.

One evening, Louisa was enjoying a sedate evening in the parlor, determined to get some rest to quiet her aching joints. She worked distractedly on a bit of sewing while in her mind she chanted over and over the meter of a poem she had submitted to a Christmas anthology. Marienne was reading, perhaps the hundredth chapter of Anthony Trollope's latest novel. Some foreign travelers, residing at the hotel as tourists and not as patients, poured over travelogues and theater announcements. In the far corner Herr Hahn puffed on a cigar and regaled the young businessmen with an escapade that sent them into fits of laughter. Mrs. Cutney bent over her crewelwork, but seemed hardly able to hold the needle. She stood to stretch, but her movements were interrupted by a sudden attack of fidgets and she excused herself abruptly. Louisa's eyes followed her. She casually rose and gave her goodnights to the others, then nearly bolted out of the room in pursuit of the woman.

The dear needs help. I hope she will let me be her confidante, finally, Louisa reasoned. She tried to overtake the ailing woman at the staircase, but her goodnights had caused delay and Louisa's neuralgia hobbled her. She stood with one foot on the first step, but her thigh cramped miserably.

"Such a face of pain you have, but not so deep as our friend." Herr Hahn appeared beside her at the foot of the stairs. He had also noticed Mrs. Cutney's discomfort.

"I hoped to offer her some assistance, but you see …." Louisa smiled wanly.

"Vee all have some trouble, no? Let's go together and see if vee can help our patient." He offered his arm and they climbed the stairs together.

Mrs. Cutney had already reached her door.

"Mrs. Cutney, can we have a word with you?" Louisa called from the landing.

"Gracious, you see how fatigued I am tonight," was the reply and the enigmatic woman slipped into her room and bolted the door.

Louisa rapped lightly. "Would you like us to do anything for you?" she asked gently.

"I would like you to leave me alone." Inside, they could hear her pacing, a fast tread that was interrupted only when she stopped abruptly to moan. The only other sound was sighing, pathetic and full of woe, rendered deeply as if to expiate a heavy care.

"She is either in excruciating physical pain or having a darkening of her mind, or both," Louisa lamented. "I suspect she will be wandering tonight. We won't see her at breakfast and yet tomorrow she

95

will be calm and controlled when she presents in the afternoon for her treatments." Herr Hahn registered no surprise when she mentioned the wandering, but also offered no thoughts.

"Herr Hahn," Louisa said before they parted at the landing, "the burdens that the guests carry here are overwhelmingly sad. Not the least distressing is your brother's condition. Does Doctor Miller give any hope?"

"You see that the city itself does vonders for Augustine. The baths help vith the aches for a leetle time. But Dr. Miller says that the inflammation is not only in his joints. It has collected in his kidneys, his lungs and his heart as vell. Already he has begun to retain fluid in the lungs. He gets breathless easily. At night, he sits up on three pillows."

"I am sorry." Louisa paused. She had to say what she knew to be true. "The end will be hard for him. He tries so to be independent. Will he stay for more treatments?"

"He vants to stay for his art. There are some lectures on the new vay of painting that he vill attend at the League and Dr. Miller has already measured his hand for a device that can hold a paintbrush. He vants to paint so desperately. He vill stay another month. I promised his mother that I vould have him home by Christmas." His face was calm and he kept his head up, looking sober but pragmatic. *He is approaching the business head on.* Louisa patted his arm reassuringly and turned in for the night.

Marchesa Contini was one patient who seemed to be benefitting from her stay at the Hygienic Bath Hotel, but whether it was from the treatments which had been abbreviated for her level of comfort or if it was the caring hour that Louisa spent with her each morning would be hard to say. Louisa had become a favorite with the gray-haired soul, who insisted that she be called Carlotta. Louisa kept the conversations simple, restricting herself to the weather, what she would like for tea, how snug she found her new tippet. Sometimes, she challenged the elderly woman's concentration, to see if there was any improvement in her focus and recall.

"Do you know what day it is today, Carlotta?"

The aged face showed a vacant look, followed by a slight moment of confusion, rummaging about in the deserted memory, and then in relief she answered, "It's good to see that someone else has my problem, dear. I can never remember the day of the week either!"

Louisa laughed with her and changed the talk to Carlotta's favorite memories. These invariably ran to the briefest but happiest time in her life, the short honeymoon in Italy, which ended in so much tragedy. In Louisa's view, not the least loss was the sacrifice of this woman's poetic voice. "Do you miss your poems, Carlotta?" she asked.

"How can I miss them when they are always with me?" The eyes were clear and unafraid. "Con sospiri, incanti e dolci sussurri," she recited. There was such beautiful lyricism that it did not matter if Louisa's smattering of tourist Italian could not interpret the literal words.

"Con sospiri, incanti e dolci sussurri," Louisa repeated aloud. It was as soothing as the mantra she had been seeking.

"Now don't go reciting that in public. You know Federico is so protective of my treasures."

"Do you regret never getting any public appreciation for your gifts?" Louisa probed carefully.

"I do get recognition. All the nuns and the teachers flatter me. My fiancé sings my praises. Mother says it is my poems that attracted him first."

And yet he silenced those songs, Louisa thought. *He wanted them only for himself.* Like so many generations of women before her, Carlotta had subjugated her talent to domesticity. *Her poems were her progeny, just like my stories.* Louisa thought of those stories she had abandoned, that lay unclaimed in the pages of Frank Leslie's newspapers. Louisa felt ashamed, confused, even frightened by the way she had stifled her own words. She had no husband to silence her. She had done it on

97

her own.

"I would like to hear more of your poems someday," Louisa said to the marchesa, almost groping for her own consolation. Again, the vacant look, the fearful eyes, the craning for a thought, trying to fill in the past. Louisa took to reading her the poems of Wordsworth and Longfellow until the quivering head nodded comfortably to sleep.

As days went on, Marienne never overstayed her hour away, which she used to make progress on her own writing. Still, she was too shy and unsure of her work to let Louisa see any bit of it. On the other hand, little by little, the marchesa began to open up under Louisa's encouragement. The old woman searched her memory and her soul for the words she had created and loved. They got to reciting little snippets of rhymes. Carlotta would begin and she would teach Louisa to respond with the next line.

"Di notte penso a me," Carlotta began.

Louisa rhymed back, "Nella braccia de te, nelle braccia, nella braccia …."

Marienne appeared at the door. She looked at Louisa with surprise. "Who told you that poem?" she asked pointedly.

"Why, your aunt, of course."

Marienne shook her head. "You mustn't do that. *Ever.*" She was so emphatic she stamped her foot. "She kept that promise all her life."

"Surely your aunt's private chambers are not considered a public space," Louisa countered.

"But you are a *public person.*"

Was she insinuating that Louisa would repeat these words, maybe even publish them?

"Marienne, you know my celebrity is my bane. Don't charge me with that," Louisa said.

"I know, Miss Louisa." The girl seemed conflicted, but then raised her eyes to Louisa's and said impertinently, "You've told me.

98

And you say that's why you've chosen to hide who you are." Marianne swept past Louisa to her aunt's side, cradling her in an embrace so strong and determined that it seemed her arms alone would wall in the memories.

NEW YORK CITY—OPENING DAY AT LORD & TAYLOR'S STORE, BROADWAY AND TWENTIETH STREET—LADIES ASCENDING IN THE ELEVATOR.

Figure 5. **Opening Day at Lord & Taylor's Store, Broadway and Twentieth Street - Ladies Ascending in the Elevator**

Chapter 10

The Piano Player

One Sunday, the children proposed a play. Helene and Rebecca cajoled Marienne to adapt a script for them and then wheedled Casey into the scheme. They huddled in the parlor after placing a sign on the door: *Silence! Rehearsals in Progress.*

"Let's do *Little Women*, as there are exactly four of us," Helene suggested.

Casey squirmed. "I am *not* putting on any girl's clothes. I can tell you that right now."

"I can sketch a few scenes from *Marjorie's Quest*, and there are plenty of nasty characters and boys in that story," Marienne suggested, averting an awkward scene for Louisa. It was decided that Helene would reign as Marjorie, with the others playing the beggars, farmers, soldiers and do-gooders who tried to help the orphan girl.

The adults were as taken with the production as the children. "Four children are just the right number to play all the roles," said Louisa, remembering the many parts she played in the barn at Concord. "There are plenty of characters and plot twists to keep them all changing costumes like a whirlwind. I shall be the costume mistress and stage director."

Augustine painted a sheet to use as the curtain and another which depicted a country lane and a field as the backdrop. It fell to

Herr Hahn to organize the stage set, which required much moving of furniture and climbing to fix the curtain across the room. That evening, the play went off—though not flawlessly, as there was one scene in which the curtain remained open, and another in which a pile of chairs transformed into a beggar's cave collapsed, with Casey and Rebecca below.

Louisa realized that they had nearly enacted a scene from *Little Men*, with Herr Hahn as the professor. She looked at his joyful face and knew he remained oblivious. *It will be better when I reveal myself later on if he has never read my books. Maybe a few more days of this comfort.*

Mrs. Miller stomped in to inspect the calamity, checking the condition of her Chinese vase before that of the children.

"You preside over a most happy lodging, Mrs. Miller," Herr Hahn said joyfully, extricating the two players from their dilemma. "Eet is like a big family."

"This entertainment is not the type of restful evening I promise to my guests," she snapped, looking at Louisa as if she had brought anarchy to her hotel. Louisa didn't care.

Life at the hotel did sometimes feel as comfortable as her family home. After the little spat in the marchesa's room, Louisa had gotten back on a steady keel with the Marienne by including her as an equal in conversations about the interesting salons and lectures she attended. Louisa and Marienne would come together in the late afternoons to talk about writing, answer their correspondence and chat about interesting snippets in the daily papers. Louisa settled into her cozy divan while Marienne sprawled on the carpet, each scanning the late editions for the society news, the theater listings and the lecture reviews.

"Miss Louisa!" Marienne announced. "There's mention of you in the paper."

Louisa started. Could it be some mess that Frank Leslie churned up? She glanced at the banner: *The New York Telegraph*. Not one of Leslie's papers. She exhaled and said serenely, "Read it to me, dear.

Let's see what they have to report."

Marienne read the 'Literary Notes' column. *"Miss Louisa May Alcott is said to have earned $150,000 from sales of her books. This eclipses Mark Twain, Horatio Alger, Bret Hart and Henry James.* Is it an accurate account?"

"Would you believe that I actually have no idea? I'm not very good at the business side of things. I know I earn a lot of money and I spend a lot of money. I paid off a lifetime of family debt, and keep up with all the bills for myself, my parents and my sisters," Louisa said.

She wasn't particularly proud of her affairs. She always felt hounded by creditors, real or imagined. It was one of the legacies her father had passed down to her. "No worries about me, Marienne," she said, preferring to believe the look on the girl's face was one of concern and not disbelief. Louisa pointed to another headline. "If you want a woman to worry about, leave your emotion for this poor Mrs. Tilton. That neverending Beecher case is at it again."

Marienne sighed and blushed. "I've lost myself in the twists and turns."

"A magnificent reputation in tatters," Louisa said. "And I do mean the woman's, not the preacher's. He'll come out just fine. He's got his saintly sister, Harriet Beecher Stowe, sitting in the pews while he continues his thundering addresses every week. You know, I once knew the husband, Mr. Theodore Tilton. He actually asked me to write for his suffragist paper, *The Revolution.*"

"Miss Louisa, you *do* seem to know just about *everyone*! Wasn't he associated with Misses Cady and Stanton, the suffragists? Tell me your insights to his character—as an author, of course," Marienne coaxed.

"I was totally unimpressed and declined to work with him. His talk was impertinent and meandering. He had a noticeably silly way. He didn't seem to be grown up yet. I am certain that he has no clear idea of the fool he appears to be."

Louisa took the paper and read aloud from the lurid local news. "*A woman from Boston hanged herself at 291 Elizabeth Street. She had left her husband and was living with a German. Mrs. Bridey C., not speaking to her husband for a week, committed suicide by throwing herself under a train.* It's always desperate and abandoned women," Louisa grumbled. "And more: *Mrs. Ida Van D. died of an overdose of morphine.*"

"All jilted by a lover or shamed by society or riddled with guilt. These women are held to such an impossible standard that they have no idea of how to go on living when they are abandoned," Marienne observed. "I should think I would get along any way I could—a shop girl, a nanny, a companion."

"You are speaking from a comfortable position. Read these women's flaws. No upstanding mistress would invite them into her household. It's the beginning of an ever downward spiral when these women are cast off," Louisa added. Louisa shifted to the daily notices to relieve the sadness of the preceding reports. These notices were among the most amusing of all. "Time for me to get ideas brewing for some lively stories. These classified ads never disappoint me. They are so filled with needs and wants and all kinds of surprising queries." A quiet plea for a domestic position or a search for luggage lost in the depot might lead her to concoct a poignant tale or comical caper. Louisa read aloud, "*Will the Lady in plaid with the dark veil who was left waiting by her companion near the Delmonico restaurant on Monday evening, care to enter that same establishment with a gentleman who noticed her discomfort and wishes to right the wrongs of his sex? Address Robert K, _____ Office.*" Louisa chuckled. "Oh, she will definitely say yes. What should the twist be, Marienne?"

"Why, it's his wife, of course. She's been suspicious of him for years and finally caught him at his philandering."

"Excellent dramatic turn, my girl. You'll have to write that one, though I must admit I am a bit surprised at the bold plot. Too risky for my little audience." Louisa tried to keep her voice playful, though it quaked a bit. She had nearly been exposed. The story that Mari-

enne had spun might be one of her own lively tales of misunderstanding between the sexes.

Further down the column, she read, "*A first class pianist, graduate
of Warsaw Conservatory, is open for a few more lessons, either private or institute; highest references. Address: L.W., Box 10, Tribune Office or G. Steck &
CO., 25 East 14th St.*"

She read the advertisement over once, then twice, then sat, absorbed.

"Miss Louisa, are you alright? You look like you've seen a vision
of a spectral piano teacher." Marienne had startled her and Louisa
jumped. "Can I help you?"

Louisa was the caregiver, the counsellor, the companion. Like
Marchesa Contini, she had sacrificed again and again for her family. It felt strange to have someone extend a helping hand to her.
Perhaps she had never had that feeling since Beth was gone. How
sweet that Marienne was offering her concern. Before she knew it,
she began a story that she had never fully uttered before, perhaps
not even to herself.

"It's the initials, L.W., and the fact that it is a Polish piano player.
I knew someone the very same in Vevey and Paris."

"Paris? " Marienne murmured. "How romantic."

"I was thirty years old and floundering. I had written one popular book, but my prized novel was rejected and then cut up so badly
when it did get published that I could hardly recognize it. I wanted a
fresh start, but I had no money, no prospects for work. An opportunity came up for me to go to Europe as a travelling companion. Of
course I jumped at it. To see the lands of Dickens and Goethe, to
see real castles and actual dukes and duchesses! Well, it was a dream.
But, due to my charge's health, we got stranded in a hotel in a sleepy
town in Switzerland."

"Go on." Marienne sat upright on the rug, hugging her knees
and taking in every word.

Louisa switched to her storytelling style. "The hotel was quiet, the clientele boring, until one night a Polish soldier with a thin, intelligent face, charming manners and a persistent cough arrived for a stay."

"Was he handsome?" Marienne interjected.

Louisa looked down at her with feigned sternness. "I am a nurse. I knew immediately he was suffering from consumption."

"My," Marienne said. "I wasn't expecting that."

"His uniform and fragile health aroused all my maternal feelings for my boys in blue. Laddie had fought and suffered imprisonment in the struggle against the Cossack invasion of his homeland. I have never been satisfied with the time I spent in the nursing corps during the war. I had an inconvenience of typhoid pneumonia," Louisa resumed in her best theater voice. "Just barely out of his teens, Ladislas became the brother, son and companion I had often imagined. I found him altogether captivating and romantic. He was poor, lonely and ill … frankly, everything I looked for in a man."

"Then you must be in your glory here at the hotel. Mr. Augustine is like that—have you noticed?" Marienne smiled slyly. The girl had impossible romantic notions. Louisa plunged on, not certain of the success of this story. Maybe Marienne would get it all wrong.

"I gave him all my attention and care. In gratitude, he became my escort, errand boy and French tutor. Ladislas was an accomplished pianist. He was forbidden to sing on account of his weak lungs, but he played fervently in the evening, face glowing, eyes shining. We delighted each other with little jokes and notes, assisted each other with translations, and when my party moved on, we promised to meet again in Paris later in the year."

"An assignation in Paris!" Marienne blurted.

"A lark, an adventure, a spree … but an assignation? No, you're changing the story." Was Marienne listening to the same tale she was telling?

"Lark, then," Marienne acquiesced. "What happened?"

"My charge sheltered in Nice for the winter, and the promised

106

trip to Paris was delayed and delayed again. Eventually, I had had enough of the staleness of one place and decided that my end of the engagement was complete. I left my employ and headed to Paris."

"By yourself, Miss Alcott?"

Louisas knew what she was insinuating. "You've got it all wrong, Marienne. We were the very best of friends. I don't think I was ever Miss Alcott to Laddie. I think I was just Lou, but perhaps my memory is wrong about that. Somehow, he tracked me at my boarding house the very day I arrived. We went on a magnificent whirl of shopping in the capital of fashion and he selected a bonnet which I still keep as a memento."

"Paris ... you saw Paris," Marienne mooned.

Louisa assumed her declamatory style. "I felt in my element and went fearlessly on the arm of my young escort, from long walks in the Tuileries, to moonlight strolls along the Champs Elysee. I said it myself in my essay 'My Boys' ...."

"I read that essay," Marienne said, with a sidelong look at Louisa. "But I never really understood it. First you say that you loved Laddie like a grandmother, and then that you kissed him on the lips when you parted, and that you cried over the perfume bottle that he gave you."

That essay had sparked many romantic fantasies among her readers. Louisa never could explain all the pathos and emotion of that parting. Though they were twelve years apart in age, Laddie's maturity and charm and manners had made their relationship seem right. He was a dying young man and they had spent two magical weeks together.

"Did he ever say he loved you?" Marienne demanded.

Just like all the other girls. Louisa responded slowly. "Well, he always preferred me to call him by a nickname, in Polish, which I found out later translated to 'my darling.'"

Marienne was unsatisfied. "So did he aspire to be a suitor or a son?"

Louisa raised her hands in surrender. "I'm sure I don't know. That's what makes it such a compelling story. It can go either way." Marienne was insisting too much on the story having a definite conclusion.

"But Laurie loved Jo. It was Jo who didn't have feelings for Laurie … this Laddie must have been your Laurie," Marienne persisted.

"You forget that I am not Jo. And people always ask me who Laurie 'is.' When I came to write *Little Women*, certainly, I remembered my boy with his European manners, all his forlorn loneliness, his gracious, respectful attention." Louisa stood up. Her voice rose a bit emphatically. *People always misunderstand my Laurie.* "I combined Laddie's Continental appeal with the rougher, more casual manners of the boys from Concord. We had one friend, William Lane, who came from England, the only boy who romped along with us four girls. Another inspiration was one of our young acting partners, a great favorite of May's. I took bits from each to draw my character of Teddy Laurence. Remember, Laurie is half Italian and half New Englander."

"You used Laddie's charm and love of music and joined it to those carefree, local boys and created the most attractive young man. All the girls think Laurie is the dreamiest character. I like how you did that," Marienne mused. "But how sad not to know if Laddie was in love with you."

"How did I ever think I could explain this to a romantic young girl?" Louisa bantered.

"Well, did you never speak again?" Marienne sniffed a bit at being taken as a silly girl.

"Never, but we wrote for a few years. He's married and has two daughters. I know that he suffered a huge loss in the Vienna Crash two years ago, but have not heard from him since. He's so sensitive and genteel, I imagine he's a bit cowed by my celebrity now. I wish he knew that I haven't changed."

"Mrs. Miller would be able to tell him how little you put on airs," Marienne said. "Can I see the announcement?" She scanned the words. "*Pianist, Warsaw, L.W, Fourteenth Street.* You must go. You can't live your whole life without knowing for sure."

"You've got it all wrong." She shook her head at Marienne, who was rising from the rug and heading toward the door. "Laddie isn't living in New York. What in the world would he be doing in New York?" she demanded as the door slammed.

The following day Mrs. Miller sought Louisa out before her bath treatment.

"It is our policy to confer with the guests and to see if the objectives of treatment are being achieved," she said. "Of course, it depends on the full cooperation and engagement of the client. Dr. Miller has noted that you expend a great deal of energy apart from the assigned therapy."

"Perhaps Dr. Miller should be the one to discuss it with me," Louisa said.

Mrs. Miller shifted her gaze. "Surely, tramping about the city with a vagabond …."

"It's that again, is it, Mrs. Miller?" Louisa looked at her piercingly.

"You are most perplexing, *Miss May*, your subterfuge, your odd associations."

"Maybe it's my head that should be examined," Louisa said. "Better yet, off with my head!" She smiled at Mrs. Miller's startled look, then turned and entered the quiet space of the Tepidarium.

Later, at the end of her treatment, Louisa relaxed in the dark. She tried hard not to let Mrs. Miller irritate her. Enveloped in the soft cushions, she whispered a new mantra. "Con sospiri, incanti e dolci sussurri," she repeated, but the sonorous words got her thinking of a lonely, sick and amorous foreigner who had reentered her consciousness the day before.

Unlike her father, Louisa was not a dreamer. If something needed to be addressed she attacked it head on, so there was nothing for it but to go to the piano establishment on Fourteenth Street. It was a simple walk of about a half mile to the showroom off Fifth Avenue, but as she drew nearer her heart pounded and she felt as if she had run five miles. Her steps drew slower and slower. She was annoyed, ashamed and confused all in one. She wasn't about to let herself grow faint of heart or flustered. Besides, even if it *was* Laddie, he would have the same problem she always encountered with boys: they turned into men. A mature Laddie was not someone she was sure she wanted to meet. She invariably found that impudence turned to insolence, that frivolity turned to superficiality and charming boyish chagrin turned to dissatisfaction. American men, at least, she found to be more self-centered, distracted and insensitive than they were worth.

She stopped short at the door and convinced herself that it was not for lack of nerve but to examine the posters in the window. Apparently, the Steck Company had solicited a testimony from Richard Wagner and it was emblazoned in the storefront. Wagner's "great friend Franz Liszt has expressed the liveliest satisfaction" in his Steck piano and Wagner expected that the "magnificent instrument will ever serve for my pleasant entertainment."

She entered the piano emporium and immediately felt ridiculous in its hushed interior. The clerk was at the rear of the store, his back to her. She caught her breath at the tall, lithe frame, the slim shoulders, the dark hair curling over the top of his collar, a hint of a moustache as she glimpsed his profile. The young man turned to approach her. She closed her eyes, held her breath and waited.

"Can I help ya, ma'am? You okay? You lookin' for a pianer?" The thick New York accent washed over her like a cold shower. She shivered like the disappointed but brave little girl at Fruitlands who longed for warmth and settled for the bone chilling cold water shower when that was all she was offered.

"Perhaps I'm in the wrong place," Louisa stammered, forgetting her purpose there. Recovering the little scrap of newspaper she sputtered out her excuse. "I was wondering about piano lessons. I saw this announcement today."

"Oh, yes, Miss Warsinski. She's makin' a commotion."

"Excuse me?" Louisa was not following.

"Lizette Warsinski. She gave a recital at the Marble Collegiate Church two evenin's ago and I'm thinkin' she was fully booked for lessons on the spot."

"Lizette. *Lizette*. That is a woman. I am so glad. I am so very, very glad." The man stared at her. She stared back. *I am ridiculous,* Louisa thought. *What was I thinking when I came here?* The man cleared his throat. She started and roused to leave.

"Do you want ta leave ya name, should an openin' come up?"

"That won't be necessary. I realize I don't need the services after all."

As she left the premises, the clerk casually followed her to the door, and threw the bolt as Louisa turned away.

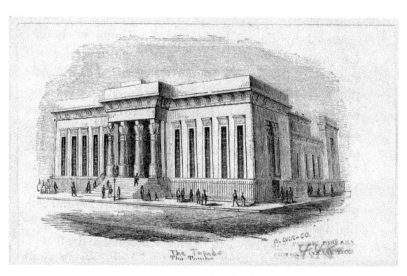

Figure 6. **The Tombs**

Chapter 11

Mrs. Gibbons

"Marienne, it's time we got serious and did a bit of good during our stay," Louisa announced one morning. "New York is a city of such stark contrasts and we have been straddling both of its worlds. We spend so much time amid the bustle of Broadway, bewitched by fashion, the modern ideas of the great thinkers, the wonder of the theater, but I can't ignore the underbelly of New York City."

"I am as eager as you to see with a writer's eyes and report on what I see," Marienne enthused.

"My family always struggled against poverty, our own more than anything. I guess I know firsthand how close many families are to utter destitution. It seems that there are as many ways to become poor in New York as there are to be entertained." Louisa brightened, thinking of an antidote to despair. "Come," she said, taking Marienne's hand. "I want you to meet Mrs. Gibbons. She is one of my mother's oldest friends, ever since their antislavery work together in Philadelphia when I was a baby. A real visionary."

"Am I really to meet one of the Alcott circle?" Marienne asked, pulling on her bonnet.

They strolled north, beneath occasional autumn trees, following the diagonal path of Broadway. They passed the uptown theaters and, further north, entrances to less luxurious hotels than were found downtown. The doorways were filled with lounging men who invited the spectacle before them and whose sole purpose seemed to be gossip. The women could hear snippets of talk about others' downfalls, unusual partnerships and fantastic court cases.

"They don't only talk gossip," noted Marienne. "They take pleasure out of repeating it, and I daresay they would even act on it if they had the chance."

"It's hard to know if they are telling tall tales or slandering someone's good name. And I don't believe they know the difference," grumbled Louisa.

The city grew less dense above Fortieth Street. As they walked the mile to 111 West Forty-Fourth Street, Louisa had plenty of time to tell Marienne about the exceptional life of Abigail Hopper Gibbons. "She is from a Quaker family, all quite influential and altruistic. Her causes are the ones dear to my Marmee and myself … the rehabilitation of fallen women, education of immigrant girls, prison reform. Did I tell you that Marmee opened a community office when we lived in Boston which placed poor women in positions of employment? We all tried to improve the women's health, their ways with their children, their literacy skills, anything that would give poor working women a leg up."

Marienne smiled and nodded. "I admire your mother and your sisters, so ready to be the protectoresses of the downtrodden," she said.

"Protectoresses!" exclaimed Louisa. "No gushing, Marienne."

They both laughed and Louisa went on. "Mrs. Gibbons influenced my mother tremendously. Being a Quaker, she started off with the Friends' combination of benevolence, concern for the needy and a belief in the independence of women. She's added to that her own theories of justice over charity. She has even gotten the government involved with funding, instead of relying on philanthropy to support her causes. She's a powerhouse of social reform. They know her in Albany and Washington."

"She sounds formidable," said Marienne. "I shall quake before her."

"She's a lamb," replied Louisa. "She's a tiny little bundle of energy in a white bonnet who always lapses into gentle Quaker 'thees' and 'thous' with my mother and other close friends."

They had already passed through the district of newer theaters, reaching a less congested area with practical new homes. "How Mrs. Gibbons came to live uptown is a thrilling story that I will let her reveal to you," Louisa said.

Finding the septuagenarian at home was never assured, given her many commitments and causes, but Louisa and Marienne were welcomed warmly by her daughter, Julia. "Mother's involved in her eternal Randall's Island dolls right now, getting ready for her Christmas run," Julia said, waving them into the parlor.

A table in the center of the room was nearly obliterated from view by a jumble of boxes, bolts of linen and lengths of ribbons and lace. A half dozen women bent over their handiwork, crocheting small dresses, sewing on button eyes, crafting yarn braids. A gray-haired, pink-cheeked woman oversaw the construction of the dolls. She bustled about opening packages, new arrivals of donated goods. The baker's boy had just entered from the back door with a pile of empty flour sacks, which Mrs. Gibbons accepted as willingly as she did the pearl sequins that the milliner had offered the day before.

"Louisa, I have not seen thee since thou were a babe, but oh, how thy dear mother has filled me with her proud tales of thy success. You are a blessing to your dear parents and a reflection of their fire." Mrs. Gibbons embraced her guests and escorted them around the table.

"What will you do with these lovely dolls?" Marienne asked, looking around curiously.

"These are the gifts which we make every year to bring to the orphans and invalids at the charity institutions on Randall's Island. I bring them on Christmas Day, and intend to continue doing it as long as God is willing to send me."

"Mrs. Gibbons, might I come with you this year?" Louisa asked, her heart melting with the prospect of helping hundreds of sick and forlorn orphans, all in one place on one day.

Mrs. Gibbons laughed. "The apple doesn't fall far from the tree. I remember thy mother in her youth always rushing to aid someone barely more needy than herself. Yes, come, Louisa. Thy fame may help the cause, too."

"Marmee's motto still is 'Do the good which lies closest at hand.' We have worked for so many of the same causes, but you have been so fearless in promoting yours, Mrs. Gibbons, that I offer any help I can give with humility," said Louisa.

Julia directed them into the drawing room, out of the bustle of industry, and offered coffee. Louisa noticed the walls of books, the desk filled with correspondence and the bust of Mrs. Gibbons's son, William. His accidental death had nearly destroyed his mother's spirit, but she had risen from that despondency more determined than ever to work for her causes.

"Marienne," Louisa began, settling down in a chair near the fire grate for a chat, "what I said about Mrs. Gibbons's bravery is all true. She and her daughter Sarah were such competent nurses during the war that they remained nearly two years at the front. They nursed, fed and mothered hundreds of soldiers."

"I suppose I was interested in protecting the contraband, as much as anything else," added Mrs. Gibbons, "especially when they were abused by the hospital managers."

"Mrs. Gibbons became so respected by the Union officers, Marienne, that her nurses were often requested over those of Dorothea Dix." Turning to Mrs. Gibbons, she said earnestly, "I've always admired you for that, your compassion combined with competence. My hospital was under Miss Dix's supervision. She was rather severe, a difficult woman to work with."

"Louisa, we know you did your part too, dear. And perhaps I did my family a disservice by leaving them exposed at home." She patted Julia's hand and urged her to tell her story.

"It was while Mother was at the front that the New York Draft riots exploded," Julia reminisced. "Those three days of pillaging, lynching and looting were the most terrifying I have ever seen." New York was never as ardent about the abolitionist cause as Massachusetts, Louisa knew.

"The mob protested at conscription orders, targeting individuals who were known to support the abolitionist cause," Mrs. Gibbons continued. "The clamor turned violent and raged throughout the city. Many innocent people lost their lives. Horace Greeley lived on our block. The mob spewed into West Twenty-Ninth Street and attacked both houses, shouting, 'Greeley! Gibbons!' Can you imagine the rage?"

"Lucy and I were at home at the time," Julia said, but seemed to halt at the awful memory. "We ran to the higher floors in terror, just as the panels to the front door were beaten in and the windows were shattered ... and we realized they would not stop at defacing the exterior only. We could hear them trampling through the broken panels, swinging clubs. We could smell the fiery torches."

This family had suffered for their beliefs. Louisa looked at Mrs. Gibbons, who labored every day for the poor of the city, likely some of the very same people who had attacked her family. The grandeur of their sacrifice made her feel small.

"The furniture was hacked and destroyed. We heard everything being overturned, books, papers, valuables ...." She paused and looked at the bust of her brother. "We recovered this, even after ... even after ... all was set afire."

Mrs. Gibbons gazed at her daughter with regret and resolve. Marienne's eyes were wide, terrified at the narrative. Louisa understood her reaction. She too was sitting on the edge of her seat. This story was magnificent, large, important. The legacy of these women was assured. *This is eminence,* Louisa thought. *This is what should be ap-*

117

plauded, appreciated, rewarded, not … not my cloying little stories.

"We climbed to the top floor, staying ahead of the destruction. The fourth floor had access to the roof through a glass skylight. My sister and I pushed and pulled each other to the rooftop and somehow escaped the mob's notice, as we scurried across the flat roofs to the final house on the block. The side street was strangely silent, and looking down, we saw a carriage which could take us to safety. We rapped on the neighbor's skylight, but the sound of our fists on glass was swallowed in the roar of the mob. We were panicked that at any moment the pillagers might explode through to the roof. The skylight creaked open cautiously. We could see the small cap and long beard of the man of the house, his wife behind him with shawl and head scarf, and a row of children, the boys' faces upturned and their ringlets swaying."

"My dear fugitives descended into the arms of a Jewish family. Their own convictions had always mirrored ours," Mrs. Gibbons concluded. "At great risk, they smuggled the girls out to the waiting carriage and away to safety. I was heartbroken when I saw my home. That pillaged, hulking shell seemed to cry out, 'It was ignorance and rum. Their children must be taught better.'"

"How did you go on?" Marienne asked Julia and Mrs. Gibbons.

"The only way I know how to," said Mrs. Gibbons. "By setting out to change the conditions that fostered the restlessness and the poverty in the first place. It is the women who control the passions of society. I have opened a halfway house for women who are released from prison, I set them up for training in jobs and raising a family, and I teach them to read. Every Wednesday, I visit the prison to see my ladies and arrange for their release."

Louisa leaned forward on the edge of her chair, about to speak. She was eager to get inside that sad and sinister prison, to comfort, to shed light on the conditions there and, as always, to have an experience that could be used in one of her stories.

"No need to say a word, my dear. I see it in your eyes. Yes, you can come with me. How about next Wednesday?"

On Wednesday, Louisa read the morning news. The city was stunned that day by reports of the arrest of a small posse of burglars, a recurring torment to the town. It turned out that the three burglars were all under eleven years of age. They had confessed to the officers that they were led to their misdeeds by a desire to emulate the characters of the dime novels they had read. This story made Louisa shudder—just two years before in Massachusetts, a violent teenager who had tortured and finally murdered several small children used the same excuse. He said he had read over sixty dime novels, relishing the "killing and scalping and tomahawking." He had even been given some favorable leniency in the press due to this claim. Louisa didn't like the alibi. She doubted that any amount of reading could change the character of a being. If that were the case, she would send her *Little Women* to the tiny burglars and assume they would begin sharing their breakfasts with the less fortunate forthwith. She wondered where the youngest criminals were sequestered.

Louisa pulled on her raingear to visit the New York Halls of Justice. The locals called this prison "The Tombs" due to its architectural resemblance to an Egyptian mausoleum.

"Would you accompany me today when I enter that horrific place they call 'The Tombs,' Casey?" she called to him as he entered, stamping his rain boots.

Casey visibly shrunk back. "No, Miss May, I can't do that," he said with a shake of his cropped head. "I promised my dear mother in heav—bless her wherever she may be," he corrected himself, "that I would never enter the shadow of those doors. I cannot enter that fearsome place." He crossed himself.

"Casey," Louisa prodded tenderly, for he never had hinted at how he lost his parents, "do you believe your mother is still alive? I would

119

truly like to help you find her, if that is the case."

"I feel that she is alive," the boy whispered. "But something is wrong. Why did she not come to find me?" His voice quivered, his brow creased and he looked so perplexed and forlorn that Louisa thought her heart would break.

"Casey, you can trust me with your story," she offered.

The lad shook his head. "Not today, miss. It makes me too sad and angry and tired. I need my spirits and my strength to get my work done today." He jammed his cap on the flaming stubble on his head and hurried off. Louisa knew that she had the key to most boys' hearts. It would take time and care, but she would find the soft little kernel inside this hard nut.

Mrs. Miller came out of her office at the sound of the slamming door. "Miss May, I must warn you about your latest escapade. It is absolutely foolhardy to put yourself in the presence of the scum and dross you will encounter at the Tombs. Only raving missionaries put themselves through such an indignity."

"Do you suppose I have not seen worse, Mrs. Miller?" Louisa replied, grabbing her umbrella defiantly.

Chapter 12

A Day in the Tombs

Cold, sleety rain slanted into Louisa's face as she tramped to the downtown omnibus. New York in November had a rare, peculiar smell which seemed to encompass all the street scene in one odor— part wet wool, part urine, part kerosene, part horse sweat and part roasting chestnuts. It was raw urban energy and grit in one scent. Louisa could identify New York if she were blindfolded and deaf with just a whiff. All the New York public seemed to struggle together on the streets on these rainy days, umbrellas to the wind, boots tramping puddles, but never slowing down.

The Halls of Justice loomed dismal and ominous. *Another foolish Egyptian construction,* Louisa noted. *I wonder what the original symbolism was intended to be … Egyptian slaves? Locked up like a mummy? The eternal resting place of the dead? But my, how very fearsome it is.* A broad flight of granite stairs led to a portico that was supported by massive fluted Egyptian columns carved with lotuses. The exaggerated lintels of the windows resembled those she had seen in engravings of the Temple of Horus. Mrs. Gibbons, with her gray dress, white shawl and white linen bonnet, looked particularly defenseless and exposed standing under these yawning eaves. Her use of the quaint familiar pronouns of the Quaker tongue made her presence at the mouth of the prison even more incongruous.

"Art thou truly ready for what is inside, dear?" she asked.

"I have seen my share of sorrow but it never gets easier to bear," replied Louisa.

"Thou art thy mother's daughter, and that is a strong compliment." Mrs. Gibbons took her arm and they marched past the guard at the front gate with a nod and into the inner courtyard. Though this opening may have been designed to improve circulation in the cellblocks, Louisa also knew that the gallows were erected in this courtyard as needed. The dark, dingy buildings were pierced with narrow slits, shedding the only light that reached to the dank interior of the place. They would have to pass through the male prison to get to the second wing, where the women were housed. A slovenly guard slid the bolt to let Mrs. Gibbons enter and scrutinized Louisa from head to toe. Louisa's cheeks burned and she could not bring her eyes to meet his.

"I will have you reported to your superior, sir. This is an eminent person and she shall have your respect," Mrs. Gibbons barked over her shoulder as they hurried along the dim corridor. *Mrs Gibbons used the word 'eminent' to describe me.* Louisa looked at the angelic woman at her side. She was embarrassed about the glory that had been bestowed on her stories while this woman labored in the shadows.

Four tiers of cells with light iron galleries ran the length of the hall. Mrs. Gibbons explained that those imprisoned on the fourth floor, closest to the skylight—which was the only ventilation in the building—were accused of the lightest offenses, assault and battery; those on the third tier, petty larceny; and the second floor housed the most violent and depraved offenders. It was all very clean, very regimented and very dark. The windows in each cell were at ceiling height and nothing but a slant of afternoon sunlight entered the place. Louisa cringed at the sameness, the dark, the boredom, the hopelessness, the unchanging eternity of the place. She understood the symbolism of the architecture now, for as she descended further and further into the bowels of the prison, she felt as if she had truly

122

been bolted and locked into a tomb.

Some of the inmates seemed to welcome the weekly return of the silver-haired woman, as if her face brought a burst of sunshine to their world. Others turned to scrutinize Louisa's form more wantonly than the guard had. Still others turned their backs completely in disgust or perhaps dejection. They seemed not to care for their own redemption, nor for anyone else's belief that they were capable of penitence or improvement.

One man sat at the door of his cell, his blue soldier's cap shadowing his face. Louisa caught his eye and honored the veteran with a salute. He returned it mechanically, but then seemed to snap to attention at the surprise as his eyes followed the two hurrying forms down the dark, tapering hallway.

The doors clanged open to the women's section and the lock and chain clinked once more as the two women stepped over the threshold and back into captivity. Once in the women's prison, Mrs. Gibbons asked the matron to show them to the cell of an unfortunate young girl, Molly Murphy. She wanted to interview the girl and see how she could best be helped. Most women were detained for charges related to domestic situations, public drunkenness, petty theft or prostitution. Molly, Mrs. Gibbons explained, had been arrested for theft, but the circumstances were particularly delicate.

In the dim cell, there was but one chair and a rough cot. Louisa stood in the faltering light, her eyes beginning to adjust to the darkness in this nearly subterranean tomb. Even the very sun was denied these inmates. In the filtered gloom Louisa could just see the form of a plump girl with fair skin and light, listless eyes.

The owner of the sad eyes could barely raise them to tell her story. "I'll start at the beginning, so you know the whole bit," Molly said.

"Go on," Louisa said gently.

"I came to New York from Ireland to be placed with a family as their upstairs maid. It was a good position. My sister had started in the same way, and she got on and married the coachman and moved to Baltimore to a better family. My missus was soft enough but oh, I was so lonely! Missus was always distracted by the children, the worries of managing the servants and with all the calls she made and balls she went to. She never seemed to see me as a real person—not a word of kindness, only something small, like 'Good day,' or 'You can go now, Molly,' or 'Today be sure to change the linen.' The master of the house, he was kinder. He noticed me more and gave compliments, which lifted me a bit."

Louisa could almost tell this story herself without hearing it. She knew from her own sad experience how a young maid could be manipulated by an employer. Her heart burned already at the fate of this naïve and isolated girl, encouraged by these rare expressions of human warmth from the man of the house.

"Sometimes, he might lend me a book from his library or leave a small nosegay, just when I was more down and careworn than usual. I did my job well. I worked there for half the year already," she said proudly. "I always collected my pay on the last Friday of every month. That was the only bright spot, besides the bit of notice I got from the master."

"So they paid you on Friday last, instead of the last day of the month," Mrs. Gibbons clarified.

"Yes, ma'am, that was always the way." Molly seemed unable to continue. "It's so hard to tell on," she whispered. She shifted her gaze to the floor and went on softly. "Soon I noticed that the master was present when missus was not. He might follow me about my work and make a comment about my looks." She blushed. "I went to the cook to ask if I was wrong to feel uncertain and ashamed of the attention from the master, or if it was to be expected. Cook shook her head, all kind of sad."

"Do you remember her words?" Mrs. Gibbons was almost as good as a lawyer.

"She said, 'It's a mighty perilous place in this house for a young girl. Master has tormented more than one and chased and coveted one or two in a way most wicked. I will keep my eyes and ears open for you. And you must do all you can to be away from that ogre.' I grew more careful. I changed my cleaning routine, spent more time in the kitchen and took the littlest child with me—she liked to tumble in the linens while I folded laundry." After a long pause, she continued quietly. "But the cook had one Friday off, the children went with their mother to the park and ...." She sat silent, trembling with humiliation and rage.

Mrs. Gibbons said the words for her. "The brute fulfilled his lust with you forcibly, Molly?"

The quivering girl nodded and continued. "I was wrecked. I raced from the house before the missus returned. She had paid me that day. The money was earned. I spent one night in a cheap boarding house. I lay awake most of the night, there was such cussing and fighting and coarse drunken conversations from the rooms about me. In the middle of the night two women entered and flung themselves, all drunk and weary on the bunks opposite. I must have dozed off for a bit, because in the morning, my money and the others were gone."

Louisa turned to Mrs. Gibbons, shaken and indignant. "How in the world are there complaints against this poor girl who has been wronged twice over?"

Mrs Gibbons nodded at Louisa and then explained the charges to Molly. "The mistress of the house, being a thrifty manager, states that the Friday payment was four days before the end of the month, and so she charges you with stealing four days pay for which you did not work."

"It's three and a half days, miss, because Sunday afternoon is my free time. I'd gladly pay it back, but it's gone," sniffled Molly.

"The woman is blind." Mrs. Gibbons now addressed Louisa. "The money bothers her more than the sudden bolt of her steady employee. I imagine she attributes it to the shiftlessness of the class in general. Neither she nor her husband had a favorable thing to say

125

to the sergeant. Then, when the girl stammered and blushed when trying to concoct a story without naming her disgrace, everyone agreed on her guilt and she was kept in detention until now, when we have come to try to broker her release."

"I have a lawyer who works *pro bono* on my cases while he studies for the New York bar," Mrs. Gibbons explained to the girl and Louisa together. "He will be able to get you released with all the discretion necessary and we will protect you in every way we can from that fiend again. Someday, you may feel strong and willing enough to think of pressing charges against him, for what he did was not only a moral but a legal atrocity." Molly's apathetic eyes showed but scant relief and Louisa could see that the girl had nearly lost all hope and self-esteem. She would be a special case for Mrs. Gibbons's halfway house.

Later, as the two women descended the forbidding granite steps outside on Centre Street, a vigorous, solid figure wrestling with an umbrella hurried up the steps toward them. Mrs. Gibbons's look of concentration faded to relief as she saw the sturdy apparition approach. "Ah, here is the lawyer I was telling Molly about. Josef! Tending to the sorriest cases, I see," she greeted him.

"As you are, Mrs. Gibbons, and ever a sight for das eyes that are hurting and hearts to be warmed. But I did not expect to see meine friend here." The man lowered his umbrella and removed his hat in deference, revealing the smiling eyes of Herr Hahn.

"Ah, so thou hast met Louisa?"

Herr Hahn looked at her quizzically. "Perhaps I was using the wrong name, Miss Lottie."

"Oh, introductions are not necessary," Louisa stammered.

Unaware, Mrs. Gibbons continued. "If thou knowest Louisa and her good family, then thou must know that the Alcotts were championing the downtrodden long before most."

"Ah, yes, the *Alcotts*." Herr Hahn made an exaggerated bow.

Louisa reddened and sputtered, "Excuse my small ruse, Herr

Hahn. It was not to deceive, but only to hope for some privacy. I really can explain the whole mistake." But as Josef straightened she saw in his eyes only kind appreciation.

"Not so very small an act, for it shows true humility."

"And the lively joker of the Miller Hotel drawing room is studying for the bar, I presume?" she countered. His eyes showed assent and acquiescence and he turned to Mrs. Gibbons to get the information about how he would proceed with Molly's case.

As Louisa listened to the discussion she was able to get a picture of Herr Hahn away from the dinner table at the hotel, where he always assumed the role of the liveliest and least encumbered at the meal. Louisa found again that she liked his energy, his natural integrity and his inattention to fashion. She listened to the staccato of his German accent and watched his nervous habit of placing his hand in and out of his coat front. She liked that though the greatcoat was slightly shabby, the wearer was not at all abashed nor concerned by the signs of his meager wealth. She liked especially that he could discuss with two women, freely and completely, legal and societal issues, never abbreviating his comments nor expecting anything but their complete comprehension and interest. He pled the girl's case to his small audience and used them as a soundboard. He looked intently from Mrs. Gibbons's face to hers, peering directly into her eyes.

Louisa had a moment of panic. She pulled out her handkerchief to cover her eyes, which were welling up uncontrollably. She turned her head and wiped the teardrops while pretending a sneeze. Herr Hahn was not the caricature of Friederich Bhaer she had been enjoying at the hotel. He was the real thing. She did not know how she had failed to see this sooner, nor how she had ever conceived of a character so perfect. *Thank goodness I am not Jo March, or I might be putting my hands into his this minute.*

"Ach, I am such a fool!" Herr Hahn struck his forehead with his palm. "I keep you fine ladies in the rain and talk of the law." He

127

sheltered them under his umbrella at the expense of his timeworn greatcoat. "Ah, we haf done the best we can and will haf the young lady to the country by tomorrow. But it pains me that the man will not be brought to justice." He concluded his comments with a sigh.

"That is a battle for another day, Josef. The girl will be safe, grow in health and have her honor maintained. That is all we can do for her now. Louisa, come along with me and I will show thee the laundry where my young ladies work and the schoolroom for their lessons and the nursery where the children are kept while their mothers labor." With that, Mrs. Gibbons was down the steps and striding resolutely to her next mission.

As Louisa turned to follow, she lingered a moment. "I am sorry. I regret that we started out in a false way."

Herr Hahn's playful grin returned. "Good day, *Mees Alcott*. Your secret remains safe with me. I think you vill find that there are many leetle secrets at the Miller Hotel." And he scurried up the steps and into the dull, gray tomb.

Chapter 13

The Abolitionist

Herr Hahn kept his promise not to divulge Louisa's secret. Since she had made it clear to Mrs. Miller that she preferred not to be identified to the other guests, things had gone as she had hoped. There were no "Jo chasers" thrusting their autograph books under her nose while she sweated and wheezed in the Tepidarium. But now both Marienne and Josef knew her real identity and she was beginning to weary of the feint. She had been able to explain to Josef how the whole episode on the train had escalated into a full fledged identity change.

He looked at her calmly, almost sadly. "It is goot for you to have some peace, maybe. You need to be away from the public." She was still unnerved by his resemblance to Professor Bhaer. She dared not mention it to him, even lightly. What would he think of her, after perpetrating a hoax, if she started calling him by a fictional name?

One afternoon, Casey stood in the hallway, turning his hat in his hands and looking down at his shoes. Louisa steered him outside to speak to him privately.

"'Fess up, boy. You look like you're ready to spill a secret."

"Miss May, there was a man outside here just a moment ago staring up at the door and he asked if I knew the tall lady with the thick hair who is stayin' here!"

Louisa scanned up and down the block to see if someone was observing them, feeling vulnerable. *Here it starts, the hunt.*

"He didn't ask for me by name?"

Casey shook his head. "I had a hard time makin' out his words. He had such funny speech."

"A foreigner? Did you tell him anything?"

"Not a word, miss. He struck me as not on the up and up," her little protector said.

Louisa was relieved that she needn't worry about Casey revealing her story, but she could not make any sense of this unsettling information. Frank Leslie's reporters would not be foreign. Being observed was unnerving. Maybe it wasn't time to remove her mask.

Several days later, a mature woman with the countenance of a cherub and a voice that pealed clear and pure as a bell joined the guests in the hotel. As the ladies adjourned to the parlor for tea, Mrs. Miller introduced the ebullient woman to Louisa.

"Miss May, this is Sallie Holley. She comes here every year for a sojourn from coastal Virginia," Mrs. Miller said. "You may be interested in her work in education in the South." The hostess left them, moving on to less radical guests.

"Miss May! Could you be any relation to dear, righteous Samuel May, the abolitionist?" asked Miss Holley, grasping Louisa's hand enthusiastically.

Louisa's face burst into a smile. She pressed the offered hand sincerely. "It pleases me when my dear Uncle Sam is remembered. Samuel May is my mother's brother. And of course I know of you, Miss Holley." The effervescent woman looked at Louisa, searching for recognition, but still seemed muddled in pinpointing their relationship. "My mother has us 'deep in the barrels' every year, sending clothing, books, gloves and linens, our scraps and what-nots to try to benefit your work," Louisa chatted as she drew the sweet-faced woman to a corner, where she waved to Marienne to join them.

As the women settled about the table, Miss Holley tried to place the connection. "Samuel's sister is Abba, now Abigail Alcott, yet Mrs. Miller introduced you as Miss May."

"It's a tiresome idea I had to keep my identity under wraps," Louisa admitted.

"I am not surprised that you fit so well into that skin. Samuel May was one of the first and most eloquent voices in the slavery debate. I keep him in my heart right next to William Lloyd Garrison, Frederick Douglass and John Brown," said Miss Holley. "So you are Louisa, the most vocal of Abigail's daughters!"

"Yes, I've always felt that it is 'the blood of the fighting Mays' that courses through my veins." Louisa beamed. "This is my friend, Marienne Ayers," she said, motioning for her to sit. The young woman nodded to the elder as she sat down at the table. "Marienne, Miss Holley was one of the first women on the abolitionist lecture circuit. She spoke passionately and at risk, for at the time it was considered scandalous for women to address men and women in one audience."

"I had the good fortune to be sponsored for education at Oberlin College," said Miss Holley, "and after graduation was chosen as a voice for the cause. It really was your uncle who was adamant about sending me, a woman, to do the good work."

Louisa and Marienne looked at the woman with some awe and respect. A college education was something that had always eluded Louisa, whose family circumstances demanded that she go out to work at age sixteen. "I have heard what a radical school Oberlin was a generation ago—women and Negroes were accepted into the student body," Marienne said.

Miss Holley nodded. "Perhaps even a progressive college could not prepare me for my strange existence, though. Always crisscrossing the north, owning nothing, boarding with sympathizers and staying ahead of secessionist advocates." She looked almost fatigued with the memory. "It was ten long years that I raised my voice, lecturing, raising funds and trying to encourage those who were not in motion yet."

"My mother often said that you spoke most fervently regarding the plight of the slave-woman," Louisa said.

"The thought that they would never be able to protect their children motivated me and all the women to action most of all," said the abolitionist. "Louisa, your mother was one of the brightest and most devoted to our cause and would have made as fine a spokesperson as anyone."

But she was burdened by a philosophical husband who had no presence in reality and had to attend to keeping her children alive rather than focus on greater aspirations, Louisa thought.

"Miss Louisa, I feel as if I have lived life in a bubble compared to you, who have known and worked with such luminaries," Marienne marveled, stirring her sugar cube into the tea cup. Louisa chafed again at the extent of her own fame, so much fame that she feared for her privacy, and yet the total anonymity of this worthy woman. *Would that I could shine some of my light on her work!*

"Miss Holley, are you still laboring for the cause?" Marienne asked.

"Yes, once slavery was struck down," Sallie explained, "I just went on doing all I could to raise up the freed blacks. The slaves had been freed but had no employment, no housing and no education. With my dear college friend, Caroline Putnam, I went to the northeastern shore of Virginia and started our institution for the education of emancipated slaves."

"So far from any city center and so remote from your Northern supporters?" asked Marienne. "Have you enough assistance?"

"We work as stoically as we can, assisted by the freedmen. Of course, Caroline and I are ostracized by the landed Southern community. We grow our own crops for food and barter for all we cannot produce."

"Marmee always says that the Holley School is open 364 days a year, with only Christmas as a holiday," Louisa said. "Is that what brings you here to take the bath cure? Surely, your stamina is strained

132

by the work."

"Oh, it's a grueling life for the two of us, with no assistants and really no socialization besides the former slave families, but we have one powerful solace. Every year for a month or six weeks, I come for a respite in New York. I approach my sabbatical like a schoolgirl on her first holiday. I see every show, attend every lecture, eat ice cream to my heart's content and shop and ride and visit and dine with all the freedom I deserve." Miss Holley glowed.

"It sounds like you relax at a faster pace than you labor," Louisa joked.

"Not very different from yourself, Miss Louisa," Marienne said.

"You ladies can help me with the second objective of my trip north. I need to drum up reserves and donations from friends, family and supporters. With your connections at the papers, with publishers and society folk I think you could be useful." Sallie had a list of retailers who offered unsold wares, pots and socks and extra lengths of muslin. She relied, she told them, on one retailer who offered her a dozen outrageously plumed and fringed fashion hats.

"Sallie, what on earth will you do with such finery at the school?" Louisa laughed.

"These hats are some of my best bartering agents," Sallie explained. "Every year when I return, the local landowner's wives know that I have only a dozen hats from New York to sell. They all want one and so the value of each goes up and up. I've traded firewood for the whole winter for one hat, and another time, had the entire retaining wall and fence repaired."

Rebecca entered the lounge to clear the tea service. With a cry of delight, a rush of skirts and a huge embrace, Miss Holley had her in her arms. "How does my little scholar get on here? Will I be able to send you to the university soon?" Sallie beamed at Louisa over the girl's curly head. "I've known Rebecca and her family almost since she was born. She's a genius, you know. We had to send her north because she outstripped all my teachers' capabilities."

133

"I'm studying math and science and philosophy, Miss Holley," Rebecca gushed. "Helene says I am ever so much better at public speaking. I want to make you proud about that, knowing that it's your special gift. I'm going to work my hardest to get to college, or even study medicine, if I can do it."

"Rebecca is one of your students, Miss Holley? Now I am the one who feels in a bubble," Louisa said. "All my hope in the strength of women's capabilities is right here in your simple example. The attention of two devoted school teachers has opened possibilities to this girl. It's a women's manifesto in action."

"Sounds like you will be writing it into one of your stories soon," whispered Marienne to Louisa, smiling as she shook hands good night.

When the parlor was empty, Sallie nestled in the settee to tell Rebecca and Louisa all about how the girl's brothers got on at school, what was happening in the town, and how the strawberry and melon patches had yielded the largest crop ever that year. She heard in turn about Rebecca's lessons, her simple chores and the growing friendship with Helene. When the two were quite satisfied that they had remembered to relate everything, Sallie turned to Louisa with plans for her itinerary. "I always promise myself to get to Central Park on the first sunny day of my visit, and the night is so clear that I believe tomorrow will be such a day. Every time I come it is grander than before and I believe it has almost reached completion now," she said. "Come with me to the park, Rebecca, as it is Sunday and Mrs. Miller allows you the afternoon off." Turning to Louisa, she said, "Will you join us?"

"Absolutely, and I have a protégé of my own who I am sure would ache to come as well."

Chapter 14

What Happened in Central Park

The following day was sunny and brisk and the four set off by barouche to Central Park. Casey wore a new plaid scarf and Rebecca a red woolen beret. Louisa approved of their new finery, gifts from Miss Holley. "Sallie, you are an incurable philanthropist in both big and small ways, I see!"

The coach travelled north on Fifth Avenue, joining a cavalcade of Sunday drivers who flocked to the light, open air and vistas of the park. At Twenty-Ninth Street Casey began to crow. He pointed to a large gilt cock on the spire of the Dutch Reformed Church. "We call it the Church of the Holy Rooster," he quipped. The ladies tried to look displeased at his blasphemy, but struggled to thwart a laugh. They ascended the elevation at Murray Hill and could see down the full length of Fifth Avenue to the green expanse of the park. The avenue was lined with palatial hotels, sumptuous club-houses and the magnificent Cathedral of St. Patrick, its two towers still incomplete.

As they reached the higher realms of Fifth Avenue, the city mansions gave way to less enticing suburbs. Louisa noted that the city grid of streets and avenues was being extended relentlessly up the entire expanse of the island. Here on upper Fifth Avenue, New York looked like a small village exploding. If a property owner had built a home on a slope or hillock, the level of the street could be cut below it, leaving the home dangling on a precipice above the new grid.

Central Park covered an area northward for two and a half miles and stretched across the island from Fifth to Eighth Avenues. The design was such that the crosstown traffic was carried on sunken roadways, unseen by anyone strolling the bridle paths and walkways above. The gentle curves and archways gave way to lawns and gardens—the Mall, the Terrace, the Ramble and the Lake would all present a different view.

"I have been to this park every year for the last ten years. I have seen it grow piecemeal from rock and sodden soil, really from some of the least appealing and commercially useless land in New York, to this idyllic place," said Sallie. "Everything you are looking at was put here by man, save those massive boulders that run down the center of the park like a spine."

"I read that they were left here by a glacier that moved across the island in some long ago ice age," said Rebecca.

More than the elegant landscaping, Louisa reveled in the throngs who took their relaxation there. Fine women in furs strolled with their little dogs along the pathways. Boys shouted and tore about the bases playing New York-style baseball. Couples rowed on the pond and shop girls read or napped on blankets in the late autumn sunshine.

The carriage continued down the long, straight Mall, overspread by russet and golden elm trees. There was a cool, metallic glint in the air, the autumn breeze of the island, a combination of saline breezes from the harbor and the fresh crystalline feel of slate and schist. Pigeons cooed, as they did everywhere in the city. A hawk skimmed overhead. On the edge of the pond a white egret stretched its neck. Nature in the midst of the city: it was a marvelous, almost jarring interlude from the urban life.

Louisa was forever going over different outcomes for her novel *Rose in Bloom*. This park reminded her that one of the messages must be about health and exercise. Looking at the two youths in her charge, she didn't need to deliberate much more. Living in the city had invigorated her, but she saw the constraints it placed on the children who often lacked a space to exercise and enough fresh air to avoid winter ague.

Along the broad byway of the Mall, Louisa noted the statues of famous poets and writers. She was happy to see her favorites, Shakespeare, Schiller and Walter Scott, but grumbled, "There's not one woman honored along the entire Mall."

Casey looked surprised and curious. "I'm wonderin' when a lady writer will be as famous as these chaps." He said it with an almost wistful sincerity that touched Louisa.

At the Bethesda Terrace, elegant sloping stairways led to a grand plaza at the edge of the lake. A fountain with a delightful angel marked the center of the plaza. "Now *that* gorgeous statue was done by a woman artist!" Louisa exalted. This time Casey looked satisfied, but forgot the lessons of art and genius when he spied the toy sailing boats bobbing in the waters around the fountain. The children descended from the carriage to join the other children at the granite edge of the pool.

Sallie remained seated with Louisa and admired the angel. "She's refreshing and powerful and soothing all at once, just like the water flowing through the fountain."

This was the first work of public art in New York commissioned from a woman. Louisa's thoughts wandered to her sister May. She had told Louisa that the artist Emma Stebbins could find no sculptor in America who would allow her in his studio or a place to cast the bronze, requiring her to complete the work in Rome. "May, our youngest sister, longs to go back to Europe and study sculpting and painting, Sallie. In the right atmosphere I am sure her talent would flourish."

Louisa began to feel guilty, as she always did when she was enjoying herself. May was on duty at home attending to feeble Marmee, and by now Father would have returned from his travels. Not that he was a bother, but there was something maddening about his serenity. He always drifted through the house like a spirit. But his tranquility depended on the particular meals he requested and the long evenings with friends who needed cider and cakes to be replenished. Did any one of them ever think how those cakes appeared? From the marketing to the baking to the serving, so many moments extorted from his daughters' true work. The chores must suffocate a girl as spirited as May. She would sketch hurriedly between Marmee's naps, or perhaps paint a scene on a flat rock she had retrieved from the river. *No one's talent should smolder on the hearth*, Louisa thought. *If it takes an Italian studio to make the fire flare, then May will have her lessons and her European life.*

The edge of the lake bustled with activity. An artist had his easel set toward the west. Something about his painting stirred the crowd.

"There's Mr. Hahn!" Casey cried. On the border of the lake, Augustine leaned forward in his wheelchair, working with such single-minded concentration that he did not see them pass. The women asked the driver to stop a moment and clustered around the artist, joining his small crowd of admirers and critics. He worked laboriously, his brow furrowed. On his right hand he wore leather bands around his wrist and palm which attached his paintbrush. He dabbed paint in short strokes, using the motion of his elbow and wrist instead of the unreliable grasp of his damaged fingers. With these fervent dabs he captured the sun on the water, the sheen of the vibrant foliage, and its reflection in the pool. At the foot of his easel sat a duplicate painting: the same vista, with a bold, glaring morning light, making the water shine, the reflection barely visible in the golden gleam of the sun. Robert was nearby, preparing a third canvas.

The crowd murmured at the rapidity of the unfolding painting. "It's not art," one man grumbled. "He didn't even sketch or plan his scene."

138

"It's almost an illusion," another said. "The paint only suggests the shapes, but the color and light complete the picture."

"It's more real than any painting I have ever seen," said a young woman.

Louisa stood behind Augustine's right shoulder. "My sister described this kind of painting to me. She saw it in Paris last year, but I could not understand her explanations. She called it indefinite—raw, mere shapes and dabs of color. I see now that words fail. Your mist makes me shiver and your sun glints so that it makes me squint. It's extraordinary. It's as if I see an infinity of colors."

Augustine gave her a grateful nod and tilted his head to consider the change of light. He mixed more black into the blue on his palate. "It's called Impressionism. No one in New York has tried to create this French style of painting. I am out to prove that the south of France does not have an exclusive right to spectacular light."

Louisa had not seen Augustine so invigorated since he extolled the beauty of Grand Central Terminal on their first day in the city. His fevered pace worried her. His face was wet with sweat from exertion. "We are continuing up to the reservoir and can collect you on our way back," she suggested.

"Thank you, but I would like to do one more painting in the late afternoon light."

She adjusted his muffler more snuggly to shield his throat and pulled his lambswool blanket down to cover his legs. He twitched with pain as he raised his wrist. He asked Robert to reposition his chair to adjust for the declining sun.

"The man intends three paintings in one day. He paints as fast as the light can change!" an observer in the crowd noted. Augustine accelerated his strokes, adding wet paint on wet paint, two colors side by side, creating a glow both familiar and singular. Whether it was urgency or serenity that propelled him, Louisa could not decide.

All four returned to the carriage to circle the autumn meadow. The field was not yet ready to surrender to winter, sending up shoots of reddish grass and dry, brown reeds. Deep in the center of the park, they circled the great receiving reservoir.

"I grew up near the Frog Pond in Boston," Louisa said to Sallie. "I could run my hoop around the whole pond without stopping. It was made for human scale. The aspirations of the city that built Central Park are huge and expansive and confident. Boston is like its park, more reserved and modest. I am sometimes not sure where I belong. I want to remain a practical New Englander but seem thrust upon a stage that I need to—want to—accept."

"Oh, Boston is not that modest. That educated set there! I went to one of your father's conversations once and I never *could* talk with Boston people. My mental faculties seem completely paralyzed when I am in their company." She quieted and looked searchingly at Louisa. She lowered her voice. "Many would be puzzled to know that the mother of the most heartwarming home in the country seems so unanchored, so undomiciled, almost."

"Home always stretches out its arms and pulls me back in, Sallie. Even if I kick and balk," Louisa added. "I never lose sight of home, no matter where I am, or who I think I am."

Rebecca and Casey hopped down from the coach and ran alongside, playing a game of tag, darting quickly from side to side. Louisa knew how magnificent it could feel to gallop until one's mind was clear. She never felt so free as she did when she ran through the woods behind Orchard House. When she ran, she let all the negative thoughts go—all the anxiety about money, all her family's expectations and all her own disappointments would drain from her tense muscles.

But things were different now. Writing and charity work consumed her. "I fit in so many places that I seem to settle in none of them. I am all over the place, physically and mentally. My energy jumps from one thing to another, from one place to another. I write essays and letters and short stories and poems and novels. I work for the women's vote, for the pensioners' benefits, for children's aid and hospitals for the blind and the crippled. I envy your single vision, Sallie, to choose a cause and to do it wholeheartedly instead of piecemeal as I have. Scatterbrained—that's what I am."

"No, you are working your head off," Sallie said. "You came to New York for a respite, and you throw yourself into new causes and new projects. You above all shouldn't forget that you are mortal and run the risk of being made immortal with your frenzied pace."

Rebecca and Casey continued their game. Passing parents held the hands of their children, watching the fun. Nannies interrupted the steady route of their perambulators, pausing to smile at the two friends romping in their carefree and innocent game. The lighthearted youths played with freedom and grace. They seemed unburdened by labels or expectations or restraints.

But Casey was stopped by a saucy tart, suddenly turning to her escort, remarking, "Golly, what's that hooligan carrying on about with that little darkie?"

A startled Negro nanny frowned at Rebecca as she came up short in front of her. "Lord, chil'! What you doin' with that Paddy?" she demanded.

Louisa jumped to her feet in the carriage. "Our children are being abused," she cried.

Sallie stretched out her hand to detain Louisa from descending. "No more abused than they have already been before, nor less than others in their situation. Underneath, New York is not so very different from eastern Virginia. We find the same intolerance and ignorance."

The two children remained still. Casey's fists curled and Rebecca threw a protecting arm over his shoulders, drawing him gently back toward the carriage. With a motherly tone, she said, "My grandmother used to tell me, 'It's not what you are called, but what you answer to that matters.' Don't listen to them, Casey."

Louisa, hovered defiantly in the carriage, keeping her eyes on the children as they slunk back arm in arm. She clenched her lips, for her natural bent was to speak without censure, to use words to dispel injustice, and always challenge wrong. She closed her eyes and counted silently to herself, recognizing her great flaw and the ways her mother had helped her with her anger.

"They will face this again and need the strength to do it with dignity and purpose," Sallie said. "You will speak, Louisa, but not now. Do it with your writing. It will reach the whole nation that way." Coming from the little woman known for her great voice of change, Louisa looked at her, uncertain. Sallie spoke again. "Believe me, dear, even in rural Virginia both landowners and freedmen read your books."

Louisa stretched her arms down to hoist the children into the carriage. They tumbled in, Casey scowling and Rebecca near tears. Louisa could not stifle a glare at both of the women. "If they weren't both ladies, I would have knocked their blocks off," Casey spouted.

"That would solve nothing, son, except to make everyone feel their poor opinion was justified," said Miss Holley.

"Well, I'm not going to accept things that aren't right, I can tell you that!" he sputtered.

On the quiet ride home, each seemed wrapped in thought. Louisa noticed the Irish policemen who walked their beat proudly. They passed stores with Negro proprietors. The crowds seemed genial, inclusive. None of this had saved the children from scathing prejudice. Casey, who had been sitting with his head bowed, looked at Rebecca covertly as she stared almost rebelliously ahead. At fourteen, the girl was small for her age. She caught his furtive glance. Her hard exterior crumpled, her lip trembled and a tear dripped down her cheek and off the center of her chin, which quivered softly. "My grandma says I was born a slave." She turned to Casey. "I don't remember any of that."

"Your folks, your grandma, they remember, though," Casey said. A few moments later he blurted ardently, "Rebecca, I vow to always work to change things for the better."

Louisa drew both children to her protectively. It seemed that this willowy girl had the strength of steel and this crusty boy was as soft as nougat inside. "Let me tell you a story," she offered, and soon had them rapt. Of course, her story had a pair of mismatched friends, a hilarious misunderstanding and a good reward for doing right in the end. Miss Holley smiled at her. Sometimes, a story was just what was needed most.

Returning down Broadway at dusk, New York vacillated between shadows and magic. Lights sparkled in the shop windows. Smokey bursts of kerosene lamps blazed over the sidewalk vendors. Theaters with giant reflectors over the entrances sent radiant light streaming across the avenue and up and down the block. The huge hotels flooded the street with brilliance from the hundreds of lamps in the lobbies, yet there were long swathes of darkness between.

As the carriage turned into Twenty-Sixth Street at dusk, the shadows cast by the flickering lamps only dampened their spirits more. In a few orbs of gaslight, people hurried home: two blonde girls, a swarthy Italian family, and an Eastern priest with flowing beard, black robes and a kalimavkion atop his high forehead. Louisa scanned the dark spaces, too. There, a tall, lean man with a pale face and a thin moustache turned swiftly away. Louisa saw only his dark back receding from her, casting a series of shadows that grew and merged as he plunged into the darkness.

Figure 7. **Supper at the Newsboys' Lodging**

Chapter 15

The Newsboys' Lodging

Despite the events of the day before, the quartet of lively young people who circled about the Miller Hotel seemed to Louisa a microcosm of New York's eclectic population. Casey, the Irish orphan, was the constant companion to Marienne, the grandniece of an Italian marchesa. Marienne, realizing that it helped her to hear her poems and essays read aloud, only shared them with Helene, the daughter of an American actress and a German composer. Helene continued to help Rebecca, the daughter of slaves, with her lessons, and Rebecca always saved some hot buns and a cup of coffee with frothy milk for Casey when he came in after breakfast to collect Louisa.

All the children had a spirit of generous camaraderie that came from youth, tolerance and optimism. Everywhere around them, they saw opportunity for hard work, positions opening to women and the possibility of education for all. Louisa was certain that these plucky youths, like the ones she was crafting in her new novel, seemed determined to claim their rights to any branch of study or labor for which they would prove their fitness.

Her mind worked constantly on the thread of her next novel. She paced the front parlor, deep in thought. In *Rose in Bloom*, she continued Rose's story as her heroine faced impending womanhood and the attractive boy cousins who would enrich and complicate her life. Louisa did not want her Rose to settle. She would travel the Continent as Louisa had, be an energetic philanthropist like Mrs. Gibbons and a capable guardian like the marchesa, all before she would contemplate being a wife.

She went upstairs to visit Marchesa Contini. The door to her chambers was open and Louisa paused to look at the slumbering old woman and her industrious niece. Marienne sat at the desk near the window, reviewing some papers. When she shuffled the yellowed papers back and forth they crackled with age. She reviewed one carefully then began to compare it with some words she had written in her ledger, scanning back and forth between the two sheets.

Louisa knocked on the open door and stepped into the room.

Marienne jumped up. "How long have you been there spying on us?" she challenged, snapping the desk closed.

"Not spying, dear, admiring the tableau of the diligent ward and her content guardian," Louisa said, surprised at Marienne's assertion. "It's time for me to relieve you for your walk."

"Fine." Marienne locked the desk, grabbed her shawl and stomped out of the room.

Louisa stared after her, exasperated. She was used to little tempests between herself and her sisters, but Marienne's disagreeable streak went beyond friendly quibbling. She had lashed out at her more than once with a meanness and disrespect that was startling. Sometimes Marienne seemed awed by Louisa's presence, her prominent acquaintances, her fame. Other times she treated Louisa like a prying fusspot. So far, Marienne had been discreet at the hotel about Louisa's identity. But this mercurial girl did not seem the safest guardian of Louisa's secret. Louisa looked at the marchesa, softly sleeping. The woman was unable to remember anything but her own early life with her sisters. Louisa sat down beside the snoring woman and pulled out her pad to write to Anna and May. Immediately, she felt grounded. Home was the safest place of all.

146

Louisa had promised to visit Casey in his own improbable home. The newsboy was quite dear to her and she was ready to do anything to help him. Perhaps May's flippant comment about the street orphan was correct.

The next morning, Louisa sent Casey off to his paper route with the intention to meet him later in the day. "It's time I made good on my promise. I understand your pride in your work and accomplishments, and I am eager to visit your lodging, too. I will meet you down on Duane Street this evening to see this paradigm of young men's industry." Casey jumped the stoop with an extra leap and disappeared around the corner.

Louisa arrived downtown late in the day. Casey's abode was a modern red brick one standing five stories high. Under the eaves of a gently sloping roof a sign declared "Home for Newsboys." She had contacted the superintendent and matron of the Newsboys' Lodging, Mr. and Mrs. Charles O'Connor, earlier in the day in her guise as Lottie May. They were used to society people coming to the home to make a donation, to hire a lad or even to select a sturdy boy to adopt.

They showed Louisa the facilities on the first floor: a kitchen, laundry, reading room and a massive dining room with long tables and benches, spare and clean.

"It's the warmth and food, a wash and a good night's sleep that attract the boys," said Mr. O'Connor. "Then we go to work on their education and training for work."

Dusk was falling when Casey returned to the Newsboys' Lodging, gathering with the other newsboys after their day of work. The boys, all brash and slangy, joking and bursting with energy, began to file in and, with great pride and flourishes of theatricality, locked their meager possessions—a cap, a kit, a bag or tattered coat—into lockers. Next, they slid any pennies they could spare from their earnings into their savings banks, a favorite ritual.

"Look, Miss May." Casey showed her the special walnut table for their savings. "There's a big drawer inside with little compartments. Each boy has his own box with a slot on top for us to slip in our coins. The boy who saves the most every month gets a three dollar bonus to sweeten his profits."

The boys trooped off to the washroom and presented, one by one, faces cleaned and hair combed for supper. They jostled in the hallway outside the dining hall until Mrs. O'Connor could inspect and admit them. She explained, "Lodging and food cost six cents a day, unless a boy tries to creep in late. There is an extra five cent fee if a boy arrives after nine o'clock, ten cents if he arrives past ten, and a bed will be denied if anyone tries to get in after eleven. This keeps the boys out of trouble at night and encourages them to come in rather than spend their money on the theater and in pool halls."

The boys spoke in an easy slang of their own. Louisa saw them communicating in special signs and secret nods as they tore about the lodging. Casey explained some of their antics. "We've got our own professional way, you know, of calling out the news. We teach the younger boys how to place their hands on their cheeks and throw their voices above the wind."

"I've heard that call," Louisa acknowledged. "Even above the perpetual ruckus in the city streets, that searing call travels. It whistles so high and piercing that it can be heard above the din."

Casey nodded at his brethren. "These fellers are a regular group of bricks. There ain't one who wouldn't share the last penny he's got. We look out fer each other and always repay our debts. It's the newsboys' honor," he said solemnly.

"I've heard the newsboys are also known to be heedless and raucous," said Louisa, smiling at the rough but sharp-eyed ragamuffins about her. "Someone even told me that you are known to drink coffee, lager and pop all in one day." The boys hooted.

"Maybe when we are at the theater," one chimed in. "The Old

148

Bowery Theater—we've renamed it 'The Newsboys' Elysium.'"

"I love the theater, too," Louisa said. "I'll bet you boys sit rapturous before tales of daring and exploits, all cheers for scenes with catastrophes and duels. But should the scene turn romantic, it's thumbs down, I imagine."

"The best was *The Red Robber of the Blue Hills*," said a portly fellow who had gravitated to her side.

"I guess you never saw *The Pirate's Daughter*," cried an older boy from the stair landing.

"I've heard you are paradigms of virtue compared to the bootblacks," Louisa said.

"We newsboys know how to stay out of trouble. We never lie, steal or break the law. But we don't blab neither. Our motto is 'Mum's the word,'" said Casey. "It ain't right to gossip or meddle in others' affairs, unless they ask fer help." Despite his affable way, there was very little that she knew about Casey aside from his unmitigated optimism and gentle heart. He guarded his past stoically. Still, Louisa was comforted again by his declaration to avoid gossip and tell the truth.

We never lie. The declaration seemed to challenge her. She was still Miss May to him, and she felt an imposter in this place, for it was just the sort of thing Louisa May Alcott would write about. She was uncomfortable with Casey's earnest words and cast about for a different topic.

"Tell me what plans you have for your hard-earned savings," Louisa said, turning to the two lads on either side of her.

"Well, miss," said a serious looking chap with a cowlick, "though I'm an orphan, I have a grandmother who is ill and I work to keep her looked after."

The second boy, a tall, sturdy fellow with a confident air, explained, "I'm saving for a trip West to make my fortune. They've got more land than people in Kansas."

"I suppose that 'Going West' is another step up the ladder for an industrious and adventurous newsboy," said Louisa to her hosts. Louisa had sent Tom, the troubled son in her book *An Old-Fashioned Girl*, out West, and had him return improved and successful.

"Yes, families in the West often need extra hands on the farm or to manage the household chores," said Mr. O'Connor.

"A little detachment of homeless children will be sent off together on an Orphan Train to a village in need of child labor," explained Mrs. O'Connor, as they walked together toward the dining hall. Casey skipped just ahead of them, his light step and joyfulness propelling him even late in the day.

She turned to Mr. O'Connor. "In Massachusetts, there are laws protecting children from manufacturing jobs."

The kind superintendent's shoulders sagged as he said gravely, "Our poor children can work in factories making envelopes and gold leaf, tobacco and twine. They are exposed to dangerous machines and impure air. Even five-year-old children are employed to make artificial flowers."

In comparison to those conditions, Louisa knew that the Newsboys' Lodging was as benign and healthful as a Bronson Alcott school—of course, with the exception that this school was thriving. *A man before his time.* Louisa sighed to herself, for her father's failed schools had meant more work for her and her weary mother.

On the way to their supper, the boys jostled each other and called out so that Louisa could hear that they had nicknames for each fellow. Fat Jake, Carrot Nose and Lightfoot were all accounted for.

"You never told me your nickname, Casey," Louisa said. Casey blushed as red as his pate.

"It's Buttonholes," he admitted, "because I am one of the only boys who can make a proper buttonhole here. I guess I've become the unofficial tailor to the fellers."

"He's awful good at letting out seams," said Alfred, the portly boy.

"And patching elbows and mending tears, I see," added Louisa, looking about at the well-mended jackets and cardigans. Alfred showed Louisa the buttonholes Casey had repaired on his jacket. "This is tricky work, Casey, with the lining and the interfacing. How did you learn to sew so deftly?"

"I used to help my mother and she taught me all I know. I couldn't bear to see her sitting up nights to get the work done so I tried to help in my little way." Louisa could not remember another boy who had taken note of his mother's sewing basket and tried to alleviate her chore.

Casey's skill was appreciated by the boys, who needed to have their tattered clothing repaired over and over again. They paid him a penny for each buttonhole he fixed and soon Casey had a small pocket of savings. Alfred jingled a pocketful of coins. "I'm on my way to owning a sweet potato cart," he said. "But for now, I sell to my buddies. If I buy baked sweet potatoes from the vendor in a three dozen lot, I can sell them to the boys fer a penny less than they're charged from the carts."

"We always know where to find him at noon," said Casey.

"So, by the end of the week, I've done the lads a favor and pocketed a profit for myself," Alfred concluded.

The boys approached their supper of bread and cheese with the same energy and spirit they had at the theater and on their paper routes. Huge tankards of milk were passed around and no one was denied seconds.

Louisa was touched to see that Casey had a special way with the youngest boys as they settled about the table. He gave each a personal word or two and a pat on the back, leaving each little fellow following his movements with a look of gratitude as they watched the older boy greet his friends. "I know how hard it was for me to start out, with no one to look out for me," he explained with the confidence of a year of street life under his belt. "I don't want the little chaps to feel alone. A word at the right time can pick up a bloke's spirits." He was part counselor, part protector and part mother hen to the younger ones.

After supper, Casey showed Louisa the schoolroom and sat down at a desk along with the other boys, who pitched into their lessons. 'Speak the Truth,' proclaimed a sign at the front of the room, and at the back, 'Boys who swear or chew tobacco cannot sleep here.' Louisa roamed the edge of the book-lined room, which doubled as their library. There were the boys' beloved Horatio Alger tomes, and, she noted, her own *Little Men* and her collection of stories called *Aunt Jo's Scrap Bag*, both dog-eared and worn. Her books seemed to be as popular here as Cooper and Stowe, even Dickens, if their threadbare covers were any indication. She suddenly felt duplicitous in her relations with Casey. *Speak the Truth.* The sign seared her honest soul.

Casey joined her after handing in his essay well before the other lads. He was a fluent writer already. "After lessons, there's a lecture of some kind, most nights," Casey explained. "Tonight there is an art lesson, and music and sermons are on tap for the rest of the week." The sensitive boy looked into Louisa's troubled eyes. "You seem a bit peaked, Miss May. Are you okay?" She really wasn't the actress she thought herself to be. She tousled the boy's hair with a thin smile.

It was close to nine o'clock and tired lads began to climb the stairs to tumble into their bunk beds, snuggling under blue blankets. "My lads are so fatigued that rows hardly ever break out," Mrs. O'Connor whispered to Louisa. "When they arrive here, many boys can barely recall the time when they slumbered soundly in a real bed. Not one of them will forget the nights they spent shivering in a box under an overpass, or in the crawl space of an abandoned cellar, nor do they ever want to return to that life again."

As the boys were saying their good nights, one approached Louisa with a snigger. "Are you the lady who lets Casey get a shampoo and bath every week so he comes in smellin' sweeter 'an a sugar plum?" The sassy vagabond looked older than the others. "He never needs to shower with *us*, because of his special friend."

"I am Casey's employer and hope that he considers me a friend as well, but I cannot be congratulated for his hygienic arrangements," Louisa answered, but had a hunch about where the bathing could occur.

Louisa closed her eyes and settled herself. She owed this to Casey, who was as transparent as glass and as honest as Abe Lincoln. She plunged on. "Boys, it's time I told you that I am Miss Louisa May Alcott, who wrote that book you all enjoy, *Little Men*," she announced suddenly. Mrs. O'Connor gave a little whoop and her face flushed with excitement. As the boys gathered around, she searched for Casey's face in the crowd, finding it and reading his incredulous look, full of confusion, embarrassment and recrimination. She reached for him but he sidled away to the back of the crowd.

"I must've been as hard as Dan when I first got here," one appreciative reader spoke up. "We have music lessons once a week, too, you know and Charlie Toonz here plays the fiddle good as yer feller in the book!"

"Gosh, miss, we've got a school most as good as yer Plumfield fer sure, right fellers?" One boy summed up their feelings. In the bustle and roar surrounding the announcement, Louisa promised the boys that she would come back and read some of her stories aloud to them.

A general huzzah went up from the boys.

Casey stood, stunned and silent.

NEW YORK PIER OF THE BROOKLYN BRIDGE, 1876

Figure 8. **New York Pier of the Brooklyn Bridge, 1876**

Chapter 16

Casey's Tale

As the newsboys teemed about her, hustling off to bed, Louisa drew Casey aside. He raised his downcast eyes to hers, his eyes welling with tears.

"I'm sorry it came as a shock to you, Casey." His eyes shifted right, then left and his cheeks flushed bright red. "It's still the same between you and me. We're pals," she added. Still, the boy resisted her. "I thought you would be a bit more excited than this."

He straightened his shoulders, stepped back away from her and cried out, "You never told me that. You weren't honest."

"You are right, Casey. It *was* a lie to make up a false name. And because of my lie, I suppose I have only blundered and offended people along the way," Louisa said. "I did not want to disturb the quiet of the hotel."

"What's that got to do with me? All this time I thought we were friends and you never told me."

"I wanted to leave who I was behind. I didn't want people to see my name and not see me. You may have felt the same sometime in your life." Casey stiffened even more and wiped his glistening eyes with the inside of his elbow. "Now you know the truth and Herr Hahn … and Miss Ayers and Miss Holley … so I imagine my game is up." Louisa smiled wanly.

"Herr Hahn? Herr Hahn and Marienne know? I have been the only fool, then," he sniffled.

"I'm sorry, Casey," she said. "You see how the boys charged about me. It might be like that when we roam the streets if people were to know where I was staying."

Casey jammed his hands in his pockets, his face downcast, then began to look thoughtful. His eyes widened. "Maybe that queer man who lingers about the hotel knows, too," Casey said. "I'll be mum as a doornail, miss. Your secret is safe with me," he said, recovering his energetic demeanor.

"Thank you for your protection. But I suppose I am ready to be Louisa May Alcott to you and all the others," Louisa said resignedly. "I am not good at keeping secrets. Besides, this whole charade is tiresome to me now. I won't hide behind a mask anymore. We shouldn't have secrets between friends."

At this announcement Casey became inconsolable again. He sniffled and let loose a torrent of hot tears. What had she said now to hurt him?

Drawing him into Mrs. O'Connor's office, Louisa sat Casey down on the horsehair settee. Casey wiped his tears with the back of his hand. "I'm sorry, miss ... miss ...." He looked at her in confusion.

"This is not just about my secret, is it, Casey?" Her mild, deep eyes looked down at the shaken boy, tender and true. "Come now. What's troubling you? You can tell 'Aunt Jo,'" she said with an encouraging smile.

Casey sobbed twice and cleared his throat. "I guess I have a story, too," he said softly. "You want to hear it?"

Louisa nodded and sat back to hear the tale.

"My folks were from Ireland—you know that already."

"Tell me their names," Louisa prodded.

"Timothy and Bridget," Casey sniffled. "In Ireland, everything was bad off, they tell me—no food, no work. Once my pa found work on the docks, the only thing they wanted was to get their folks here, too," Casey began. "The old wooden piers of New York where Pa worked were rotten."

Louisa frowned. "Every week, I read a notice in the paper about how the city's Common Council makes a payment to an owner for reimbursement of a lost horse. They fall right through the crumbling boards of the city docks," Louisa said. "It is treacherous there."

"Not only that," Casey added, "Ma was always worried that he would get bludgeoned or thrown over by the 'river thieves.' They might do anything to get at expensive cargo—sometimes even clean out a whole ship."

Casey sat silent a moment and then smiled a bit. Louisa leaned forward to encourage him. "We lived in a small house and our rooms let out to the yard. My mother was happy that we could plant our own potatoes and cabbage. From the windows, we could hear our neighbors and the sound of the brogue. On Saturday evening there were dances with fiddles and jigging and whiskey for the men. But I liked being in our warm kitchen most of all, the smell of the soda bread baking ...."

"I know that scent too, Casey. It's the aroma of a mother's love and care, of feeling safe and secure."

Casey's lip quivered. "I was always happy on my way to school. I enjoyed reading and music the best. They wanted me in the church choir. They said my voice sounded like an angel's and that it would rise up to the seraphim." His ardent speech made Louisa suffer with him for those lost moments of pure serenity.

"I'll bet it did," said Louisa.

"Ma sent the steamer tickets to her folks." His face darkened. "I think they packed some of their best things, their linens and good wool. We waited and waited for their ship. Then we heard some bad stories, some talk among the other families who had heard of a storm and a sinkin' ship." Casey trembled and leaned up against Louisa's side. She put both arms around him. "Finally, we got a telegram. They were both drowned, but the chest with the linens was beached along the shore." He paused, for it seemed the rest of the story was even harder to tell.

"Poor child!" Louisa exclaimed.

"I never remember my mother crying, but I never did see her smile again. She began to sit long hours at the window, swaddled in all the woolens and linens from that trunk," Casey stared at the floorboards and gasped out the words more than he spoke them. "She would rouse a bit when Pa came home, and drink the broth and potions he brought to coax her to eat.

"It went like this for months, no muffins, no garden, no singing. One day, she dragged herself from the chair and began to sew. She sewed little garments, little blankets, and knit some tiny booties. I sewed and sewed with her to be near her, to help lift her sadness."

"With each basted seam and hemmed corner, you hoped that you were stitching together everything that had been ripped apart in your family." Louisa sighed.

"One night, my ma's old fears came true," Casey said softly. "She was sewing by candlelight when the messenger came to the door, turning his cap in his hand and shifting side to side, like he had somethin' real bad to say, but couldn't do it. He didn't have to anyway, fer Ma was wailin' and screamin' already."

It didn't take a writer's imagination to fill in the scene. *The wail that Bridget let out was a deep and plaintive cry from the depths of a grief that was already pulling her, dragging her into an abyss.*

*"*The men were huffing with the weight … the weight of Pa's body. *"*

A huddle of men, grunting with the effort of lugging a pallet, crossed the threshold. The lower body was crushed and oozing, the eyes glazed, the chest still rattling. Timothy was not dead, but there was no hope for him.

"Pa could only groan and sweat and toss," Casey bawled. When his crying slowed, he continued the story. "I ran to hide behind the bed. I couldn't look at Pa's face. He stared and stared into Ma's eyes. Every time he groaned, she screamed. Every time he gasped, she panted. They had the same sweat on their faces. They musta been in the same kind of pain. They both looked like they were dyin'." Casey was spent with emotion and had no more tears.

"All that screamin' brought the neighbors to the door. 'Why the poor thing's gone into labor from the shock of it,' one said. But it was too early for the baby to live and so …. On the same night that my father died, my little sister took her first breath and then her last. Mother just turned her head and screamed and screamed again, this time without any pain in her body. Oh!—it was the deepest, saddest sound I ever heard."

Louisa could only shake her head.

"'Tis a shame,' the old lady next door whispered," said Casey, dramatizing the scene. "'Her mind's gone with fear and misery and despair. She's wandered away from reality. She's got no one left but this little creature.' The ladies looked at me cowering behind the bed. 'There's nothing for it but to send them both to the asylum where they can get care,' someone whispered."

Casey sniffled and caught his breath. "I had lived my whole life in a warm home with sun and muffins and two parents. I had heard only the worst stories about the asylum. Children were separated from their mothers, even on … another island," he cried. "I knew I would not see my mother again in that dreary place.

"I looked at the whispering women and I panicked. I heard the screams of my mother, repeating and echoing, and ran. I ran and ran and ran. Away from the screams, the blood, the dead baby, the mashed body of my pa, and most of all from the sad faces of the women who looked at me with the kind of look that made me know I would be dragged away to the children's asylum."

The sounds of the lodging had diminished to silence. Mrs. O'Connor peeped into the office and nodded to Louisa over Casey's slumping head, then quietly closed the door. Louisa and Casey sat together, side by side. She had a protective arm over his shoulder and with her other hand offered him her handkerchief. She dabbed at her own eyes more often than she did the hiccuping lad's cheeks.

"That's when I started roving the town with the other fellers," Casey continued.

"You slept in burnt out buildings, boilers and old carriages with the other little vagabonds?" Louisa gasped.

"We banded together. My new friends were merry and sharp," Casey said, recovering some bravado even as he avoided her question. "And they were nice to anyone younger or poorer."

"Was there no one you could trust? No teacher, no priest? How did you survive? How did you not starve?" Louisa clutched him to her.

159

"Aw, you wouldn't believe how much good food the rich throw away." He shook off her embrace. "The alley behind the Astor House is the best place to get meat. They toss whole parts of roasts," he said, brightening. "Life wasn't half bad during the summertime. But when the winter weather came, misery gripped me. The others yapped when I decided to go to the Lodging, said I was givin' up my freedom. But I was too cold and hungry to think about larks and liberty then."

"And you never went back to see if your mother had returned?" Louisa asked.

Casey shook his head. "I've got boys who do that for me and no one has seen her since they took her. I asked at the asylum once and they wanted to know why I was interested and I got afraid they would take me and I never went back."

"You know I can make inquiries for you," Louisa offered.

"Thank you, Miss May—um, Miss Alcott." Casey sighed.

"Call me Miss Lou. I've always just wanted to be Lou."

"But it sounds like a rough little boy," Casey said, another sob catching in his throat.

"There was a time when I wished I was a boy." Louisa smiled sadly.

"Bah! You! Such an elegant and famous lady!"

"I suppose I will have to take that as a compliment, my dear boy. Would you like the elegant and famous lady to help you with your search for your mother? "

"Oh, thanks again, Miss Lou, but I have someone who is doing that very thing for me now."

Louisa raised her eyebrows. "Is it someone who will do the job for you? Do you think they will uncover the truth?"

The newsboy recovered a smile. "Oh, they'll figger it out," he said. "I know for certain that sometimes things right before our very own eyes are the last thing we see."

160

Chapter 17

Murray Hill

Louisa motioned for Marienne to follow her out of the breakfast room. The November sunrise was just whitening the fronts of the buildings across Twenty-Sixth Street. Louisa huddled behind a verdant fern and handed her young friend two journals, *The Youth's Companion* and *The Independent*. She drew her finger down a column of print and across the byline, *L. M. Alcott*, saying, "I promised Casey I would give up the charade, and these stories will be one more chink in my wall. And if Helene and Rebecca see these tales they will put two and two together and figure out that I am in New York. Besides, I intend to write about my day in the Tombs next, and then I will be completely exposed."

"You've been productive, Miss Alcott," Marienne said after she scanned the stories, "using your impressions of the schoolgirls who join us on the streetcars for 'My Little School Girl,' and designing a happy ending for the destitute vagabonds we observe everywhere in 'Letty's Tramp.'"

"Everything that rattles my brain can come out on the page. I just need to let the steam out before I boil over." Lizzie bustled by with a tray of silverware. "I could do a story about that!" Louisa motioned to the cutlery tray.

"About a hard-working servant girl? I can see you do that," said

Marienne.

"No, I would animate the spoons and forks and have them teach a lesson to an unruly boy," Louisa joked, but made a mental note to use tableware in a future short story.

That evening, Louisa invited the children and other guests into the parlor where she read aloud her story about the little schoolgirl on the streetcar. As the story ended tragically, there was a quiet pause at the end. "Such a perfect story," Helene noted. "Tell us, who is the author?"

"It's me, actually," Louisa admitted, spreading the paper wide for all to see her name.

Then there was a general hubbub and chatter and wondering that spread about the room. For a moment, Louisa felt as she had in the early years when she brought a story home to her family. She would read it to them breathlessly. At the conclusion, how they would applaud and comment and rejoice at her success. These kind people were just as congratulatory, every one smiling as they marveled at her in their midst. She felt relief immediately. She was surrounded by friends now, not intruders or busybodies. They had every right to the truth. They could not invade her privacy because she welcomed their intimacies.

Mrs. Miller looked smug. *Here come the broadsheets,* Louisa thought.

"Shhhh!" This startling warning came from the corner where the marchesa sat in the shadows. "Not in public, dear. Do not read in public."

Marienne went to her aunt's side, looking at Louisa with masked eyes.

"The truth vill come out," said Herr Hahn, puffing thoughtfully on his cigar as he sat musing before the fire. A smoldering log collapsed into ash, sending sparks flying up the chimney. He spoke to no one in particular as he breathed his thoughts into the air along with the cigar smoke, but he elicited a reaction nonetheless.

Casey shuffled and pulled his hat down over his eyes. Rebecca edged over to stand behind him, one hand on his slumping shoulders, looking defiant. Was she there to console the boy, incriminate him, or ask for his protection?

Mrs. Cutney coughed and pretended to be absorbed in the newspaper. Louisa felt the room was charged with unspoken insinuations. Herr Hahn had implied once before that the Miller Hotel housed some unknown secrets. Hers might be the least surprising of all.

Mrs. Miller broke the tension with a broad and mannered smile. "I recommend that each of you make use of our library. I believe that every one of Miss Alcott's books for young people is represented there," she said.

At the mention of the famous books, Mrs. Cutney recovered her usual languid demeanor and extended her hand to Louisa. "I always felt that your Beth and I would have made fast friends."

Louisa held her hand warmly. "Beth was my favorite, too. Thank you for loving her." Louisa had the hopeful thought that with her affinity for Beth, perhaps this mysterious woman's outings were humble visits to the needy.

"I shan't ever be able to show you one of my stories," Marienne asserted, playing up her innocence of the secret grandly. Helene ran to get the book she was reading, *Eight Cousins*, and asked for an autograph on the spot.

"My Miss May is the famed Miss Alcott!" Augustine declared, winking at his brother.

Louisa's revelation actually liberated her comings and goings and made it easier for her to sprinkle exciting talk that she had heard at the literary salons and on the lecture circuit into her conversations at the Miller Hotel dinner table. Mrs. Miller beamed at being able to tout her famous guest to the new diners. Marienne and Helene wanted to hear about the luminaries who might be encountered, especially at the salon of Mr. and Mrs. Botta, the family friends Marmee had recommended.

"So you spend your evenings with the publishers and thinkers of our city?" Herr Hahn seemed impressed with the remarkable connections that Louisa had made so quickly.

"I try to hold up my end of the conversation but generally feel overwhelmed with the lofty sentiments I hear," Louisa admitted.

"Oh, if Mr. Edwin Booth would appear one night, would you speak to him for me?" Helene asked.

"You say that Mrs. Dodge attends? How I should like to have her autograph," swooned Marienne.

To get to the Bottas' home, Louisa loved ambling uptown through Murray Hill, a neighborhood of townhomes and families where she felt more comfortable than on the grand and impersonal avenues. "If I ever lived in New York, this would be the place for me, Marienne," she said as they walked together one evening to the salon. "These noble brownstone townhomes remind me of Beacon Hill in Boston. I suppose Boston is a bit more restrained. These homes aren't large but have the look of Italianate palaces. Look at the wrought iron railings and high stoops." The little plots of land between the front gate and the lower entrance were landscaped in miniature with potted trees, asters in planters, small statuary and children's wagons. Wool merchants, bankers, oil dealers, importers—the men who made New York work lived here.

"Just imagine: this entire neighborhood was once a single estate," Louisa said and launched into an amusing tale of the origin of the locale's name, Murray Hill. "During colonial times, the Murrays owned a farm that covered all the land from Madison to Third Avenues and Thirty-Third to Thirty-Ninth Street. Their home stood on one of the highest hills on the island. When the lanterns blazed it was almost like a lighthouse, it was such a familiar guidepost."

"There is still a pleasing slope to the neighborhood, despite the grid cutting it down," Marienne noted as they ambled to the very spot where the old homestead had stood, now populated by a row of city domiciles.

"Mrs. Murray was an unsung hero of the American Revolution.

The British made a surprise attack on the colonial troops. Mrs. Murray and her daughters went into action, diverting the British by inviting General Howe to rest and take tea with them, entertaining the Brits sufficiently to allow the American troops to escape and regroup. The next day, the reassembled American army defeated the British in a battle at Harlem Heights. Will women always have to wield their influence though wiles and subterfuge?" Louisa asked. "When will we finally be allowed to participate fully in being citizens?"

Marienne's face brightened and she glanced about at the sloping crossroad as if looking for a memorial to the clever women.

Murray Hill was now becoming a center of the literary and artistic thought in New York. No one was more responsible for this than Mrs. Botta, whose Saturday evening salons brought together people from all nations, as long as they had emerging ideas and scholarly or artistic pursuits. She was another of the remarkable women of New York who seeming to come from nothing, and with only the power of her intellect and her determination had become a champion of the arts, as Mrs. Gibbons had become of the downtrodden and Miss Holley had become of the freed slaves.

"Despite her Italian name, Mrs. Botta was born in America. Her given name is Anne Lynch. She started out working as a governess," said Louisa.

"Don't all the intelligent women get plugged into that hole?" asked Marienne.

"I was saddled with that same job when I was much too young. I suppose it's not the worst way a young writer can support herself."

Before they arrived at Thirty-Seventh Street, Louisa explained more to Marienne, "Mrs. Botta started publishing poems and reviews in periodicals and just with that, began her weekly Saturday evening collations for young writers and thinkers. She had no social position and no fortune, yet she attracted the great intellectuals of the city, Herman Melville, William Cullen Bryant, Horace Greeley and Margaret Fuller."

"I wonder who will be there today," said Marienne.

Louisa had kept her best revelation for last. "Edgar Allan Poe was a frequent visitor and first read 'The Raven' when he was unknown at Mrs. Botta's salon! No one else was championing him then. He came and read it hesitantly."

"Hesitantly! I can't believe that! How do you come to know that he was not as fearless as he later was known to be?"

"Father attended the Bottas' salon when he visited New York twenty years ago, and the story about Poe and his readings was one of Mrs. Botta's favorites."

"I heard that she is also blessed with a true romance."

"You're just like my mother!" Louisa exclaimed. "Happy to hear about a woman's accomplishments and then asking about her love life." Louisa, so immured against the possibility of marriage, saw that her mother still harbored that wish for her daughters. The last scene in *Little Women* made it abundantly clear that Marmee was not comfortable with the thought of her daughters becoming *New Women*—self sufficient, professional and free of male connections. Mrs. Botta's match kept Marmee from despairing over Louisa and May's unmarried state.

"The Bottas met in Europe when she was nearly forty years old," Louisa continued.

"And so now their salon is filled with the educated, international set ... and so much accomplishment in one woman!"

"Not only intelligence but artistic genius! Augustine would be happy to know that she sculpts in her home. Some of the shields and busts you will see are her own work. When I compare my achievements to Mrs. Botta's, I always feel lacking," she admitted.

Marienne shook her head. "You will be the most famous person in the room and you still feel inconsequential."

Louisa and Marienne entered the wood paneled entrance hall at the front of the house. Their silk skirts rustled softly as they climbed the grand stairway piled with books, statues and flowers in alabaster urns. It led up to the twin public parlors, which they had glimpsed from outside though the full length windows. Chandeliers shimmered and fringed damask curtains framed the scene.

At the top of the stairway was Mrs. Botta. "Louisa! Let me embrace you like a daughter, for your dear parents' sakes," she said, clasping her in a motherly hug. She then turned to welcome Marienne. It was impossible not to fall under the charm of Mrs. Botta's hospitality.

In the parlor, flickering lights revealed cabinets with glass doors, ancient books, fragments of mosaic, pottery and bronzes, and piles of books in every corner. The hosts radiated peace and warmth, reflected in their kind attention to each other as well as to their guests. If Professor Botta began a sentence in Italian, his wife finished the thought in English. If a visitor struggled to keep up with the conversation, they found another who spoke the same language and made things comfortable for both.

"He is so absorbed with her," Marienne whispered to Louisa, as she watched the Bottas glide about the room arm in arm. "Is that what you mean about European men? With his long hair and chiseled face, he is quite handsome. I can see that Mrs. Botta has made a lovely match."

Louisa often entered salons with a momentary feeling that she was out of her depth. She felt less cosmopolitan, less educated and less facile at foreign languages than the other guests, though she could hack her way ruggedly through a word or two in French and German. But here she could maneuver between conversations, even those in a foreign tongue, for there were enough travelled people about to warrant interpreters and the eager discussions never flagged. Marienne pressed near her side. She seemed ready to reflect the glory of her mentor. Louisa saw that the girl yearned to be accepted in this sphere. Marienne gaped at the magazine editors, writers and literary critics about her.

Dr. Stoddard, the editor of *The Atlantic*, hailed Louisa. "Have you thought over my offer to print your next serial?" he asked.

She smiled at the editor and shook her head. "I am promised to Mrs. Dodge, and overwhelmed at that," she said.

"Ah, attending to the tender readers again," Dr. Stoddard said. He had cut to the root of her own discomfort. He was offering her a stage for adult readers and she was equivocating. *Little Women* appealed to all readers, but perhaps she had never recaptured the immediacy and candor of her *Hospital Sketches*, nor the ebullience of her shocking adventure tales. She stood, concentrating and considering her own successes and secrets.

Mrs. Botta grabbed her arm. "No brooding here. Come and share your blunt and humorous observations. Here is our most celebrated author," she announced to the crowd. Louisa's gray eyes twinkled as she launched into a story explaining her fear of exercise machines.

As Mrs Botta bundled them off later on, she gave Marienne an enthusiastic hug and chided Louisa, "You have kept us in the dark about this charming woman. Bring her again, and any more spectacular protégées you may be hiding." Marienne lowered her head in humility but could not hide her grateful and eager smile.

One Saturday, Louisa decided to bring the Marchesa Contini to the Italian household, hoping that the sound of her native tongue might spark recognition and memory in the frail woman's mind. The marchesa was generally calm and smiling now. Agitation had left her during her weeks at the Miller Bath Hotel.

Mrs. Botta immediately took charge of the marchesa, speaking softly to her in Italian and settling her in a comfortable chair. Marienne looked lovely in a dress of purple silk with a black sash and ruffles and trimmed all over with black passementerie and lace.

"Come, Marienne," said Mrs. Botta. "I want you to meet some young women poets."

Marienne looked longingly in the direction of the women talking in the corner, but shook her head. "No, I must stay with my aunt, as she might get confused," she said.

"I am in charge of your aunt tonight," said Mrs. Botta. "Here, I

168

will introduce her to a little band of Italian musicians who will delight her. She will be amused and content." She offered Marienne an ice and lemonade and drew her off to be introduced to some women writers. The girl appeared remarkably self-possessed as she joined their conversation about the finer points of a new poem.

Louisa lingered near the marchesa, who seemed alive with memories as her countrymen peppered her with questions about life in Genoa of sixty years hence. She became Carlotta, the school girl again, and then Carlotta the poetess and young wife. She spoke in Italian and the circle around her remained attentive with respect for a long life of hardship. No one pressed her for facts she could not recall, for her stories were picturesque and quaint. Someone called for her to recite a poem. With Mrs. Botta by her side, she began to recite in a lyrical voice. Louisa had just picked up the phrase that the two liked to repeat together, "Con sospiri, incanti e dolci sussurri," when Marienne rushed in agitation to her aunt's side, her face full of unrest.

"That's enough, Aunt. Please stop—you know you should not be repeating this in public. Please stop," she pleaded.

The old woman's eyes turned to the girl's and then turned inward. There was a battle for a thought, casting about for some awareness, and finally, failing that, a blank look and a shrug. After that, the marchesa could not be induced to regale them with any more memories or any more stories. Louisa's soft entreaties, which usually placated the distraught woman, could not draw her out. Louisa was frustrated that the promise of an evening which had started as gentle therapy had ended with the same scared and vacant patient.

Marienne refused to be cowed by Louisa's look of disapproval. "You are forgetting, Miss Alcott, that my aunt has committed never to repeat those poems in public."

When did this girl become not only a ward but a warden? Louisa thought. "She is among friends here, Marienne. Let her sing," she suggested gently. But the girl sat by her aunt's side for the rest of the evening, answering all the questions directed her way and diverting the conversation from her aunt's past.

Even Mrs. Botta's simple embrace could not coax another smile from the marchesa that evening. As she helped to wrap them in their cloaks in the hallway later that night, she nodded to Louisa and said, "Bring these ladies again, for I think the conversation did some good for poor Carlotta and the girl shows promise. You might do well by bringing them separately," she suggested, "though I doubt the younger will let the elder out of her sight."

As she settled Carlotta's scarf and gave her one last hug, the elderly woman whimpered and whispered, "Mama."

Louisa could not hide her irritation at the girl's behavior. On the carriage ride home, she pressed her to explain. "Your aunt was opening up so beautifully to her past, smiling and remembering. You cut her off from those memories."

"You know she vowed to her husband never to recite her poetry in public," Marienne said firmly. "If she were in her right mind she would not have broken that promise. I have to protect her and have her do as she would want to do if she had the capacity. It is not right to coax words from the mouth of a doddering woman."

"These words are part of her identity, her soul," Louisa said. Still, she felt in no position to press the point, burdened as she was with her own deception about her early stories. The marchesa had spent her whole life protecting her promise. Louisa was just as bent on protecting her own legacy. *Perhaps I need as fierce a custodian as this girl.*

The marchesa, meanwhile, was staring at the carriage floor.

"I'm sorry, Marienne. I see how much you care for your aunt. But how good it was to see her alive with her memories!" Then, turning to the elderly woman, Louisa asked tenderly, "Can we get you anything?"

"Federico," was the answer. "I want Federico." Her eyes swung past Louisa's, searching the black clouds outside. She seemed to disappear into a profound darkness of doubt, duty and dreams.

Chapter 18

Bijou's Wish

Louisa's routine continued, though at a fevered pace that suited her spirit. That she could keep it up surprised her. Perhaps the treatments were improving her health. She had less joint pain and had gained weight, and the constant neuralgias she experienced at home were gone.

Louisa saw a bit of all her own struggles in the challenges faced by her friends at the hygienic hotel. The infirm and afflicted clients, Mrs. Cutney, Augustine and the marchesa, the artistic young girls, Helene and Marienne, the energetic Sallie Holley, stolid Josef Hahn and invincible Rebecca—all illustrated many angles of her own makeup. She looked at the talents and challenges of the good people around her, and as always, hoped to honor them in a character or a plot twist in one of her tales.

Herr Hahn was in the final days of preparing for his New York bar exam. He was being mentored by a respected public advocate firm located near the hotel. The firm agreed to do the court filings of the cases he was uncovering at the Tombs, along with other litigation pertaining to exploited women which Mrs. Gibbons unearthed.

"How did your German legal work prepare you for these sad cases you are seeing in New York?" Louisa asked one night at the dinner table.

"Those with no voice are everywhere the same," Herr Hahn began. "Have you heard of the Kulturkampf in mein country? Eet is Mr. Bismarck and the politicians trying to shut the Catholic Church from power."

"I have often been conflicted on that institution myself," said Louisa. "The Church itself has such influence and wealth, but the poor and humble who worship there seem to be some of the most downtrodden in society."

Herr Hahn nodded to her. "That eez it. It was the people who vorshipped who needed legal protection … not the beeg power. Ve set up civic groups and did legal defense for churches and local clergy."

"I expect that you will be sought as a community organizer and expert in government and church litigation here. Once you complete your bar studies, you will be an asset at the New York firm in their work in advocacy of all kinds," said Augustine.

An embarrassed flush colored Herr Hahn's kindly face. He waved the compliment away and turned to help the marchesa into her chair. "Miss Louisa, I have a new client. I cannot divulge any information, but I thank you for the referral." He nodded and winked her way.

She looked around the table but no one smiled back. None of her society friends would seek a lawyer, either. *Casey!* Her heart was hopeful and grateful, for she knew that Josef would search diligently for the child's missing mother.

Louisa's effort at mentoring Marienne was bearing fruit, too. The girl's writing was becoming more confident as she exchanged ideas at Mrs. Botta's salon with other young writers. Louisa had many good talks with her about methods and voice, so it was gratifying when the girl finally came to her one evening in the library with a revised manuscript and laid it before Louisa cautiously.

"I must get your opinion before I dare to send my little story out into the world," she said.

The engaging story about a pair of sisters who planned a Christmas surprise for their elderly landlady made Louisa smile. Marienne emulated her style and did it well. "This will be welcomed by an editor for their holiday edition," Louisa said and then set about suggesting a few improvements. "Make sure you use good, strong words," Louisa said. "Say things in the simplest way possible and your meaning will be understood."

Helene needed to practice her lines for an upcoming performance. She cajoled Casey and Louisa to rehearse with her one afternoon in the parlor. Casey again refused to play the feminine roles, so it fell to Louisa to be both the foolish mother and the addle-brained daughter.

Louisa scanned the script. "This play is about a family not unlike the Shaws in my *Old-Fashioned Girl*," she said. "Who have they got to show them the way out of their constant scrabbling to be at the top of the social ladder?"

"It's my character, Fan-Fan," said Helene. "The youngest son."

"You're playing a *boy*?" Casey said, his voice ending in an exaggerated inflection, which caused him to redden.

"I am glad your character has some sense. I suppose that will be easier for you to be a boy than for me to play these poor specimens of femininity," said Louisa, though she threw herself wholeheartedly into the roles, sporting a fur boa about her neck and walking with the exaggerated Grecian curve of the "elegant."

Herr Hahn peeked in to see what the clamour was all about, just as Helene was saving Louisa's character from absconding with a ne'er-do-well played unconvincingly by Casey. Louisa twirled her boa in an exaggerated circle, waving at Casey as she exited the scene. Herr Hahn smiled broadly. Louisa straightened and blushed.

"Charming, charming," the lawyer said, but then he looked directly at Louisa. "Continue, mein Schatz, you are most intriguing this way."

Mein Schatz. My treasure! He wasn't smiling anymore, but looked at her almost plaintively and closed the door. Louisa paused in mid-

173

stride, staring at the portal. Had he really spoken so tenderly? To her, or to the silly character she played? *This accursed boa!*

Soon after, Louisa and Marienne went to the theater to see the play. Casey came to meet the ladies afterward to escort them home. Backstage, Helene greeted her friends in full costume. As Fan-Fan, she was garbed in a dark gray knickerbocker suit, brown oxfords and a flat, plaid cap which hid her curls. The transformation from Helene to the young son garnered Casey's endorsement.

"I'd never know you were a girl, really," he said approvingly.

"You seem so proud that I was a boy for even just a few hours. What's wrong with being a girl? I am more gratified than anything to be a young lady who can make money and help my mama, too."

Casey fell silent. He worked so hard to support himself and Louisa knew that the disappearance of his mother was a weight that hung about his heart and tightened with every memory. She knew, too, that the story of Helene and her famous mother, Matilda, was not nearly as sad as Casey's poignant one but it had enough love and sorrow in it—and scandal—to fill the newspapers for some time.

As they all walked home, Louisa began the tale, hoping that the friends would come closer in their shared loss. "Your mother is one of the most famous actresses in the country, certainly the most renowned Camille." She coaxed Helene to tell her story.

"Oh, yes, she played Camille in France and brought the role to the American stage. She owned the boards because no one had ever seen such style as Mama's."

"I remember the critics used words such as 'electrifying' and 'explosive' to describe her acting," Louisa enthused. "My father took me to see her perform in Boston years ago. I was completely startled by Matilda's first stage entrance. The audience could not decide if she sucked a lozenge to quench a cough or to show her character's illness. It seemed all too natural to be acting!"

"Mama was the leading lady of the New York theater and my papa is a famed conductor and musician. He lives in Europe now," the girl added. Louisa and Marienne glanced at each other. They knew from the gossip of the time that several years after the birth of their daughter, Matilda's husband left the family, returning to Europe with his wife's wealth. "But she's sick now, and has no strength for the stage. She gives acting lessons, when she can. She lives in a single room. We were very poor before I got this contract at the theater."

"Golly, Helene, you always act like such a princess that I thought you *were* one," said Casey uncomfortably.

"Acting—that's the thing!" she admitted. The two walked on, their heads inclined toward each other. Casey's hands were jammed in his pockets and Helene's expostulated dramatically. "One year, the actors and producers offered a benefit in Mama's honor. Edwin Booth, my idol, gave a performance. I was so glad to be able to see my mother worshipped by the whole community of actors. They raised enough money to keep our small room, pay for her medications and doctor fees, and keep me in school."

Now, two years later, the little girl was helping to support the invalid mother, as she became in turn the darling of the New York theater scene. Louisa had read a review that called Bijou Heron's performance "the greatest theatrical production in America today."

Helene was signed to work with the great theater impresario Augustine Daly. This year, Mr. Daly was holding a benefit performance and he had a special role for Bijou to play. The clients of Dr. Miller's Hygienic Hotel were invited to the theater to see the spectacle. The happy group trooped together to the theater, just two blocks away on Twenty-Eighth Street and Broadway, to see their little star on the great stage. The theater was renowned for its rich terracotta carvings and individual seats, instead of the benches used in older theaters.

"Can we come back in the summer?" Casey turned to Louisa, ruffling through the pages of his program. "In the summer, Mr. Daly's theater even has fans blowing over great chunks of ice to cool it down!"

It was Rebecca and Casey's first time at the theater. This huge auditorium held over fifteen hundred spectators and the children seemed to gaze around at each and every one of them. They delighted in the posh surroundings, gaped at the ladies in satin and lace, and eyed the popcorn and candy in the lobby cases. As the lights were extinguished and the wave of silence passed over the crowd, Casey leaned over to Louisa and whispered, "Someone is staring at you through some funny little telescopes!"

"Never mind, dear, I've gotten used to people staring at me."

"But this isn't one of your cracked girls or their mothers … it's a *man!*"

"And thank you for reminding me what a singular instance that would be, my chaperone!" laughed Louisa. Louisa's answer appeased neither the boy nor herself. She had an ominous feeling but she hushed Casey as the lights lowered and the curtain opened on a charming scene.

The stage set was all in miniature with a lush garden, a Venetian lagoon and a minuscule balcony, onto which Helene appeared as Juliet about to call to her lover. Romeo was played by another child actress attired in an elaborate costume of velvet and furs, while Helene wore a simple white dress, making her irresistible to the crowd.

Casey leaned over and whispered, "Helene's mama made her that dress herself." Louisa squeezed his hand, knowing that he remembered his own mama whose sewing had ended in a sadder fate. The two tiny lovers recited the famous poetry as the audience suspended disbelief and surrendered their enchantment to the charming performance.

Casey leaned forward. He seemed to be absorbed with both the words and the conceit. When Juliet spoke the lines, "What's Montague? It is nor hand, nor foot, nor arm, nor face, nor any other part belonging to a man. O, be some other name!" he slumped back in his soft chair with a smile and a chuckle. Rebecca thundered her applause for her nightly reading coach as the two little thespians completed their curtain call.

Louisa was pleased that the magic of the stage had enthralled both of her guests. Shepherding them out of the theater, Casey suddenly grasped her hand. "Miss Louisa, I'm not sure—he turned away so fast—but the man who asked about you outside the hotel, he just left ahead of us." Louisa craned toward the door, but didn't even know who she expected to see. Was one of Frank Leslie's hacks stalking her?

After the performance, Louisa invited all her hotel friends to a supper to celebrate Helene's success. The venue of the party was to be part of the surprise. The three youngsters locked arms, their heads nodding and bobbing as they bubbled over with excitement of the evening. Margaret shepherded them along the crowded street.

"How ever do you have the courage to speak in front of so many people?" gushed Rebecca.

"I'd say that Romeo chap, that's another part that some able young feller got gypped out of," said Casey. "Do all the girls get to play boys parts?"

"It's curious," answered Helene. "In the old times, when women could not perform on a stage, the women were played by young boys. Now the girls play the boys. I suppose it's confusing!"

"You have no idea!" said Casey under his breath.

Helene was concentrating on the route, following the procession of friends down Broadway. "Why, Miss Lou, we are getting so close to Mama's home. I even think the men with the basket of fruits have stopped at her door," she added in confusion.

"Where else should we celebrate tonight, dear, but with the one who has given you all your talent, all your direction, and all your honest emotion?" asked Louisa.

Green boughs with ribbons and sprays of white camellias hung around the humble room, brightened with candles, as an honor to the great actress's greatest part. A long table had been set down the length of the single room, and a bouquet of alyssum, asters and carnations in pink and yellow hues waited for Helene as a centerpiece.

The table was piled high with bowls of pears, grapes and apples, towers of nougats and caramels, and buckets of ice cream in white coffee, burnt almond and maraschino flavors. There were cakes with powdered sugar on top and buns with currants and cinnamon, still warm from some decadent late night bakery. A cheery servant girl in a white apron passed around hot coffee and cider. The guests were boisterous, all discussing the surprise with glee and appreciation. Helene acted as hostess, introducing her frail and tragic mother to all her friends.

"Just see, Mama, here is Rebecca and Herr Hahn and Miss Marienne." She clapped her hands and presented each one. Matilda played her part formidably, using all her powers of deception to conceal her fatigue and indisposition, and with real joy and delight welcomed all her daughter's friends to her simple home.

Louisa took Matilda's hand and said kindly, "I am like a schoolgirl fanatic in front of you, madam. It is a lifelong dream of mine to meet you."

"Thank you for the interest you have taken in my daughter. It's an honor that we both cherish. I think we've read every one of your books," replied Matilda with a voice still resounding with exquisite diction. "Yes, even *Work*, where the little actress has her life imperiled by some kind of mishap on the stage. You certainly shouldn't make our profession out to be so treacherous."

If Louisa had been Casey, she would have let out her own low whistle and a quiet "You have no idea!" but instead she smiled at Matilda and promised to write a tale about a little performer with a happier outcome.

I've written worse than that about the theater, Louisa thought, remembering her hidden stories which abounded with fallen and challenged actresses. One of her earliest stories had a jealous actress perpetrate the murder of her rival on stage. Another had sent her husband falling to his death when she cut the cable to an aerial stage platform. But Louisa's personal favorite was her chameleon-like character, Jean

178

Muir, who as an actress masquerading as a governess enters an affluent home and beguiles every man in the household into relinquishing their fortunes.

Louisa and Herr Hahn surveyed the bright faces of the mother and faithful daughter. "I don't suppose nuptial finances are in your line, Josef?" Louisa prodded.

"No, I have studied that this case has too sadly been settled in the courts." The lawyer frowned.

"How could the man leave with the woman's honestly earned fortune?" Louisa asked.

"There was a question of a prior husband who was intent on coming to claim Matilda's plenty, and the courts ruled that all would go to Maestro Stoepel," Josef said. Louisa smiled at this delivery, for Josef's labored accent was nowhere to be found in his reply, as if he had memorized the very line from court briefs he had studied.

"I can only imagine that knowing the inevitable abandonment by her husband, the mother felt this would be the only way to protect her assets for her daughter. Perhaps she had a premonition about her health," Louisa deliberated. "It's a painful thing to see. This unremitting illness has brought down her appeal so much and drained her stamina for the stage. Still, there is a simple way for mother and child to be together for now, and I have arranged it all with Mrs. Miller today," Louisa confided to the lawyer. "Matilda agrees and Dr. Miller has already consulted on her case. She is coming with us … back to the Miller Hotel!"

When the party broke up later that night there were no adieus until the morrow, for Herr Hahn bundled Matilda's emancipated frame into his arms and carried her downstairs to the waiting carriage. Then all the others whooped and ran and marched back uptown, clamoring up the cobblestone street, singing silly songs and making noise as if it were the New Year.

Later, as they parted on the landing for bed, Josef gave a tilt of his head in salute to Louisa. "It is a very goot thing that you do for our leetle Bijou."

"My mother always told us that if we cast our bread upon the waters, it will come back buttered," Louisa said, deflecting his appreciation.

"Ah, yes, *thee* Alcotts, as Mrs. Gibbons says," he chuckled.

"Josef, you are of the same mold, only your 'do-gooding' happens every day, a bit at a time, while I swoop in on occasion and make a grand flourish."

"I like the svooping," said Josef with an approving look.

"Well, all my 'svooping' can't make things better for poor Matilda. Imagine having all her fortune stolen by her own husband!"

"Ees it the fortune or the husband which is the vorst loss?" Josef asked.

"How can a court, a law, protect such an abomination? What kind of a law only shields half of the population?" Louisa was in one of her "fighting May" moods. She stewed about the destiny of women in general, completely disregarding her own tender fate.

"Eet seems that such a bad law might need to be broken," said Josef, almost as passionately.

Louisa stopped her one sided rant and looked at him more closely. "Really, Josef, have you been studying law or reading Thoreau?"

"I vould read your Mr. Thoreau if eet vould make you happy." As he bent and took her hand to say goodnight, his burly head obscured the light from the sconces on the wall. Louisa saw only shards of light emanating around his head like a halo. They paused together, holding hands in the shadows of the gaslight, and Louisa, thinking of the doomed Matilda, whispered, "But … Matilda … I fear that Dr. Miller will find a very big challenge on his hands."

"Vell, such is true for many of us, you know." Josef pressed her hands firmly, then dropped them. He shook his head and turned his sturdy frame to lumber down the hall.

Chapter 19

The Mentalist

The arrival of Matilda Heron at the Eli Miller Hygienic Hotel was the beginning of a sparkling change to the dinner table. Matilda knew an eclectic array of writers, producers, actors and artists who descended on the hotel once it was reported in the papers that "Mrs. Heron is now reconstructing at Miller's Turkish Bath Hotel." Louisa sensed that Mrs. Miller regarded her as the agent of a not-so-subtle change to the clientele of the hotel. When Louisa had arrived, the table was heavily populated by asthmatics and nervous people with tics, but now it thundered with loud theatrical voices and racy jokes. Louisa suspected that Mrs. Miller was cowering over her reputation as the matron of a "first class health institution with quiet rest times." *Serves her right for getting what she asked for. I don't think it will be long now until we break out the Montefiascone*, Louisa chuckled to herself.

One curious visitor was Washington Irving Bishop, a young mentalist. He was small and jittery, seemingly a bundle of nerves and skin, so sensitive was he to all movements, sounds and noises. At dinner, Matilda questioned him. "Didn't you travel as the stage manager of Anna Eva Fay, before her fraud was exposed?"

"Yes, madam," the man replied politely. "And I was the one who exposed her."

"I love a good exposé! Tell us your story, please," she urged the young clairvoyant.

"Miss Fay was one of the most renowned vaudevillian spiritualists, and as I was her stage manager, I was privy to the fraud. I could not tolerate the charade, the way she duped people, turning their hopes against them. Yes, I divulged the tricks of the spiritualists and turned entirely away from the movement."

"Show us one trick," Helene pleaded.

"It's far too silly for anyone to believe. Shall I reveal one, madam?" Bishop asked her mother permission to give an example. Matilda nodded.

"You have to remember that people who went to these shows wanted to believe in spirits—also, that everything was done in a darkened theater," said the mentalist, blowing out the candles and beckoning to Lizzie to turn down the gas jets. He took the hand of Helene on his left and Marienne on his right. "Now take the hand of the person to your left and right," he instructed. "This exercise only astounds if we are absolutely certain that everyone's hands are being held firmly." Louisa took Augustine's hand gently into hers, feeling the warmth of the swollen joints, and on the opposite side, Mrs. Cutney's cool and flaccid palm.

"Now does anyone have a spirit they would like to conjure?"

"My husband," whispered Mrs. Cutney.

"Please, madam, it is for the children, just to demonstrate," Bishop said.

"Perhaps we could contact my pony, who died when I was young," said Helene.

"We must concentrate very hard," the mentalist said, smiling.

In the dim light, Louisa peeked through her lashes while the rest seemed to bow their heads and concentrate in belief. She scanned around the table and met Herr Hahn's glare. His eyes snapped with fury. She nodded to him slightly.

BAM! The table shuddered with the strength of the blow. Even the mentalist started in alarm.

"I think the pony is under the table," said Helene, her voice quivering.

"It is only mein foot," declared Herr Hahn angrily. "That is the vay with these deceptions."

Helene sniffled a little in fright and confusion.

"There, there, mein Schatz. It was a cruel idea."

Louisa's head whipped in Herr Hahn's direction. She reddened and lowered her gaze. What a fool she had been. His sweet words were just a reflection of his generous nature. That was all.

Herr Hahn could not stay angry for long and turned apologetically to Bishop. "Ah, mein friend, excuse me. I have been like a stubborn pony too."

"No better way to expose the fraud, sir. My thanks," he responded.

Later, in the parlor, the ladies gathered around the unusual guest while chamomile tea was served. "And if you are not a spiritualist now, what do you call your skills?" asked Matilda.

"I have a knack for mind reading, which I do through interpreting muscle tension," Bishop said seriously. "I do not pretend that my gift is a supernatural phenomenon. Rather, it is an innate sensitivity I have to reading thoughts through bodily clues. I like to call it 'muscle reading.'" With his curling brown hair, light blue eyes and pale skin, his acute attention and slight frame, the young man was likely to convince many impressionable women that he was a sensitive interpreter of inner thoughts.

"Tell me my thoughts on spiritualism," Louisa challenged him.

"I can guess your leanings just from your dare, but I will do an honest assessment," he said as he took Louisa's wrist in his hand. He pressed his two fingers on her pulse and his thumb

183

on her forearm and looked into her deep, almost melancholy eyes. He frowned and declared, "You are more than a skeptic; you reject spiritualism completely. Not only that, you have a bad experience with someone or something related to spiritualists."

Louisa nodded and she withdrew her wrist from his, protectively. She was surprised at the accuracy of his assertion. She detested people who claimed to hear knockings from the dead or to have their writing usurped by a spirit from the other world. For her, it was clear that death ended life in this realm. The last thing she would hope for Beth, or for anyone who had made the glorious passage, was to have so little to do in the afterlife that they came back to knock on wooden tables in the dark of a séance. He had hit to the core of her belief immediately. There would be no secrets for long in the presence of this clairvoyant.

"My family was touched by a charlatan," she said. "It's not an easy thing to talk about." She walked slowly to the window and looked out at the moonless street scene.

"You can't bring us to the brink like that and leave us hanging," said Augustine, who expected a clever story.

Louisa was pensive, hesitant. "We had a childhood friend who was accused of deception and imposture at two séances."

"Certainly, there are many who have had the same claim against them," said Matilda.

"It's just jumbled up with a lot of family losses … and I am still angry about it," said Louisa, turning back to the roomful of expectant faces.

"I remember that your father was sorely disappointed in the young man, Frederick Llewellyn Willis," Miss Holley reminisced.

Once the name was mentioned, Louisa found the story tumbling out. She sat back down on the divan near Augustine and spoke deliberately. "Yes, he came into our lives at our darkest time, just after we had left Fruitlands. He was a gentle boy who liked to play with us girls. He was an orphan and my mother took a liking to having a boy around. He would spend school breaks with us when we lived in Concord and later, when we were back in Boston in our leanest years, he would board with us while he went to school. It was while he was in divinity school at Harvard that he heaped some dishonor on himself."

"Nothing that tarnished your father's saintly image," Mrs. Holley interjected.

"My father was just recovering some dignity with his 'Conversations' after years of ridicule. We couldn't afford for more derision to come our way and we really never mentioned Llewellyn again."

This mentalist was too young to recall the sensational story from Boston of 1857. "I remember something of this when I was in Boston that year," Matilda affirmed. "A young man was expelled from Harvard Divinity School. He never denied that he was a medium, nor did the Harvard faculty fault him for this, but that he was duping his audience, that the 'demonstrations' were actually tricks, was the issue."

"And there was something much worse than any humiliation that might have befallen my family," Louisa added passionately. "We had another reason for a more virulent dislike of Llewellyn. He went on to write a treatise, which he claimed was supernaturally inspired, of Theodore Parker's words and teachings from beyond the grave."

"Theodore Parker! Our reformer, abolitionist, our proud leader!" Miss Holley exclaimed. "Llewellyn besmirched him?"

"Oh, Sallie," Louisa exploded, "when I was making my way as a writer, I would go to Parker's home on Sunday nights, sit like a mouse in the corner and listen to the glorious words of hope that swirled about." She told the others, "Parker would always take my hand, recognize me, ask after my parents and encourage me to return. I hardly needed the encouragement, for I longed for that talk and those principles."

She shuddered at the memories of the lowest day of all, so low that she thought to throw herself in the Mill Dam. She could not tell the story of how she stared at the waters, thought of her family and finally recovered her senses. The first place she thought of as refuge was Theodore Parker's home.

"Parker saved my life physically and metaphysically. To have a spiritualist, and one who lived and loved and grew alongside my family, defile my hero ...." Louisa stopped speaking because she feared her own rage.

"And to complete the betrayal, Llewellyn now boasts that, having been the solitary boy at home with the Alcott girls, he was the model for Laurie. Never—not ever, not once, at no time, did Llewelleyn resemble my Laurie," Louisa averred. "So, dear Mr. Bishop, if you ever encounter this man on your mentalist circuit, please, do expose him for the fraud he is."

Bishop nodded, bowed and turned toward the impassive Mrs. Cutney, who hovered about the edges of the group, as diaphanous as a spirit herself. "My dear madam, would you like a muscle reading?" he asked her. Mrs. Cutney smiled that sad smile, shrugged that slow shrug and held both hands behind her back. *This is my chance to get the story about where she wanders,* Louisa thought.

"Come, come, dear." Louisa placed her hand on Mrs. Cutney's back, gently urging her forward. "I've done it, now it's your turn. It's really very simple. Doesn't hurt a bit." She took Mrs. Cutney's right hand and placed it in Bishop's. Mrs. Cutney's eyes were wide but she barely seemed to breathe.

Bishop grasped her wrist gently and closed his eyes for a few moments. Finally, he opened them and said, "You have a craving for something very rare, something that is slightly dangerous, but very wonderful, too. I cannot quite place what it is ...." He closed his eyes again and stood trance-like. His hand gripped Mrs. Cutney's wrist more and more firmly, until she cried out and, with a gesture of impatience and fear, pushed him from her. The young man tumbled like a board to the floor, as pale and translucent as a ghost.

Mrs. Miller jumped to her feet with a cry, overturning the china cups on the small table in front of her. Agile Rebecca, who was always nearby to be of service with the drinks and fans, was the first to reach the prostrate man and placed her hand on the front of his neck to feel the pulse. Dr. Miller was at her side immediately. "The pulse is feeble and breath shallow. This is more than a faint. I believe he is in a cataplectic trance," he stated. The doctor gave orders for restoratives and had the young man brought to bed. Amidst the disorder and chaos of the moment, Louisa saw Mrs. Cutney reach into her pocket and check for a small wad of paper. Grasping it frantically, she slipped from the room, leaving a faintly acrid odor in the air.

It was several hours before the young mentalist came to, none the worse for the experience.

The next day, Louisa came into Dr. Miller's office. "I hope you saw how very capable Miss Grant was in our urgent moments yesterday," she told the doctor.

"Her unflappability in the emergency was appreciated. I have been underestimating the young woman," he agreed.

Mr. Bishop stopped by to confer with the doctor, looking fit and healthy. He waved Louisa to stay seated and explained, "This was not the first bout of unconsciousness I have had. These episodes have occurred during my exhibitions, and seem to be brought on by deep concentration. I intend to carry a note in my pocket, to warn people that it might be hours before I regain my senses." He added quietly, as Louisa wondered if he had a premonition. "I am worried that an autopsy might be ordered if I should appear dead."

"That is a most extraordinary thought, Bishop," the doctor said sharply.

"I sense things, you know. I worry, too, about what it was that Mrs. Cutney needed so desperately, but I do not foresee her appearing at the dinner table again on the evenings I might visit."

Chapter 20

Sorosis

Louisa peered at herself in the hallway mirror, trying to tilt her new bonnet to just the right angle. The towering concoction of plum silk and black velvet rippled with ribbons and a cascade of violets. She had told the milliner that she would accept no exotic feathers on her new hat. She had seen feathers, nests and even complete birds on women's heads in the city. Fashion was one thing and cruelty another.

"Bring it forward and tilt the back up," Marienne instructed. "It makes you look impossibly tall that way. Who are you trying to astonish today?"

"Not astonish—just blend in," replied Louisa. "I am a bit daunted. I am going to the formidable group of ladies known as Sorosis."

"What's Sorosis? You do look a bit unnerved."

"Ah, it's a grand story and it's got all my favorite elements: haughtiness exposed, women's triumph over the lordly establishment—and Charles Dickens to boot," teased Louisa as they entered the parlor. At the sound of Louisa's "storytelling" voice, Rebecca and Helene paused from their recitations and joined the others for the tale.

"It began about ten years ago, the last time Charles Dickens was in the States doing a reading tour. I saw him in Boston myself that time. My idol fell flat for me: he was aged and foppish, with a weak voice. No matter. The tour was a huge success. At the end of it, the Press Club of New York organized a dinner to celebrate the man.

"Jane Croly, who has invited me to speak today, asked to attend the dinner. She is on the editorial staff of *The New York World* and a famous syndicated columnist."

"She is Jenny June! I have told you girls about her columns discussing the place of women in the working world and her view of marriage based on equality between the partners," Marienne interjected.

"She has just written a book on the topic," Rebecca added. "I saw it at the Astor Library. She calls it *For Better or Worse: A Book for Some Men and All Women.* Isn't she awfully clever?"

"Fanny Fern asked for a ticket as well. Fanny Fern! The highest paid columnist in the country! And they were both denied, because the Press Club is a male institution," Louisa continued. "Later, the Club reconsidered and because both women had husbands in the organization, they relented. But the women declined, of course, stating they had not been treated like gentlemen."

"And now they have their own meals and lectures?" Helene asked.

"Exactly. Mrs. Croly organized the literary and journalistic women into a group called Sorosis."

"I know what that means," said Rebecca, putting on her cloak to leave for school. "It's a botanical term for a fruit created from multiple flowers on a single stem."

"Glorious," said Marienne. "Women cooperating together, bringing forth a harvest."

"Yes, it symbolizes all the sweet and healthful power of women working in solidarity," said Louisa. "The club now meets at Delmonico's, the very scene of the first rejection. Before this group, the restaurant did not allow women to dine unaccompanied by men."

"It's perfect for you. What's the problem?" asked Marienne.

"I am so abashed when I stand before a crowd. I talk too fast, my voice rises to a strident pitch, I get red in the face, and altogether just try to get to the end of the battle without embarrassing myself."

"Miss Louisa, just tell them a story!" Marienne suggested. "You'll be fine. Especially with that hat."

Delmonico's restaurant was one of the oldest and decidedly the most elegant eatery in the city. Its sedate brownstone facade was pierced by arched windows framed with lace draperies. The wrought iron fence before it sheltered a garden with evergreens and potted plants. The carriages clattered to a stop on the cobblestone street, depositing energetic and fashionable women. Inside, Mrs. Croly welcomed the guests. She was an ebullient, lithe woman of about Louisa's age who spoke with a slight English accent. "We've grown to almost one hundred members, and it looks like today is one of our largest gatherings. The ladies are absolutely delighted to have you with us."

Just what I feared, Louisa thought, and smiled nervously at the women about her.

Mrs. Croly rose and gestured grandly to indicate Louisa seated on her right. "Members, I am proud to present to you the most successful woman author in America." Louisa scanned the faces of the women in the grand private dining hall of the most prestigious restaurant in the city. Around the bouquet-filled tables were writers, businesswomen, physicians, fashion experts, scientists, editors and educators. All that stood between them and their luncheon was Louisa's remarks. Marienne's words reassured her. Nothing came easier to Louisa than telling a true story, laced with hyperbole.

"I learned a lot at Vassar College," she began lightly. "Oh, I never attended college …." *Why did I even bring it up in front of these educated women?* "But now I find that I have an open invitation to speak there and also, uncannily, that my books are kept on the library shelves. I told the librarian that my 'Little Women' are poor little things with few advantages and are rather bashful, like their ma." The women laughed softly and looked expectant. Louisa was certain that this bashfulness was all on display. "The last time I 'attended college' four hundred students mobbed me and I was completely overwhelmed by the autograph books, albums, kisses and handshakes. The girls pressed me to make a speech. As I never was and never intended to be a speech-maker, I asked the girls if they would be satisfied if I just stood on the dais and turned around slowly. Hooting with energy, the girls agreed, and there and then 'the most successful author in America' revolved quietly for her fans. And so, dear ladies, I offer to revolve for you as well."

She did speed up her delivery at the end and heard her voice get pitchy, but she was done. Thank goodness no one asked her to pirouette. The ladies clapped politely and whispered kind words to her and Louisa regained her seat with relief.

Her ordeal over, she settled down to her meal with Jane and her influential friends. They spoke fervently and wisely about their desires and goals to empower women to help, educate and uplift other womenfolk.

"Women must be educated and they must believe that they have a place in the world before they set themselves up as the caretakers of a home and a family," said one.

"Jane, you are a perfect example of all that a woman is capable of," said another. "Four children, managing the women's section of a city paper, editor of *Demorest's* ...."

"Books written, clubs encouraged, always on the forefront of women's fellowship," enthused another.

"Perhaps just say *womanship*," Jane suggested.

"I know a young lady who needs to see how you work and how you accomplish it all," said Louisa. "She wants to be a writer but desperately needs guidance on the basics of writing for her audience and remaining true to her own vision."

"Bring her to me," Jane said. "I will take her to the newspaper office and show her what a woman can do with her pen in this city."

Louisa brought Marienne to *The New York World* offices the following day. Jane met them with a curious smile. "Now, one of the important things I do is to read every major newspaper in the city, to see their slant and what they include or miss. Don't blame me—I didn't report it," she said to Louisa as she handed her the morning journal. There was a small mention in the lecture review section of her offer to revolve at Sorosis. *That finishes off my anonymity in the city,* Louisa thought. *Someone at the meeting yesterday tattled to the press.*

Marienne attended office hours with Mrs. Croly regularly. She told Louisa one morning after her walk with Casey, "Mrs. Croly is the perfect mentor. I felt I had nearly lost my voice before she started to instruct me in her cogent writing skills. She is so adamant about the communion that exists between all women, that we have a special language to use with members of our own sex."

Louisa felt that Marienne was appropriating some of Jane's linguistic traits and answered plainly, "She has good common sense and a real desire to instruct young writers. And to pass on what she's learned."

Louisa saw Marienne groaning and struggling in the hotel library in the evenings, scratching out and rewriting passages, still unsatisfied. "Mrs. Croly has given me some assignments to practice writing in a journalistic style," she moaned. "This realistic writing is all too hard for me, so unlike the poetry I love to write." Marienne cast her pen down.

"It took me ten years until I found my style," Louisa encouraged. "Nothing improves your authorship more than trying to write in all different ways. Keep scribbling, The more you do, the better you will be."

It was Jane's idea to have Marienne come to a Sorosis meeting and read her poetry between two lectures. While the ladies usually discussed health and sanitation issues, conditions in hospitals and foundling asylums, women and property rights, and equal education of the sexes, Jane decided that a literary interlude would be welcome. Marienne blanched and sputtered, "Please don't think I am not completely honored, but I am so unworthy of this. I am not prepared to share my poetry."

"No artist ever thinks their work is done, especially a true artist. Come and be embraced. You will not find a more welcoming and gentle audience than this one," Jane assured her.

Marienne wore a simple black gown with a small white ruffled collar. Her hair was pulled back into a tight knot at the nape of her neck. Louisa understood that she was intent on making herself seem older, graver and more serious than her winsome appearance would imply. The few tables in front of her were occupied by women who buoyed her with encouraging looks and polite attention. She started in a small voice, but her oration was perfect and gained strength as she proceeded:

He was a fancy of ecstasy

Who entered my world with sweet felicity.

Bold, yet kind, he appeared

The first blithe afternoon he neared.

His face a handsome visage seen,

His form with youthful, vibrant mien.

All his power drawn from blessed youth

Embracing privilege, station, yet truth.

A regal form, a vision glorious,

I halted, waited all timorous.

But once I viewed him close at hand

His princely clothes yet clothed a man.

He strode with rugged hearty power,

His simple way showed love could flower.

With sighs and charms and whispers sweet,

A heart, like mine, with rapture beat.

He longed, he loved, he sought to woo,

Humane, caring, faithful and true.

Good, honest, plain and calm

With smiles and kisses, his simple balm

And then the man truly was seen

Unencumbered by title, earthbound, not mean

Tethered to cares of all mankind,

Deciphering the mysteries that weary every mind.

Existing like Adam, but striving for heights

With strength and skill to illumine the nights.

A man yet kingly all the same

Encompassed in the sinew of his frame,

A dreamer, a lover, a learner and still

Much grander than a single man's will.

The room was silent.

"Oh, Lord, what have I done?" Marienne whispered, and then, with a small cough and a sigh, the room reverberated with applause. The girl blushed red. her eyes filled and she wobbled, faint and slightly shaky. Louisa threw her arm about the trembling girl's shoulders and, with a wink to calm her fears, guided her back to her table. She settled into her chair, took a large gulp of water and stared down at the starched tablecloth.

"Remarkable maturity for her age!"

"Such deep emotion. Where does it come from?"

"That's a very well constructed piece of poetry." Louisa smiled, for the comments from the women justified her opinion of the girl's talent. Marienne sank back in her chair, as relieved as Louisa had been after her speech in front of the same body.

"Mrs. Botta would be the one to get her connected to all the right literary people," someone suggested. "She always has an intern or an apprentice or a student in her ken." So, although she was not present, it was decided that Mrs. Botta would be the very one to champion the new poetess.

"Let me take your manuscript, dear. I will be at the salon this Saturday," said Mrs. Paterson, as she slipped the papers from Marienne's trembling fingers. "Come now, dear, you look as if I've drained your very life blood. You *do* have a copy of this at home, I am sure."

"A copy? Why would I have a copy?" the young girl stammered. Marienne looked ashen and then revived herself. "Oh, yes, I have my notes and scratches. I just would like to take this sheet and make it even better before Mrs. Botta sees this."

"Nonsense, Marienne, it's pure genius already. Don't be so humble. And Mrs. Botta will be your grandest support and advocate. She knows how to get the best from everyone and *knows* the best of everyone, too," Mrs. Paterson added. Marienne looked bewildered, her eyes following the forceful woman as she sashayed out of the room, waving goodbye to her friends with the precious sheets folded in her hand.

The week following was Thanksgiving, which Louisa cherished with all her New England upbringing. New York had its own Thanksgiving tradition with parades of people dressed in costumes, Pilgrims and Indians, beating drums and blaring horns as they marched through the streets.

The Bottas invited her to dinner. The roast turkey stuffed with chestnuts and oysters took its place at the head of the table, while the sideboard was laden with the weight of partridge breast flanked by an English mutton and roast prime rib. There was oyster-crab bisque, a diamondback terrapin, corn fritters, cranberry jelly and asparagus in hollandaise sauce. Vanilla soufflé, mince pie and the almighty pumpkin pie finished the meal.

The guests were as varied as the menu. Louisa enjoyed the reminiscences of an old German, an ex-consul to Washington. She wished that Josef were there to hear the tales, and supposed that he was working alone at his desk, studying or writing advocacy letters. The party continued with music and singing, then a look at an album of stunning photographs. The evening ended with champagne toasts. The revellers departed down the magnificent central stairway, where the candles, the art, the flowers and books overflowed, as abundant as the feast and generosity of the Bottas.

Louisa, descending on the arm of Professor Botta, clasped his hand and smiled with contentment. He handed her ceremoniously to the butler, who held Louisa's wrap. Mrs. Botta was extending her congenial wishes to the other guests as they left. That made her sudden movement to stop Louisa's exit all the more surprising. "Louisa," she whispered, "I need to talk to you." She pulled Louisa into a small office at the bottom of the stairs.

The motherly concern on Mrs. Botta's face was evident. "I have a hard thing to tell you, dear. It seems your apprentice, the little ward of Marchesa Contini, is a fraud. The poem she read at the Sorosis meeting and which I hold in my hand is not her own work."

197

Louisa was stunned. "How do you know this, and whose work it is?"

"This poem is the very same one that Carlotta Contini recited to me in Italian at the salon several weeks ago, the time when Marienne interrupted her so abruptly."

Louisa scanned the scribbled lines "With sighs and charms and whispers sweet," she read aloud.

"Con sospiri, incanti e dolci sussuri," the two women phrased together. There was no doubt. *That thankless little ingrate.*

Marienne had been waiting for Mrs. Botta's correspondence about her poem, so when Louisa returned from dinner and asked the maid to see if Miss Ayers was available for evening tea, she readily came to Louisa's sitting room. The fire was petering out and the room was slightly cool, but Louisa's hands quivered from more than the chill as she drew their tea. Marienne, sitting and taking the teacup, cried, "Oh, Miss Alcott, you look so drawn and sad. What is it? Are you unwell?"

"No need to worry about me, dear. It's you that I am concerned about."

"Goodness, don't worry about me." The girl sat back, looking relieved. "Is it Mrs. Botta? If she finds my poems lacking, I am not concerned. I know I have a lifetime to keep working on my craft and with all the example and instruction I get from you and all the others I know I will improve."

"Rather, she finds the poems excellent," Louisa said. "The poems, as I said, are not the worry." The girl looked at her quizzically, placing the teacup down with her own shiver. "It is the provenance of the poems that we are concerned about," Louisa said firmly.

"What are you accusing me of?"

"Certainly, the phrases seem close to those I have heard your

198

aunt recite. Did you translate her poems?"

Marienne's shoulders flinched, but her face remained impassive. "I read her poems, of course. I may have repeated a phrase or two without knowing it," she said without much conviction and clutched both hands in front of her. She looked like a supplicant asking for mercy.

Louisa started more softly. "Mrs. Botta says she heard—"

"—the whole thing." The girl flung her hands out. "Yes, I recited the whole thing. I work and toil and moil about but nothing so pure or perfect comes to me," Marienne said, fighting back tears, but with an impassioned tone that Louisa understood.

"Yet you have been the protector of the marchesa's legacy all this time, keeping her from reciting her own work openly," Louisa chastised.

Marienne stood and paced toward the fireplace and then spun around, eyes flashing. "You have no idea how I feared being judged. The more I read Aunt Carlotta's poetry the more I knew I could not create anything as beautiful and alive as that," she said with down-cast eyes. "How would you know, when everyone idolizes you, what it feels like to be so unsure, so inferior?"

"Don't use my fame as your crutch. I worked for every bit of my recognition." Louisa was startled by her own insistence. *She knows nothing about my public's opinion or my fear of being exposed.*

Marienne slammed her fist into her open palm. "I won't, I won't have you reproach me." With each *won't* she slammed again. "I am all alone in this world. My aunt is of no use to me any more. This was my chance to make an impression. I took my opportunity, that's all."

Louisa was taken aback by the girl's vehemence and her lack of remorse. Marienne turned away, covering her face with her hands and began to shake with sobs, her bravado spent. "She was blocked from reciting her poems, but I made no such promise to her husband. I will have to make a living somehow. I don't know how I will survive … if Aunt Carlotta is gone."

Louisa began to soften toward the girl. She took the young woman by the shoulders, turned her gently and cupped her hands on each side of Marienne's wet face. "You have been placed in a position of opportunity. Mrs. Croly has taken you under her wing. She will not abandon you, nor will I or Mrs. Botta. Don't waste this chance to do honest and useful writing. Make a name for *yourself*." Louisa would not let the girl pity herself. She understood the force of her intense desire to achieve, driven by the need to support herself. All Marienne's desire for fame, the need for expression and the worry about the future reminded Louisa of her own youthful trials. Louisa found she was weary of the same struggle that was repeating itself in this girl a generation later. "Marienne, you are living a life that has included heartbreak, duty, family love. If you speak with your own voice, you will have much to say. Use your own heart, your own imagination and your own struggles. The words will come."

"Does everyone know?" stammered Marienne, embarrassed, removing herself from Louisa's grasp.

"Dear, Mrs. Botta and I will have to share it with Mrs. Croly. Promise me and all of us who encourage you that you will work all the more on your own voice and your own legacy." Seeing the girl's dejection, she added, "Do not leave here abashed. You have been corrected. That is all. You are young and I am glad that I was here to protect you from a worse fate. We 'scribbling women' must stick together."

The girl straightened her slumping shoulders and looked up into Louisa's eyes and said, "I am ready to accept the help and assistance these women offer. But save me the lecture on honesty. It doesn't ring well coming from a woman who spent a month under an assumed name."

Chapter 21

Behind a Mask

Louisa had no intention of abandoning Marienne, despite the younger woman's arrogance. She felt all the more that the young ward needed guidance and nurturing. Marienne continued to attend office hours with Mrs. Croly, and went to the salons at her home and Mrs. Botta's, still touted as the young protégé of Louisa May Alcott. But there was no doubt that the friendship between the two was strained. Louisa was willing to forgive Marienne's harsh words, but the girl remained insolent and distant.

At Mrs. Botta's one Saturday, Marienne made a point to stay apart from Louisa, chatting with the young poets and writers she had started to befriend. Standing close to Louisa was the thunderous Mrs. Paterson, who had championed Marienne at the Sorosis meeting and channeled the poems from the girl's hand to Mrs. Botta's. "Tell me, Miss Alcott," she said loudly, "how has your young poetess gotten on?"

"Just as she should, ma'am," said Louisa quietly, "studying and listening and reading and writing."

"Studying the great authors, I presume," said Mrs. Paterson. "Or maybe some less well-known poets."

Louisa had to leave this conversation. She was not sure what the woman was implying or what she knew. Louisa turned regally and crossed the parlor, selecting a chair against the wall where she was half hidden by an effusive bouquet. She sat and scanned the room. Louisa suddenly felt apart from the low rumble of conversation about the great new thoughts and discussions of the latest achievements. Marienne sat on a small divan and conversed in an animated way, though her eyes roved suspiciously. Across from her, Mrs. Botta was saying something firm to Mrs. Paterson, who turned to leave. Before she did, she sent a piercing look across the room in Louisa's direction.

Louisa had the distinct thought that she was being implicated in Marienne's fraud. She could not shake the worry that Mrs. Paterson knew about Marienne's plagiarism and worse, that she believed Louisa had condoned it. She was certain Mrs. Botta had not spoken. It was foolhardy to think she was being scapegoated for Marienne's mistake. Still, the thought of being accused of a deed she had not committed was intolerable to Louisa. No—it terrified her. She started to sweat and her head ached. *What if that loud woman speaks? What if she thinks I have done the same?* Louisa felt that the good turn she had done a young woman was about to be exposed as a charade of falsehoods.

Louisa did not feel well enough to stay. The hum of voices echoed in her skull. She approached Marienne. "I have had one of my attacks of neuralgia, and need to go home a bit early."

Marienne rose. "I am sorry, Miss Louisa. Let me get your things and we will leave."

"No need to interrupt your fun, dear," Louisa said. "I will catch a cab and send Casey to collect you in an hour." Louisa wanted to be seen leaving without Marienne. It would be best if she wasn't her champion in all things. She could not risk her literary reputation in protecting the girl's. She waved to Mrs. Botta from across the room and descended the opulent stairs in a rush.

In the carriage ride home, Louisa tried to calm down. Surely Mrs. Paterson knew nothing. The comment about the lesser poets was merely about the conversation of the day, the *poet du jour*. Perhaps Mrs. Botta had refused her a copy of the poem Marienne had recited and that's what sent the large woman off in a huff. Marienne's plagiarism hadn't been revealed. Louisa still felt vulnerable. *I am not at all as authentic and genuine as the American public wishes me to be.* Long before she came to New York, Louisa had started living a double life. Coming to the city was a mistake. There was too much publicity and peril here.

That evening set off a bit of a setback in Louisa's recovery. She felt an ache between her shoulders which she couldn't shake and a growing nausea. She slept poorly and when she did sleep, she had anxious dreams about small children reaching their arms out to her and claiming to be her own. She stayed home for two or three days in a row. She spent an extra session each day in the sauna. Casey came with her newspapers and asked if he could run some errands. Rebecca brought her broth from the kitchen in the evening. Eventually, Louisa began to relax.

Marienne came with a small poem she had written. "It's completely my own and yet I am satisfied with it. Thank you for believing I could do it," she said, leaving the sheet and a single rose on Louisa's bedstand.

Louisa exhaled for the first time in days. *This entire affair has been a figment of my own imagination*, she assured herself.

The next day when Casey came, she was dressed and ready for a jaunt. "Let's go, Casey. I am ready to walk about the walls of the reservoir on Forty-Second Street. The day is clear and we will see the hills of New Jersey."

Casey smiled and grabbed her hand. "Race you to the street car!" he challenged.

Louisa was back in stride, ready to take on her role as the composed yet energetic authoress. One evening at Mrs. Croly's home, she met a jocular man connected with the city government in some way.

"Miss Alcott, I will be the envy of my little women at home when they hear that I have spent the evening in your company," he said.

"And have you not opened the pages of my books yourself?' she challenged.

"What now! Do you think I can live in a household with four women and not know what they are about? I admit I have read the works, and have come away enriched by the sweet sentiments, as well as the important truths, hidden in your stories." He went on to compliment her on the realism of her *Hospital Sketches*. A boisterous woman chimed in on the metaphysics of her adult novel, *Moods*. Others were vocal about the homespun wisdom they cherished in the March family series.

While Louisa, behind her calm eyes and glamorous silks, appreciated the enthusiasm of her expanding audience, she immediately chafed. The secret she hid from her admirers—the body of pseudonymous work that lay in printed newspapers, scattered in tabloids and women's magazines across the country over two decades—seemed to dangle in front of her, still. She doubted any of them would feel the same about her secret publications. Her illegitimate children. Would she never get any peace until she acknowledged their existence?

Louisa sat in a highback chair and Jane offered her a cool beverage. Behind her, three men whispered together. "Frank Leslie intends to resurrect the Tilton-Beecher connection in his paper with an illustrated timeline," she heard the first man say.

"He takes it out of the church and bedroom and right into every man's parlor," said another.

"Even Leslie's own illustrators call their work 'artistic filth,'" added the third.

Louisa cringed at the power of those white sheets of typeset paper produced in Printing House Square. The papers and the gossipers continued to heap public scorn and humiliation on no less a personage than the abolitionist and preacher Henry Ward Beecher, the most famous Protestant minister in the country. The locals called his church "The Grand Central Station of the Underground Railroad," and because of him, Brooklyn wore a halo of respectability and piety. But once the papers had reported the private allegations even many years after the alleged affair, they and the reading public, would not let go. And there was that name again, Frank Leslie. He seemed ready to defile everything he reported. Only this questionable man's discretion stood between her literary reputation and exposure.

Louisa longed to shake off these worries. She thought of her favorite salon, Miss Mary Louise Booth's, uptown near Central Park. There, she always felt comfortable, carefree and beyond scrutiny. Mary was as tender as her sister Anna and as lighthearted as May. A visit to Miss Booth's was like going to a party at a young girlfriend's house, surrounded by bouquets in large vases and canaries in cages, bound scrapbooks and their great Maltese cat, Muff.

"I shall go to Mary's," Louisa decided. "I will be pampered there."

Chapter 22

The Wildman of the West

The demanding rap on her door disturbed Louisa's concentration. She hurried from her disheveled desk to attend to the urgency. Flinging the door open she found Lizzie, shifting from one foot to another. The girl offered Louisa a calling card. "Mrs. Miller would like you to come down and see the visitor right away."

Joachim Miller, Byron of the Sierras, the card read. Louisa understood the mistress's insistence. "She's concerned about the long hair, I assume."

"And the cowboy boots," Lizzie added.

"And the gold tipped cane, I would think, also." Louisa enjoyed imagining the look on Mrs. Miller's face when she admitted the visitor. "But Lizzie, I absolutely cannot see this person. You will have to ask Mrs. Miller to tell him to leave."

"Really, ma'am?" Lizzie's eyes grew wide. "Is he that much worse than the others?" Louisa wanted to laugh at her melodramatic response. But honestly, he *was* that much worse.

There were a lot of ways to describe Joachim Miller—a poet, an eccentric, a charade, really. This bard had fashioned himself as a dashing character, calling himself the "Wildman of the West." His poetry was dismal and derivative, and she was absolutely certain that he was "a licensed libertine," as she remembered her neighbor in

Concord, Julian Hawthorne, had labelled him.

"It's a long story, Lizzie, but the important part is this: he's left two wives with no means of support, both with a number of children. Now he travels about the country and Europe, living the life of a celebrated writer and trying to make liaisons with anyone who will tolerate him." Louisa could go on but Lizzie blushed, took the card that Louisa offered back to her, and turned to deliver her difficult message.

Louisa could not stifle her urge to see this man she had heard so much about. Matilda's room looked out onto Twenty-Sixth Street. She knew that the actress spent most of her day quietly with Helene if the child did not have a rehearsal. She sped down the hall, then tried to appear casual as she knocked on the door. The minute Helene opened it, Louisa tumbled in. "To the window, to the window," she cried. Hiding behind the damask curtain, she pointed to the figure of Joachim Miller as he stood on the top of the steps, looking bewildered and chagrined. His shaggy brown locks fell from a broad brimmed, high hat as he swaggered away.

"A *cowboy*? You know a *cowboy*?" Helene laughed.

"Actually, I refused to meet him," she said firmly and turned to Matilda, who was propped up on the daybed. "He's a philanderer who left his first wife, an American Indian, after two children, lured a young poetess into marriage with him, then left her with three young ones. He battles her in court over child payments, insinuating that the last child is not his. And *he* is the one who has been traipsing about the Continent, spending lavish amounts and playing the Romantic Poet."

"Calm down, Louisa, you're taking it all too personally," said Matilda.

Louisa's decision to refuse his acquaintance ran deeper than merely protecting her own reputation. The story of the jilted wife had always riled her and she had never been sympathetic to men who abandoned women. In her story which won Frank Leslie's prize, the

206

unsavory Gilbert Redmond wooed his old flame while he cast his young wife aside and he suffered for it. She was not about to give Joachim Miller the satisfaction of acting cavalier with her. She absolutely intended that he would recognize the snub as coming from an upright woman who supported a move toward women's equality in marriage—and furthermore, one who had the public's ear on topics related to the family.

That evening, Louisa dressed for a more tranquil salon than Mrs. Botta's intellectual gala or Jane Croly's journalistic affair. She was determined to fulfill the promise to herself that she would go to Mary Booth's and have a relaxing time for a change. Marienne would not be invited. Louisa went to the front hall mirror to adjust her scarf. Herr Hahn stood near the fire in the drawing room nearby, poring over a sheaf of papers. She had rarely seen him attend social events. "Josef," she called, "you spend too much time on your work. You should come with me."

He looked up through his monocle, as if recalled from the Halls of Justice and surprised to find himself in a New York parlor with a chattering woman. She half hoped he had not heard her. When it came to delicate moments, she was famous for saying the wrong thing at exactly the wrong time. Would he think her impetuous offer too bold?

His faraway look turned to one of pleasure. He put aside his legal briefs and said, "Eh, vat vould this old Teuton have to say in such a place?"

"Not old, just very wise," Louisa answered. "You are just the sort of hard-working man some of these thought slingers need to meet."

It took a bit of cajoling, but not long after, Louisa was handing Herr Hahn over to be introduced around the salon by Mary Booth. He looked comfortable with the handsome woman on his arm. Mary wore her gray hair in elegant rolls about her head and her pale complexion highlighted huge blue eyes. She showed him some of the treasures she collected from all over the world: urns from Japan, old silver from Norway, jewels and gems from Mexico.

Mary's evening salon was filled with music, performances, readings and good conversation. The home had three connecting parlors where authors, singers, statesmen and publishers circulated the rooms in a convivial way. Mary let Josef examine a case with the hair of Shelley, Keats, Byron and Leigh Hunt, and the shelf of books she had authored and translated.

"Miss Booth wrote a history of New York to be used as a school text," Louisa said. "But when she brought it to a publisher, he sent her home to expand it. Well, she worked on that little book for so many years that it grew to a thousand pages."

"Now her *History of New York City* is acclaimed as the first and last word," said an admirer nearby.

Josef perused the bookshelf. "These translations, even a history of France, in six volumes …."

Mary pulled de Gasperin's *Uprising of a Great People* off the shelf and handed it to Josef. "At the outset of the war, this book advocated for the abolitionist cause. I burned to do something, just as Louisa did. She went off to the front and I decided to translate this book."

"Mary's publisher would print it only if she could translate it within a week, so she came home and did the opposite of the first book. Instead of struggling over it for years, she did her work in no time. Within two weeks the book was being printed. You are tenacious and unrelenting, Duchess," Louisa said, using the pet name Mary's friends called her.

"We are not amused." Mary struck a stately pose and laughed.

"I believe you are a leetle amused," Josef said, indicating the ebullient scene around them.

"Mary," said Louisa, settling down in one of the many delightful corners where a private chat and a joke could be shared in confidence behind a tasseled curtain. She motioned for Josef to join them. "Do you realize how you conquered New York in the same way that I set out to conquer Boston? Each from our cold attics, members of the exploited sisterhood of seamstresses." The cat leapt onto Louisa's lap, circled comfortably, and settled down.

"But stitched into the vests and shirts of our girlhood toil were our dreams of a time when we would be respected and published, if not rich and famous. And look, look where we are now," said Mary. "You, the acclaimed author ...."

"And you, the editor of *Harper's Bazaar*," Louisa finished.

Mary prodded Louisa. "I have a poet I must introduce. He wants to meet you desperately. Don't blame me if he falls in love with you," she added mischievously. "He does fall in love with someone every time he surfaces here." She jumped up and took Louisa's hand, drawing her to the next parlor. Josef followed with a bemused expression.

Louisa stopped halfway across the room, shocked to see Joachim Miller staring at her with an insolent look. "Mary, is that ...?" Louisa said.

"Oh, he's nothing but a showman, Louisa," Mary said as she was called away by the ring of the doorbell.

Miller lounged on the couch, his flowing brown hair and beard giving him the unmistakable look of a frontiersman. The man gazed longingly about himself, surrounded by a bevy of mooning women. His handsome face was too perfect for Louisa's taste. He wore a velvet jacket and embroidered pantalones, as if he had just arrived from a hacienda in Mexico. He turned his dreamy eyes to her and rose lethargically. He was tall, but partly due to the high-heeled jackboots he wore. And were those Bowie knives slung across his waist?

He took a few long steps and raised her hand to his lips, saying, "At last, I have hunted down the maiden Diana. I am so sorry that I found you indisposed when I called on you."

"Not indisposed, just opposed," Louisa said coolly.

He remained unruffled. "But I forgive you for the slight." He kissed her hand lightly, with facetious gravity. Louisa wanted nothing more than to box the ears of this conceited puppy. She didn't understand why Mary let him attend, except for the fodder it gave for twittering later on when he left. She was above battling with this rake. Louisa politely disengaged her hand and was about to move on to another corner when he shifted his stance to prevent her escape.

That the phlegmatic poet had bothered to make such a hasty movement sent a stir through the crowd nearby. A young man coughed and a shrill giggle arose from one of the women near the couch.

"I have long desired to hear a bedtime story from your very lips, Miss Alcott," he said loudly enough for all to hear. There was a gasp, then a few titters from the women surrounding him. Louisa stood in the center of the room, all eyes on her. She burned with humiliation. Was he mocking her public persona or casting aspersions on her virtue? Her spine straightened.

"I don't intend to tangle with a wild man." The words didn't come out as she intended. There was a chortle from Miller's entourage. *I've left myself open for this cad.*

Miller made a little growling noise with his throat. "But I would certainly like you to try," he smirked, kissing his lips in her direction.

Louisa was hot enough to blow steam. "You are as vulgar as you are rude," Louisa spewed. "I have a good mind to—"

"—say 'goot night' and be going." Josef was at her side and gently pivoted her toward the door. He stopped midroom and turned back. "You, sir, eef I know the term … you, sir, are a *humbug*."

The eccentric poet stared at the sturdy German. Louisa still smouldered, glaring back. Miller raised his hand as if to make a point but instead he gulped and sat down sharply. Louisa noted the change in his composure. His hauteur turned to timidity. Coloring briefly, he tried to resume his languid position but the jackboots would not resolve to a picturesque angle. The little entourage of adoring women surrounded the offended poet, shaking their heads over their shoulders as Louisa and Josef turned to leave.

210

Louisa hid her smile behind her hand and hurried out of the room, bursting into laughter as she entered the hallway. "Josef! You were perfect! That's exactly what he is—a humbug, nothing more and nothing less."

"I think perhaps a beet more, but it will do for thees company," Josef said, offering Louisa her wrap.

The two stood on the granite stoop and breathed frost into the clear New York night. A horse and carriage clopped down Fifth Avenue. On Saturday evenings, the avenue was filled with revelers walking or riding to the posh clubs or to the newly-constructed mansions across from the park.

"Do you mind walking a few blocks first?" Louisa asked. "I have got to clear my head."

Josef nodded his consent. "Your health seems completely restored and mine ees not so bad either." They stepped to the sidewalk.

"I don't understand why Mary takes his presence as a joke and I am so offended," Louisa said as they turned left onto the avenue.

Josef took her arm and they walked a bit in silence. "Vell, it offends you morally." They passed the impressive wrought iron gate posts of St. Luke's Hospital at Fifty-Fourth Street. The two story central chapel glowed in the blue-black haze of the city. *Morally— and now personally.* Louisa was still mortified by the muddy torrent Miller spit out at her and could make no answer. As if he read her mood, Josef added quietly, "That fellow is a swine."

One block further was the Catholic Orphan Asylum of St. Patrick's and across from that, the excessive, scandal-ridden mansion of the infamous Madame Restell, a suspected abortionist. Philanthropy and profanity stood side by side in this city, behind the same architecture, nearly at the same address. Anything could be hidden behind a mask of propriety in New York.

"My sister May thinks I have a problem with men," Louisa blurted. She colored a bit and hastened to add, "Actually, May thinks I

211

have a problem with *everyone*. I can't play the social games she says are necessary."

"Games, no; but courtesy, yes," Josef offered tentatively. Seeing her glare, he added, "Ach, you were right not to accept his call. You do not need to be seen vith someone who diminishes you."

"He has abandoned two families and yet is accepted in society quite unobstructed by any repercussions. Let a woman try that!" Louisa fumed. A careening policewagon raced by on the avenue and Louisa waited for the racket to die down.

"Ah, yes, the false marriages." Josef nodded.

She took a breath. "There was a frantic moment when I was small—a time when we thought our father wavered about his marriage and children, too. He was so smitten with the thought of re-configuring society into one happy family."

"Such an optimistic philosophy," said Josef, looking warily at Louisa as if he had just opened Pandora's box and was about to reap the consequences.

"Such ideals he had! Even in Germany they must have heard about his failure at Fruitlands?" Louisa asked. Josef nodded but could not get a word in as Louisa continued. "The poor man had to give up all his utopian dreams. Imagine giving up utopia for our prosaic existence. It was pathetic."

"And who picked up the pieces for the good man after each failure?" Josef prodded gently.

"My mother … and I," Louisa said. "His career and reputation are much restored now that he can add to his travelling 'Conversations' that he is the 'Father of the Little Women.'"

"So any change to your reputation vould besmirch his, too," Josef summed up.

Louisa shook her head. It wasn't only a personal thing. "It's not just about my family and our esteem. You must understand … the whole submissive position that women accept." She considered, then spoke carefully. "In Concord, when I was growing up, I wit-

212

nessed the convolution of another family abandoned by a husband in pursuit of the poetic muse. You've heard of William Ellery Channing?"

"Ah, another poet," Josef laughed. "Now ve are establishing a pattern."

"He was more renowned for his friendship with Mr. Thoreau. After a few years of marriage and children, he began a wandering, self-searching existence that always led back to long saunters in the woods with Henry. His discarded family was taken in by his sister and her husband, Thomas Wentworth Higginson."

Josef looked blank.

"Higginson, the abolitionist, writer and war hero, and Thoreau. My idols," Louisa continued. "But neither of them, both beacons of enlightened thought, seemed able to impress on Channing the untenable position he had caused his wife to endure. They both allowed the husband to act dishonorably, yet maintain his status in society, their friendship and the public's good opinion, while the abandoned wife suffered condemnation and contempt."

"Of course, a rejected wife has no legal or social standing."

"We've seen that with poor Matilda Heron, the two Mrs. Joachim Miller and Mrs. Tilton's story, too."

"Ah, the wife vas treated like a possession by her husband and a simpleton by both men," Josef said, shaking his head.

They had reached the bulk of St. Patrick's Cathedral. The Collegiate Church of St. Nicolas and Jay Gould's magnificent home were down the block. Gould was one of the richest and most ruthless men in New York. *Again, malevolence and success, hand in hand. One could be a scoundrel yet maintain the highest social standing here, right beside the emblems of piety.*

Louisa climbed the steps of the cathedral and sat on the top one. Josef followed and sat a step below her.

"So, vith the state of things, vhat's a voman to do?" Josef asked.

"She's to do *everything*," Louisa insisted. "Write epistles, go to meetings, send money, change laws."

Josef chuckled. "That's *you,* meine kleine Aufruehrerin," he said, resting his elbows behind him and throwing his head back to look at the stars. "You are a most charming pot stirrer. Some might say changing laws ees a crazy idea."

Louisa glanced down at him, stirred and surprised. "I never said I was sane."

Louisa could not see his face in the dark. "So vith marriage in the legal rut eet is, I take eet you have rejected that condition completely?" Josef asked quietly.

Have I? "I know for certain that it causes women who were unable to fend for themselves to preserve the proprieties in public, no matter how hot a hell their home might be," Louisa said. Hugging her arms about herself, she swung forward. "Besides, I love my liberty too well to relinquish it for an establishment. I've worked all my life for my family and never intend to let anyone else have rights to my earnings." She pulled her knees up to her chest, rocked back and exhaled a long, breathy whistle. "As Mercy said in *Pilgrim's Progress,* 'I might have had husbands afore now … but they were such as did not like my conditions.'" She had deflected his question with a joke. *What is wrong with me?*

She only had a view of Josef's profile, and he still stared up at the stars. He was as close to the ideal of a man that she had ever conjured. He seemed to be a modern day knight of honor sprung from the pages of a Scott tale, with only a duffle filled with papers as his jousting weapon.

Josef stood and climbed to the top step alongside her. He took her hands and helped her stand. Now she was one step below him. Her two hands remained clasped in his. "Eet would be a fine thing to work together to change the laws."

"That's a serious job, Josef."

"Ah, vell, marriage is a serious thing."

She had never seen him look so determined, nor so tender. He

214

was looking too earnestly into her eyes. Louisa pressed his hands, as much to encourage him as to console. He leaned closer. Louisa turned her head down and away awkwardly. Josef was left leaning into an array of silk violets and velvet bows on the top of her bonnet. Louisa frantically disengaged her hands and grabbed Josef's arm, pulling him down the steps to the avenue.

"Why are we still standing here? To change, then!" Louisa declared, hailing a carriage home.

Figure 9. **American Sketches: The Ladies' Window at the New York Post Office**

Chapter 23

Letters

Once back in her room, Louisa could not settle down. Her conversation with Josef had brought to the surface her antipathy to marriage as an institution. The laws were clear that a marriage union subjugated one human to another. Most women, she knew, gave up their freedom and autonomy without a thought.

Her parents' marriage had been unusual from the start. They shared high ideals, lofty aspirations and absolute commitment to each other. They set about to make a perfect kind of union, one that society could emulate. And yet, it had not been an easy relationship.

She had a sudden desire to write to her father. She could not write to ask his view of marriage, but starting her letter, the words flowed. She told him that New York was rich and filthy, cultured and rude, progressive and overbearing. Sprawling hastily at her desk, she began to fill pages with descriptions of the lectures she had attended, the theater she had enjoyed and the people she had met. He would love to have her repeat the names of Mrs. Botta, Abigail Gibbons and Sallie Holley.

I'm writing as well as entertaining myself, so this has been a most profitable and successful season, Louisa wrote. *I am much healthier than when I arrived and everyone says I look years younger. I am receiving so much attention that I am afraid I shall come home a first class peacock.*

She reluctantly added the latest gossip. *Tilton's daughters have left their mother stating that they feel their father is in the right. Marriage, hypocrisy, women's rights (or "wrongs," as Marmee says) are so muddled in the Beecher-Tilton case that everyone associated with it is tarnished, but Mrs. Tilton—well, she is destroyed.*

An adult relationship between men and women was impossible, given the legal constraints. There was no possibility of subjecting herself to that. Still, Louisa could not shake from her mind the words that Josef had spoken. He had promised to work at changing marriage laws.

She paused and thought of her abstracted father, his intentions so often misunderstood. She imagined the rank gossip of the New York tabloids and the way they might demean the dreamy philosopher and added, *I cannot recommend that you come here for your Conversations, for people are too busy to think and only gossip prospers in this town.*

Louisa considered the things she had not told her father. She could not bear to mention Casey, for she knew that May would exclaim, "I *knew* she would find a street urchin to adopt!" She would not discuss Matilda and Helene, for Anna and Mother would worry that Louisa could slip into the carefree and dissolute life of the theater, which had always attracted her. She couldn't bring up her interactions with the mentalist, for Father would worry about her wits and good sense.

Most of all, she did not mention Josef. Every time she thought of some way to include him, the comment seemed to miss the mark, to diminish him in a quip or a funny story and not get to the essence of his personality. She did not, in any case, want them to place too much importance on or add any sentimental weight to their friendship.

The next morning, she walked to the post office. New York was one of the several hundred cities in the country that had door-to-door mail service. The town was just too large for someone to write

"Miss Alcott, Bath Hotel" and hope that it would be called for in the office. It needed a proper street address and number for delivery here. Still, it was her habit from Concord to walk to the post office to deposit her letters and call at the window in case there was anything for her. The city, like other large cities, had established a Ladies' Window where women could collect their mail without fear of male scrutiny.

Louisa grabbed her stack of mail and turned from the window, pushing her way through the calamitous, rushing crowd. Once outside, there was little chance to collect herself as the careening hacks, the barking vendors and the rumble from the elevated train tracks on the next avenue assaulted her senses.

Glancing up and down the street she spied two of her cast of characters from the hotel looking suspiciously about themselves, as if they were about to steal into an alley. Rebecca and Casey had just exited a seamstress's establishment across the way. Casey carried a brown parcel, and looked sheepishly around him. The seamstress rushed out behind them and handed him a smaller package. She seemed to give them both a few words of explanation, then took Casey's face in her hands and whispered something. Both children threw their arms around the woman and hurried off in the direction of the hotel.

"Another secret!" Louisa mused. "If it's not gossip, it's secrets in this town!"

She shuffled her mail as she walked far behind the two children. She recognized a funny package from Anna's boys, a letter from Thomas Niles, her publisher, and a crisp envelope that looked like an invitation from Mrs. Croly. One other envelope remained in a florid, unfamiliar hand. She glanced at the return address.

Frank Leslie.

She stopped midstride. *Here it comes.* Louisa turned off Twenty-Sixth Street, the children forgotten, and headed to Gramercy Park. She sat quietly to face what was coming.

219

Dear Miss Alcott,

My wife and I hope that you are enjoying your interlude in New York, though 'interlude' is perhaps too idyllic a word for the pace that you have endured during your stay. But what would one expect from the jungle when the lioness is in its midst?

Dear woman, it is hard for me to wax poetic. I am a journalist and a businessman and so I will get straight to my purpose.

We once enjoyed a useful and profitable relationship.

I have not been able to secure one of your stories in the last five years. It is of great interest to do so. Of course, you understand that I have the publishing rights to your previous stories. Perhaps we will be forced to rerun them if we do not get new work from you—with your legal name as the byline, of course.

I would greatly desire to speak to you about terms.

Sincerely,

Frank Leslie

Every fear and worry about her respectability and reputation stared back at Louisa in the words of this letter. Frank Leslie was threatening to expose her anonymous sensation stories. She stared at the paper in her hand. The words blurred and her eyes burned.

Perhaps if she wrote him a new story he would be satisfied. But would he really be content with a cosy moral tale? He couldn't force her to go back to her lurid style—she would never do that. She could not ever concede to this request.

Perhaps she should write to Mr. Niles. Something could be worked out, man to man. No, this was not a man's issue, for a male author would never be put in this position. Louisa must handle this in her own way.

If not man to man, perhaps this could be handled woman to woman. Miriam Squire Leslie managed her life like one of Louisa's audacious heroines. She seemed to use every bit of knowledge, guile and strength to get what she needed. And she did not seem reluctant to use any method that suited her. But Louisa did not know enough about Mrs. Leslie. When she had her victim where she wanted, would she be relentless or just?

In Louisa's stories published under Miriam Squires's watch, the heroines were courageous and resourceful. None of them would concede to the sexual power plays of their partners. One committed suicide rather than submit to a tyrannical marriage; another mesmerised her wandering lover with her dancing. Rising abruptly, Louisa bolted toward Broadway and hailed a hansom cab. "Five-Thirty-Seven Pearl Street," she told the driver. "And wait for me, please. I won't be long."

When Louisa entered the newsroom, the aroma of cigars and coffee assaulted her. She knew this place, this smell, these sounds. The newspaper den had not changed much from the smoky rooms in Boston where she had tentatively left her first manuscripts, back when she was at her most optimistic, yet most vulnerable. The room clamored with the tapping of ticker tape, orders barked by the daily editor, and the scrambling and scratching of pens.

A burly clerk with a visor looked up at her indifferently. "You in the right place, ma'am?"

"Would you announce me to Mrs. Leslie?"

"Who'd I be announcin'?"

"Louisa May Alcott."

The room fell silent. A dozen heads turned in her direction. A frosted glass door opened suddenly and a woman emerged. She was magnificent. Her thick brown hair was parted to each side and cascaded over her forehead in waves. The dark eyes were accentuated with deep liner on both lids, making them seem impossibly large. Her waist was cinched to a miniscule taper. *Did she work like this all day?*

"Miss Alcott." The woman extended her hand and at the same time gestured for Louisa to enter the office. "To finally meet you after all these years of collaboration." She closed the door and motioned for Louisa to sit. As she settled herself behind a great ebony desk the tapered waist disappeared and the eyes grew piercing.

"Thank you, but I needn't sit. My cab is waiting," Louisa said.

"Are you like your friends at Sorosis and all the other women's clubs who shun my society, but adore my work?" Mrs. Leslie asked sharply.

"Miriam—let me call you by your name as a sister," Louisa said. "You know I have the most respect possible for all you have done in a man's world. You've achieved what is an ideal of mine—creating a place for women writers and readers. Your magazine for women offered me an audience I cherished. Thank you for championing my work even before I was famous."

The editor's face softened. Louisa was heartened.

"I have learned that people who flatter are about to beg," Mrs. Leslie said, making Louisa squirm. "Is it about my husband's letter?"

"The work I did for your husband's papers is an altogether different story," Louisa said. "I'm not proud of it."

Miriam Leslie's eyebrows shot up.

"He and I have a history that … is uncomfortable," Louisa said.

"Frank Leslie prospers on uncomfortable," his wife returned.

"The stories I wrote for him before I became the 'Children's Friend'—I can't be associated with them anymore. Now that you and he are … so intricately entwined … you understand."

"Do you, of all people, see me as my husband's mouthpiece?" Miriam shot back.

"A lot has changed for me since I last published in one of your husband's journals. And that story would shock my gentle readers. It was the one about the boating party who all took hashish. It would ruin me now."

"Louisa Alcott, you've retreated to the tame, have you?" she challenged.

"We've both got the same goal in mind," Louisa said, placing her hands on Miriam's desk and leaning forward urgently. "You have the women's attention and I am going all out for the children. I have the key to that right now and I am going to open that lock. We have got to change minds together about what women can do and be."

"Yes, working for a new order." Miriam stood and looked out the window. *A new order*. Louisa had heard much about this at the Women's Congress, but had not seen it mentioned in the Leslie publications. Miriam remained at the window. City Hall, its impressive fountain, the taper of the island at the Battery were in her view. With her back still to Louisa, she said, "I am imagining the Giantess that will be in our harbor one day," she said. Louisa was startled. This wasn't the direction she expected from Mrs. Leslie. "What a noble woman the woman of the future may become!" the editor said as she turned back to Louisa, determined and defiant.

Louisa had unexpectedly discovered a sister in alliance with her own aims. She thought not the less of the eyeliner and the cinched waist, for the aspirations of the soul inside were grand. "I'm giving up a lot to fight this fight," Louisa said hesitantly.

"Like your 'blood and thunder'?" Mrs. Leslie said.

"Tell me, which was your favorite?"

Miriam sat and thought a moment. "The one where that lecherous rake torments the young mademoiselle on the train. In the end, he seems quite tormented himself by her presence, hardly able to control himself, and then, the coup de grace ...."

"... the mademoiselle is a spunky garçon! I am glad you like that one. It's innocent, really, compared to some of the others."

"And yet, you have gotten right to the crux of the matter. Once the child is arrayed in male clothing, all the harassment stops."

"It's interesting what clothing says about us," Louisa said. "And what men do to women when they think they can get away with it." Louisa looked at Mrs. Leslie, awaiting her verdict.

"Yes." Miriam cleared her throat. "My husband was interested in rerunning some of your older work. But I am beginning to see those types of stories wouldn't be received well with your name attached to them now," Miriam said in a businesslike tone as she looked down and rustled some papers. Louisa's instincts had been right. Miriam would not turn on her. Her heroines never did betray another woman. "People would be affronted, confused," Miriam continued, looking at Louisa calmly. "The time is not right for you and me. Perhaps again in the future ...."

"The stories in the other publications ... your husband?" Louisa pressed.

"I assure you, he is completely under my thumb." Miriam smiled, making a grinding motion with her thumb on the desktop.

Louisa took Miriam's hand. "Thank you for protecting me." She turned to go, but added slyly over her shoulder, "And I can get you into a Sorosis meeting any time you like."

Miriam shooed her out the door. "Louisa May Alcott, you are out to tame me too!

Chapter 24

A Desperate Woman

A few days later, the city was captivated by the news that the notorious corrupt politician, William "Boss" Tweed, had escaped from prison and seemingly evaporated into thin air. The conversation at the dinner table ranged from amazement to disgust.

"How can a man of that size and fame just disappear?" Helene marveled.

"In this town, money can buy anyone and anything and often seems to triumph over justice, as in this case," Louisa said glumly.

Boss Tweed, all six feet and three hundred pounds of him, had ruled over everything and everyone in New York City through embezzlement, bribery and plain coercion. He was the commissioner of public works and in that capacity siphoned off millions of dollars directly from the city construction projects.

"Some say he stole 45 million, others 200 million, used it for himself and his cronies and to bribe everyone to look the other way," Augustine said. Robert had folded the newspaper into half for his invalid charge, down the long direction, making it possible for Augustine to manage turning the sheets himself. Louisa had seen people in New York do this to keep the pages ruly on the streetcars. "After the first trial ended in a hung jury, Tweed was finally convicted and sent to prison."

"Eet is a funny kind of jail he attends," Herr Hahn added.

"Somehow this Boss of New York managed to get the courtesy of a daily afternoon walk in an uptown park. His wardens then accompany him to his Fifth Avenue mansion for dinner with his wife," Augustine continued. "Yesterday, on his afternoon sojourn, Tweed just vanished."

"Ahh, vell, people cannot hide from their troubles forever," Herr Hahn mused. "And did not your poet Emerson say that every act has its compensation?" he addressed to Louisa. *Was Josef reading Emerson, now, in addition to Thoreau?* Marienne coughed, looked abashed and colored briefly. Maybe the girl was ready to repent her own action, aware of the consequences, but Louisa had seen precious little humility from her yet.

Two elderly women, new to the table but already reigning over it with their disapproval, snickered and nodded and cast glances at Mrs. Cutney. The solitary, silent woman raised her eyes and looked at them impassively. They were a pair of spinsters who had arrived at the hotel a week before. The Davenport sisters had the same thin nose, the same pewter hair pulled tight into a bun and same sagging shoulders, differing from each other only by the exceeding thinness of one and the uncomfortable corpulence of the other. They were undergoing treatments for asthenia and gout, as each disease fit their individual physiques. They also shared the same unwavering narrow-mindedness and inflexible opinions.

"It's an inside job," came a disgruntled voice and a grunt from the end of the table where the Davenport sisters sat. When Louisa looked their way, they were both glaring and shaking their heads so it was impossible to know which had spoken and which had grunted, though she supposed it really didn't matter.

After a few days of disdainful observation, the sisters had formed an opinion about Mrs. Cutney and her occasional sudden wanderings at odd hours. They bustled together to Mrs. Miller's office one morning while Louisa was in earshot, putting on her cloak in the hallway.

"Madam Miller, you have made one of the most unconscionable errors that a hostess could conceive: you have allowed an adventuress to board under this roof," they averred together.

"I assure you, Miss Alcott is eccentric with the associates she keeps, but she is not an adventuress," Mrs. Miller lowered her voice and looked furtively in Louisa's direction.

"We'll talk about Miss Alcott presently," the thin one cawed.

"We mean Mrs. Cutney, with her comings and goings," the heavy one squawked.

Mrs. Miller looked dumbfounded. "Mrs. Cutney is the most polite and self-effacing guest we have. I will not entertain your comments."

"And speaking about entertaining, there are altogether too many actors and other artists at the dinner table," began Sister Slender.

"Along with that rowdy woman who claims to be an author," ended Sister Stout.

Later that day, Louisa saw them trying to take the marchesa into their confidence as they sat in the parlor gossiping about the other guests. Marchesa Contini, with her childlike smile, told them that she thought her mother would be coming with Angelina to spend the weekend. The two old ladies snickered and murmured to each other. "Add that to the list of hotel deficiencies. Now there are mental defectives residing here, along with the other misfits." Louisa bit her lip and turn away, disgusted.

Louisa was in one of the quiet cycles, her body sending her the warnings that a bout of rheumatism would be on the way if she kept up her fervid pace. She decided to spend the week in her room reading *Faust* and an edition of the *Journal of Speculative Philosophy* containing a series called "Letters on *Faust*." She convinced herself that she had always had a fascination with German literature and Goethe in particular—and not that she had been influenced by her German friend.

Josef was studious to a fault and stayed in days at a time, reading in his stockings with the door to his room open, a cup of tea at his elbow. He never seemed to stop his own fervid pace and she wondered if his health would be compromised by the amount of responsibility he continually assumed for others. In the afternoons the house was still, with all the guests either at the baths, resting, or out on brisk walks. Louisa liked the cozy warmth of her small room and sat curled on the settee, a basket of apples at the ready.

The furtive sound of a stifled cough in the corridor and soft footsteps approached the stairway. Louisa guessed it was Mrs. Cutney on one of her secretive expeditions. Louisa had never had a private moment with Agnes and felt ever more certain that the enigmatic woman was undeserving of the aspersions the Davenports had thrown at her character.

Louisa poked her head into the hallway. "Ah, Mrs. Cutney, I hoped it was you. I was just aching to get a good walk myself and I see you are about to go out. Would you mind if we walked together for a bit?"

The woman blanched paler, if that were possible, and turned her glittering, teary eyes toward Louisa as she stifled a yawn. She stood still, as if considering, and then aroused herself and with a sudden movement, approached, leaning close to Louisa's face and said in an agitated voice, "Rather, if you could, you should beg me to stay!"

"By all means, then, I beg you remain, and offer to you all the comfort I can. Come into my rooms and let us have a good chat, and perhaps I can do something more to help you than just talk."

"No, delay would be dangerous for me in the end, very dangerous." The woman's words, along with her eyes, darted wildly. Louisa saw a faint wisp of perspiration on her upper lip and brow as Mrs. Cutney, with a flustered movement, tried to brush past. Louisa sought to detain her and lightly grabbed her wrist. She felt the goosebumps under the woman's clammy skin and knew she had to act.

Louisa, with her tall, powerful frame, swiftly enfolded the woman in a firm embrace. Mrs. Cutney struggled briefly and then crumpled into her arms, spent and submissive. Louisa drew her forcibly into the room, closing the door, securing it, and barring the way with her back to the door.

"Dear Mrs. Cutney, you are ill."

"More than you know, more than you know," was the reply. "I must get my remedy."

"Allow me to get Dr. Miller," Louisa offered.

"No!" The shaking woman drew away from Louisa's reach. She grew more agitated and began to scratch herself deeply and hopelessly.

Why had she not seen it before? The nighttime wandering, the teary eyes, the jerking movements, the scratching, the sighing. Now the reason for the clandestine journeys became clear. "Agnes, I know all. I see the signs. You are withdrawing from opium!"

"Let me out of here. You have no idea what you are saying," Mrs. Cutney hissed.

"I see the dilated eyes, the clammy skin, the agitation, and now I understand your wanderings at all hours, even to the Five Points."

The poor woman crumpled to the floor. "You cannot know, you do not know … the craving … the pain."

"My dear, I do," said Louisa. "I assure you, I *do*." In her compassion, she dropped to the floor beside the trembling woman and grasped her hands. "When I had typhoid, I was treated with laudanum. After that, whenever I had my aches and neuralgia I would need it to get any peace, any sleep. There were times when I tried desperately to cease taking it and would return again and again to the sweet delirium it gave me. Finally, I had to stop it completely, but it nearly drove me mad to resist it."

The woman looked at her incredulously. "Do you really know? The retching, the twitching, the pain and the vomiting? The longing, the desire …? Let me out of here. I am suffering." Mrs. Cutney rose, but staggered and clutched the chair to keep from falling.

"I never took such a high dose that I had those dangerous symptoms," said Louisa. Agnes swooned. Louisa caught the woman in her arms and helped her onto the nearby sofa. "You are in grave danger. I must get you medical help. Dr. Miller is not the one, for he does not deal in medicinals."

"Do not go. Do not leave me," the woman pleaded. "I feel I will die without this infernal crutch and I will die with it, too!"

Louisa could think of only one adult in the house compassionate and discreet enough to send on the mission for medical help. She raced down the hall to Josef's room. One look at Louisa told him the situation was urgent, and after a brief explanation, he grabbed the battered coat and was out the door to find the doctor. Returning to the abject woman, Louisa promised, "I will not leave you through any of your trial, Agnes. I have nursed many a worse case than you, of all kinds."

Louisa calmed Agnes on the sofa, massaging her limbs, coaxing her to take a sip of cool water and covering her with a thin blanket as she tried to get her to rest.

"Oh, that I should come to this," the woman moaned, sitting up urgently and beginning to rock fiercely back and forth. "After my injury, our terrible accident, laudanum was prescribed. That poison! I am done!" She rocked and twitched some more. "I didn't care if it was to relieve the excruciating back pain or the dreaded insomnia … the grief … the tincture promised relief of many kinds and I needed it desperately."

"Yes," Louisa commiserated. "I know, I know. The little drops brought such a welcome sleep. They can wrap you in a fog where the searing pain becomes a dull ache …."

"… and the dreaded heartache becomes an indolent worry for an hour or two," Mrs. Cutney moaned. "The treasured two drops became four and I used those four drops again and again several times every day."

"And when the doctor saw the contents of the vial diminish so rapidly, he gave you a stern lecture but repeated the receipt." Louisa knew this story, too.

"Each time the drug wore off, there was pain and longing, and the need for the medication loomed greater." Agnes tossed on the chair wiping her forehead with a twisted handkerchief. "The next time he was to visit and I saw the nearly empty vial, I knew that I could not bear the coming lecture nor the possibility of losing my one true respite."

"You found a willing pharmacist?"

Mrs. Cutney nodded, her eyes angry and then ashamed. "But soon my cravings increased and knew not the bounds of the pharmacy's business hours. That was when, in desperation, I went to the Five Points and began the clandestine procurement of my poison." Mrs. Cutney fell back, exhausted.

Herr Hahn returned not a half hour later with the eminent Doctor Knight from the Hospital for the Relief of the Ruptured and Crippled. *There could not be a more piteous or fitting name for an institution,* Louisa thought. She pressed Josef's hand gratefully and he turned discreetly to exit the room as she closed the door behind him. She was relieved that Josef had brought Dr. Knight, as he was renowned for his compassionate care of the most miserable, always with an eye to diet, comfort, exercise and gentle encouragement. Dr. Knight requested that Dr. Miller be present for the examination and consultation, for the care would unfold in his facility.

Agnes repeated her story to the two physicians. The kind consultant shook his head when she admitted the dose she had been taking. Dr. Miller was nonplussed. "My training and profession repudiates the use of any medicinals," he began, "but this suffering woman presents a pathetic case."

By this time Agnes was sweating, her eyes and nose running, her limbs twitching in agitation. Once or twice she held a handkerchief to her lips as if to squelch the nausea.

"It could be fatal to withdraw the opiate abruptly," said Dr. Knight. The two physicians agreed that a course of opiates, carefully administered in diminishing doses, would be required for the care of the patient.

"You must be watched vigilantly and the dose of laudanum carefully reduced. You will need an expert nurse to see you through this," Dr. Knight warned.

"I am a nurse." Louisa stepped forward. "And I will guard her like a sister."

So began the painful vigil. Agnes thrashed violently when the cramps and abdominal pain gripped her. Louisa had specific instructions to watch for prostration and feeble heartbeats and then to administer the deadly tincture in lessening amounts. Agnes begged for more to bring the relief and euphoria she craved, but Louisa guarded the little bottle firmly and set the limits.

Mrs. Miller let it be known that Agnes Cutney was indisposed but her condition was not contagious. If a scream or moan could be heard from behind the closed doors Mrs. Miller ensured her guests that it was from the grip of colic. Whenever Louisa asked for fresh sheets or a cooling compress to be brought up the proprietress glared at her as if this too had been brought on by Louisa's indiscriminate friendships.

Several days passed as the struggle in the sick room unfolded.

The seagulls, blown wildly off course, cried close to Louisa's window as she huddled inside, hovering over her charge. Louisa had become used to the blustery, damp winds of New York. Situated as it was at the mouth of two rivers that emptied into the Atlantic Ocean, the town was wracked by gales when the wind blew in the northeasterly direction. The inrushing tides flowed brackish up the west side of the island and seagulls shrieked mournfully as they were pushed on the gusts of the wind. The gulls landed on the docks and waited for the wind to shift and find a way back to the open sea, singing their plaintive air. Louisa found their call neither melodious nor comforting. But their melancholy calls brought Louisa to the window to look out at the dreary scene.

There was a cold drizzle. It was not a day to be out without an umbrella. She studied the people struggling in the wind and rain, heads down, mufflers pulled over their chins. One face looked up through the driven rain. A solitary boy, poorly dressed for the weather, stood with his cap soaked and his collar turned up against the elements. He trod back and forth across the street, the same ten steps, to and fro. She recognized him as the loud-mouthed ruffian who had interrupted her lunch with Casey several weeks ago. He clapped gloveless hands against his arms to warm them and stamped his feet, looking about him and always glancing at the door of the Miller Hotel then up to the second floor window of Mrs. Miller's room.

He looked impatient at first, then alarmed, and finally, utterly miserable. He started across the street as if to address his concerns to the proprietress and then returned to stamp his beat.

"Agnes," Louisa said, "your messenger is here."

The woman moaned anew and pulled the pillow over head. "I have told them never to come here. That is why I always collected the infernal toxin myself. I cannot bear this humiliation, nor this torment."

Louisa grabbed her Macintosh, taking care to put the medicine vial in her pocket, slipped out of the room and charged down the stoop and across the street. The boy looked startled and made as if to run, but Louisa stopped him with her rebuke.

"I know you! You are that sassy leader of the gang of hooligans who likes to pick on smaller boys! I see you have gotten yourself into a bigger situation than you can handle."

"I am only here to collect a debt, lady, so I don't know what sityation yer goin' on about."

"Precisely that. Your lady customer has up and left. She told me you would be coming and you are to know that she does not need your … product … anymore."

The boy blanched. "I am ruined! I'll be strung up for sure if I don't collect the money she owes! It's bad enough how they treat me when I lose a customer, but not to get the money for services rendered … a chap can run, but they will find me anywhere."

Louisa put her hand on the boy's shoulder to comfort and steady him. His scrappy veneer was cracking, uncovering a child who was fearful, quaking and abused, another blameless child lost in the underside of the city.

"We will get you the money, but you should take this as a turning point and get out of your line of business. I see that you are not ruined yet. With the right place and structure, you could become a useful lad." She pulled her tiny writer's pad and pencil from her pocket and began to write, then tore off the page and offered it to the soaked boy. "Don't go back to those people tonight. See this lady tomorrow morning and she will set you up. Be ready to work honestly and fairly and you will get on."

The sneer on the boy's face turned incredulous, and then with embarrassment and relief, he took the scrap of paper on which Louisa had scribbled Mrs. Gibbons's address.

"I got so far down … that there didn't seem anything left to me …." His voice faltered. "Thank you, miss," he said simply but the sob that choked him tore at Louisa's core. He scampered away in the rain. Louisa wondered which hovel or basement he would slink into tonight, and hoped that his resolve remained with him in the morning. She doubted her scrap of paper could change his life. Her heart wanted to run after him, but her responsibility remained with her patient on the second floor of the Miller Hotel.

That evening, Agnes slept fitfully. The ordeal had left Louisa's stamina stretched to the limit of exhaustion, her nerves frayed so that her very hair seemed to ache. She splashed her face with cool water and looked into the small mirror on Agnes's dressing table. Her eyes were bleary and her head throbbed. A solitary lamp flickered in the far corner of the room and in the soft gloom the reflection wavered. Looking back at her, Louisa saw the haggard face, teary eyes and sunken mouth of an opium addict. The stoppered bottle was at her fingertips. Louisa knew the ecstasy and welcome oblivion it offered. She glanced at the stuporous woman and with trembling fingers grabbed the bottle in both hands.

A moment later she stood at Josef's door, banging wildly. No matter that it was the middle of the night, no matter that she looked a fright and he was in his nightcap, she needed a respite somewhere. He stood placid and sturdy, his broad, calm face encouraging Louisa. Only his strength and integrity would protect her.

"Josef, take this vial from me! I am so weary I am frightening myself. I can't be near this accursed potion a moment longer." Louisa was explaining too much or maybe not enough or maybe she need make no explanation at all.

Josef took her face in his hands, and looking into her eyes, steadied her. "You are not only filled with the charity, but also great courage. To face illness is hard, but to face demons is agony." Was he speaking of Mrs. Cutney's demons or her own? Louisa slumped against his broad chest. She wanted his arms to embrace her and stop the shivering in her soul. Instead, Josef pushed back a loose strand of her thick hair and lightly kissed her forehead. "The kind nurse has devoted so much to her patient that she is beginning to suffer. Let me do the goot vork tonight and keep the vigil by the sick and you vill call for a hot brandy and take a very deep sleep," he said, putting her gently aside.

Louisa trembled again and wiped her nose with the back of her hand. "There, there," Josef crooned, taking her by the shoulders. "Thees vork is too hard. I have been a fool to leave you for so many days with thees worry." She wobbled from weariness and strain. His arm was strong around her waist, supporting her. His soft brown

235

eyes showed concern and disquiet. Or was it heartbreak? She felt she should speak now. He bolstered her, he assuaged her, he comforted her.

"Josef, I—"

"—am too tired to talk now," he finished.

"Josef, you," she began again.

"—are as solid as a bear and vill take thees burden tonight."

Why was he talking about a bear? She hadn't said anything about Professor Bhaer, had she? Exhaustion and stress were muddling her brain; she had not meant to say any of the things that he put into words. The headache and trembling had her in a state of confusion. Josef escorted her gently down the hallway, supporting her teetering frame and delivering her to her door.

"Rest," he whispered. "It vill be better in the morning."

Chapter 25

Transcendent

Not long after, Louisa and Josef attended to Agnes Cutney's farewell. She was leaving for a rest home recommended for cases like hers. The Davenport spinsters smirked and turned away when the white apparition of Mrs. Cutney passed down the stairs and out to the waiting carriage. Mrs. Miller hoped that some decorum would return to her establishment.

Louisa arranged the blankets around her patient's thin frame and gave her an encouraging hug. "You have survived the worst, Agnes. Remember that we are here for you when you need us, myself and Josef …." How naturally she had put herself and Josef together as a pair.

In the ensuing days, the decorum Mrs. Miller sought still did not reign over the hotel. A new sound of tramping feet and lively salutations came from the front hall. Louisa sat in the library, but the constant racket of the doorbell made her throw her book aside to go see about the commotion. Rebecca escorted a young man to the parlor and the doorbell rang again. At the sound of the third insistent ring Mrs. Miller threw open the front door herself. She looked at the disheveled, bohemian young man up and down and sighed.

"Are you here for Miss Alcott or Mr. Hahn?"

Louisa thought that her literary and theatrical acquaintances were a tad more polished than Augustine's dissident friends, but Mrs. Miller seemed to lump all the new callers in one bundle and labelled it "peculiar." Lately, the young men who flocked to the hotel parlor in the afternoons came in broad brimmed hats, slouching boots and fraying capes. They bore on their faces earnest and wild expressions and in their arms, canvases wrapped in dirty linen. They monopolized the parlor for an hour or two, gesticulating urgently, arguing, debating or emoting.

Louisa found the Davenport sisters chortling behind the door to the salon, eavesdropping and shaking their heads. "I believe they are anarchists," whispered the thin one. "I hear them expostulating about a 'manifesto' and a 'New Age.'"

"No, they are thieves, planning a heist," said the portly one. "I am certain they mentioned a 'huge breakthrough' and are very determined to get it."

"It's worse than you ladies have imagined," Louisa said, passing by them to join in the parlor conversation. "These gents are from Bleecker Street." The two ladies looked shocked and bustled away, either to preserve their dignity or alert the others that libertines from the artistic boarding houses to the south had invaded.

At the center of the tempest sat Augustine, focused and absorbed, discoursing vehemently and pointing out the advances and discoveries inherent in the canvas put before him. The young men had learned that Augustine was espousing work done outside of a studio in the open air, depicting the play of light and the change of atmosphere. They scrutinized his canvases and urged him to go further. "You're on the brink of a masterpiece, man."

"Don't back off—you need to go further."

This talk worried Louisa for after they left, Augustine seemed in a fever to begin a new painting, a painting that would need to be completed without stopping, to capture the very light of the moment. He pushed himself hurriedly into the cold December weather and ended up panting and gasping for breath, spent and weak.

238

Louisa saw his unmistakable deterioration. His legs had begun to swell. He could not lie down for rest, but needed to be propped on two or three large cushions to keep his head above his heart. "His heart ees failing, Dr. Miller says," Josef confided. "First, his kidneys do not vork, then the veakness in the heart cannot keep up with the fluids and the lungs collect the vater. It's like drowning vithout a pool."

"I have seen digitalis used for this," Louisa offered.

"This he tried, but the nausea and loosening of the bowels was too severe."

"Morphine, then, will ease his breathing." Despite the tragedy of Mrs. Cutney's addiction, Augustine had no such possibility, for his life was nearing the end.

"He wants to vork too much. The morphine makes him groggy so that he vill not take it in the daytime. He vill take the relief only at night."

Louisa finally begged Augustine to stop painting outside in the wan winter light. "I am certain that the gaslight glow on a young woman's skin would be just as glorified a subject as a setting sun, Augie. Look about you for suitable models."

Augustine began work on a huge canvas, a double portrait. It was usual for Matilda to be found reclining on the divan in the parlor, her daughter at her side, reading aloud to her mama, or the two lying in each other's arms, turning the pages of a new fashion edition. Matilda was the perfect model, for her own frailty kept her listless and static on the couch. The stillness of her body was belied by her piercing look which seemed to search into the unknown, into the afterlife, into infinity.

The winter sunlight came through the sheer gauze window panels from the right and cast a ghostly white on the face of the ailing woman. Her deep blue dress contrasted with the pastels of the slipcover. She held a book in her hands but stared out the window. The girl huddled at Matilda's side, her plump legs tucked beneath her, her little arm flung up beside her mother on the couch. Helene's head angled downward, concentrating on the words as she read aloud. Another glow, the firelight which was out of the plane of the painting, colored her face with a ruddy brilliance. The two were side by side but seemed to breathe two different atmospheres, each to be made of different flesh.

"It's beautiful," Louisa marveled.

"It's not my masterpiece," Augustine announced firmly.

Nighttime scenes began to interest him. He captured Rebecca and Helene during their stairway studies. He focused most of all on the darkness surrounding their little halo of light, as if the girls were safe for the moment, unaware of the gloom pressing on them from all sides. He kept an easel near his bed and dabbed tiny paint sketches of smokey shadows in his room. Herr Hahn, keeping late nights as he studied for his examinations, allowed Augustine to paint him by candlelight while he concentrated on the tome before him, seemingly oblivious to observation. The small sketches that Augustine produced frightened Louisa. Josef's frank countenance was there, his concentration, even his magnanimity. But she could not discern in these doleful sketches Josef's sturdy vigor, his optimism, nor his energetic, busy temperament. They were stunning works of genius, but there was something so mournful and so sinister lurking about the edges and creases that Louisa could not bear to look at them.

Louisa liked to keep Augustine company now that he worked indoors in the afternoons. They would sit together at the window of his workroom, he behind his easel, she in a comfortable chair, her writing box on her lap, each dabbing and jotting as their inspiration flashed. When they worked together, the energy of the universe seemed to center around them.

Louisa kept up a scant chain of chatter just to be good company as she scribbled a few thoughts on paper and Augustine assaulted his canvas. "Your mother will be happy to see you next week when you return for Christmas," she said. " I am sure she's missed you dreadfully. It will be a grand homecoming."

A grunt in response and then the constant *dab, pause, wipe, dab, dab,*

240

dab, splash from behind the easel.

The mismatched brotherhood of the young American and middle-aged Teuton were becoming increasingly dear to her. "I am thinking of how you are the inverse of my famous character, Teddy Lawrence. You have a European father and an American mother," Louisa said to the back of the canvas.

"And how I yearn to amble around Europe in pursuit of my masterpiece," Augustine replied, smacking his fist on his swollen knee, which elicited a grimace.

"Have you read my girls' book, too, Augustine?"

"There's something for everyone there," he answered. "For us men, we plunge on to see which fine March girl Laurie will win."

"Like a prize in a game. Don't taunt me, sir; it's the part I am the least fond of."

Louisa liked the charged atmosphere of genius that seemed to fill the room in Augustine's presence. She wished some of it would inspire her. But today, the character sketch she was working on would not come. She put her papers aside. Louisa stood to stretch and catch a glimpse of Augie's painting. His window faced west and the sunglow was visible over the slate rooftops of Twenty-Sixth Street.

"That light, you've captured it! It's brilliant—sublime, I would say."

He continued dabbing, sweating and gasping. She wiped his brow with a damp cloth, and he kissed her palm in return. His face was deeply anguished.

"My brother, has he ... spoken to you?" he asked softly.

Louisa stood still, as if hesitating on a threshold. Safety lay in the space where she stood and uncertainty across the brink. "Spoken in what way?" Louisa asked.

"I see he has not," Augustine replied. "It is not my place to mention it. It is like Josef to be so ... taciturn. But for me, being perhaps so close to ... eternity ... I see things more clearly, more urgently."

Louisa sat down. Her heart pounded, making her ears burn. She took some deep breaths to calm herself. She settled back in the streams of the sunglow. Could she dare to believe what Josef would profess? When he spoke, who would respond—the public or the private Louisa? She needed to know, right now, who she was. She might be the successful authoress, the ardent suffragist, or the humble weaver of homepeace.

Her heroines never relied on intuition. They used their wits, their intelligence and their savvy to solve dilemmas. Louisa was reasoning, as if she could puzzle her way to an answer. For once, to believe that what she felt in her soul was the truth, that she might perceive, without fully understanding, her true self and the best answer. She suddenly grasped the philosophy her father and his friends had tried to make the world understand. To trust the spirit, find the truth within. *If he speaks, I will be open. I will not argue. I will listen.*

Augustine adjusted the strap on his orthotic device. He mixed his gold and orange colors and dabbed lightly. "It's curious," he whispered. "My point of light is receding further and further away. This luster seems to taper to infinity, almost drawing me forward into a tunnel of radiance."

Louisa saw his face illuminated, as if the sunglow from his canvas reflected celestial beams. "The light, it is so magnificent … it seems to buoy me above the room," he gasped. Louisa looked at him, alarmed, for she knew that the exertion was extreme and his wild talk reminded her of the passage that her sister Beth had faced. He was still dabbing, dabbing, creating his masterpiece. Louisa picked up her pen and began scrawling, her fingers flying.

"Augie, I think I have it!" she announced, as she wrote with her heart. "One can't reason about everything. I realize the only thing is to be transcendent! Transcendent!" There was no response from behind the canvas. "Augie? Augie?"

"Transcendent" was the last word she spoke to him. Augustine's head slumped forward on his chest, the tip of the paintbrush strapped to his withered hand still reflecting the color of the setting sun and the radiance he had achieved.

242

Chapter 26

The Finest Christmas Eve

Josef had promised to have Augustine home by Christmas.

"I never thought the boxes I vould send to Albany for Christmas vould be so burdensome or so sad," he said to Louisa as they set out on a snowy day to accompany his brother on the first leg of his final journey home. Josef had decided that he would not travel to the Albany home he had never entered. "It will not comfort the grieving mother to know that this lumbering old seed of her husband carries on while her young son lies in a casket," he said to Louisa.

Louisa walked arm in arm with the grieving brother to the depot. They began in overcast skies that soon opened up to a soft, light snow flurry. The snow swirled lightly, dappling the atmosphere with white and silver, sterling sparkles that lay on their shoulders and their hat brims. "Augie's here with us, Josef," Louisa said, "for I never saw snow like this before. It's his eyes that help me see this wonderland of color, more gorgeous than nature itself."

The children walked solemnly along with the carriage that carried Augustine's coffin. They had been the models for most of Augustine's last compositions, and their sorrowful countenances reflected the way he portrayed them in his last days. "I have the last painting carefully wrapped and vill keep it in my sight for mein whole life, but I worry about the large paintings that I cannot safely send with him,"

Josef said. "Those paintings that Augie gave his life for."

"I am sure that Mrs. Botta will be able to help place them in a prominent gallery. And Augustine's disciples will see to it that his work is not forgotten," Louisa reassured him. The buildings before them seemed nearly to evaporate, almost to melt into the atmosphere, nebulous and indefinite in the glittering brightness. They had reached Grand Central Station. Augustine had never come back to paint his vision of its shining display at nighttime. The pale sun on the snow-covered glass panes refracted into shades of gray, violet and taupe, mottling the marble floor of the waiting room.

"You're right," Josef sighed. "I see Augustine here, too."

Robert, faithful to the last, bowed slightly to Josef and said, "May I extend my condolences once again?"

Josef grasped Robert's hand and elbow and held on empathically. "Mein goot man! You have been the actual brother with your care and sympathy to our Augustine. Never would I deny that your loss is greater than mine!"

Robert's face showed his anguish only for a moment. He cleared his throat, turned to his sad duty, and left. Josef watched the casket disappear down the platform, with misted eyes.

Louisa pressed her lips close to the rumpled head bowed down in sorrow beside her. She whispered, "Always, you will see him in the blush of spring, the waving grasses of summer and the vibrancy of autumn. He's not suffering now. Don't you suffer too much. You have done all you could." In truth, she had suffered this same loss and found that she sometimes felt closer to her Beth now than before she died.

Returning to the hotel, the tiny funeral cortege filed solemnly by the empty wooden wheelchair that Augustine had left behind. "Thees children need something to lift them up," Josef mumbled to Louisa. But her own spirit was hurting for her friend's loss—and her own, for she was already missing Augustine dreadfully.

A few solemn days later, in the quiet part of the afternoon when the Bath Hotel's guests were napping or relaxing after their treatments, Louisa heard the front door slam. This was followed by some hushed giggles, a thud and the sound of something being dragged across the parlor floor.

"It sounds like some insane caper is being enacted in the parlor." She smiled. Throwing off her writing cap and pushing her papers aside, Louisa's curiosity led her down the hallway to investigate.

As she descended the curved stairway, a whiff of pine wafted up the front hall steps. The giggles came in louder peals, interrupted by grunts and pants. Poking her head into the parlor, she saw Rebecca and Herr Hahn wrestling with a shrouded carcass. With the last knots of rope conquered, the limbs of a feathery evergreen tree stretched out to engulf half the room.

"Josef, that is the most magnificent Christmas tree I have ever seen!" Louisa nearly leapt into the parlor. She loved Christmas, though her Massachusetts upbringing had not included a decorated tree in the house. Seeing the tree, the sheepish look on Josef's face, the wide eyes and parted lips expressing Rebecca's excitement, Louisa was overcome with sentimental thoughts of the family at home and this misfit pair in front of her who were secreting a giant tree into a health establishment.

"What do you imagine Mrs. Miller will say about this?" Louisa chuckled softly.

"There cannot be a woman so cold that she vill reject the joy thees vill bring to the children," Josef answered. "And not only the children, it is mein own joy that I make, as vell." Josef's timid look turned dewy-eyed and Louisa knew the loss he felt. Christmas meant family, and he had just been wrenched from the brother he knew too little. He seemed to be wistful, almost disconsolate for something he could not obtain.

"I have a fresh basket of apples to string up on the boughs," Louisa interjected too jovially. "And let's ask Lizzie to pop some corn for the garland. We can make a shopping trip for some treats to add to the tree and I am sure Mrs. Miller will allow us some of her candles." Josef's mood began to brighten. She and Rebecca bundled up joyfully to procure the purchases. "Put your endearing charm to good use, Josef. Get to work on our proprietress." She winked at him as they went out the door.

That evening when the doors were thrown open to the parlor, Mrs. Miller *was* smiling and the guests were astounded at the sight of the glistening tree, bedecked with wreaths of popcorn, apples, oranges, sugary hearts and gingerbreads, sets of mittens and horns of candy, little toy whistles and ducks that could squeak. The children clapped their hands and reached for the treasures. The adults congratulated Herr Hahn on his achievement and Dr. Miller proposed a toast with some sparkling cider, making the evening a decidedly festive one for the Hygienic Institute all around.

After dinner, Louisa approached Josef as he stood beside the cheery fireplace, his hands clasped behind his back, head tilted as he peered intently, surveying his success. His eyes were devouring the tree, eating it up with his gaze, inhaling it with his senses, hungry for the sight and smell of this sparkling and fragrant pine. "You must miss your home very much at this time of year," Louisa said, softly touching his arm.

"There are many things I vill miss soon, too," he said, passing his hand before his eyes. His usual vitality seemed quenched. Then he looked at her with such a doleful glance that her heart shuddered. His eyes were more than sad. They were sunken with worry and fatigue.

"My colleagues vant to celebrate with me thees night because I have passed my bar exam," he said, recovering his genial demeanor.

"Josepf! How can you be so humble about something so wonderful? Why didn't you tell us sooner?"

"We had our sadness here and there is just so much more to be done, so much to try to do, and my part may be so leetle. But tonight we celebrate. Vill you come as my guest?"

"There is nowhere I would rather be this Christmas Eve," Louisa said sincerely. Truly she felt drawn to his side, though she did not know if her role would be to celebrate or support him.

It was a perfect Christmas Eve as they stepped out together, for a light snow had begun to fall and their breath shone before them in wispy puffs of frost. The gentle carpet of snow silenced the city sounds as their carriage took them down the Bowery to "Kleindeutschland," the German quarter.

"Do you know that this 'Leetle Germany' has more people speaking the German tongue than most towns in mein Fatherland?" Josef told her. "Perhaps you spend a year in thees four hundred busy blocks and never vill hear a word of English." The street signs here were in German and everywhere Louisa caught the sounds of the sweet German accent. She could also see the reflection of German industry as they passed the establishments of shoemakers and tailors, upholsterers, furniture and piano makers. Unlike the glitz and commerce of Broadway, the Bowery was the avenue of the working class. Here were dry goods shops, cigar shops, ready made clothing and hardware stores. Fruit vendors stocked for the Christmas celebration displayed rich profusions of exotic grapes, juicy pears and vibrant oranges all from some tropical clime. The confectioners and the toy stores had dragged half their wares out to the street, setting up booths as quaint and picturesque as any German *Christkindlesmarkt.*

"Josef, I feel as if I have been whisked off to Dusseldorf," Louisa cried as the soft snow fell on her lashes and the sounds of cranking organs and hearty voices raised in song reached their muffled ears. They passed an array of festive beer halls, lager saloons and music halls. She was charmed by the gaiety of the crowds strolling in and out of the buildings, bedecked with bright scarves and top hats. Others, ready to celebrate the holiday, hurried homeward, their baskets laden with delicious treats and packages under their arms. Children tried to collect enough soft snow to start a miniature snowball fight.

The pair alighted at the Atlantic Gardens, the most renowned beer hall in the city. Families, couples, groups of young friends streamed in and out of the gigantic doors which entered into a huge vestibule filled with booths selling food and small gifts from Bavaria. This lead into an even larger hall, where great chandeliers illuminated the boisterous scene.

"I admit I have never been in a beer hall or tavern before," Louisa hesitated.

"Not a tavern, no—no, thees is the wrong idea. In the *biergarten* we have only family joy here, no drunkenness. You vill see," Josef protested.

Louisa stepped into the immense vaulted hall, easily accommodating three thousand people, all eating, drinking, conversing and laughing. This was not a tavern serving tipsy dandies or licentious old sots. The beer hall was a lively family resort where neighbors gathered together to celebrate and relax, play dominoes or billiards, sing and dance. The glowing chandeliers and flaming brackets along the walls lit the full arch of the curved ceiling, frescoed in Old World splendor. Apart from that luxury, the place was plain, practical and clean, a right reflection of the lives and character of the people who enjoyed it. The floor was sanded bare and the tables were rung with simple, sturdy high-backed wooden benches. Thousands of friends and well-wishers swarmed about the tables, along with their tidy children.

Josef's friends and colleagues gave him a rousing cheer as he approached their table. The wives and daughters drew Louisa into their kinship and offered her a stout glass of *gluhwein*, the festive wine mulled with spices of the season, and passed around heaping trays of *lebkuchen*, the holiday cookie. The spicy, warm gingerbread with its hint of honey and a hard sugar glaze combined all the favored flavors of Louisa's childhood. She looked about contentedly. "This drink is already warming my cheeks," Louisa said to her hosts.

"Yah, you glow like the wine," said a friendly old woman, and she shifted across the bench to let Louisa slide beside her to enjoy the music and festivities. Louisa watched Josef greet his countrymen with warm embraces. The men stood arm in arm together in an intimate, brotherly way as they conversed. She compared this to the ways of American men, who would have stifled their emotions into a loud *hello*, a clap on the shoulder or a stiff handshake.

A giant orchestrion, immense enough to fill the whole room with sound, pumped out folk music with a throbbing beat. Couples danced to the polkas that groaned through the pipes. Louisa had never been a dancer. Though she might thump out the tempo frantically with her toe, her limbs would fly all akimbo when she tried to take a whirl. She waved Josef away with a laugh and he grabbed a wholesome young shop girl for a spin on the dance floor. Louisa turned to a little one at her knee and to the child's delight, engaged in a cheerful game of pat-a-cake.

To the right of the orchestrion, on a balcony above the dance floor, was a small band heavy with brass instruments. The tuba and accordion had prominent positions, as required by Teutonic folk music. The maestro tapped his baton and the entire atrium hushed. Only a few sweet notes were necessary, and then the room vibrated with the voices of all. Their songs gave voice to treasured melodies, the well-known airs of their homeland. "Lutherhymne" and "Das Deutsche Vaterland" were sung first. Christmas carols followed, familiar tunes filled with nostalgia. All raised their voices to sing "O Tannenbaum" and, prayerfully and hopefully, the simple "Stille Nacht." Neighbor turned to neighbor, parents to their children, lovers to their dearests. They seemed inspired by the beauty of the old traditions and the hope of the season. "Peace on Earth," one man wished aloud. It seemed that anything was possible on Christmas.

Louisa looked for Josef's face. Not finding him among those at the table, she roamed the grand hall slowly. At one end of the hall was a sparkling Christmas tree, adorned with the special German glass globes that reflected the brilliant candlelight. At its base was a charming nativity scene. Kneeling before it, Josef's head was bent, his lips moving silently. He seemed, in his deep devotion, to be petitioning his Creator for something in a most fervent way. His brow was wet with sweat and his cheeks glistened with a few errant tears. He shifted heavily, took a deep breath and crossed himself. Though he had worked for the Catholic cause in Germany, the thought that he was of that religious minority had never occurred to her. For the second time that evening, his energy seemed spent. And for the second time, he passed his hand across his face, closing his eyes. He kept his palm against his lips for a moment, lost in thought.

Louisa stepped to his side and placing her hand on his shoulder, said, "You have a great sorrow that troubles you. Tell me, if it will lighten your burden."

"Ah, it's just that there is so much to do and not enough time," was the sad response, as Josef gestured for her to kneel beside him. The brown eyes were filled with such an expression of sadness and submission that Louisa longed to nestle his head on her shoulder and provide the comfort that she had always given to her wounded boys in the war. *Wounded—that is what he is*, she thought. *Could it be that he is ill?*

"Josef, are you well?" She searched his face.

He shifted his eyes, glancing downward over the wood carved figures of the Holy Family in a desperate way. Then he sighed. "Louisa, I have been distant with you. I am suffering from a tumor that cannot be healed. I came to the Hygienic Hotel with the leetle hope that the cure would rejuvenate me, and it has. It has allowed me to continue my vork for thees months," he said, then added hesitatingly, "and to meet you."

"It cannot be a fatal tumor. I do not believe that! Look at you, look at your strength! There is a not a sign of illness about you," Louisa chaffed. "And besides, there are other types of treatments. You must not rely on this water therapy to cure you; it's for nerves and muscle aches, not for malignancies. You should see a surgeon. You need a medical evaluation. I will take you to Boston, where the great hospitals are …."

250

Josef placed his finger on her lips. "I have done all that, mein Engel. It is quite, quite hopeless. That is why I need to vork all the more swiftly and devote myself to the leetle bit I do while I can. That is why I cannot be to you everything I could have hoped." Josef's eyes looked deeply into hers and Louisa clung more closely to his side. If only her sympathy and strength could change his fate.

"Josef, you are Catholic. Perhaps your faith will help."

The afflicted man shook his head. "I am not knowing anymore what I am. I am so lost sometimes."

"Don't give up on your belief in the sweet stories and the promises of eternal life, even when those stories seem only a shadow of a truth," Louisa said. "Come. I have someone who can help you, I am sure."

The night had turned still and starry, as they bundled under a blanket in the coach that sped uptown to Fifty-Ninth Street. The doors of the Catholic church were just opening to release the joyful believers after the celebration of the midnight mass. The choir was still lingering over the final notes of the "Alleluia" and the pastor was shaking the last parishioner's hand.

"Come and meet Father Hecker. He has faced all the most piercing questions and has come out serene." Louisa drew Josef up the broad steps.

Father Isaac Hecker stood tall and placid at the top of the stairs. He was thin and pale and bespeckled, but his blue eyes gleamed as clear as the daytime sky. His long beard and pockmarked face shone calm and nearly mystical. "Isaac, it is Louisa," she said. "We need your counsel."

When Louisa was a child, it was Isaac Hecker who had sought the counsel and good will of the Alcott family. He was a young man when he came to Fruitlands, torn between a philosophical and a religious passion. Louisa was a topsy-turvy girl running in the copse on the ridge behind the homestead. She knew immediately, even then, that Isaac was different—saner perhaps, though he was even less of

251

this world than the others.

Now, standing on the snow-driven steps, the clerical man spread his arms in welcome. "Louisa, I would recognize you in a moment. Your eyes are still as sparkling and your voice as clear and unambiguous as in those summer days in Utopia." Louisa and Father Isaac embraced.

"I have often thought back to the blissful picture of family life on that farm and remember those four energetic girls and their dutiful mother. You women were the towering achievement of the place."

"You were with us in the summertime, Father, our idyllic heyday before the troubles set in."

"A-ha! I always said there was not enough fruit on those trees for the name of your colony! But you have weathered those trials well, I see. Tell me about your mother and father," he said, drawing them into the warm, candlelit foyer of the church.

"My mother remembers you as the only considerate man who, after working harder than any of the philosophers in the fields, still had the energy to come into the kitchen and knead bread with the women," Louisa reminisced.

"And your father, he thought I was not devoted enough to the philosophy, that I was interested in the world too much," Father Hecker replied. "I was a young man … I still liked to eat," he joked.

Louisa felt Josef move close to her side. "At times your face would glow with ecstasy, and I sensed your serenity," Louisa said to the pastor. "It gave me some peace and stability to have you there, for even with your visions and mystical experiences, you seemed more grounded than the others."

"In the end, the misguided social missions failed me. I suppose I was not looking to reform relationships on earth, but man's relationship to God," said the priest. "I found the best path to God here in the Catholic Church." The cleric looked down at his white robes. "Yet, you see, I still dress like your eccentric Plato, in a white linen tunic." The thin face smiled.

"So, Isaac, are you a Catholic or a Transcendentalist?" Louisa asked.

"Child, you know too well that before I entered the seminary I lived with your Mr. Thoreau. But now the Pope has appointed me to convene my priests in a new order."

"A new order ...." Louisa repeated softly. The very same words that Miriam Leslie had said to her, yet with a totally different meaning. *Maybe the words Josef had said could be turned a different way too,* she thought desperately,

"Father, my friend Herr Hahn needs your advice," Louisa said, gently drawing Josef's arm through hers. They stood together as if to face the priest's benediction.

"How can I help you, my son?" The gentle minister leaned closer, ready to give counsel.

Josef looked almost shamefaced from Louisa to the priest, then looked plantively at Louisa to rescue him. "I may have brought Josef here for help too insistently," Louisa said. "I'm famous for that."

"Just like your dear mother, Louisa." The priest's serene gaze held her in his warmth for another moment. "Always following the philosophy of simple charity."

Louisa scoffed and waved away his attention. This wasn't about her. It was Josef who needed guidance. The contemplative cleric smiled gently at her as if she was still the angry girl who roamed the hills and wrote furiously in her journal to relieve her mind of doubt.

"My child, I have long wanted to tell you that your four little women trooping through the snow on Christmas morning to bring their breakfast to the poor German family, your Mr. March going off to minister to the souls of the war wounded, your Marmee suppressing her anger every day, your Beth visiting the sick, even dying from the contagion she contracted, they taught more people about our Lord Christ than all my energetic sermons across this whole country have. Your March family is charity in action."

Louisa wavered slightly on Josef's arm. This religious man had read her book as a spiritual tale. Perhaps people were finding messages and levels of intent in her simple story that spoke to them in ways that Louisa had not fathomed. *The same words, but a different meaning.* She had always seen *Little Women* as a saccharin rendition of her own upbringing. But what if an upbringing among philosophers, abolitionists and literary geniuses had caused her to produce something extraordinary? She had written hurriedly, almost furiously, biting at the indignation of writing a book for girls. She did it because of the expectation that it would be popular enough to pay some bills. She did it because Mr. Niles promised to publish her father's *Tablets* as a concession to her efforts. She did it because once the memories were recalled she could not stop herself from spinning the sadness into poignancy and the heartache into heartsease. She had come to assuage Josef's need and had found her doubts about her own worth erased.

Josef was pressing her hand and smiling at her. His twinkling eyes signaled pride and his firm grasp gave her encouragement. But there could be no such comfort for him. "Father, my friend is dying," she said bluntly.

"And I find my faith is not so strong as I vill need," Josef sighed.

The gentle giant turned to Josef and placed his hand on the ailing man's head. "I will bless you and ask the Lord to keep you for as long as is His wish," he said. "I myself have been diagnosed with leukemia." Louisa gasped at the thought of another hale man oppressed with disease. "That was five years ago," he said with a smile. "And the Lord is not done with me yet."

He drew Josef into the soaring caverns of the church, advancing through the shadows and stopping in the gentle halo of light that surrounded them at the foot of the grand altar. Father Hecker grasped Josef's hand, encircled his slumping shoulders, and bowing their heads together they began to pray.

Chapter 27

A New Way to Spend Christmas

New York weather never promised to be delightful in December, but Christmas morning dawned particularly chilly, wet and windy. Louisa woke with a heavy heart and wondered if she could stay in bed, avoiding the holiday completely. She pulled the covers off her head and looked out the window at the gray clouds streaking across the sky. She knew that today there would be no soft, glistening snow to coat the gritty truths she had uncovered. She wanted to pull the bedclothes over her head and avoid thinking about the unjustness of Josef's diagnosis. So many people were suffering physically right within her circle: Josef, Matilda, Marchesa Contini, Agnes Cutney and even Father Hecker. She rolled over, looked at her silver watch and groaned. She had promised to meet Mrs. Gibbons at ten o'clock and wondered if she would have the stamina to do the deed she had promised. She had agreed to go with the good Quaker woman to Randall's Island and spread Christmas cheer among the orphans there.

Today was the date of Mrs. Gibbons's annual outing to distribute the dolls, toys and books she had assembled on her dining room table for months. When Louisa had volunteered, the thought of enlivening the scene at the orphanage was appealing. But now that the day had arrived, leaden and threatening to match her hopeless mood, she grumbled to herself about the commitment. It would be a frigid ferry ride to Randall's Island and the stops would include the idiot asylum as well. As she stepped out into the wind, Louisa thought she was a complete philistine compared to Mrs. Gibbons. The dear old woman had been bringing joy and hope to hundreds of sick and abandoned children for thirty years. Surely Louisa could not begrudge one day.

Louisa rushed over to the East River wharves, the city shrouded in fog, her only bearings the endless grid which discharged her at the far eastern edge of the island. The miserable last block, which headed toward "The Charity Pier," skirted the city hospital: the gloomy granite building incongruously named Bellevue. The last block was usually populated by the most destitute beings in the city. Today, it was empty.

This easternmost edge of the same Twenty-Sixth Street on which the Miller Hotel stood was called Misery Lane between First Avenue and the river. Here, the infirm, the alcoholic, the insane and the destitute would line the street toward the piers, hoping for transport to the hospitals and almshouse on the islands of the East River. Mrs. Gibbons had warned her that the Department of Charities and Corrections ran the only boats that were permitted to access the institutions, spread over three islands, north of Fiftieth Street and stretching nearly to the Bronx. Three times each week, a little steamer left the pier with no clamoring crowds, only bearing the unmarked coffins which were slated for burial in Potter's Field.

She met Mrs. Gibbons on the dock, along with a small entourage of helpers. A savvy activist, the good Quaker invited the press to cover the event. Usually she had the mayor or the commissioner of health along on the outing, but this year she had as her golden carrot a full-fledged celebrity.

"Gentlemen," Mrs. Gibbons announced, "I am delighted to tell you that Miss Louisa May Alcott is participating in our work today." The little horde of newspapermen crowded about Louisa.

"Would you say that Christmas won't be Christmas without any presents?" asked one cheekily.

"Are you intending to become a patron of the charity institutions here?" asked another. Louisa, embarrassed as always by the attention, only nodded and smiled at the reporters, but gave them no usable quotes, causing them to start again with a round of unanswerable questions.

As soon as they were aboard, Mrs. Gibbons tackled the rotund commissioner with a little sermon about issues related to the children's welfare. She had captured him in a position from which he could not escape, and she demanded his full attention for the entire ride. The reporters tried to get Louisa to make a statement but she waved them toward her hostess. Let them question the commissioner about his budgets and Mrs. Gibbons about her needs. She deflected the attention to the plight of the orphans.

The fog was thick and haunting. "We'll be helped by the lighter traffic on the river today, due to the holiday," said the captain before they departed. "We cannot even see our destination just ahead in the river."

The clouds seemed to cast a mournful shadow on the specter of the unpitied dead, the faceless lives that had been ferried across these waters. The masts and hulls of ships appeared out of nowhere and the boat skirted ominous chunks of ice conjured by the cold winter weather. The deep knell of a buoy, a sharp whistle and the lapping sounds of a paddle wheel all reached Louisa's expectant ears before any rivercraft came into view. Sailing vessels glided silently by on their way to the Long Island Sound. Across the river, the mansions of ship captains lined the waterfront at Hallett's Cove, while at the Manhattan docks, passenger steamers hovered like rocking palaces.

Arriving at Randall's Island, Louisa spied a familiar slouched cap and freckled face descending the steep steps from the pilothouse. "Merry Christmas, Miss Louisa!" Casey greeted her.

What is this clever ragamuffin up to? she thought. *Hitching a ride on Christmas morning to the most dismal acreage of the city?*

"So you will be my escort and bodyguard even on this pious holiday, Casey. Do you never take a moment's rest?"

"Well, I've got better things to do than loll about on a day off. Besides, it was capital being on the top of the ferry. Did you hear me sound the horn?" Casey shifted some small bundles under his arm and Louisa immediately recognized the brown parcels as those he had collected at the seamstress across from the post office two weeks before. His mission here was one that he had planned and not some sudden lark.

The arrival of the boat, the unloading of the boxes filled with sweets and goodies, the carriage brought round for Mrs. Gibbons and Louisa—all attracted the attention of a few older boys. These poor chaps had been too long in the orphanage and waited year in and out for the arrival of the sweet, motherly woman who brought them one day of joy. They ran ahead to alert the others, one little hunchback leading the way, crying, "She's come! She's come!"

As they approached the chapel, Mrs. Gibbons gave Louisa a review of the hospitals and homes on the island. "This entire island is dedicated to the care of children. After our greeting in the chapel, we will go to the nursery," explained Mrs. Gibbons.

Mrs. Gibbons smiled encouragingly at Casey and Louisa. "We go to the idiot asylum afterwards. There are several hundred young people there. We say 'young people,' for most of them never achieve more than a toddler's understanding, though they can remain here up to age thirty. That is the hardest part of our work today. I hope thou will not be distressed by what will be seen." With Louisa's empathetic heart, there was no doubt that she *would* be distressed, but also that she would lend the most help she possibly could. Giving on Christmas was her family's tradition.

The chapel was warm and festive, with garlands of pine and candles blazing. The children burst into applause at the sight of

Mrs. Gibbons and she smiled at them like their own grandmothers would, if these abandoned little things had a memory of one so dear to them. Someone whispered that the tall lady with the thick hair was the mayor's wife, and so Louisa was able to relax in anonymity again. The children assembled in rows by size order to perform their songs and speeches. In front were the little girls in blue frocks and white aprons and the small lads in white pinafores; behind, the older girls wore pink calico and ribbons while the big boys wore gray suits. A bashful lad got up and recited a Christmas poem, which turned out to be the one Louisa had written for an anthology of children's verse, *The Horn of Plenty*, just published for that Christmas season. The words,

"Waiting, watching, listening always

With full hearts and tender eyes,"

described the scene in front of her. But as she scanned the faces, so many of the "tender eyes" were blighted, so many of the physiques defective.

The orphans who had made it to Randall's Island were the fortunate ones compared to the street children, for they were fed, clothed, educated and made ready for the trades. Still, Louisa pitied these misshapen, scrofulous children. Their parents might have died of hard toil or hard drinking, with fevers from tuberculosis or cholera, or damage from careless accidents or exposure. In short, their parents had died of poverty.

The children were served a special dinner of turkey and pudding, peas and corn, mashed potatoes and gravy. Louisa watched Casey scamper about the hall like an excited puppy. He was as attentive and encouraging to these poor children as he had been to those at the Newsboys' Home. He moved from table to table, distributing the custard pie and cranberries for dessert, stopping to pat a small lad's head, or press the hand of a quiet little girl. The children were enthralled with the sight of a successful orphan who had a job and a sturdy pair of new shoes. This little waif was hardly better off than

259

they were and yet he was all smiles and energy. Casey had as much zeal and optimism as he had on the day Louisa and he had met. Instead of drowning in his sorrows, he seemed unsinkable. Of all the precious friends Louisa had made in New York, she felt that Casey was the dearest. *He's perfect.* She smiled to herself. *Perhaps this little fellow is the man I have been searching for all my life.*

It was not yet completely clear to her, nor to Herr Hahn, that Casey was an orphan. The lawyer had found no record of Mrs. McDermott's death in the health department registers. Had she expired undeclared in a charity hospital, or could she have survived her ordeal? It was possible that Casey's mother was searching for him in the city among those shoeless gangs of pathetic boys downtown.

After dinner, the gifts were presented, sending up another round of cheers and applause on Mrs. Gibbons's behalf. She passed down the children's ranks regally, bowing left and right, but in her little black bonnet and waterproof she looked like a peculiar kind of angel to these grateful children. The reporters left after the official proceedings, except for one young man. He, along with Casey, helped to haul the boxes filled with gifts to the infant hospital and lent a willing hand in all the activities.

The joy of the orphanage was the highlight of Louisa's day, for now the difficult part began. She smiled bravely as she lugged her box of dollies to the sick and afflicted children in the hospital but her heart ached. Crippled ones hobbled on their crutches to see the bounty. The blind half crawled in the direction of the bustle, while the many bedridden children stretched their hands, pleading for attention. One little unfortunate with a bandaged skull and eyes that seemed not to see turned her head towards the commotion, all the movement the child could muster. Louisa placed a doll in her crib, close by her little body so that she could feel it, if not gaze at it contentedly. She caressed the child's cheek and rearranged her bedclothes. There was so much more these children required. Finally, she placed a sweetie in the voiceless mouth, leaving the child with a smile on her face and herself with tear-filled eyes.

More haunting than even those at the nursery were the faces and moans of the idiot asylum, their next stop. Louisa recalled Thoreau's sentiment, "You may perhaps have some pleasant, thrilling, glorious hours even in a poor house. The setting sun is reflected from the windows of the almshouse as brightly as from the rich man's abode, the snow melts before its door as early in the spring ...." Louisa knew that this poetical thought could come only from one who had not felt the sorrows of the inhabitants. She noted that the thin winter sun barely penetrated the filthy windows and the snow at the door was trampled to slush and mud, mixed with spit and urine.

The matron prodded Louisa forward as she hesitated at the threshold of the large room, circled round with half-grown men, children rocking methodically in their own world and young women cuddling their new dolls. There were shrieks of excitement at the toys and books and in the commotion, a young girl had an epileptic fit, followed by two others who lost consciousness. This required a general hiatus in the revelry, though not a lot of consternation on anyone's part, while the assistants ministered to the distressed. The care of the attendants and nurses made Louisa realize, fully for the first time, what her sisters Anna and May had dealt with every day. As young women they had taught at the Syracuse State Idiot Asylum, never complaining, doing what they must to send money home to the family "sinking fund." Louisa had always been jealous of them for getting away from the everyday drudgery of existence in Concord. Now she comprehended the full extent of their sacrifice. How did those sweet girls handle this misery and remain the uncomplaining dears they were? It hardly seemed possible to encounter these scenes day after day and remain sane. She turned to the nearby suffering faces, understanding the depth of sacrifice her sisters had made to keep their own family together. She treasured again the sweet complacency of Nan and the bright, hopeful beauty of May. Forcing a smile, she cuddled the children about her.

After all the commotion subsided, the reporter helped to collect the unclaimed items, preparing a box that Mrs. Gibbons would give to the staff for their children at home. Louisa looked for Casey, wondering how he had managed to face the nightmare of the blank faces, dumb smiles and awkward screams. He was so capable that she had forgotten his youth in the face of such pitiable circumstances. He wasn't in sight. She hoped that he had not fled, overcome.

Mrs.Gibbons was across the room talking to a young girl in a dark green dress with a black shawl and a pretty bonnet of pale green, trimmed all around with sprays of faux orange blossoms and gentle lace. Louisa had not noticed the girl before. Her delightful appearance seemed incongruous in the pitiful surroundings. She was too young to be an attendant at the asylum, too elegant to be one of the charges, and she had not come on the ferry passage. As Louisa approached, she vaguely recognized the girl. There was something about her slim shoulders and thin neck, the pale complexion and assured stance.

Looking down at the girl's sensible boots that belied the femininity of the outfit, Louisa cried, "Casey, you look an absolute picture of girlhood! What are you doing in this fine costume?"

Mrs. Gibbons answered in a whisper, "I have added one more stop to our mission today, Louisa. We are also going to visit the Women's Lunatic Asylum on Blackwell Island, where the ferry will necessarily stop as we head south. There is a strict rule that no males of any age are allowed to be in contact with the women in the asylum. Don't reveal our little lie, for Casey has a special mission there."

Louisa understood. Casey would be looking for his mother among the deranged and irrational women. She stared at him over and over. The transformation was uncanny. He did not change his demeanor or his voice—he was just Casey in a dress, and yet he seemed a natural girl.

The lunatic asylum's glorious entry soared five stories to a gigantic dome. The walls were made of bluestone and a spiraling stairway colonnaded all the way to the cupola lined the rotunda. Two wings splayed out at right angles from the atrium, forming the women's and men's wards. The matron, apprised of Mrs. Gibbons' request in advance, had collected all the women so named Bridget McDermott—the Bridies, the Mary Bridgets, the Birdies—and placed them in the public lounge. The sight of a half dozen dismal women, some crying, some stony-faced, others calling out, "Come here, deary! Come visit me, pretty girl!" was heartbreaking. Casey, with Louisa on one side and Mrs. Gibbons on the other, their arms locked and their gentle support sustaining him, moved from one sad being to another.

The child trembled as he made his way toward each bereft form. Lifting each sad face in his hands, he would look into their eyes and find no resemblance to the mother of his memory. One woman gazed past the child with a frightened stare, started and then cowered. Another whispered to Louisa, "My husband put me here. I am not insane—you must believe me." While the matron gently shook her head Louisa knew that her claim was not impossible.

From the far corner, a slim, slumping figure, her visage in the shadow, her voice soft and incredulous, threw her hands to her breast and called, "Katie! Is it my Katie?"

The matron grunted, "She hasn't spoken this whole year."

The child stopped trembling, pulled away from the protective arms of her friends and threw herself on the gentle, downtrodden form. "Mother! Mother! It is your Katie! I have come to take you away from here!" The wretched mother and the sobbing daughter clung to each other.

Louisa took in the scene and shot a glance at Mrs. Gibbons, who smiled back sheepishly. Louisa sat down on the nearest chair, a sturdy wooden contraption with leather straps on the arms and legs. She surmised that it was used to restrain the most senseless patients. "Well, I might as well be strapped in, because I have been the least sane of the whole lot, it seems. My little newsboy has been a girl all this time?"

She looked at the mixture of joy and protection that Casey, now Katie, exuded and saw the same resolute, motivated youngster she had always known. How in the world had she missed this? The clues were there all along, the fascination with Bijou's costumes, the showers away from the other boys, the sobbing when she found that Louisa had been disguising her own identity. Even the brown parcels from the seamstress were finally revealed in Katie's fine outfit.

Mrs. Gibbons beamed. "Sorry to keep thee in the dark, but Katie insisted. She would not have revealed her true identity yet if she did not find her mother. She was not ready to give up her home at the Newsboys' Lodging."

Katie was at her mother's knee. The dazed woman stroked the child's face, saying, "Katie! I thought I had lost you! I thought you were gone!"

"I thought the same, Ma! But once Herr Hahn found a name like yours in the ledgers, I had some hope." Katie poured out her story to her mother in a sudden rush. "I've been saving to take you away from here. I save sometimes two dollars a week in the bank at the Lodging. If I can prove that I can keep you in a safe room and care for you, they will let me take you out. You will get better surrounded by sunshine and all my good friends."

Mrs. Gibbons leaned over and whispered in Louisa's ear, "When Katie ran away from her home the night of her father's death and her mother's breakdown, she learned that she was safer, and surrounded by stronger allies, if she dressed as a boy." She approached Mrs. McDermott and placed a gentle hand on her shoulder. "My dear, Katie has been living at the Newsboys' Lodging. That is why your inquiries at the orphanages were fruitless. I suppose no one would have thought of looking for your daughter at the boys' lodging."

"And Josef, has he been part of your ploy?" Louisa asked Mrs. Gibbons.

264

Mrs. Gibbons nodded. "Katie came to me the very same afternoon we visited the Tombs. Something which thou said got her thinking. And I set the good advocate to work. The pennies in the Lodging bank should not be needed. Herr Hahn is working on an even bigger plan for Katie and Mrs. McDermott."

"You look thin, Ma, and so pale and sad," said Katie. "I'll get you out of here soon."

"And you look strong and healthy," said the mother. "Thank God for all who have helped you." She stood, wobbling, and held out her hands to Mrs. Gibbons and Louisa.

Gently, Mrs. Gibbons spoke to the mother and child, helping them separate until another day. She led Katie out of the room, the little girl swooning with the turmoil and emotion of the day. Louisa spent a few moments with the dazed mother. Her upbringing and her nursing experience had given her facility with people in the throes of mental illness. Louisa admitted to herself, too, that she had struggled with "the blue devils" much of her life. She had written about struggles with insanity in her novel *Work* and in several of her short stories.

"It is not only Katie's hope that you will recover with her kind attention, it is a strong possibility, Mrs. McDermott. You need kindness, care and rest, and it will all help your mood. You and Katie will be together very soon and half your grief will be relieved. What a strong and passionate little sprite she is. She seems invincible."

When Katie emerged from the asylum to meet the party at the ferry, she was again clad in her newsboy's clothing. This transformation of the young girl and the reappearance of the newsboy did not escape the eye of the young reporter. "So tell me, lad, what was that all about? The girl's clothing, I mean."

"I don't know whatcher talkin' about. Yer way off base," Katie responded in her blunt street slang. Louisa suspected that the reporter was not convinced and wondered if his report of the visit of the kind Quaker and the famous author would include the tale of a mysterious metamorphosis as well.

The ride home was one of rejoicing and laughter, with Louisa admitting her ignorance and Katie crowing about her own acting abilities. "Now you know why I am so good at buttonholes and why I cried so much when you said you wanted to be a boy, too," Katie added. She would return to the Newsboys' Lodging for now, at her own request, while Herr Hahn and Mrs. Gibbons worked their magic.

"There now, I feel better for the next year," said the indefatigable Mrs. Gibbons as she bustled off from the dock to her next charity. "I intend to be here for another thirty years, and if I am not, then my children will be. Thank you, Louisa and Casey." She winked.

Later, alone in her room, Louisa munched an apple for her Christmas dinner, having missed the meal at the Miller Bath Hotel. She had witnessed unspeakable misery, along with innocent joy, among the children at the asylum. The moving scene of reconciliation between the mother and her child had nearly overwhelmed her. But it was the realization that yet another of her truths had been shattered that left Louisa feeling unmoored and drifting. Boys or girls, health or illness, decorum or debauchery—she seemed not to be able to tell one from the other here. Nothing was what it appeared to be in New York.

She wondered what might be her next surprise.

Chapter 28

Theatrical Moments

"Will you be going to the theater again tonight, Miss Alcott?" Matilda Heron asked on that last Tuesday in December as Herr Hahn helped her settle at the dinner table. The Miller Bath Hotel dinner guests continued to be drawn heavily from the local theaters, attracted by Matilda's and Helene's celebrity, and staying due to Louisa's ability to animate the conversations.

Louisa nodded. "My favorite moments in New York are those I have spent at the theater. And I admire no actor more than your favored Mr. Edwin Booth," Louisa said to Helene warmly. "I am going to his performance of *Julius Caesar* this evening."

"Aye, the reigning actor of our time!" interjected an agreeable impresario. "Edwin Booth has no equal in his portrayal of Shakespeare's prince," he asserted, raising his glass to toast the legacy of the actor.

"I saw Edwin Booth more than once as Hamlet. I will never forget the last time," Louisa said in a somber tone. "It was April 1, 1865." Few in the theatrical world could miss the impact of that date. Two weeks later, the country was stunned by the assassination of President Lincoln by Booth's younger brother, the actor John Wilkes Booth.

"John's headstrong activism showed in his style of acting," said

Matilda, who knew the attributes of both brothers' acting styles. "John was dark and fiercely handsome, full of intensity and devilry. Edwin's style is filled with reflection, artistry and naturalism."

The impresario waved his hands. "After the assassination, Edwin received hate mail and threats of violence, even fearing his own death should he resume the stage."

"For his first return in *Hamlet*, he did not make a stage entrance," Matilda said, "but appeared seated in a chair, his head bowed in his hands. Full of sorrow and regret, he won the audience's devotion."

"He continues to perform to sold out crowds, but does not take a curtain call," the man said. "He feels it risks exposure to violence."

Later, Louisa walked by herself the few short blocks to the Fifth Avenue Theater, shivering in the cold. She missed her little escort, but thought it imprudent to have Katie about after hours. Katie, of course, had bristled at the idea that she was a less suited escort once her true gender was revealed. "What happened to your idea of letting girls work at any occupation to which they desire and are suited?" asked Katie.

"And why would it be improper for me to be about alone, but not for you?" countered Louisa. And then they conceded together that indeed, neither of them were certain of what would be best and that the whole issue was "complicated."

Louisa was joining a group of friends to see Booth's performance in *Julius Caesar*. The party chatted as they filed into their seats in the center of the orchestra level. Louisa's thoughts were unsettled and she could not relax in her plush seat. She empathized so strongly with the struggle the actor had faced, that familial blight that had been none of his doing, and the general moodiness that he exuded. The performance began and the first appearance of Edwin Booth was made even more somber by the sight of the actor's left arm hanging helplessly at his side. This was a remnant of a stroke seemingly brought on at so young an age by his smoking, overwhelming cares and unrelenting intensity. Gradually, though, the gentle and natural elocution made the familiar words seem new to Louisa and she began to fall under the spell of the Bard and the beguiling actor.

In the third act, the allure was shattered. With incredible violence, Caesar was struck down. A noticeable gasp rippled through the crowd at the brutality of it. Surely, everyone knew the myth that Brutus had cried, "Sic semper tyrannis!" at this moment. These were the very words that John Wilkes Booth had declared after firing a single shot into President Lincoln's skull. Louisa felt anxious and drained. She could not understand how Edwin had the stamina to face the innuendo of that harrowing epithet. At every performance, he must have remembered his brother's deed and gone on to perform his own rendition of a leader annihilated. Perhaps it was a metaphor for what John Wilkes Booth had done to the President, the country and his brother's career. It was all too heavy for Louisa and her attention flagged.

It was then that she had the distinct feeling that she was being watched. This had happened to her before in this same theater, the night of Bijou's performance. She scanned the upper boxes, but in the darkness her search was futile. She trembled a little and tried to hide behind her fan. She felt eyes following her from all directions.

Suddenly, the audience was thundering its applause. The play had concluded while Louisa sat in her gloomy contemplation. The curtain came down and there were no extra bows or curtain calls. The lights came up and as Louisa collected her wrap and rose to leave, she was certain that she saw a thin figure of a man draw quickly out of view behind the red curtains in a box just above her. Whoever was concealed behind the curtains wore fashionable buff-colored gloves and did not reappear. This furtive surveillance startled her nerves and made her uncomfortable, as if the very walls had watched and whispered. The ominous feeling increased.

Louisa made her apologies to her companions, declining their invitation to join them for refreshments after the performance. The aching double tragedy of the play and the guilt that the poor actor seemed to bear weighed on her and she felt she would be disagreeable company.

Her room at the hotel was a cheery sight. The fire had been set and the maid had arranged a small tea tray and her things for retiring. Though she had made it clear that she needed no assistant to attend to her clothing, Mrs. Miller still tried to insist on a personal maid for her needs. Louisa was ever frugal, preferring both to save money and ensure her privacy. She could mend and repair her clothing as well as any young domestic. Her wants were simple indeed compared to those the proprietress expected of her as one with so much celebrity, so she was surprised when there was a knock on the door and the evening maid entered, carrying a small tray with a calling card.

"Excuse the intrusion, miss, but this excited young man would not be turned away." Louisa had a sinking sense of alarm, as any visit at this late hour made her worry for the well-being of her loved ones at home. She braced for bad news.

A thumping as of someone coming up the stairs two at a time sounded in the hall. The girl looked alarmed. All guests were to be met in the parlor. With a quizzical expression, she went on with her message: "He said you would not turn away your Big Son."

Laddie. Louisa threw the card aside without looking at it. The little maid stood looking confused as Louisa, abandoning all decorum, gave a whoop, threw the door open and embraced the young man at the door jamb where he had pulled up to be introduced. Louisa drew him into the room with a vigorous yank, alternately laughing and crying while she smothered him with kisses, tousled his hair and held him at arm's length to look him over.

"Why didn't you write to tell me you were coming?" she demanded between hiccoughs and sobs.

"I make big surprise like the time you come to Paris." Ladislas Wisniewski had indeed blossomed into a healthy, handsome man, with no sign of the lingering cough and wan visage that he had worn in Vevey after his wartime ordeal. He stood before her in evening

270

dress with curly black hair, a small crescent moustache and an irrepressible grin. "My mama send me to complete a business works she had, and as she be comfortable right now with the wife and children, I stay to see this so magnificent city."

A tinge of a blush rose nearly to his forehead. One of Laddie's most agreeable traits was his courtesy. He was always a gentleman in the parlor at Pensione Victoria, smoothing over awkward pauses and inviting friendships. He wouldn't be one to discomfit others with any complaints about his own situation. Louisa knew this gentle soul enough to sense that there was a more delicate and perhaps more pressing reason for his arrival in New York and his dalliance here.

He plunged on with his explanation. "I think to give lessons to pay for my trip home and then, I see in the paper that you are here—there was written about a women's meeting—and I know I must find you!" *So something good had come of the Sorosis newspaper report,* Louisa thought.

"Poor boy, and you find me a crotchety old spinster, come for the cure at the baths," said Louisa.

"You are always the best laughing, best joking, best playing girl I know!"

"And you, now a father of two daughters! I am dying to know all about them. You must have a photo for me. No? Well then you will draw me a picture with words and I will become their Aunt Weedy for sure!"

She drew him to the settee, dismissing the astonished night maid. Soon their words were tumbling out, in a rush to fill the gaps made by more than ten years of separation. He supported his mother and family, whom he doted on. After losing a small business, the family returned to Paris, where they lived at the moment. They vacillated between there and Prague, for he had lost his small fortune in the Polish stock market crash. Louisa sensed that this financial instability was part of his errand here in New York. She admired that he remained cheerful and optimistic. How like a Plumfield boy he was!

271

"Whatever became of your translation of *Vanity Fair*?" Louisa teased.

"You tell the too cruel joke, Louisa, just like in old days. You hear my English is not good to make translation."

"It's just exactly the same as when we last spoke," Louisa said. It was uncanny how little he had changed, while she felt eons away from the balcony along Lake Leman. In truth, she felt some pity for Ladislas. He tried all his life to do his duty. He had provided for his mother by teaching music and he was doing the same now for his wife and children. He seemed to be frozen in time, as if he had not accomplished anything in the ten years since they had last held each other's hands. The fact that she had become the most recognized author in America hung between them, yet unspoken.

"I never meant to lose track of you, my boy, but there has been a lot to occupy my mind. You have no idea how tiresome publishers are." That sounded more pretentious than Louisa desired. She paused, then said, trying to regain the natural flow of their conversation, "Will you be in town long?"

"I believe the works I come to do will be complete by the end of year. I will sail home as soon as the weather makes good enough in the spring."

"We will have scads of time to spend together, then!" she exclaimed. "Let's pick up where our Paris adventures left off!" She meant it enthusiastically and innocently but again, there was an uncomfortable pause.

Laddie grinned. "I am married man, Louisa. Do not be too much bold!" Louisa was glad he alluded to that irrational kiss lightly. She laughed. He had broken the ice and they were dear friends again.

"You are still a scamp, I see, and will try in every way to make ridiculous insinuations and jokes."

She called for more tea and toast, which occasioned a questioning look on the prim night maid's face when she returned and suggested that they descend to the public drawing room. Laddie's beguiling innocence had cast the same net around Louisa's heart that he had fastened in Vevey. She beamed upon him with eyes filled with affectionate pride and shooed the maid to her duties.

The two settled contentedly into the green and yellow cushions of the divan, like two gossiping crones, for a good, hearty talk about family and future. Louisa told Ladislas that she would be sending her sister May to Paris in the spring and that she would love for her to meet his mother, wife and girls. Laddie told Louisa that the girls had all her books and would rave to have an autograph from the mother of the *Little Women*. They commiserated together about their aging parents and their fierce desires to provide for all their needs. Louisa suggested that before Laddie returned home he should travel to Concord and meet her revered Marmee and gracious, philosophic father. Most of all, they decided to do some unusual sightseeing together in New York. Plans were made for an excursion, and with more hugs and caresses, Ladislas was bundled off into the New York winter night.

Louisa gazed around contentedly. The evening which had begun with so much trepidation at the theater had ended with complete warmth and comfort. That was when she noticed that Laddie had left behind his gloves. Naturally, they were fashionable and buff-colored.

Figure 10. **Interior View of Augustin Daly's Fifth Avenue Theatre,** **New York**

Chapter 29

Liaisons

It was only natural that as Marienne attended the bustling salons at Mrs. Botta's and Mrs. Croly's that she would attract the attention of young men who were charmed by her youthful enthusiasm and intelligence. Two or three came to the hotel to call on her and each time they sat decorously in the parlor, taking tea in the afternoon, or joining the guests in the evening after dinner. Mrs. Miller was conflicted between her role as hostess and guardian of all respectability.

One evening, as they were leaving the dining room, she consulted her husband and Louisa, as the girl's mentor, about the protocol that should be observed. "Miss Ayers's guardian is not competent to chaperone these calls," she said. "I shall not tolerate any impropriety under my roof."

Louisa rolled her eyes. "And what exactly do you think they are speaking of in hushed tones by the fire?" she challenged. "Because I can tell you it's about Whittier and Bryant more than lovering."

"Miss Alcott is right, dear. The girl is quite level-headed and she has always been discreet."

"But what of the young men? I know nothing of them. We have to do right by the girl."

Dr. Miller was used to placating his wife. He scanned the parlor and fixed on Herr Hahn's practical face. "Here, here, dear. We will enlist the good lawyer. His interrogation skills may come in handy."

Herr Hahn took to his assignment genially, though he doubted the cause. The next young visitor to arrive at the Miller Hygienic Hotel must have wondered what the relationship was between Marienne and the aggressive German fellow.

"Hello, young man." Josef extended his hand to the sheepish candidate while Marienne blushed. "I am Herr Doktor Hahn, and you are …?" Louisa had never heard him introduce himself with his title before. He was laying it on a bit thick.

The young man mumbled a response.

"Ah, and your line of business is …?" he added, standing with his hands behind him, under his coattails.

Another mumble.

"And vhere is this fine city do you live? Vith your family? I see, I see. All right." He stopped short of inquiring about intentions.

Marienne glared at Louisa, who raised her hands in surrender and shook her head. "It's not my idea. Don't look at me for proprieties," she said.

Marienne tossed her head and continued into the parlor.

Shortly after this new protocol was in place, Ladislas arrived in the early afternoon to pick up Louisa for their first adventure in the city. "To the tip of Manhattan today, Laddie!" she greeted him, but then noticed the gathering clouds. "Perhaps I should go back for my Macintosh," she said, returning upstairs to her room. "It'll take a minute. Have a seat."

Laddie sat on the grand mahogany bench, idly twirling his bowler hat in his hands.

When Louisa returned to the upstairs landing, she saw Josef enter the hallway, looking at a dossier in his hand and heading toward his pile of mail on the front table. She took a breath and paused there. *My goodness, I have not introduced them.*

"Hello, my young fellow," he said, looking up in that absentminded way of his and extending his hand to Laddie. The "young fellow" rose and shifted his hat to the left hand to offer his own in return. "Here to see our young lady, I presume?"

Louisa smiled. Laddie looked confused. "Yes, monsieur. We are off to see the great Brooklyn Bridge today."

"Alone?" Josef asked. "Why do I not know of thees?"

Laddie moved his hat to his other hand. Josef focused on the golden band on his fourth finger.

"Do you think I vill let her traipse about the city vith a married man?" He sounded almost indignant.

Louisa clattered down the stairs. "You two are as befuddled as any clueless old guardians in a short story," she began, taking each one's hand in hers. "*I* am the young lady in question, not Marienne," she said to Josef. "This is my dear friend of many years, Ladislas Wisnieski." She turned to Laddie. "And this our resident knight in shining armor, Josef Hahn."

The two men looked a bit foolish and chagrined, but recovered gallantly and offered their greetings. Josef retained a bit of his protective stance, and Laddie—did he look jealous?

"I'm sorry, my goot man, if I sounded harsh. A misunderstanding, that is all," said Josef.

"Miss Louisa is worth the fighting over, though," Laddie said with that impish look.

Louisa smacked him lightly on the head. "Off with you, you scoundrel!" She looked at Josef. His face was calm, but she felt his unease. He might have got on better continuing the interrogation. Intentions? Character? Was he looking at her with disappointment? Ever since she knew of his diagnosis, she didn't want him to have a moment of discomfort. Still, she turned and accompanied Laddie out the door.

Louisa and Ladislas set out by omnibus to the tip of Manhattan. They both acquired seats, but the bumpy ride was slow going.

"Your friend is a bit stiff, no?"

"Principled, disciplined—traditional, perhaps," Louisa said.

277

"Not your type, I think," Laddie teased.

"Let's drop it, Laddie. He's dying. I can't bear it," she said and shifted her gaze out the window at the gray day.

They arrived finally at that rousing spot where the broad harbor opened into the ocean. Louisa breathed deeply to try to erase the lingering worry about Josef's disapproval. The waters churned as violently as her emotions. At high tides, the lapping and surging water gushed up the two rivers that surrounded the island, changing the direction of their flow as the freshwater met the salty and the two merged for a time until the ocean pulled away and the great rivers discharged their contents serenely into the sea again.

The very swirling and mixture of tidal forces seemed a symbol of the city that looked toward Europe, accepted its best and then spewed out its own heady achievements for all the world to take. The Rhine, the Thames, the Seine—none of the rivers that Louisa had seen in Europe compared to this throttling, massive Hudson River that sucked in the sea and then turned its own tide against it. The constraints and formalities of old Europe were submerged in the freedom and spontaneity of the New World. With Laddie beside her, she felt how narrow his opportunities had been compared to her own. Laddie, rollicking in the swirling breezes, looked as if his trip to New York could brighten his prospects and his future.

They stood on land reclaimed from the harbor. A sea wall protected the Battery from the roiling currents, which looked out to Brooklyn, Governors and Bedloe's Islands, Staten Island, and beyond that to the Jersey shore. Ocean steamers, oyster boats and clipper ships surged in the restless waters. The dignified promenade that swung around the tip of the island led on the right to Coenties Slip, which still retained the stepped Dutch rooflines of the first European dynasty in the city. Toward the left was South Street Seaport, where the huge masts and bows loomed, pitching down to almost touch the rooflines of small buildings already one hundred years old. To their backs lay the rumbling audacity of Manhattan. Down the Narrows the seas stretched across to the European Continent, and on the right the whole breadth of the United States spread out behind the cliffs of New Jersey, reaching nearly as far westward as the ocean stretched east. On their left, spanning the second river, stood the elegant towers of the new East River Suspension Bridge.

"What do you think when you look at this bridge, Laddie?" Louisa asked.

"That tower makes everything on both shores look like toy. It stands like elegant lady, like church with its pointed arches." Laddie threw his hands in the air and raised a salute of praise to the incredible size and majesty of the tower. "Now I understand how you say it is a cathedral in the open air!"

They had walked east along the waterfront and were by now just level with the rising platform of the Manhattan tower.

"I think about something different altogether. I think of the human sacrifice that went into making it," Louisa said.

"You talk like men were fed to lions."

"They might as well have been. The elder Roebling was killed in a boating accident on one of these wharves. His son took over and got Caisson's Disease, crippled for life. His wife is in charge unofficially now. She's overseeing everything. Yet the husband is getting all the credit."

"They always do," said Laddie, looking a bit fatigued with her gloomy history.

Louisa scanned down the shore to the foot of the Manhattan tower, just beginning to rise above the waters of the high tide. At the riverfront there was a small wooden foreman's office and she half expected to see the billowing skirts of the dogged Mrs. Roebling inspecting the progress. "I am absolutely convinced that Emily Roebling is the first woman field engineer in the country," she said.

That a woman had become ascendant in the construction of the Brooklyn Bridge was a fitting complement to the next great structure that was going to rise in the harbor, on tiny Bedloe's Island in the very midst of the sparkling waters. The island lay in the center of the harbor, to the right of the bridge and in their direct line of sight.

"In Paris there is an announcement about a gift for these waters," said Laddie. "They will build a great statue called 'Liberty Enlightening the World.' It is to be gift, people to people. Monsieur Bartholdi had already cast a model of the right arm of the great statue, holding a lamp of welcome."

"I have seen an engraving of the proposed statue in the papers here," Louisa said. "This Colossus will be a woman, so instead of power and arrogance she will express goodwill, hospitality and maternal concern."

Laddie started to roll his eyes at her. "With the giant lady statue and the giant bridge built by a lady and the more giant lady author, I wonder where the place is for the men?"

"I refuse to let you invent some unwarranted sympathy for the lords of creation," Louisa said. "Just look at that rot this morning about a woman unchaperoned in the city. It wasn't Josef's idea. He knows I can't stand that type of thinking."

"You never could." Laddie smiled.

"It reminds me of our two weeks together in Paris. We went everywhere together, unconstrained. And yet women haven't come far enough in society to sit with a young man in a snooty parlor without people gossiping," she said. "I am so glad that I never let that sort of thing stop me." She sat on the ledge of the seawall. Laddie stood with his hands in his pockets and looked off across the water.

"You always be big person with new ideas. There is never a woman like you," Laddie said. "So different, as you say, from the women in my country … my own mother … my wife."

"There you go. Am I more like your mother or your wife, or just some wild monster from a far off land?" Louisa laughed.

"More like the lady Colossus you speak about," Laddie said, with a smile. Then, pulling her up from the little stone wall, he complained mockingly, "Louisa, you make me think of so much new ideas my head spins."

"Poor Laddie, you always were the feeble one," Louisa said, massaging his temples gently.

Louisa's relationship with Laddie had always been one free of introspection or guile. They were merely two friends who had invariably relied on humor and joy to unite them. They had had enough of the technological wonder of the bridge, the fractious commercial comings and goings of the ships, and the broad landscape. Louisa and Laddie walked off arm in arm to plan another lark.

"When my father was in town, he had his head read," Louisa said. "I propose our next trip should be to a phrenology studio. There may be a bust of his wise skull on which I can compliment him. And perhaps we can get some explanation of your own spinning head."

When Louisa returned to the hotel late that afternoon, Rebecca greeted her with a slight nod. "Mrs. Miller asked me to send you to her office."

"Sounds like I am in trouble again." Louisa shrugged.

When Louisa entered the office, she found Mrs. Miller behind her desk and Marienne at the window, turned away from the door.

"Yes, Mrs. Miller?" Louisa asked with a curious glance at the girl's back. Marienne turned. She smiled, widened her stance and crossed her arms.

Mrs. Miller did not offer Louisa a seat. She rose herself. *Is this to be a boxing match?*

"Miss Alcott, this is most unfortunate, but I have heard a report that we must address. Miss Ayers—" she began.

"That young man you entertained in your rooms. Perhaps I am not the only one who needs a chaperone," Marienne blurted.

This insolent girl is pouting and I am the victim of her anger.

"Marienne, you know me. You know what I stand for. Why do you choose to think something salacious?" She turned to Mrs. Mill-

281

er. "This is ridiculous, Mrs. Miller. The girl owes me an apology. My friend is a dear, dear acquaintance from long ago."

"And yet, Miss Alcott," Mrs. Miller interjected, "there must be some reason why you attempted to hide who you are. Why you came here incognito, so to speak."

"I've heard your story about the Polish boy." Marienne looked triumphant. Louisa had told her little romance story to the wrong person. This girl who had already nearly tarnished her literary reputation was hurling reckless information. One thing Louisa had learned from Marmee's placement office was that some women just refused to be helped. Marienne was one of those.

"What are you getting at, Marienne?" Louisa snarled.

The girl shrugged. "Just looking at the world with a writer's eyes. Looking at how relationships get complicated. How things aren't always as they seem."

Louisa had heard enough. "Don't talk to me about writing, you hypocrite," she said and turned to leave.

"Herr Hahn always says, 'The truth will come out' …" Marienne rallied back.

"And don't ever use that blessed man as your defense."

She slammed the door.

Chapter 30

Mind Reading

Louisa took a deep breath and knocked on the marchesa's door. Marienne opened it a crack, as if she was wary of an intruder. "It's time for me to sit with your aunt," Louisa said with effort.

"I don't need your help. And you can tell that to your little newsboy, who isn't even male. For a woman who worries about her reputation, you keep some odd company."

"I'm sorry you came to this, Marienne. I just want you to know that Mrs. Croly agrees to stand by you as a mentor. She's more willing to work on hopeless cases than I am, I guess," Louisa added.

"Some women just have more integrity than others," Marienne retorted and closed the door.

Miss Holley entered the hallway just as Louisa turn away from the door. Her shoulders slumped but her eyes flashed. "What do you do when people accuse you falsely, Sallie? I am sure you are shunned all the time in your good work."

"Just knowing you are in the right helps," Sallie said. "But people do make such a mess of things when they mistake one's intentions." Sallie dragged a large basket of linens to her door. "I'm just about ready to pack up and get these donations back to the school. I'll probably leave next week."

"Getting back to where you belong," Louisa said. "You know,

that sounds inviting."

When Laddie came to pick her up for their next adventure, Mrs. Miller glared from her office. He tipped his hat to her and she averted her eyes. If she had known that they were on their way to get their heads read she would have reacted even more strongly.

Though the intense interest in phrenology that had swept the nation two generations before had long since peaked, the Fowler and Wells Phrenological Cabinet, on the corner of Beekman and Nassau Streets, was still one of the most visited attractions in the city. The small museum was now run by a descendant of the original Fowler Brothers and tended more toward the entertaining than the scientific. The establishment offered lectures, tours and a gift shop. The two friends paid their admission fees and feigned scholarly interest in the displays.

The exhibition contained replicas of head types that had been collected by one of the movement's early proponents. The skull casts ranged from pirates to presidents to Julius Caesar himself. Busts were everywhere, especially the symbolic phrenologic busts of white ceramic, with blue lines delineating the areas of the different human faculties. Louisa was silently happy that her father's visage did not appear anywhere in this circus. Displays of mummies and paintings of famous people and their phrenologic attributes cluttered the room.

Louisa had to pull Laddie behind a glass and walnut cabinet to get him to stop staring at a patron with a bulbous head examining a sign that read, "Professional Examinations Given When Desired ... Will be Found most Valuable and Exceedingly Interesting."

"That would be an exceedingly interesting skull to examine," Louisa said, stifling a laugh.

"How very amazing your big head must be, too, Louisa," Laddie needled her.

"And how very curious your little one would appear." They both burst out laughing, nudging each other toward the examination chamber. "If my *philoprogenitiveness* outstrips my *self-esteem*, I will be

284

ashamed to admit it," said Louisa, reading from the head chart nearby.

"And if my *adhesiveness* overshadows my *conscientiousness*, I will must shall to deny it," countered Laddie. "Let's have good big laugh and read our reports aloud."

Louisa, with her high brow, prominent cranium and deep eyes would be a phrenologist's delight. She sat quietly, restraining a giggle as the master measured her head with a craniometer, a special kind of caliper that swung from ear to ear, gauging the bumps and crannies of the skull. Then, the examiner used his fingers to scan the skull. With a few murmurs to his amanuensis and some jotted notes, a report was developed. Whether it was valuable or interesting, as advertised, remained to be seen.

Back in the anteroom, she waited for Ladislas. As he emerged from the examination room, his ridiculous grin and childish demeanor infected her with mirth and they smirked like schoolchildren as they exchanged their folders. "Ladies first, so I will read yours," Laddie said with a laugh. As he read, Louisa was so taken aback by the accuracy of the description that she thought that Laddie must be interjecting his own narrative. Or perhaps the examiner had recognized her and summarized what he might know about her from reading the papers.

"Faith, hope and charity very large, especially the latter. Friendship, remarkable. She has more friends than she wants, bears others burdens & lets them impose on her through her strong sympathy and generosity. Conjugal love very marked, capable of all things for the man she loved." Here Laddie made ridiculous eyes at her.

"A devoted wife and mother."

"Wrong!" shouted Louisa.

"Adores children and wins their heart at once."

"Well, that's the philoprogenitiveness bit," said Louisa.

"Loves praise but can go without it if her will or principle makes it seem right. Leans to the ideal, yet from certain motives can be very practical. A good

285

nurse from her magnetic & sympathetic power. Has the gift of language, is dramatic and witty. Strong passions but can control them. Dual nature very marked, but the higher predominates through culture & moral sentiment. Great powers of observation & mimicry. A good talker but not a speaker. Intellectual faculties developed largely, but great benevolence prevents entire devotion to intellectual pursuits."

"That's me putting my great novel on hold to write something that sells for Marmee's new rug," Louisa said.

"Conscientiousness large & will also, and the two conflict. Great vitality & a fine constitution, yet liable to overdo as the spirit is ardent and sometimes headstrong. A person who can row against the tide & like it. If she wrote a story, no one could tell how it was coming out as it would be sure to take an unexpected & unusual turn. Love of nature, reads character well & has great intuitive perception."

Except when I am in New York, she thought.

"Understands without study & knows things by instinct. A remarkable head."

"Hooray, Louisa, your much big head is a remarkable one!" hooted Laddie.

"Let's see what study of your pea brain reveals," said Louisa as she began to read the traits affirmed by Ladislas's skull.

"Charm and playfulness are essential traits, always polite & accommodating, winning & attractive. Did you bribe him to write this, Laddie?" she ribbed.

"Is a fluent, easy and ready talker; conveys ideas finely. In which language?" Louisa jested.

"Fond of fine things, & all that is beautiful, loves luxury. Has strong desires to accumulate property & uses influence over friends to obtain favors. Sets a great deal by the enjoyments of the appetite. Well, isn't this a lot of rubbish!" exclaimed Louisa. She stopped in mid-sentence, closing the portfolio and handing it to Laddie.

The gentle Pole blushed to his hairline, but gracious and humble as always, he insisted, "No, Louisa, this was our game; now I pay the price." Seeing Louisa's discomfort, he stoutly determined to read aloud his own report in spite of his faulty inflection.

"Disposed to act honorably, but may at times adopt a rule of expediency where self can be benefited. In time of prosperity is buoyant & hopeful but if adversity thickens becomes discouraged & grows gloomy and desponding. Is ordinarily good natured but if provoked to anger, sharp and severe. Is respectful in the society of the other sex, yet has little warmth of love. Outward appearance is all smooth & affable, though intentions not so easily understood. There is too much 'make believe.'"

In the silence after the last words, Louisa shifted uncomfortably but with a playful tilt of his head, Laddie tried to look contrite and became the charming boy who bedeviled her on the balcony at Vevey. He asked, "Is this why Jo March never married Laurie?"

Louisa breathed a sigh of relief. *The scamp! He really wasn't going to take this seriously, thank goodness.* "No, Jo March wasn't interested in marrying anyone, as you can plainly see."

"But near one year after turning sad Laurie away she become engaged to that dusty old professor!"

"Must I explain Professor Bhaer to you too, Laddie? He was everything that Jo felt she needed to become the woman she longed to be. With his learning, he gave her the education she desired for herself. As a German, he brought everything Romantic ... and his moral certainty about God and the worth of humanity and dignity of the poor ... it was everything that Jo—no, that *I*—wanted to add to myself." Louisa stopped, confused. While she was tumbling headlong into her justification of Professor Bhaer, it was Josef Hahn she was imaging.

"And you are the one to have such good skull!" Laddie laughed. "The dusty Bhaer would have a ponderous one." Louisa winced. Laddie's outburst brought him back to his own dilemma. "But Laurie still only become the man who follows after his little wife and watches as Jo and Bhaer have big school and big hearts and big family."

"And I'm sure I changed the shape of my head by using it as a battering ram all those years, forcing my way through life and fighting for everything worth having. You are still a young man. I am sure your head can still be molded."

Laddie brightened again. "Bravo, Little Mama! I will become man worthy of Jo March!" He always could be winsome and petulant and irreverent all at once.

Louisa was suddenly a little ashamed of her lecture on persistence. "Goodness, with all this preaching your Little Mama has officially become Marmee and is ready to sermonize you straight into decent behavior."

"I hope your real Marmee was not so strict. I would be feared to meet her."

"Oh," Louisa replied, "I put Marmee in there for the adults and the critics. The children know to skip over those parts and get straight to Jo and Laurie's next prank."

"And so will we!" he exclaimed. "We will skip this naughty part." And tucking Louisa's arm into his, he dropped his folder into the trash as they ventured out into the gray December day on Broadway.

By the time the two approached Louisa's hotel, they had accumulated souvenirs and packages from shops and gift stores along the way. One block south of the hotel, on Madison Square, stood the elegant and imposing Hoffman House. Louisa had not been into its formidable bar because it was open to women only once a week. This being the day of the feminine invasion, Louisa needed to fulfill a promise to May. The couple entered the masculine haunt boldly. The mahogany paneled salon was arrayed with crystal chandeliers, stuffed moose heads, grand mirrors, tapestries and Turkish carpets. The chairs were carved from heavy wood with red leather seats and a half nude water nymph plunged into a gurgling fountain in the center of the room.

None of this was the cause of May's interest, however. Louisa was sent specifically to report back to her sister on the famed painting by the French master Bouguereau which hung on the center wall of the salon. The painter considered *Nymphs and Satyr* his most important work. That it hung in a bar room, even an elegant bar room, was a testament to the titillation it had caused. The massive painting depicted four life-sized, voluptuous nude women, frolicking and taunting an equally nude satyr. The women pulled his hair and dragged him, resisting, toward the cold water. Louisa realized that May would be awed by the sculptural quality of the women's bodies, by the twisting shapes which revealed all aspects of the human anatomy, and by the sly way the painter had turned the legend on its head by having the satyr being the one affronted. But Louisa, never an art connoisseur and always easily shocked by licentiousness, would not have minded if the red velvet drapery which often covered the picture were pulled closed tonight.

The Hoffman House was also famous for its cocktails. The Hoffman Martini was its signature drink and Louisa, having delayed her decision about the prohibition of liquor to another time, called for two of the dry gin and vermouth libations. The maître d' was chagrined when Louisa politely closed her women's menu and poured over the gentlemen's, which listed the prices of every item. As the chef had not condescended to translate the names of any of his productions into legible words, Louisa needed Laddie's translation, and as Ladislas seemed not to have the funds to pay, he needed her generosity. She listened as he ordered in his perfectly charming French. They feasted on oysters and green turtle soup, followed by Long Island brook trout and croquettes of lobster. Their conversation overflowed with goodwill and intimacy. Laddie always spoke of his little wife with warmth and respect. His New York business remained murky to Louisa, as did his financial situation. They laughed together about Louisa's hunch about the pianist L.W.

He asked about her plans to remain in New York. "I'll stay as long as I feel well and until I am tired of the frivolity," she admitted. She realized, too, that Laddie was the only spark of gaiety in her New York world just then. Dessert came, consisting of two kinds of ice,

289

apricot tartelettes and macaroons, all accompanied by champagne. Laddie had always managed to make life sweet and effervescent.

They sauntered home, jostling each other under a single umbrella. A heavy rain had sprung up and they had hard work avoiding the puddles that glistened on the cobblestones. They hopped like children from curb to curb, rattling their purchases and splashing a little in the largest puddles. Finally, pausing at the top of the high hotel stoop, bundles awkwardly clutched between them, the torrential rain battering on the umbrella, Louisa sensed with some confusion that she had been in this exact situation once before. Where exactly had this happened, and more to the point, with whom? The answer flooded her with amazement and then foreboding. This was the wonderful love scene between Jo March and Friedrich Bhaer, the triumphant moment when doubt and misunderstanding slip away and the two profess themselves betrothed, as well as thoroughly drenched.

Despite Louisa's height and stature, Laddie bent his head close to her ear and whispered plaintively, "Louisa, can I see you again?"

Louisa's heart fluttered for a moment, then was steady. She did not know if he was her dashing boy looking for another lark, a lonely foreigner needing a hand, or a suitor—and a very inappropriate one at that. Somehow, she remembered her skull traits. *Conjugal love very marked, capable of all things for the man she loved* was one she did not believe herself. *Leans to the ideal, yet from certain motives can be very practical* suited her much better, she thought.

She drew herself up a little taller. "I will be at Mrs. Croly's on New Year's Day. Will you call on us there?"

With half closed eyes, Ladislas inclined his head, with a gentle nod that could have been either assent or concession. He handed her the umbrella and walked slowly off into the rainy night.

Louisa still trembled a little, but shook her head sadly at his shivering back as he disappeared. *Intentions not so easily understood. There is too much 'make believe,'* she thought.

Chapter 31

A New Year's Surprise

Clang! Clang! Kaboom! Rat-a-tat-tat! The racket broke out suddenly in the blustery night. *Craaack! Kaboom-boom-boom! Clang! Craaack!* The residents of the Miller Hygienic Institute hoorayed and sang on the roof of the hotel at the stroke of midnight. Fireworks showered in the distance over the riverfront. The sounds of church and fire bells, firecrackers, horns, pistols and even booming cannons reverberated across the city. The noise from New York's furious welcome of the New Year was ferocious.

Louisa spread her arms and gave hearty wishes of health and prosperity to the children. Katie, Rebecca, Marienne and Helene, four girls together, their faces shining with delight, were ready to welcome a new year and a new world. Then, descending from the roof, she entered the drawing room to comfort the marchesa, unsettled by the noise, and arrange Matilda's shawl to envelope her in softness and warmth. Josef stood by the fireside reading a legal report, content to make the best of his holiday by spending it to help others. Louisa respected his calm decision to work to his capacity while he was well and able. She tried her best not to distract him or tempt him with amusements or escapades. Perhaps that was why Ladislas had come into her life at this time.

New Yorkers were about to begin a day of celebration and raucous visitation. Women stayed home accepting callers, while the men streamed from house to house making required social calls and desired visits to friends. Louisa had accepted an invitation from Jane Croly. It was the custom to invite several single ladies to play co-hostess. Jane Croly had invited Louisa to help her brave the on-slaught and to freely invite any guests she would like to visit. If La-dislas arrived it would be neither unusual nor noted.

As soon as Louisa had been invited, she surveyed her wardrobe. The black silk dress she had purchased on her first days in the city had been worn dozens of times. She knew exactly how to spruce it up and spent the next two evenings adding gold braid to the vest and skirt. She remembered all the ways that the Alcott sisters had needed to camouflage their wardrobe, painting slippers to look like satin, turning the fabric of old clothing to remake a skirt. She thought about how May and she had prepared her wardrobe for this sojourn in New York. Perhaps her time here was winding down. Sallie had mentioned home and now it called to her. Maybe she had been just as fashionable as her urgent, artless spirit would tolerate. It might be time to stop playing the sophisticate and get back to her business of grubbing along in the garret. It could also be that this spectacular social obligation for the New Year celebration at Jane Croly's home would be her grand finale.

New York was sure to show its attraction to excess today. At least Jane wouldn't succumb to the craze of having the hairdresser arrive at midnight to coif the hair of all the ladies in the house, nor would she enlist a popular punch maker who travelled from one fashionable house to the next making the latest favored concoction. Louisa was glad to accept her level-headed friend's invitation where she expected that good conversation and ideas would prevail over nonsense and flirting.

Louisa descended the curving staircase, the gold braid glistening on her suit and her hair piled in a sophisticated knots on the back of her head. Josef sat near the fire in the parlor. She crouched by his chair. He looked at her with a sad, quizzical smile.

"Josef, come with me. You will love the kind of talk that goes on at Mrs. Croly's."

"No, Schatzi, it is better that I stay in mein slippers vith my hot tea and a blanket."

"You are feeling worse." Louisa's forehead creased with worry. "I can stay with you."

"No, no you belong out there," Josef said. "Never vould I be the cause of so much disappointment in your hosts. They need your blunt and urgent kind of chat."

"Sometimes I feel I am just tilting at windmills."

"No, you are slaying dragons." He squeezed her hand, then gave it a little pat as if to encourage her.

Impetuously, she bent over and kissed him tenderly, quite regardless of everything but her own heartache. Josef's eyes did not show surprise but he didn't smile. He just looked at her in a blank, hopeless way. She adjusted his tie in a manner so similar to how she had nursed his brother that she shuddered. *This is getting insufferable.* "Get your rest, sir," Louisa said almost desperately. "Don't wait up for me."

When Louisa arrived at the Crolys' at noon, she had settled her emotions and looked almost regal in her fine black and gold suit. The other co-hostesses were young single women and Louisa felt like the grand dame among them. Jane had such a bright and charming manner that they all were set at ease immediately. Even Louisa began to relax.

The Croly home was one of the surprisingly spacious and handsome four-story brownstones in Murray Hill, for which the neighborhood was famous. Four homes had been built on a lot usually designated for three, making the rooms slightly less wide than usual and the receiving salon at the back of the first floor particularly long and narrow. There were windows only at the far end of the room and the length was lit by candles and gas jets. Even in midday the room was dim.

Jane's eight-year-old daughter Vida quickly monopolized Louisa's attention. She drew her favorite author to a comfortable armchair and sat on her lap in the familiar way that children usually assumed with Louisa. She usually set out to charm them with her sparkling wit. She would never talk down to them or tell them something that was not true.

"So, are you such a smart lass that you read my silly books by yourself already?" Louisa asked the adoring girl.

"Mama insists I read them aloud to her. She says it is so she can help me with the hard parts, but I think she enjoys the books as much as I do," was the astute answer. Vida went on to tell Louisa that she had heard there were "too many boys" in the latest book, which she had not read yet. Louisa promised to assuage her disappointment by sending her a signed copy of the offending book.

Louisa could see that the young hostesses were nearly as excited to meet her as the child had been. She tried to set them at ease by making friendly comments. "Jane, our hostess, is loquacious, but has such a quiet voice you may not be aware of that trait. And her peculiar mannerisms come from being dreadfully nearsighted. She may seem delicate and feminine, but I have learned that she is just gathering her bearings," she joked affectionately.

"But look at the dear! She always acknowledges her dual roles as mother and journalist," Louisa proclaimed, looking at Jane surrounded by her children. Louisa recognized that the balance Jane managed between her domestic and professional life was something that she herself had never achieved.

It seemed that the clock struck noon at the same moment that the doorbell shrilled. "Watch this, Louisa," Jane warned. "These first guests will be very young men. They are the ones who seem to embark on their quest early, with the goal to make the most visits possible in one day. They approach the day as if attempting a feat."

"Perhaps it is a testimony to your good sense and an affirmation of your noble character that they will not come later in the day and insult you with any insobriety," suggested her husband.

"Or maybe the chaps have heard that your buffet doesn't hold out," her son Herbert opined as he hovered near the table laden with small sandwiches and ham timbales, potato salad, chestnuts and filberts, pickles and dried fruits, plum and bread puddings, ginger drop cookies and reigning over all in the center a rose cake, decorated with real blooms.

Indeed, the young men did enter the drawing room in clusters, making small talk, amid their white ties and nosegays. They devoured some food, sipped tea or punch, and bowed out in as short a time as possible, attending to their long lists and pack of calling cards. Their efforts resulted in peals of laughter from the women and girls as the door shut behind them.

Louisa admired the beguiling way Jane greeted her guests and with a few words made each one feel that they were the most eagerly awaited. She watched her hostess's slight figure move from group to group, offering a small silver tray with glasses of punch made from a light, nonalcoholic wine. Most guests seemed surprised and delighted that Louisa May Alcott was available for conversation and camaraderie that afternoon. In turn, Louisa felt it was possible she was seeing more energetic and learned men than she had at any of the salons she had attended.

The ladies smiled and chatted for nearly twelve hours. Louisa thought they must have welcomed two hundred guests. The men were mostly from the journalism field, but also actors, politicians, dramatists, poets and even the Russian general counsel, a good reflection of the influential people that the Croly family knew. Louisa remembered the invitation she had extended to Laddie and wondered about his absence. She had offended him on parting, she was sure. She felt uncomfortable about the prospect of seeing him in this society. His suave European manners would not fit well with the practical, earnest talk that had surrounded her all day. It was better he had not come.

Louisa finally collapsed into her carriage past eleven, thinking of a tub of warm, fragrant water in which to soak her aching feet. The day would have been much too gruelling for Josef. Before turning in, she checked outside his door and paused to hear his soft, regular breathing. He was comfortable.

After her soak and a good cup of hot tea, Louisa relaxed in her dressing gown, another luxurious purchase. It was a rich green flannel with a broad lace collar and cuffs. Brilliant green and gold tassels hung from the belt and cord at the neck. She snuggled into the soft corner of her couch, sorting through her New Year cards and messages.

Louisa began to worry about Laddie's absence. There was not even a note from him. She regretted that she had allowed him to walk home in the rain without an umbrella. He could have a chill or fever. There was no one to care for him in this city, and she did not even know where he was staying.

It was after midnight when she was startled by a hard rap on the door. She opened it a crack and saw the evening maid with Ladislas behind her, his hand on the door to stay any attempt by the stout woman to bar his entry. It was clear that she had instructions from Mrs. Miller to keep the inappropriate tête a tête in Louisa's private quarters from occurring again.

Laddie's contrite face was half covered with a magnificent bouquet of hyacinths and white tulips. *Where had he found such exotic flowers in January?*

"You rogue!" Louisa chastised him. "You had me worried half out of my wits!"

"That is exactly as I always like you best," answered Laddie with an intriguing sparkle in his eyes.

"Tell me what has kept you from me all day!" He looked uncomfortably at the maid, who had planted herself in the doorway, like a guard dog about to pounce.

"I have something to say that could not be said except when we are alone." Laddie's demeanor changed and he grew suddenly serious.

"Thank you, Maggie, for bringing my guest. Can you fetch us some tea and cakes? And cold water in a vase for these gorgeous blossoms." Louisa allowed Laddie to pass into her chamber and firmly sent the maid on her errand. Laddie presented his floral apology with a gentle flourish and a kiss on each cheek, the European greeting. He seemed to have fortified himself with a dose of whisky which Louisa could faintly discern on his breath. He looked about for a comfortable spot and seizing on the small spinet in the corner, he settled there with a look of relief and began to play softly. The maid bustled in noisily, as if to make her presence decidedly known, setting the tea down with a clank and storming out.

Laddie played, placid and serene, while Louisa arranged the flowers in the vase. The whole scene was domestic, even romantic. Louisa's thoughts went back to the music room at Vevey, where Laddie's passionate playing would end each magnificent day. They had always understood each other, had always complemented and protected each other. The scent of the hyacinths, a drug-like perfume, reminded her of the garden walks along the lake. How different life would have been had they remained together always. How many times had she heard how every female heart that ever cherished *Little Women* had imagined Jo and Laurie together? They were her greatest literary creations, drawn from a harmony past conventions, past limits, past labels.

"You play so sweetly and bring back such tender memories that I almost see how Jo and Laurie might have continued on together as a pair," she whispered softly, into the flowers.

Laddie stopped his quiet music and rose. "I am glad you say these words, Louisa. It is for real why I must speak to you. I wish I could speak the better English to tell it more clear. Your Miss Jo, she came to New York to seek her fortune, no?"

And instead, she found her partner, her soulmate, Louisa thought. Was that what Laddie was trying to express? Her hands flew to her heart and then she stretched then out to stop him from uttering what was better left unsaid. It would be pointless for him to divulge his love after all these years. He was a married man with children. Their time had passed; they could never reverse their first parting, and there was no future for them on either side of the great ocean.

"I also come to New York to seek a little fortune, maybe. Louisa, you used our romance to make much gain. You see that I am big reason your story make much money."

"It's a loving portrait, *moja droga*." Louisa used the endearing term Laddie had taught her years ago. "All the young ladies are wild about Laurie."

"That is other reason why I ask you to give me what I should earn."

The icy tone he used sent a shiver down her spine. "Laddie, surely you are not saying that my portrait of you in *Little Women* would entitle you to profit?" The realization struck Louisa like a bolt of lightning.

"'Entitle' ... I do not know this word, but I know you have never thanked me well for your success."

Louisa crumpled to the settee shaken, embarrassed and furious. Her wistful dreams of a moment before were fully betrayed. She stared at Laddie beseechingly and then her cheeks began to burn. Anger rising, she shed her romantic notions without a qualm. Louisa's energies were immediately marshaled to protect herself, her legacy, her family.

Ladislas approached the back of the sofa and firmly placed his hand on Louisa's shoulder to detain her there. "Miss Alcott is very famous with the young people and always teaches them how to behave and be kind. 'Aunt Jo's' fans would not want to know that she spend two weeks without a duenna in Paris with a very young dandy ... there are many stories that I can write, too, Louisa," he whis-

298

pered.

This confused and feckless young man was threatening her autonomy and her livelihood. Her innate sense of justice, her fierce advocacy of authors' rights, her strong solidarity with the plight of women's emancipation tumbled together with the memory of the struggles she had endured to achieve success. That success was all her own and she shared her profits with only those she loved. Louisa, the "fighting May" regained her sense of survival, smothering any tenderness she had felt moments before.

"Ladislas, we were dreamers. You would pervert that memory?"

"I do not think you would want my tales to be told. Maybe what I remember is different from what you remember."

"If you have a need, if you came to me honestly, I would never deny a friend—but instead you threaten me with extortion." Louisa shrugged his hand away from her shoulder, stood and turned to confront him. Her eyes snapped and her cheeks blazed with indignity and shame. How could she protect her name and her honor? She had worked all her life to live in a charitable, blameless way. She had asked her young fans to be wholesome, noble and honest. The children who idolized her would not be shielded from the vile story that would inevitably be emblazoned across the newspapers, Frank Leslie's most of all: "Miss Alcott, 'the Children's Friend,' blackmailed by ex-lover." The truth about whether that love affair had occurred or not would not be the story. The story would be her pristine character unfolding in public view.

She wanted to fight the base insinuations he was threatening to reveal. She wanted to put an end to the slavery of women, the subjugation of their humanity to mere objects of desire and possession. Why should she let this man humiliate her without repercussions?

And yet, she sighed. How many times had she learned during these weeks in New York that a man's honor would not be tarnished by treachery to a woman? She thought of how snide and vile the newspaper accounts would be. She knew that Ladislas would cast himself similarly to the men who walked unscathed by public opinion, Channing, Miller and Beecher. She knew that her position was not very unlike poor Molly Murphy's, used Elizabeth Tilton's or abandoned Matilda Heron's. Their full stories would never be told in public, and neither could hers.

While Louisa grappled with the threat to her own reputation, she realized that she feared even more for another individual inextricably involved in this mess. There was a character she desperately needed to protect. She would not, she could not allow the greatest male creation of her entire literary output, Theodore Laurence, to be drawn and quartered in public. Laurie belonged to Louisa and to all the girls who sighed and cried for him.

Gentle Laurie was sick and boisterous, lonely and outgoing, impetuous and polite all at once. He was a wheedlesome, cajoling, fun-loving boy … a whirligig with refinement. The March women did not need his protection but he offered it unasked, the way a good man should, gallantly and respectfully. Ladislas had been so when he was younger. This condescension, this rage, this ugly domination had not blemished their relationship in Vevey. This person who threatened her was not her Laurie.

She lashed out at Ladislas, who turned pale at her tone. "You are a craven, hard-hearted and small-minded person. You are not a bit like the Laurie I created and none of *my* little women would tolerate you for a second. I thank God that I am not your wife because my property, my gift, my creations, would become your possessions. Fortunately, I am in sole possession of my talent, my wits and my money. My lawyer will be in contact with you and send you a satisfactory amount. Please go and do not ever try to contact me again."

Ladislas put out his hand to grasp Louisa's but she retreated from his embrace, and swung the door open. "Louisa … we are friends," he stammered.

"We *were* dear friends. Friends are devoted, honest and true. You are none of these things. Go." She almost pitied his confusion and

300

shame. There was no amount of money that could possibly assuage his humiliation. He rushed from the room, moved swiftly down the hall, clattered down the front steps and out into the night.

Louisa did not answer the maid's knock when she came to collect the tea tray. She was at her desk, her head sunken on her folded arms, sobbing. She wanted Marmee but knew she would never tell this story even to that most understanding soul. She would lock this episode away from her creative mind and keep her image of Teddy Laurence separate from the conniving, greedy, insolent person who had so nearly ruined her life.

This detestable scene with Ladislas was a microcosm of what New York seemed to be. Everyone hoped to profit by another's industry, appearances were more valued than truth and the past was always explained away in the light of a bigger, headier future. *Frank Leslie's Illustrated News* would have made a full edition of her downfall, sold at a special price and hawked on every corner. She knew that she had barely escaped scandal and dishonor on herself and her family, but only by capitulating to baseness. She was profoundly tired of being away from home.

Everything in New York had turned out to be the opposite of what she expected. All the paradoxes played in her brain over and over again. An earnest young writer was a plagiarizer, a staid woman an opium addict, a newsboy an orphan girl, a fine, robust man was ill, and the most cherished, romantic relationship of her life was a sham.

Figure 11. The New Hoffman House, Madson Square

Chapter 32

The Stories are Written

When Louisa woke the next morning she had made her decision. Her heart, her mind, every bit of her being was ready to leave New York. She was never one to rail at separations or departures. Once Louisa decided on a change, she would get to work on the details. Moving was in the Alcott blood, and deliberation was not one of Louisa's traits. The family had moved four times before she was two and twelve times by the time she was six. Three months in a location was a definite home. How different from their family friend, Mr. Emerson, who had stayed in one place and collected his brightest companions around him. "Here we are," he wrote, "and if we tarry a little, we may come to learn that here is best." No, the Alcotts had a way of making home anywhere they found their loved ones, anywhere they gathered their friends, anywhere their hands could toil and their minds could rest. By that definition, the Eli Peck Miller Bath Hotel had been one of Louisa's homes.

Louisa looked at the stack of invitations on her writing table. She knew that as Miss Louisa May Alcott, the eccentric authoress, people expected her changes in mood as well as her unpredictable physical disability. No one would think it amiss if she excused herself from New York society abruptly. She sat down and scribbled resolutely: *I regret to decline … unfortunately indisposed … A sudden call from home*

… My schedule does not permit …. There were a dozen ways to pardon herself from the commitments, all of which seemed inconsequential to her now. She sincerely hoped that there was nothing left for her to uncover in New York, no further secrets and no further discoveries.

Louisa was not surprised by the summons to Mrs. Miller's office. The proprietress was standing, grim and steely beside her desk. She greeted Louisa with a grimace.

"The night maid has told me that you flouted our house rules with that young man again."

"Excuse me?" Louisa had enough of this overbearingly self-righteous woman. "It seems that you forget who I am."

"I hardly think *you* know who you are, Miss Alcott, or whoever you plan to be today," Mrs Miller said.

"I am preparing to leave in a few days."

"As you must," was the firm reply.

Mrs. Miller looked relieved when Louisa informed her of her imminent departure. Louisa had an urge to tell her that she intended to book a stay every fall season, just to see the look of dismay cross on the face of the sanctimonious woman. "I'd like to have the use of the parlor Tuesday afternoon," Louisa said instead. " I wish to invite my New York friends to a farewell tea." A momentary look of terror flashed across the proprietress's face, but she nodded angrily and assured Louisa that all would be in order for her celebration.

There was a general feeling of bustle and departures in the Miller Hotel that week. Sallie Holley was ending her sabbatical, ready to return energized to Lottsburg. Before she left, she wanted to settle Rebecca in a better position. The menial chores at the Miller Hotel were not up to the capabilities of the young lady and her schoolwork needed to come before household duties. Miss Holley and Mrs. Gibbons were going to come together to consider ideas for the young scholar's further education. Katie's necessary change of living situation and education were also to be discussed. The Alcott home was a natural place for these girls who needed guidance. Louisa had a quiet thought that Concord, with its excellent school system and aura of intellectualism, might be the place for them.

Miss Holley and Mrs. Gibbons were already in the parlor along with Rebecca and Katie. Louisa was still pleasantly smarting from being bamboozled by these two sly girls. They had managed to pull off hiding Casey's shower arrangements from both her and Mrs. Miller. Louisa still looked a little aslant at Katie to see if the perky newsboy she loved was intact and was pleased to see that every nuance of his personality remained in the steadfast and energetic girl before her.

The front door slammed closed, heavy snow boots were thrown off and Herr Hahn strode in looking like the rooster of his namesake, about to burst his feathers. He was practically crowing. Louisa had not seen him so full of energy and delight since his struggle with the balsam tree on Christmas Eve.

"Thou looks as if there is good news to be told," Mrs. Gibbons said, welcoming him.

"Ah, the search has gone vell and I have goot, goot news for our little Katie," he replied. Sitting on the edge of the big cushioned chair, he took the girl to his side. Her red locks were just beginning to curl about her forehead, making her look daintier than ever. She looked into his broad, honest face with incomprehension and wished her greatest wish.

"Katie, when your father died, his friends on the wharves knew that they needed to do something for your poor mother and yourself. They applied to the Common Council of the city," he began. Seeing her confusion, he explained further. "The city oversees disasters on the docks and wharves and has a fund to help people who are hurt there. The goot vorkermen also vent to the benevolent association of the new Longshoreman's Union. They know there could be help there, too. But the authorities could not release the money to your so sick mother. They searched and searched for you, but no Kathleen or Katie McDermott ever showed up in the poor

305

houses, police stations, hospitals, or —"

"Or in the Newsboys' Lodging, because she could not!" Katie joined in.

"That is the big truth, Katie. You disappeared to the whole vorld, you ... how do you say ... *varnished?*"

"She did have a certain sheen about her, but I think it would be better to say she *vanished*," Louisa interjected. After laughter and smiles, the spirit of the whole room was enlivened by the prospect of the next announcement.

"So, my so shiny girl, you have many hundreds of dollars in a trust fund for you. Eet is enough for you to have small rooms to live vith your mother for some years and also money for your schooling."

Katie climbed into Herr Hahn's lap, encircled his neck with her arms, and beaming through tears, she said, "I could never have hoped for so much. Thank you, thank you for finding my little fortune! I will be able to live with Mother and go to school, for I intend to be a newspaper writer and maybe even an editor in the future. I've already got my foot on the first rung of that ladder." All of Katie's well-earned confidence and can-do attitude glistened in her castle in the air.

Everyone had an opinion about how Katie could achieve her goals. The doctors had given an encouraging report about her mother, for they felt that the broken woman would inevitably improve from her deep depression now that the beloved daughter had been found. All indications seemed to point to the happy prospect that with months or years of tender care, Katie would again know at least some of the sweetness that had existed between the mother and daughter, back when they sewed together, sang together and lived in happy oblivion before the family tragedies. Mrs. Gibbons knew a quiet home where the landlady had experience with people from the mental asylum and would keep a watchful, caring eye on the frail young mother. Miss Holley felt that Rebecca could help with the care of Mrs. McDermott in the evenings and that would free the girl to attend to a more rigorous course of study. She had set her sights on a medical career and the caregiving skills she would need in the profession would be fostered by her attendance on Mrs. McDermott. The girls could live together, go to school together and share the simple nursing duties. Louisa knew they were ready to face that challenge with their combination of sympathy, optimism and strength.

As Miss Holley was leaving in just two days, there were preparations to be made, reservations to book and bags to pack, and all pitched in to help with the arrangements. Louisa went to lend a hand with the packing, carrying with her a slightly frayed and discolored parcel. She handed the little package to Miss Holley, almost like an offering.

"I have a contribution to your hat collateral. It's a little old-fashioned, but of the finest Parisian design," she said with the smallest of sighs and the greatest of efforts.

"It's sweet, Louisa. Any young girl would love to have this," said Miss Holley, carefully positioning the hat on the top of the last barrel.

"Make sure the new owner is young and full of dreams." Louisa smiled. Then she wrote home to May.

I am leaving New York, which has managed to begin to irritate me. I don't regret my stay for I have learned and seen and admired much, & the unseemly parts I have rejected. I will cherish my acquaintance with the many courageous ladies who set the example here, and the few very good men.

Tell Marmee and Plato that I will arrive on Wednesday.

Yrs, Louisa

PS: I donated my little French hat to Sallie Holley's fundraising efforts. I have gotten rid of the old, tired memories for some very wonderful new ones.

She could hear May's whoop—"Tell me all!"—but she never would.

The next afternoon, Louisa presided over her small tea party for the dearest friends she had made in New York. Jane Croly and her little Vida came with a basket of oranges, which they said, with a cosmopolitan flair, was for the upcoming Chinese New Year. Professor and Mrs. Botta came, bringing with them a bouquet of lilies that infused the salon with a sweet fragrance. Mary Booth brought her favorite bird in its gilded cage to sing to the young ladies. Herr Hahn settled Matilda on the sofa where she was able to survey the parlor aglow with candles and filled with the warmth of true friendship.

The four girls clustered together, sharing their plans for the next year. Marienne was to be an apprentice to Mrs. Croly. She would work at the magazine and learn the role of proofreading while attending to her own growth as a writer. Louisa hid her disquiet with the girl and offered her congratulations. The indomitable Mrs. Botta had offered to oversee the marchesa while Marienne was at her office hours. The soft sounds of the Italian language that were often heard in the Bottas' home would be soothing to the elderly woman, who remained serenely distracted. Matilda and Helene were moving to comfortable quarters near the Union Square Theater where Helene would perform next season. Everyone knew that the young actress would need her greatest strength and spirit to fill the role she would need to play that year. It was the one that so many daughters would need to perfect: a role that required ministering to the burden of illness, hearing the confidences of the dying and bearing witness to the legacy of the mother after her death.

Louisa saw the bright hope on their four faces and the calm magnanimity of the strong women who had helped to make their dreams reality. She turned to Josef. "Everyone is in their place thanks to you and these dear, practical women." Louisa smiled at those around her.

Josef spoke first. "Louisa, you still do not see that eet was your big heart that saved Katie from the street life."

"It was you who steered Marienne away from wrong and toward her writing career," Jane reminded her.

Mrs. Gibbons smiled and added, "It was thee who brought Helene and her mother together."

"And which books did Rebecca have in her pocket most of all? You must know that it was your books that inspired her to keep working and striving, because of the example of the hard-working and bright young women found there," Sallie concluded.

And with that, the four grateful little women surrounded Louisa, embracing her in their pink, freckled or ebony arms, showering her with thanks and promising to be all that she had encouraged them to be. "Why don't you pledge to meet again in one year, dears, and share with each other all you have learned and achieved?" she suggested.

"We will, Miss Louisa, we will!" they agreed. Louisa was certain that these gifted girls were wide awake and ready to use their freedom and their opportunities well.

Only her future with Herr Hahn was unspoken for.

He walked with her to the hallway and reached for his hat. "Don't put on that hat and walk to the depot unless you are resolved to get on the train home with me," she said with a thoroughly aching smile. *It's not a joke.* "Josef, I've said, 'Come with me' before to this or that salon, but those same words have a different meaning now. *Come with me*," she pleaded. "How my father would love to have a German scholar under his roof, and Marmee would have a bit of hope for her spinster daughter."

"Ees this the way the New Voman makes a marriage proposal?" He grinned.

"Oh, not a formal proposal," Lousia bantered back. "I can't make a move like that without checking with my lawyers and my financial counsellor and my publisher. Especially the publisher. I don't think 'Louisa May Rooster' would look well on the book bindings."

Josef smiled down at her benignantly, serene in his purpose. "My vork is here for as long as I have strength to do it. I am in a guut, restful place."

"I am going back to Concord, at least for the time being," Louisa said, as if realizing finally that she would not be bringing any of the dear girls back to her family circle, nor this cherished man. "You might find me there or in Boston, or the seashore in the summer, but I always go back to Concord."

"If we had met ten years ago we vould have been such goot partners," Josef said with a sigh and moist eyes, taking her hands.

"If we had met ten years ago, I would not have thought a serious, foreign Catholic was meant to be my partner and would have paddled my canoe furiously in another direction."

"And I vould have thought the frantic American lady who rowed like a man was too frightful," he countered with a smile, but his head bent closer to hers as he looked into her expressive, haunting features.

"Ten years is a long time," Louisa sighed.

"People do not change so much. Eet is the body that changes," Josef answered sadly, releasing her hands. "If I blossom up to goot health in six months, I will come to Concord and meet your so famous family." He was so kind to make the parting optimistic, for Louisa knew it was more likely that in six months he would need a devoted and steady nurse. She was willing to be that to him. She hoped that she could rely on Mrs. Gibbons to call her when that time came.

But at present, the time had come for Louisa's departure. She turned back to the parlor and surveyed her friends.

"When you return, you can revolve at a Sorosis meeting any time!" joked Jane.

"Come back again and make some history in this town and I will have to rewrite my book!" said Mary.

"Will I meet you here next winter, Louisa?" asked Sallie.

Louisa thought not. She had tried the waters here, and though she had sailed confidently through the social and literary engagements, she had come unmoored by the twists in all her relationships.

She had spent the last evening expunging her journal and discarding any correspondence from Ladislas. Maybe she had come to New York with as many secrets as she had uncovered. An actress, she knew, always played a double life.

"Perhaps," Louisa said.

The memory of the last scene she and Ladislas had enacted together at the depot in Paris, the one that she had treasured for a decade and that had been besmirched by his unscrupulous blackmail made her ask that no one accompany her to the station. She descended from the carriage at the same intersection where she had encountered Casey—so long ago, it seemed, that her world had been turned completely around.

The white light of the metropolitan atmosphere sparkled like diamonds and was as cold and sharp. The January air still took her breath away. It was as frigid and biting as the conversations at the salons. The sunlight streamed like bands of silver, a fitting reflection of the city's essential focus on wealth, money and investment. The granite buildings built like fortresses had a diaphanous aspect, as if aware that their time was transitory, and change was inevitable.

So it was that she arrived alone to the gleaming arch of glass and steel and looked about to board her train. Louisa clutched an armload of books in her left elbow and raised her right arm to signal to the porter, who was approaching with her trunk. As she marched toward the departing track, Louisa overheard four travelling girls whispering together, their eyes wide.

"Why, with her swirling skirts and armful of books, her determined step and strong arms, she looks like the Giantess that Bartholdi is planning to erect in the harbor," gasped the oldest girl, recognizing the famous authoress and nudging her companions forward.

The youngest, still in her schoolgirl frock, murmured, "I *do* think she is the most dignified figure I have ever seen!"

"I have heard she is the kindest dear ever, and would do anything for a child who is in trouble," added the second.

"You girls put her up as the model of all that is noble and pure in womanhood, but *I* heard that she is an accomplished actress and all that dignity is just a part she plays. I see her eyes sparkle and I think she is ready to dance a jig or challenge us to a footrace—only she is bound by her performance to keep still," said the third, a robust and open-faced girl who looked ready to sprint around the block just for fun herself.

The fourth girl, not much older than the others, but with a most inappropriate bonnet burdened with frills and feathers, said, "Oh, it's worse than that. *I* heard that years ago she had a lover in Switzerland and he was scads younger than her, too!"

The train blew its horn three times. A bold burst of steam escaped from its smokestack outside of the station as the engine began to rumble. Four pairs of eyes, four gentle sighs, and four little women watched as Louisa ascended the train as if to a pedestal and turned to them with a kind and unfaltering gaze. She stood on the top step, looking down at the expectant girls.

Then, Louisa slowly nodded toward the first two, tapped out a hornpipe on the metal grate for the third girl and with an exaggerated and dramatic pause, winked mischievously at the last and disappeared into the railcar for home.

Epilogue

In late September of 1875, Louisa May Alcott arrived in New York. We know from her journals and letters that she stayed at Eli Peck Miller's Hygienic Bath Hotel, she spent time at the Tombs, at the Newsboys' Lodging and visited Randall's Island with Abby Hopper Gibbons on Christmas Day. She attended lectures, the theater and salons at Mrs. Botta's and Mary Booth's gracious homes. She visited Central Park with Sallie Holley, who was staying at the same hotel, and befriended Mrs. Jane Croly, with whom she attended a Sorosis Meeting and greeted guests on New Year's Day. She had her cranium "read" by a phrenologist, though not at the Fowler and Wells cabinets, and went to the theater to see Edwin Booth perform.

In late November, she wrote to her father, "I like New York very much, and feel so well I shall stay on till I'm tired of it. People begin to tell me how much better I look than when I came." But by mid-January, she left abruptly and never savored an extended New York trip again.

This is a work of fiction, but all biographical information about the individuals mentioned above, as well as the background history of Louisa and her family, is based on the facts found in the books listed in the sources that follow. Helene "Bijou" Heron was a real actress whom Louisa did see perform that year. A theater critic of the time places Matilda Heron as recuperating at the Miller Turkish Hotel, and at the same table as Louisa and the mentalist, W.I. Bishop. Rebecca is my fictionalization of the character "F" whom Louisa describes in her short essay "My Girls." Isaac Hecker was a member of the commune at Fruitlands and lived and ministered in New York in the mid-1870s. The facts mentioned about Frank and Miriam Leslie, Llewellyn Hovey Willis, Joaquin Miller, Edwin Booth and the Roebling family are authentic. The other characters and situations are all fictional.

In the spirit of plagiarism that Marienne Ayers perpetrated, the astute reader may see that her poem, "He was a fancy of ecstasy," is William Wordsworth's "She was a phantom of delight" turned upside down as it might have been written by a woman. The Bouguereau painting that Louisa and Laddie viewed had made a splash at the French Salon a few years before Louisa's visit to New York, but did not hang in the Hoffman House bar until a decade after this story took place.

Ladislas Wisniewski was a real person whom Louisa befriended on her first trip to Europe. He was one of the young men whose characteristics she used to create the fictional Laurie in *Little Women*. In 1873, Louisa wrote in a letter, "my Polish boy Laddie (or Laurie) has turned up in N.Y. alive & well with a wife and 'little two daughters,' as he says …." There were plans for him to visit her, which never seems to have occurred. At about that time, she instructed her publishers to pay him $400. Though these intriguing facts could not possibly correlate to the dates of her New York visit, I have taken the liberty of creating the wildly imaginative encounter between the two in New York. I apologize if I have offended either the descendants of Mr. Wisniewski (who remain untraceable to me, as he had only daughters) or to the legions of avid readers who still believe that Jo should have married Laurie.

Louisa May Alcott's recipe for a successful story was to start with a framework of true events, reflect a decidedly feminine viewpoint, include a moral tale which rewards acts of goodwill and kindness, and never to let greed or ignorance be the victor. If readers see any similarities to the current story, know that it was purely intentional and lovingly created. Alcott readers and scholars will find phrases from and allusions to many Alcott stories sprinkled throughout. Like jewels, they sparkle and leave a trail of light and beauty that enriches and illuminates the messages of this work. It is my hope that recognizing those lines is one of the subliminal pleasures of reading this book.

Finally, it should be evident to all that this story is an homage to the work of Louisa May Alcott. It is from her books that generations of readers have learned that dreams are achieved through industry and patience, that one need only to look about to find those who require assistance, and that women working together in a broad sisterhood have the power to make their own lives, and the world, better.

In that respect, Louisa and the Lady of the Harbor have more parallels than the four young travelers noted, for the message of each has been to embrace those in need, to shine a light in the darkness—and always to keep a book close to one's heart.

Suggested Reading

The primary sources are all the published works of Louisa May Alcott, including adult and juvenile novels, essays, short stories and poems.

The Alcotts

Anthony, Katherine. *Louisa May Alcott*. New York, London: Alfred A. Knopf, 1938.

Bedell, Madelon. *The Alcotts: Biography of a Family*. New York: Clarkson N. Potter, Inc., 1980.

Herrnstadt, Richard, ed. *Letters of A. Bronson Alcott*. Ames: The Iowa State University Press, 1969.

LaPlante, Eve, ed. *My Heart is Boundless: Writings of Abigail May Alcott, Louisa's Mother*. New York: Free Press, 2012.

---. *Marmee and Louisa*. New York: Free Press, 2012.

Matteson, John. *Eden's Outcasts*. New York and London: W. W. Norton & Company, 2007.

Myerson, Joel, and Daniel Shealy, eds. *The Journals of Louisa May Alcott*. Boston: Little, Brown and Co. 1989.

---. *The Selected Letters of Louisa May Alcott*. Athens and London: The University of Georgia Press, 1995.

Reisen, Harriet. *Louisa May Alcott: The Woman Behind Little Women*. New York: Henry Holt & Co., 2010.

Saxton, Martha. *Louisa May Alcott: A Modern Biography*. New York: Farrar, Straus and Giroux, 1995.

Stern, Madeleine B. *Louisa May Alcott: A Biography*. New York: Random House, 1996.

Stern, Madeleine B., and Kent Bicknell. "Louisa May Alcott Had Her Head Examined." *Studies in the American Renaissance*, 1995, pp. 277-289. JSTOR.

New York City

Bender, Thomas. *New York Intellect: A History of Intellectual Life in New York City*. Baltimore: The Johns Hopkins University Press, 1987.

Ellis, Edward Robb. *The Epic of New York City: A Narrative History*. New York: Marboro Books, 1990.

Homberger, Eric. *The Historical Atlas of New York City*. New York: St. Martin's Griffin Third Edition, 2016.

---. *Scenes from the Life of a City*. New Haven & London: Yale University Press, 1994.

McCabe, James D. *Lights and Shadows of New York Life*. National Publishing Company 1874. Facsimile Edition, New York: Farrar, Straus and Giroux, 1976.

Nevius, Michelle, and James Nevius. *Inside the Big Apple: A Streetwise History of New York City*. New York: Free Press, 2009.

Oppel, Frank, ed. *Gaslight: New York Revisited.* Secaucus: Castle Books, 1989.

Others

Bacon, Margaret Hope. *Abigail Hopper Gibbons: Prison Reformer and Social Activist.* Albany: State University of New York Press, 2000.

Bishop, Eleanor Fletcher. *A Synopsis of the Butchery of the Late Sir Washington Irving Bishop.* Philadelphia: Selden & Marion, 1889, www.iapsop.com.

Brown, Joshua. *Beyond the Lines: Pictorial Reporting, Everyday Life and the Crisis of Gilded Age America.* Univ Calif Press, 2006.

Burrows, C.H. *Phrenological Description Of — As Indicated by the Developments of Body and Brain.* Lincoln, IL: Herald Print, 1870.

Chadwick, John White, ed. *A Life for Liberty: Antislavery and Other Letters of Sallie Holley.* New York & London: Putnam, 1899.

Croly, Jane. *Sorosis: Its Origins and History.* New York: J. J. Little & Co., 1886.

Donovan, Cornelius. *A Handbook of Phrenology.* London: Longman's, Green, Reader and Dyer, 1870, https://archives.org.

Elliott, Walter. *The Life of Father Hecker.* New York: Columbus Press, 1891, https://archives.org.

Frisken, Amanda. "Obscenity, Free Speech and 'Sporting News' in 1870's America." *Journal of American Studies,* 42 (2008), 3, 537-577.

Fuller, Hiram. *Grand Transformation Scenes in the United States.* New York: G. W. Carlton & Co., 1875, https://archives.org.

Giblin, James Cross. *Good Brother, Bad Brother: The Story of Edwin Booth & John Wilkes Booth.* New York, Clarion Books, 2005.

Hinesdale, Guy. *The Present Status of Hydrotherapy and Other Forms of Physical Therapeutics.* Stanford: Lane Medical Library, 1885.

James, Edward T. "Mary Louise Booth." *Notable American Women 1607-1950: A Biographical Dictionary, Vol. 1.* Cambridge: Harvard University Press, 1971, pp. 207-208.

Janik, Erika. *Marketplace of the Marvelous: The Strange Origins of Modern Medicine.* Boston: Beacon Press, 2014.

McCullough, David. *Great Bridge.* New York, Simon & Schuster, 1972.

Morse, Caroline M., ed. *Memories of Jane Cunningham Croly, "Jenny June".* New York: Putman, 1904, https://archives.org.

Willis, Frederick L. H. *Theodore Parker in Spirit Life: A Narration of Personal Experience, Inspirationally Given.* London: J. Burns Progressive Library, 1873.

"Servant of God: Isaac Hecker." *Paulist Fathers.* www.paulist.org/who-we-are/our-history/isaac-hecker

"Washington Irving Bishop: The Magician Killed by an Autopsy." *Atlas Obscura.* www.atlasobscura.com/articles/morbid-monday-the-magician-killed-by-an-autopsy.10 March 2014.

Acknowledgements

My gratitude is endless for my friend Jane Cavolina, who said to me, "You know so much about Louisa, you should write a book!"

Always, love and thanks to my husband, Garry Yee, and children, Laura, Michael and Julie, for their encouragement and forbearance. Just like the Alcott family, they always tread lightly when I am in a vortex, give me a wide berth when I am writing, tolerate my excesses and passions and congratulate me on my little successes. My parents, Robert and Bridget, gave me the tools to actualize my dreams, whether they understood them or not. Thank you to my rock of a sister, Carole, who never judges, always supports, and Aunt Charlotte, who gave me my first copy of *Little Women* and cheered on this little homage.

To Kim Mora, who was the first one to actually read an early draft of this novel all the way through and had enough good things to say that she kept me optimistic (back when this book was big on facts and thin on plot), I give my appreciation. To Kevin Searcy, who foresaw the book and was always confident in its successful completion, I give my love.

To the sister-in-law with my same name, whose comment ("Don't you think you should leave that topic to the experts?") both challenged and motivated me to study harder, read more, listen to other Alcott scholars and unravel every thread, I give my gratitude. Some have called me an autodidact and I agree that I have an honorary PhD in proving I can do whatever I've set out to do.

My thanks go out to the generous circle of scholars, fans and readers of the work of Louisa May Alcott, who embody Alcott's vision of a gentle circle of women embracing and assisting each others' interests and achievements. I found that embrace at Orchard House in the yearly Conversation Series, in the online messages of the Louisa May Alcott Facebook Group for Fans, Readers and Scholars, in the scholarship of the Louisa May Alcott Society and in the positive community fostered by Susan Hoyle Bailey at her blog, *Louisa May Alcott is My Passion*. Thank you to Joel Myerson for his permission to replicate the entire phrenologic reading of Louisa's head, which was first published in *Studies in the American Renaissance* (1995), pp. 277-289. Quotes from some of Louisa's letters, though often paraphrased and embellished, are from *The Selected Letters of Louisa May Alcott*, edited by Joel Myerson and Daniel Shealy, and used with permission from the University of Georgia Press.

Most of all, thank you to my generous editors, the lovely ladies at Pink Umbrella, Adrienne Quintana and Merry Gordon. This book exists because of their commitment. They believed in the concept and themes of this book back when it was heavy on biography and history and part travelogue of New York. Their insight was laser focused and their suggestions sparked a lively change. With their nurturing, this book blossomed. I wish that Louisa May Alcott could have known the cooperation and sisterly solidarity of a publishing house run by women.

Book Club Questions

1. Everyone seems to have an opinion about the city of New York. Some consider it the pinnacle of modern civilization, others see it as an overwhelming collection of civil problems, others disdain it as extravagant and elite. What was your prior opinion of New York? Has it changed?

2. Which character transformation surprised you the most? What were the reasons you did not see the change coming?

3. In your opinion where does Louisa "belong" the most?

4. Anne Lynch Botta, Abigail Hopper Gibbons, Jane Croly and Mary Booth were famous and accomplished women who had not only local but national reputations. Had you heard of any of these women before? Why do you think their legacy is unknown to us?

5. *Little Women*, which surprised even the author with its popularity, has never been out of print. Have you read that book? If not, why not? If you have, did you see some of the themes of *Little Women* reflected in this book?

6. Louisa wrote her early thrillers under the pseudonym A. M. Barnard. Can you think of other authors who have hidden part of their repertoire behind a pen name to preserve their literary gravitas? Do you think that Louisa was too sensitive about her "blood and thunder" stories?

7. Louisa May Alcott never married but portrayed both perfect and broken marriages in her work. Discuss the personal and societal issues that may have impacted her decision to remain single.

8. Miriam Squire Leslie carried on the Leslie Publishing empire after her husband's death, actually saving it from financial ruin. She changed her name legally to Frank Leslie. In her will, she left her fortune to women's suffragist causes. Louisa could not have known any of this at the time. Does this information surprise you? Why do you think Louisa was hopeful that Miriam would be her ally?

CPSIA information can be obtained
at www.ICGtesting.com
Printed in the USA
LVHW031503160220
647097LV00001B/106

MAR   2020